THE DARKNESS OF PLACATA MONTIS

DLM JOHNSON

THE DARKNESS OF PLACATA MONTIS

DLM Johnson

The Darkness of Placata Montis

Cover art: Ajla Huseinovic

Editor: Shalu Gupta, Your Co-author

Publisher: D. L. Finn

Library of Congress number: 2022907484

ISBN Print: 978-1-7329662-6-0

ISBN eBook: 978-1-7329662-7-7

ISBN Hardback: 978-1-7329662-8-4

AUTHOR NOTE

First of all, thank you for finding your way to opening my book. Writing is really hard, and honestly, we just want to be able to share a world with everyone that exists without our minds. For me, I had such an amazing support system guiding me along every step of the way, but a few of those humans took a little extra time to get me there.

For getting this whole thing started, I'd like to thank Jared "Kumquat" Merrill. You made me believe my words were worthy. Kelsey Charlotte. Your eyes showed the light that I hope many others find through my words. Paul. You gave my words the push they needed to be able to be seen by the world, and not just by those who understand my odd ways of speaking. Lauren. You took the time you didn't have to point out one of my major writing flaws. You helped me to level up. You added another tool to my bag. I am forever grateful. D.L. Finn, Mom. You provided me with all of the support and encouragement needed to get my book out into the world. Seriously, above and beyond what I needed to get it here. Ajla Huseinovic. Your amazing ability to capture my words and put them into a stunning cover. I couldn't have asked for a more perfect representation of my mind. Shalu Gupta. The editor of my words. You brought coherency to my words and broke down that final wall so that I could finally cross that finish line. You are all absolutely amazing.

And to everyone else who has supported me along the way. Friends (Special shoutout to Nella, Flick, Sean. Alexandria, and Amy for keeping that intense encouragement going when I wanted to throw in the towel. You guys rock my dang socks off). Beta readers. Your time has meant more to me than you could possibly imagine. Thank you for your continued support. I hope my words fill your minds the way your support has filled my heart and soul.

CHAPTER ONE

The night was heavy as a storm consumed the sky, casting a chill into the unusually humid air. A lightning bolt shot across the clouds, momentarily revealing a breathless figure lurking in the shadows among the trees. Her green eyes widened with frantic searching as she supported herself against the unforgiving bark. When the world went silent again, a gust of wind blew the rain sideways, stinging the bared skin of her arms as she shielded her face.

In the distance, a raven cawed continuously, as if in warning, and a rumble of thunder answered, shaking the ground. The electricity-filled sky joined in on the conversation, brightening the surroundings enough to reveal a large, crooked house in the distance. The raven's persistent beckoning called through the chaos of the sky, capturing her attention.

When the shadowed night returned, the woman crept from the shelter of the trees, chancing the dangers of being revealed. A quiet step onto the rocks of the beaten path caused the excess water to squeeze from the sides of her leather shoes. She paused a moment, listening in the silence between the unrelenting rain as it cascaded down her clothing.

A whoosh traveled through the air, capturing wet chunks of hair, whipping them on her face. With a sigh, she shifted an arm to protect her head again, her darting eyes scanning her surroundings. A branch crashed to the ground behind her, fueling her anxiety. The tightness in her chest forced shortened breaths while dark spots filled her vision.

Taking a moment to center herself, she willed her body to push forward through the ache of straining muscles. Finally, she reached the looming dwelling, hesitating outside the large door. Glancing around, she met the gaze of a raven, and it cawed loudly, seeming to encourage her forward. Though she was desperately seeking shelter and protection both from the rain and all that threatened her, her shaking hand hesitated as it reached out to ring the doorbell. A moment later, the unnatural cracking of wood behind her forced her arm to jump to the button, bringing forth a classical song.

Retracting her finger, she quickly angled herself to run if the person inside didn't reach the door in time. As steps approached from both sides, she quietly pled for the face on the other side of the door to be gentle enough to trust, if only for a little while. The racing of her heart kept her adrenaline pumping through her veins while she waited. Her drenched clothing weighing less heavily than the anticipation of the situation. When the handle turned, she glanced once more at the rainy darkness.

Her eyes widened with fear as the dark form shifted out of the thick trees at the forest's edge. She pushed against the wood of the opening door, throwing the human out of the way to step inside, and quickly locked the entrance. Closing her eyes and turning, she slid her back against the smooth wood of the door to sit, water dripping from her sopping clothing. Holding her breath and a hand out to quiet whomever she might have endangered, she listened intently, calling upon her magic to assist. When there was only the sound of the raging storm, she let out a breath. No lurking darkness or figures descending from the rumbling heaven had captured her yet. It was peaceful, though only for a moment. It wouldn't take long for anyone, or anything, to figure out where she had gone.

While she calmed her pulse, a warm breath tickled her bared upper arm. Whoever let her in had gotten close enough to where their body's heat radiated into the chill of her flesh, warming her for a moment.

However, a quick shift from them sent a gentle breeze through the air, producing a shiver on her wet arm. The person then awkwardly cleared their throat to speak, but no words filled the silence. This hesitation piqued her curiosity, daring her to look into the face of her savior. When she raised her head, a man was squatting down before her.

With a furrowed brow, she analyzed the features. The golden orbs peering down were gentle like an empathetic friend, and something familiar lay in his gaze, but her racing mind could not place it. His playful smile and twinkle in his eye made her feel welcome, but the subtle frown gave away the uncertainty of his thoughts. The longer they remained in silence, the more evident his expressions became.

Her clothes stuck to her as she came to standing rapidly. Noting his swift response to her movement, she wiped her muddied hands on damp clothes before reaching out to shake his. The looming stranger's palm swiftly formed into her own while he smiled.

Though her hand tingled from the contact, she held a firm grip, letting her gaze travel to his face. His crooked smile was framed by a day-old beard and unkempt brown hair. She lengthened her spine to lessen their height difference, struggling to fill her body with confidence.

When his gentle smile shifted, she released her grip and attempted to form a tight smile. At the same time, her fingers groped ambiguously for the door handle in search of a viable escape. At that moment, she was unsure whether she wanted to escape his probing eyes more or the thing that was outside.

"Thank you for letting me in," she finally said, more quietly than intended.

Grinding her teeth in frustration at her still breathless words, she let out a nearly imperceptible growl. He continued to smile softly while taking a small step away from her.

"You're welcome."

The words melted off his tongue and relaxed her enough to release her jaw's grip. That familiarity struck her again, but the neurons in her brain were too busy firing off warning signals to skim the files of her mind for a face she was sure she knew.

The raven bellowed again just outside the window as the man

peeked past her to look out the stained glass next to the door. A frown tickled at his brow this time, and his lips twitched before he spoke to her.

"Mind telling me what type of danger you brought to my house?" He nodded to the door behind her while clasping his hands behind his back; a nearly imperceptible smirk tugged at his lips.

She winced slightly and analyzed her chances of running back outside, feeling the chilled metal of the handle against her fingertips. He was right; she had put him in danger by coming here, but would she make it worse by leaving now? She attempted to craft some believable story as she peered into the kind eyes that kept distracting her.

"Well," she started slowly.

The danger that had become an integral part of her life caused pause. She should tell this man to throw her back out into the rain and separate himself from everything she carried. In the past, when she had grown close to someone and told them her truths, they were inevitably endangered. The empty pain that was left behind wasn't something she had the capacity to experience again. But, through the tangled thoughts etching her mind, she decided to leave her fate in his hands. If he chose to let her stay, she wouldn't have to take the blame.

"You see..." she hesitated again when a shiver passed through her body.

She released the handle, telling herself that the icy touch of the metal in her palm caused the tremble. Clearing her throat, she stepped away from the door. Even the slight movement forced the pair to rotate their positions. The new angle placed his back against the wall while it provided her with open space, giving her more of an advantage. Taking a deep breath, she re-centered her focus.

"I come from a land much different from yours," she said with a reignited confidence. "A land where magic exists and mythical creatures walk. And out there," she pointed towards the door, "is what we call The Darkness. It moves in the shadows. And I..." she paused, searching for the right words, "pissed it off. I really don't want you to get hurt, so the sooner I can figure out an escape plan and get out of here, the quicker you will be safe. It shouldn't hurt you once I'm gone... It's after me, not you. Do you have a back door, perhaps?"

A flash of fear quickly passed over his face as she spoke, though he hid it well. When a massive crash rumbled the door, he grabbed her by the arm closest to him and promptly pulled her through the house without a word. His anxiety seemed to pass through his hand to her arm, causing her skin to fill with goosebumps.

"LET. ME. GO!" She struggled to wriggle herself free.

Adrenaline begged her to get away, but he turned to face her in a frenzy and grabbed her other arm, pulling her towards him with both hands. He squeezed her flesh with urgency but did not cause her pain. Instead, the look in his eyes revealed a hint of determination and something else she couldn't quite place. His nose was barely an inch away from her when he finally spoke.

"We have to get to my safe room! NOW!"

The drop of his controlled features stole her breath while the recognition forced its way closer to the forefront of her mind. Then, sensing the urgency, she allowed a barely perceptible nod, and he quickly responded to the movement. He took her hand in his own before starting up a half-run pace through the hallways.

Her body pulsed as it pleaded for her to remember who he was. A thousand questions raced through her mind while he dragged her along. How could he know that they needed to run? Why had he chosen to help her? What was it about his presence that soothed her more than she cared to admit? The dizzying pathways pulled her in and out of awareness as she fought a sense of impending doom.

"We're almost there." His voice effectively broke through her anxiety and tugged her focus back.

The strange hallways reminded her of a hotel from one of the many horror films she had been exposed to in this magicless world. The walls which filled the spaces between the matching doors were a blur of maroon, gold, Seafoam green, and some other strange pastels. She recognized some of the designs as she let her vision settle: Fleur de lis, damask, and paisley. While she had been outside, this apparent mansion had seemed nothing more than a large bungalow. Still, the twisting walkways strained her senses when she tried to remember a larger abode in the flashes of lightning.

Finally, they reached a door, and he released his grip on her hand.

Some sort of mechanism by the handle scanned his finger and eye, then waited for him to speak the phrase: "All is not as it seems."

Well, he wasn't wrong about that.

As the first set of doors opened, she reluctantly followed him. There appeared to be no way out, yet he continued with only a slight glance to make sure she followed. As he confidently moved towards what looked like a dead-end, he disappeared. Stopping dead in her tracks, she held her breath as the door slammed down behind her. She was trapped. Her heart raced, and she could only gasp every time she tried to take in oxygen. As the room started spinning, a hand reached through the wall, pulling her to the other side.

CHAPTER TWO

She fell forward, unable to move her legs. Luckily, her trained reflexes allowed her to land safely on her hands and knees. The dull hum of the room provided something to concentrate on as the harsh lights slowly came into focus. She blinked several times to clear the moisture blurring her vision with a large breath.

A warm hand grasped her shoulder before a soft voice spoke gently next to her ear, "I'm sorry. We needed to get to safety. That door would not hold it off for long."

Once again, there was a strange tingle where his hand had been, and she fought the urge to feel more of his touch. Clenching her jaw, air hissed its way past her teeth before being held captive in her lungs. As she let her eyelids fall shut, an image of Yggdrasil formed in her mind. She imagined the tree sprouting as the roots weaved into a protective Celtic knot. The image activated her magic and allowed her to listen to his heartbeat as her breath slowly released. His rapid pulse filled the silences between the reverberation of his footsteps when he began pacing.

"I guess I owe you my thanks, then." She glanced up for a moment.

The instant her eyes found his face, she knew he wasn't an immediate danger. But the exhaustion from everything else threatening to take over her body suffocated her mind. So she let her eyes fall shut again, willing her mind to focus.

His pacing fell out of its rhythm a breath later, pulling her attention. The steps grew louder until she felt his warm breath on her neck, but no physical contact was made. Instead, she could sense a hesitation radiating from him again, and his silence caused her curiosity to win the best of her. So, with one last deep inhale, she carefully opened her eyes, looking directly into his.

"I know all of this seems strange to you," he practically whispered. "Why would you ever expect a reaction like someone pulling you through their home when you just told them that magic exists?" he laughed, gently tapping his teeth together.

When she simply stared back at him, he grimaced, then started pacing the room again and would stop from time to time, then merely grunt or sigh. She let her eyes follow his shadows and shoes around the room but was reluctant to lift her head fully. Finally, after the third pass of his muddied boots crossing her line of sight, his quiet mumbles became actual words again.

"You see, I, uh. Well, I know where you ran away from. The land," he hesitated, coming to squat by her. "Placata Montis."

She snapped her head up to look at him.

He faltered a moment before continuing. "Um. Anyway. The Darkness. I br—, I don't—, I don't think we met by accident." His laugh seemed forced as he closed his eyes. "And I'm sure what seems like a short time for me here has probably felt like a lifetime back home, but it was the only way I knew to protect my people." His voice was barely a whisper.

She scrutinized his face as her seemingly permanent frown deepened. His solemn expression was smooth while the final uncertainty left his brow. Allowing her eyes to trace the defined lines of his jaw, her breath hitched; the recognition of his face forced its way to the forefront of her mind. When her gaze reached his lips, the realization hit her completely, like the gusting wind pounding against the sides of the house.

"No," she started. "That would make you..." her words faded away as she shook her head, not wanting to believe it.

He opened his eyes to look directly at her and gently asked, "You remember?"

"You can't be. You're exactly as you were when you left!" she shouted.

"Please understand that I had no—"

"Stop!" She threw her fists up and then pressed her knuckles into her temples. "It's not possible. It's not!"

She fell back onto her hands and clamored until she hit a wall, shoving her back against it while her hips lowered to the floor. Then, shaking her head more vigorously, she shut her eyes and tried to remember him. Forcing down the barrier she had built to block out his face, she let her mind travel back in time when things weren't so dark, searching for the last memory she had of him before he left.

"Um—" His footsteps got louder, so she held out her hand, hoping to pause him before he could encroach upon her much-needed space.

The last time she had seen the prince was just before he abandoned the people of Placata Montis. He had been somewhat frenzied when he talked to her parents. The tousled brown hair that claimed his head seemed more rambunctious than usual, and his typically tucked-in button-up shirt had poked out beneath his vest. Nevertheless, he had smiled at her with gentle eyes that bore some semblance of sadness while leaving. Those same eyes consistently called to her, even now. The same lips and face which stood before her. He was precisely as she remembered him being twenty-two years ago. It was as if he had been frozen in time, and now she was practically his same age or the age he appeared to be, rather. Her frown turned into a glare when she gazed upon him once again. All the resentment she held against him for running away crashed like a flood of fury, threatening to drown her in it. She squeezed her hands into fists while fighting the urge to turn one of those beautiful eyes black.

"Are you okay?" He took several steps away from her as her glare bore into him.

"Just — I need a moment, Graham."

Taking a deep breath, she released her hands and wiped her face before pushing herself to stand while looking into his eyes. As she willed her uninvited anger and fear to fade, curiosity replaced it, washing it away like mud. Moving toward him, the gentle rise and fall of his shoulders while he breathed reminded her of a story her parents had told her about an incident that left a diamond-shaped scar on the prince's left shoulder. If the person in front of her was indeed the prince, he would wear that mark. Her suspicions about this unaged version of the prince compelled her thoughts to remember how the story had gone, hoping it wasn't a story many knew.

"Hmmm," she said, mostly to herself.

Shifting her eyes to his torso, she tried to find some hint of imperfection through his shirt. Although she was sauntering towards him, almost like a predator to their prey, her eyes remained focused on his shoulder. The movement of his chest from his breathing halted as she leaned in, but he stayed in place. She nervously rubbed the leather bracer that enclosed her wrist.

She reached up towards his shoulder. "May I?"

Graham shot a glance down at the fingers that hovered over his left shoulder and tilted his head to the right as he undid the top two buttons of his shirt. Then, shifting forward with a gulp, she steadied her shaky breath while gently pulling his cotton undershirt's neck to reveal the same diamond scar that her mother had described. Her fingertips brushed over it lightly as she let herself feel the reality of everything, jumping slightly when a spark of magic left her finger.

"Holy shit." She shuddered from the contact where the vibration of magic passed between them.

His breath rustled her hair when he chuckled.

"Holy shit, indeed."

Lowering her hand from the scar, her fingers became trapped between the closeness of their bodies. A rush of blood flooded her cheeks as she ran her hand across the ripples of muscles beneath his shirt. Then, growling in frustration at her body's immediate yearning for someone she spent so many years hating, she clenched her hand into a fist and retracted it. Graham laughed awkwardly, rubbing the back of his neck and taking a step back while a touch of pink kissed his unshaven cheeks.

Grinding her teeth together, she turned away from him. The memories she had of him from before came crashing into her mind. In her youth, she had loved the prince, knowing he would someday make an influential leader. The countless hours he had spent with her parents hashing out plans to defeat The Darkness once and for all had previously given her hope. He had genuinely cared about everyone and would take the time to know people. He was involved in a way that she hadn't seen from the king. Still, after he left, her anger at being abandoned by the person she thought could help had clouded her memories, making him a monster without a face.

It had been just two days before she turned thirteen that the announcement was made that the prince had gone. However, there was no public goodbye, just a note he left behind with words that, at the time, made no sense. She had spent months trying to decipher a hidden meaning after his disappearance. Her parents had been uncharacteristically dismissive about the note, but it contained words she would never forget.

My Dear People of Placata Montis,

It breaks my heart that I must leave you like this, but I promise it is the only way I know to try to save you all. I just can't continue to help you if I stay. I am so sorry I couldn't do more for you here. Be kind to one another. The strength of many will go far. Don't trust the whispers in the shadows.

Your Loving Prince,

Graham

A guttural sound climbed from the pits of her stomach, escaping her lips as she squeezed her fists.

"Are you alright?" Graham reached out to comfort her.

"Please. I just need to process." She pulled away before diving back into her thoughts.

She clearly remembered the moment when she read his words, every emotion that shook through her body, every unanswered question that threatened to crush her bones. It didn't make sense that he would leave when what she had overheard and seen while he was with her parents only supported the fact that he wanted to fight. But instead of letting the unknown destroy her, she decided that if he wouldn't take care of his people, she would. After all, it was in her blood to lead a group of warriors one way or another.

Of the families with magic, most had the choice of becoming a

Fighter. But others were required to become one, no matter what. Her lineage forced her to become a Fighter eventually, or *Pugnatores Tenebrarum,* of what they called *The Darkness*. These malleable creatures would consume the energy and life of a person, forever making them lost to the darkness of a twisted death.

To protect the identity of the Fighters, their appearance would change when danger was nearby. The magic behind the illusion was old and powerful, and very few understood how it truly worked. Even then, it was difficult to bend it to your will, so usually, Fighters just appeared how and when the magic wanted them to. However, very rarely, a few could take control of it and look as whomever, or sometimes whatever, they wanted to at any time. She was one of those people.

She had quickly discovered that she would appear in her standard form to those in this land without magic; their eyes could not process her illusion. However, to those from her home, including The Darkness, she would appear as if she were a different person. She knew that at this moment, the prince saw her as she had wanted The Darkness to see her: small, frail, and seemingly helpless. Part of her wanted to reveal who she was, but she didn't trust the situation's safety entirely.

"So...," he cleared his throat and shifted awkwardly around to be in front of her again. "Might I ask your name? I'm sorry to say that I do not recognize your face from my days as an active prince."

He made a noise that almost sounded like a laugh but then changed to a cough. He rocked on his heels and bounced slightly as he waited, clasping his hands behind his back once again. She made a mental note that this seemed to be where he automatically went when uncomfortable. Even so, Graham kept throwing her for a loop. Usually, she was reasonably good at knowing what a person was thinking just by analyzing their face and body language, but with him...

"Um," she stalled.

With one last look into his golden eyes, she went back inside her head and contemplated which name to give him. He had spent a lot of time with her parents, especially her mother. Still, his interactions with her directly hadn't been as fruitful. She had been painfully shy around him, watching from a distance or eavesdropping. The words she could have said when she was near him were lost in her awe, so she usually just directed her attention to her parents. And while her mother and father had trusted Graham wholly, even after he left, could she afford to give out her actual name to someone she wasn't entirely sure she could rely on?

"How about you call me Li for now? It's a nickname I go by, and I don't think it's safe for you to know my true name just yet."

She growled at her inability to stop the unnecessary explanation. Something about Graham was still comforting to her, and she was having a hard time ceasing the words from all pouring out. More words threatened to spill out, but she swallowed the temptation.

As her eyes painted across his face once more, trying to gauge his reaction, she caught what seemed to be a feigned recognition of the name.

"Ah, yes. Li it is, then."

His smile was sincere, but something in his eyes seemed off like he was hiding his genuine reaction to the name. Li was desperate to trust him, but her body's tenseness to Graham warned her against it.

"Well, *Prince Graham*. Now that you've got me trapped in this room, what's the plan?"

This time, she let her usual sarcasm lace her words. If Graham wasn't going to be completely transparent, why should she? The comfort of his presence dampened her senses, so instead, she focused on her annoyance with the situation. Li hated the need to run for safety. Still, the idea of not doing anything to fight The Darkness disgusted her even more. She had let Graham lock her in a room before thoroughly analyzing her options. Now, the stress was causing Li to chew away the inside of her cheek.

"Hang on. Let me check something," Graham replied without acknowledging her tone.

Scoffing quietly at his disregard for her passive-aggressive response, she rolled her eyes and tried to let it go. There was nothing she wanted more than to yell at him, curse, scream, shout, but his blatant disregard for her rudeness squelched her fire. With a sigh, she let her attention travel back to him. Distraction quickly took over her thoughts as her gaze traced the muscular shape of his stature through the button-up shirt, vest, and form-fitting slacks.

"Li?"

Embarrassment flooded her hearing with the vibration of the tensed muscles in her face when he turned around and caught her staring. She stumbled over her words as she tried to figure out what Graham had just said to her while taming her blushing skin.

"I, uh, wha—. Ummm. What?"

He gave her a crooked smile and laughed. "Would you like to come to see this?"

Her mouth went dry as all the moisture traveled to her palms. She wiped her hands down her pants and tried to create saliva. She nodded slowly as she walked towards Graham, but he had already turned around, doing something. She quietly cursed herself for allowing her hormones to distract her from being present in the moment.

Graham silently pointed in the air, showing Li what he meant. Looking up at the large images that hadn't been there moments ago, she tried to understand what she was looking at. The screen was massive and took up most of the wall.

"Cameras."

"Yes. But not just any cameras." Graham grinned. "I have been determined to figure out how to fix the mess I left behind all those years ago; that's why I designed these to track The Darkness. I'm so close. I can feel it. So close..."

His words trailed off, and she saw a hint of sadness take over his features, followed by determination. His defined jawline sharpened, and his eyes focused as he clicked and typed with purpose. She looked closely at the skin behind the scruff on his face. There were hardly any wrinkles, especially for someone who should have been almost sixty.

"Do you mind me asking how you've hardly aged in the last..."

"LOOK! THERE!" he interrupted excitedly while pointing to the screen.

She turned her attention quickly from curiosity back to her mission. Graham zoomed in, and The Darkness was distinctly visible. She scowled as the malleable form twisted through the hallways of the mansion. Seeing the threat so close made her blood boil instantly.

Prepared to fight at any moment, she flexed her muscles while lowering her body slightly and smashing her teeth together.

Graham reached over and gently touched her arm, pulling her from her trained rage as his fingers vibrated her skin. He was bouncing almost imperceptibly with excitement. She let the tension leave her body as her eyes took in the entire room. The hairs on her arms stood at attention with anticipation.

"Watch." His smile stretched across his face.

He looked like a child on Christmas morning for a moment before he switched back to what she now understood was a trained, regal appearance. A command was completed beneath his frenzied fingers, then he placed his hand on the mouse before speaking again.

"I have been waiting so long to test this successfully," he continued, hovering the cursor over a button that said *Initiate*.

Li watched his eyes tracing the movement of The Darkness. He seemed to be waiting for it to reach a specific part of the hallway, and the closer it got, the more impatient he became. Finally, things must have lined up because he made a strange noise and then clicked. The excitement cast a crazed look in his eyes, which worried her for a moment before a horrible screech came from the screen. A white flash of blinding light followed. While she blinked the fluorescents out of her eyes, a box came into focus where The Darkness had been.

"What in the hell is that supposed to be?" her voice came out more skeptical than she would have hoped.

"I like to call it *The Dark Abyss*, but that's just because I'm bad at names," he laughed before quickly stopping as he saw her unimpressed look. "It's a box. And it traps The Darkness. We need to wait precisely eighteen minutes to see if it will hold it. Then we will gather the box so that I can run the last of my tests to see if I finally figured out a way to destroy them once and for all."

Li shook her head. There was so much information coming in and so many unanswered questions. The confusion of everything happening was causing her to become annoyed at every little thing that pricked her senses. She took a couple of steps towards him, putting her face uncomfortably close to his.

"Hold on. You prepared your home to trap one. But you've never successfully caught one before. And I'm assuming they can't track or enter this room unless they come through in one of those little boxes?"

"... Yeeeaaaaaahhh. Kind of. I mean, I've caught them before; the box just never held. Quite a few close calls," he finished with an awkward laugh while rubbing the back of his neck.

She realized he wasn't telling her everything when he shifted away from her.

"You figured out a way to trick them into coming here, didn't you?"

He nodded slowly, taking another step back.

She took two long strides towards him and grabbed his shirt in both hands, pulling his face down to hers.

"Did you know I was coming? Did you watch me out there running for my life? Did you see me get disarmed?" She paused, waiting for a response until her anger boiled again. "DID YOU?"

He gently placed his hands on top of hers.

"Let me show you just one more thing. Please," Graham quietly begged.

She let go of him and stepped back, bowing mockingly as he passed by. Her anger faltered slightly when he paused to squeeze her arm. Quickly pulling away, Li crossed her arms and paced impatiently while he pulled up camera footage.

When she saw the image on the screen, she dropped her arms and ran closer.

"WHAT THE HELL!?"

The fighter on the screen was locked in a dance with The Darkness. The picture was surprisingly clear as it displayed the magic cascading through the trees. The lightning caused the cloud-like form of The Darkness to disappear as Li alone dominated the attention on the screen. Not the portrayed magic version of her. But her true self.

"Eliana..." Graham's body tensed, "these cameras intermittently reveal the magic helping you to hide your true self while also showing the natural form you exist in. I didn't realize the effects it would have on a Fighter. I mean, it makes sense if you really think about it. Mortal devices don't typically recognize magic, and I know that magic hides your true identity. But my intention was never to expose you. I just wanted to find The Darkness."

She froze at the mention of her full name. Not only had he seen who she really was, but apparently, he also remembered her. She couldn't shuffle through the jumble of emotions to place one into words. So instead, they came across as unsure and timid.

"If you've known my true identity all along, why did you lie and pretend not to know me?" she asked through gritted teeth.

"It's not necessarily a lie. I mean, I didn't for sure know you were the Fighter when I let you in. The camera footage and the storm didn't make it easy to recognize you. And..." Graham hesitated, "when I was outside watching you, it was difficult to positively identify anything with how far away you were. I also know how important it is to protect your true self. So, I couldn't very well say anything while we weren't in the safety of this room, now could I?"

He tried to make his words light and humorous, but anger took over her emotions. She gritted her teeth and squeezed her fists tight. She had trained for twenty-two years not to let her emotions control a situation, yet all she had done since being with the prince was to allow them to lead.

She took a deep breath and let her magic ripple through her body, removing her disguise. The short black hair and brown eyes melted away. Its calming effects made her green eyes glow, and her fiery red hair floated just for a moment. As her hair gently settled back down onto her shoulders and back, it was no longer damp. Instead, the soft wave had become more prominent, releasing the twigs trapped in the tangles.

The clothes that hung loosely on her transformed into ones that clung tightly to her flesh while protecting the more delicate parts. Her dark, tight pants slid neatly beneath her shin-high, well-worn leather boots, and her leather shirt resembled something more of a corset. The multiple clasps and pockets allowed for ample storage without taking away from her figure, and the widened straps stretched to just barely cover the tops of her shoulders, leaving most of her arms exposed.

CHAPTER THREE

Graham watched Eliana with awe. The woman before him had transformed from thin and helpless to sinewy and confident. She was taller than her disguise, but only by an inch or two. The only resemblance he could find was the passion within her eyes and the deep frown that regularly painted her brow.

But this new face, this is the one he knew, glowing from courage. This one brought back memories of when Eliana was just a child, the child whose parents helped him escape all those years ago. The child was now a ravishing, confident, mature woman.

He let his eyes paint across her curves while the memories of her childish form left his mind. His gaze paused upon her fingers as she brushed the last of the dampened earth from her leather pouch. Though her hands were slightly calloused, they remained feminine. He resisted the urge to reach out and feel if their appearance held to the touch. He imagined that they would feel somewhat like suede. Soft yet tough. Weathered, yet taken care of.

"Well." She sighed, startling him out of his thoughts. "Since you say we're safe to speak my name in this metal box, then I guess it's safe enough for me to be me. But let's get back to more important things.

How in the hell have you not aged whatsoever since you ran away from us?" she remarked.

"I'm honestly surprised your parents never told you," he replied, staring into her fierce eyes.

"Told me *what*? They never told me anything while they were *alive*."

"They've passed on? That is terrible news, indeed. My condolences," Graham replied with little emotion.

"Yes," she spat. "Fifteen years ago. The Darkness killed them while they were left to clean up *your* mess. How many times did you summon The Darkness to my home like you did tonight? Hm? How do I know that you didn't leave something behind at my house that brought The Darkness there that night my parents died?" she scoffed, walking away from him.

Graham opened his mouth to speak but was quickly cut off as she whipped around.

"*You* said you'd help us fight The Darkness." She jabbed her finger into his sternum to emphasize her words. "You promised to lead us to victory, but instead, all you did was run and leave us hopeless and frustrated. So, don't give me your pity. I don't need it. All I need is to protect the people of my land since apparently you don't care to."

"Eliana." He jumped into the conversation while she recollected her breath. "I truly am sorry. I do not pity you. If anything, I regret my choices." He held her warm hands in his own, and it stirred a long-forgotten feeling in his chest. "There are still a few aspects you don't understand but know that it was your parents who encouraged me to escape. I didn't want to run. We had been working on stopping The Darkness, but it was difficult to complete tests successfully with all the magic in our land. Not to mention, it was dangerous for the people. Luckily, I found an old man who cast a spell on me to prevent me from aging until I returned to Placata Montis. So, please believe that it was the only thing I knew to do to save my people."

Her body remained rigid even after he stopped speaking, and her mouth was slightly agape. When moisture built in their hands, she pulled away from Graham and slid her palms down her thighs. He clasped his hands behind his back as she looked up at him again.

"Why wouldn't they tell me the truth?" she whispered gently. "Why would they let me stay so angry with you? It would have been so simple to tell me what you meant in your letter. What else were they hiding? It just doesn't make any sense."

He faltered as he reached for her again, deciding to give her space instead. He awkwardly rubbed his hand over his triceps, causing his rolled shirt to leave its neatly folded place. Watching her struggling with this new information, he strained to provide her some relief.

He desperately wanted to tell her the answers she craved, but he had made a promise that he wasn't willing to break, at least not for the time being. Taking a moment to contemplate the repercussions of giving her everything she wanted, he sighed with resolve. The guilt for all the unnecessary pain she had suffered was overwhelming, but it wasn't the right time.

When she looked up to meet his eyes, he could see the tears threatening to escape. He focused intently on rolling back his sleeve to just above his elbow to give her time to recover. When he finished, he glanced up at her. She held her hands over her heart, and he could see the tremors running through her muscles while she continued to fight back the tears. He cursed himself for causing her pain and instinctively reached out to pull her into a hug.

Her tensed body resisted comfort momentarily but eventually melted into his touch, and he released a breath he hadn't realized he was holding. When her shoulders hunched into him, she released a flood of emotions, his own throat tightening up in response. He squeezed her tightly, then moved one arm up to stroke her hair as the other stayed encasing her body, desperate to ease her pain. She turned her head to place her cheek against his chest and reached up to wipe her face before finally wrapping her arms around him to return the hug.

"Your parents are — were good people. They were smart and trustworthy. They would have done anything to protect the people and even more to protect you." He paused for a moment. Her face was still buried in his chest, so he returned both hands to cradle her body against his own. The motion was oddly soothing to him, and he wished they could stay there forever. "If they didn't tell you the truth, you need to trust that it was for a good reason. Based on what I saw in the forest, I'd say you used your anger and pain to learn how to become the strong, determined Fighter you are today. Your parents understood how important your part is in defeating The Darkness, and if you had known, then you might not have been able to reach your full potential. I mean, what thirteen-year-old wants to be told that the future of their land depends on their ability to reach a certain skill level so they can fulfill some foretold goal such as defeating The Darkness?" he finished with a laugh when he felt her relaxed beneath his touch.

"I guess not many would take fondly to hearing something like that," she breathed, her voice barely above a whisper. "But there were so many times they could have told me. So many times, I vowed to find you. To make you pay for all the pain and suffering that you left behind. I told them constantly how much I hated you for what you did, and they never betrayed your truths."

As she spoke, her words got louder, and she stepped away from him. He awkwardly dropped his arms by his side, resisting the urge to reach out for her again. When he tried to find the words to answer her, he was cut off.

"Did my parents make you leave because they knew it would make me the strongest fighter to defeat The Darkness?" Eliana's eyes bored into him like she could burn holes through him. "Did you have to abandon your role so I could become the strongest Fighter? Did you have to uproot your entire future just to follow some unclear vision?!"

She spat her words at him, and he flinched slightly. It cut him more profoundly than he would have hoped that she blamed herself for all of this. Despite everything, it seemed that her anger was more directed at herself than him or her parents.

"Look, we knew one day I would have to leave to conduct my experiments safely, which meant me needing to leave Placata Montis. Yes, your parents pushed my departure sooner than I would have liked, but your importance to the plan superseded any desire that I had to stay with my people a little longer." He took a breath and tried to calm his emotions. "The only thing I would have changed about how I left is to make sure that nobody felt like I was abandoning them. But we're all players in this game, and some pieces are more important than the others."

He shrugged gently while Eliana nodded with her eyes glazed over. Graham watched in fascination as hints of magic lined her fingers like a sparkler.

"Eliana?" He tried to pull her from the trance.

The woman in front of him was no longer present. Not wanting to chance to hurt her or himself in whatever was going on, he let the moment play out, stepping closer to be there if she needed him.

When she started to sway gently, he sighed quietly and leaned against the wall, silently watching as Eliana remained unresponsive to his world.

My body tingled while I relived memories from the past. The images flashed like skimming chapters in a book while the emotions barreled into me like a train. I focused hard on the memories that could confirm Graham's words. The facade that my parents could do no wrong started to drip away as the reality of my life flowed into my mind's eye.

Once I had washed away the fairytale memories of the past, I tried to fully understand the truth. Yes, my parents loved me completely, no matter how I attempted to filter it, but seeing things as they were, as they are, would have given me the answers that I needed.

It was cold outside, not quite winter. The leaves had all changed but still held to the branches. My parents whispered something off in the distance. They were arguing. I maneuvered my way around the fallen leaves, avoiding crushing them beneath my feet like I usually did, but I only caught the end of what they were saying.

"Yes, but if she can't discover that power on her own, then nothing we do will matter, anyway?"

My mother brushed a dark curl out of her eye when she responded, "We can't put such a burden on a child. We need a backup plan. Graham is close to finding an answer. I know he is."

My father scoffed.

"You put too much faith in him, Delilah. Eliana will be thirteen in a few

days. If we want her to succeed in her training, she needs to commit herself fully. She's a caring girl. I know she'll make it her mission to help the people."

"And what if she doesn't?" my mother asked, placing one hand on her hip.

"I guess then we tell her the truth and hope she makes the right choice."

My father tenderly put a curl behind her ear while my mother frowned. The same frown that had almost made a permanent home on my face.

"I still think we need to tell her the truth now and let her decide for herself."

An acorn fell near me before my father could reply, and they ceased their conversation.

The memory faded away, and I let the next one flood my mind.

It was warm now as I sat in the fresh spring air. The sun was just hot enough to relax my muscles without burning the flesh. My eyes were closed, but I felt the grass tickling the sides of my fingers. My legs were curled to the opposite side while I sat on one hip.

I lifted my face and inhaled the breeze that carried the scent of blooming flowers. I smiled softly and opened my eyes to the new life that had emerged after winter.

Graham watched in fascination as Eliana's body reacted to the intensity of her thoughts. A twitch on her face. A gentle turn of her head. The tightening of her muscles. A small gasp. A flutter of her hair as she chuckled softly. He dared not to touch her for fear of what her magic might do if he pulled her out of this trance.

When I looked around the trees, I realized what this memory was. I felt myself turning my head as I heard a twig crunch beneath someone's step. It was my mother. She smiled down at me, but her eyes gave away her concern.

"How's training going today?"

She made herself comfortable next to me, gently stroking my hair. I had come to this protective circle of trees to hone my skills but didn't start yet. I sat forward, brushed off the grass from my hands, and resorted to making noises instead of words.

"Erm. I... Uhhhhhh."

I laughed awkwardly, and she joined in, brushing a soft curl from my eyes.

"You know, Eliana, after just three years of training, you've practically surpassed our most skilled Fighters. I am proud of you, dear! You truly are something to be treasured."

I let myself look at her and saw the guilt weighing her down. Rather than remaining in the distracted version of the memory, I took control and let go of the awkward 16-year-old hormones that had flooded me initially.

My mother was trying to tell me more at that moment than I remember. Before the younger version of me replied, I heard my father call, interrupting my words. My mother snapped her head towards him and let the furrow of her eyebrows expose her fear. She quickly took my arms, forcing me to look her in the eyes.

"Don't ever forget how special you are. This isn't what we wanted for you. This shouldn't be your life. It shouldn't be planned out for you this way. I'm sorry, my sweet baby girl."

I opened my mouth to ask more, but my father appeared, and she released her tight grip. I watched the white imprint from her hand leaving my flesh. My mother's body language instantly changed. She feigned being relaxed. But I could tell otherwise now.

"Here are my beautiful girls!"

My father helped my mother up from the grass, his smile shining brighter than the light breaking through the branches of the trees. But again, I could see what was hidden beneath. I let my magic seep into the memory and reveal the unseen.

I could now see that my mother looked malnourished. The dark circles seemed to be consuming her beautiful eyes like a Blackhole destroying a shining star. Her shoulders slumped forward, and I saw the disgusted look she had towards my father. Only with magic I knew the truth now. He was no longer my father. The soft blue eyes melted away to reveal golden brown orbs peering into my face. My body jerked, and the memory faded away.

"The king." Eliana gasped and placed her hands on the desk in front of her, shaking her head.

Graham's breath caught in his lungs. What had she seen? He quickly stood upright, taking a step forward to comfort her, but as he reached out, she promptly circled her arms, and before he could even blink, she had him pinned against the wall.

"What. Did. You. Do?"

Her words felt like they were laced with acid. Each syllable she spat at him seemed to cause a burn on his exposed forearms. Graham was sure he heard it sizzle with contact, and he could smell his flesh burning. Yet when he looked down, his skin was untouched. Terror coursed through his tensed muscles.

This is her magic?

He had underestimated her skills, but everything he saw gave him more hope of success. She was causing hallucinations of burning flesh without causing any physical damage.

"ANSWER ME!" she shouted while pressing into him more, glaring into his eyes.

He gagged in response to the pressure and coughed a weak response, "Okay."

She abruptly stepped away from him when he agreed to answer, causing him to collapse forward. He placed his hands on his knees and waited for the wave of nausea to pass. After a few breaths, he slowly brought his gaze back to the space. His golden eyes focused on the glowing figure standing across the room. Her hair had gone back to floating, and her entire form sparked with electricity as the magic coursed through her body.

Graham wiped the sweat from his head with the back of his hand and sunk to the floor as the nausea was replaced with a pang of bone-crushing guilt. The realization dawned upon him that he'd been thinking about Eliana as a tool rather than a person.

CHAPTER FOUR

Eliana kept her glare on Graham as he started sliding down the wall. Her anger faltered when tears suddenly filled his eyes. She loosened her fists to release the magic she held within, shaking her head at how imbalanced her emotions were. While her hair settled back onto her neck, the heels of her feet planted firmly back on the ground.

A tense silence filled the room, but Eliana could not find the words to comfort Graham. As her innate desire to help him saturated her, another memory flooded back. With a sigh, she resolved on giving him another moment while she guided herself to the night of her eighteenth birthday.

I stood looking out my bedroom window upstairs, inhaling the crisp night air. Then, with a gentle sigh, I glanced down at a quiet mountain through the dim lights of the town, smiling at the memories of the laughter which filled these walls not even an hour ago. Another home turned off its lights for the night; I let my gaze travel over to the garden and creek which ran through our land. The beauty of it all squeezed my heart.

Turning eighteen meant that I was expected to be ready to go off into the world, create some sort of life with a family that I chose, and fulfill my destiny of defeating The Darkness. The thought of leaving my parents behind was excruciating, no matter how much I tried to convince myself a partner could mean as much as they did to me. But as it was written, my training had been completed, and I was expected to be out finding a mate. Someone that could support me in this journey.

My nose wrinkled, and my eyebrows pulled together. The thought of being romantically involved with anyone just seemed like a waste of time. The thirteen-year-old version of me had been madly in love with the prince. Well, to whatever capacity a thirteen-year-old might be capable of loving someone far beyond their own years.

I scoffed. So many wasted years, first feeling things about Graham and then trying to forget him. The heartache of even just that schoolgirl crush had cost me so many years. Besides, I had more important things to do now. A relationship was a distraction and would only cause issues. These people, my family and those that reside in Placata Montis, are the only ones who need my love and protection. No man or woman looking for my sole attention as a partner would get it. I wouldn't let myself be carried away by such distracting emotions.

A soft knock pulled me from my thoughts.

"Come in." I turned towards the door.

My father's face gently smiled at me through the crack, his eyes asking permission to enter. When I gave him a nod, he let himself in, closed the door behind himself, and sat in one of the chairs by the window.

I quickly let my magic surge through memory, but I only saw the deep wrinkles on my father's face. He looked frail and tired, like my mother. His pure form seemed exhausted, and there was an urgency. I couldn't recall noticing that when I first lived this memory. When he patted the seat next to him, I joined him.

"Happy birthday, Eliana. I guess you're not such a kid anymore, huh?" he laughed sincerely, but it never reached his eyes. "Listen, I want you to know how proud I am of you. Never in a million years did I think that your mother and I could raise such a perfect child. You have always been wise beyond your years, and I just wish you hadn't had to grow up so fast." He paused, resolving something within himself while I waited patiently for him to continue. "I wish things could have been different for you. No matter what, always know that you have made us proud. Trust yourself. You are meant for great things. I love you very much, my little one."

I caught a tear falling from his eye just before he pulled me into a tight hug. I understood now what he meant, but at that time, I just thought he was emotional about me growing up. I felt myself responding to him and cringed at my lack of awareness.

"Thank you, but I'm not going anywhere." I looked at my father while I pulled away. "These people need me. I have no plans to run away with someone and start a family. I know you and mom want me to be happy, and I'm grateful for that. But I am already happy, here, with you both. I don't need anyone else. The only other place I'd rather be is in the castle, taking away the power from the king."

He smiled with a sadness that I didn't understand as he sat back in his chair and gently shook his head.

"You take after your mother so much that sometimes I fail to realize how much you're also like me. Once upon a time, I thought I didn't need anyone else. I was going to take on the world alone. But once your mother was in my life, I couldn't remember how I survived without her. She didn't make me weak; she brought out the best in me. And in times when I might have otherwise given up, she helped me see my worth. I hope this fight isn't something you have to do alone. You were never expected to fight on your own. I know you're strong, but don't forget that you've got plenty of people willing to stand by your side."

He hugged me again, and I frowned. Why did he keep talking about doing this alone? Doing what? Why was this so important? I knew that my training was more important than most. I knew that I had the strength to help defeat The Darkness, but why would I ever be asked to do it on my own? Before I could ask, there was another knock on the door, and one helper summoned my father away. He kissed my forehead as he stood, then quickly made his way out the door.

"I love you, Eliana."

"I love you, too, Dad."

When the door closed again, I sighed and returned to gazing out the window.

CHAPTER FIVE

The sterile room quickly replaced Eliana's memory, and she let her gaze fall back to Graham, who was still shaking quietly. She pushed down the guilt fighting its way to the forefront, acknowledging that she had calmed enough to ask him questions about what she was piecing together. What bothered her the most was his lack of reaction to the information she was discovering. It didn't make sense. There had to be something more that she was missing.

With a gentle resolve, she made her way closer to him, observing his response to her.

"How is the king involved in this?" she asked him softly. "Why did he look like my dad? Why were my parents so frail? If you're so involved with helping, why did my dad keep saying that I'm doing this alone?"

When Graham only continued shaking in response to her barrage of questions, she squatted in front of him and placed her hands on his arms. He flinched slightly at her initial touch, relaxing while she let her magic cross over from her fingers into his skin. She felt his stress, guilt, and pain subside and ceased her magic. When she timed a deep breath with him, his body finally stilled, and his glossy eyes looked up.

"I'm sorry for hurting you," she whispered. "You seem to have a greater effect on me than I realized. All the anger I've held, the feelings I've repressed — I guess I hoped it would just resolve itself when I got rid of The Darkness — if I could fulfill the promises that you failed to."

Eliana paused when she felt the pain the comment caused him. With a sigh, she continued with less hostility.

"I looked up to you so much when I was a child. After you left, I felt abandoned by you. I was so sure that I, we, had all meant so much to you, but then you just... left. You know, I used to observe you with my parents," she smiled at the memory. "You were so excited about every discovery. I wanted to be just like you. Your curiosity. Your gentle caring. But then when you disappeared and my parents started losing control of everything," she shrugged. "It was so hard to watch. So hard to not know what to do to help them make it better. Then, when I lost them, my hatred for you grew out of control, and that anger drove me to go out and fight. And I did. I spent so many years thinking about what I'd say to you. And now that you're here, I can't seem to communicate what I need to...."

She removed a hand from his arm to wipe away a tear from his cheek with her thumb. Her relaxed fingers bent as she ran her hand across his temple and let it trail through his soft, brown hair. A smile formed on her lips when the hair fell back into place, refusing to accept the new home she offered it.

He returned a taut smile at her that traveled to his glistening eyes, then swallowed, clearing his throat while readjusting against the wall. Eliana took a seat on the hard floor beside him, leaving a hand in contact with his skin, focusing on the tingle while it unconsciously activated her magic.

"First of all," he started with one last sniffle, "please accept my apology for not giving you the respect that you deserved as a person. For so long, you've been the single key to defeating The Darkness, and I admit that I got wrapped up in the idea. Prophecies tend to have a way of forcing you to think there is only one way of doing things, but really, 'She alone will be the key' doesn't necessarily mean you have to do it alone. It likely means that you are the only one who can unlock some missing piece. Anyway, I'd love to get to know who you are as an adult when time allows for it."

"Oh. That makes sense, I guess," Eliana replied while a wave of blush consumed her cheeks. "And, um. I'd like that, too. Getting to know you as a person."

Graham smirked at her before continuing.

"As for your other questions, you need to understand that in the beginning, I didn't know what my father was doing. He had been working with The Darkness long before I found out."

"He what?!"

"He figured out a way to summon The Darkness and reason with them so he could use them as he pleased. I'm still not entirely sure how or when he started doing it, but maybe a little more background can help fill in some blanks and connect some of the 'whys'.

"Growing up, my mother convinced me to hide the fact that I have magic abilities from my father. His great disdain towards magic and most magical entities brought out an ugly side to him. So while my mother merely wanted to keep me safe from his wrath, it only caused me to hate myself. I mean, why would I need to hide my magic from him if it was good, right? So, after my mother passed, my father also convinced me to believe as he did. He convinced me that magic was evil," he grimaced slightly, rubbing a hand over the back of his head.

"So, it's true that your mother had magic?" Eliana gently prodded.

"She did. Shortly after she passed, your mother noticed that something was changing in me, and she befriended me. She was gentle and pure and never tried to force any way of thinking on me. She simply existed harmoniously with the world around her and, in turn, gave me a safe place to exist. The closer I got to her, the more I learned my father was wrong. Then, a few years later, when I was almost fifteen, I discovered that my mother had not died from natural causes. Nor had she died from magic like my father had claimed happened. Instead, it turned out he had been slowly poisoning her."

"Why would he do such a horrible thing? What made you think that magic had caused her death?" she asked, the words escaping her lips before she could stop them.

"When my parents first met, my father assumed that she had been like him: without magic. She didn't even know of her powers until she gave birth to me. Some complications should have killed us both during the labor, but she willed her magic into fruition and saved us. My father resented her after that, insisting she had lied about who she was."

"How did she not know?" Eliana asked.

"A royal family had adopted my mother when her parents were killed by The Darkness before she was even one. She once told me that her new family didn't want anyone to know that she was adopted, and they didn't even tell her until I was born. She did not know the strange things happening around her growing up were because of magic, and then when it just stopped altogether, she brushed it off as coincidence. Anyway, my father told me that magic was evil and that my mother was mentally ill because of it. What else did I know other than to believe my flesh and blood when my mother never said otherwise?

"My father spent years trying to convince my mother that she should give up her magic after she gave birth to me, but the more he fought her, the stronger her powers became. She didn't know how to control it, and I think her love for him and her desire to keep me safe drove her to some level of madness. So, I believed my father for a long time, but when I met your mother, she showed me how incredible magic could genuinely be. Unfortunately, my father's hatred blinded him. Or, perhaps, he was just jealous. He was the only one out of his family of five that was not gifted with magic."

"Geez," Eliana murmured.

"I know. Anyway, my hate for magic vanished when I spent more time with your parents, your family. They introduced me to the beauty of magic through stories and books. By the time I was eighteen, I finally found out that your mother was also a Fighter, which reinforced my desire to immerse myself in the magical world.

"Though your mother's training hadn't started until she was sixteen, her parents still asked her to keep it a secret from me until they were sure I could be trusted. I understood later where their worry came from, but finding out two years later stung. So, when I learned of her journey, I guess a part of me also wanted to see if my magic could really be used for good considering my family history. I spent almost three unsuccessful years trying to train myself in private. I could feel my magic, but I couldn't access it. It was frustrating as all hell."

"Couldn't access it? Is that some family trait?" Eliana interjected.

Graham chuckled.

"No. There were greater forces at work this time. Luckily, your grandparents believed in my capabilities, so they helped me when I was in my early twenties. Your grandma would always tell me, 'I can see a light in you, boy. You're destined for great things.' And I would laugh it off. But when my father got worse, I understood the validity of her words. I kept him away from the Fighters for many years while I continued the charade of being the obedient prince."

Graham hesitated, seemingly getting lost in his thoughts.

"So, were you able to finally access your magic to help?"

"Eventually, yes. But when I discovered a few nights before your thirteenth birthday that my father had been spying on me and learned about what your family had done for me, I knew our plans would need to change." Graham paused, his jaw tensing while he took a deep breath. "My father had found someone with magic abilities willing to make potions and use spells so he could change as the Fighters did, even though he had no magic of his own."

"Wait, what?"

"My father could hide his true form, changing to a specific person. One that already existed. The transformation wouldn't last long and made him violently ill, but he was determined to make natural-born magic users lose. I told your parents everything I knew. And... Well... We all agreed that the sooner I left, the quicker you would be away from the focus of his attacks. I wanted to find a way to stop the evil immediately. However, as soon as I got out of our world and into this one, I spent the first handful of years running and hiding from my father. I wish I knew what caused him to be so virulent. I want to believe that it was just jealousy. But maybe...."

His words faded away while his eyes focused on an internal image. He suddenly looked old and tired but still had a charm. His laugh lines hinted at a more pleasant time while the sides of his mouth melted down with gravity.

"Graham?"

Eliana patiently waited for more of his words to answer her questions as she felt his body rise and then fall again with a large breath. Squeezing his arm for encouragement, she watched his mouth tense slightly while his lips tried to form a smile before turning his gaze upon her once more.

"Your parents would have gone to the ends of the universe to protect you. After I left, your mother contacted me only a few times. It was difficult and always left her drained. She warned me that my father was coming to this world to find me and... told me he was poisoning you guys, too. Initially, they couldn't figure out how."

With a frown, Graham's eyes darted around Eliana's face. Just before she could interject, he continued.

"Eventually, your mother figured out the poison was in the garden. Everything they brought from there was hurting you, so they quickly protected the area. But once they started getting healthy again, my father noticed and sent The Darkness after them. They used their magic to feign their wellness around you, but I think if they would have just let you see them, they could have healed and been more prepared to fight off the evil. They used a lot of their magic to protect you. Your mother once told me it felt like her spark of life was being pulled from the depths of her core."

"I wasn't a child that needed to be sheltered from all of this," Eliana growled in frustration. "They spent so much time building me up to fight just to hide the truth of how bad the fight could be. It doesn't make any sense. I just feel like I am still missing a few pieces."

"I'm sure you are, and I'd like to eventually fill in whatever else I can, but I'm trying not to overwhelm you too much. And, I'd like to know something from you first, if you don't mind. How have you managed to escape danger for all these years? How did you survive The Darkness that night?"

She released her hold on his arm and ran a finger over her leather wrist guard before releasing a string that held it in place. After a long hesitation, her eyebrows set into a more determined frown, and she pulled the band away.

Graham gasped as his eyes settled on the flesh just below the heel of her hand. He reached out and traced the familiar shape with shaking fingers, caressing it like it was braille and had a story to tell. Her skin tingled with magic more aggressively when he touched her.

"But.... how?" he stammered while looking up at her face.

"My parents gave all the magic they had left to send me to safety. I was out in the garden training when I heard them yell to me," her focus softened while she recalled the memory. "I remember throwing everything aside and rapidly climbing the stairs. The house seemed like a giant maze. It took so long to get to them. I slammed open the door and saw them surrounded by a dark cloud. There were so many of them. My parents were holding hands, and their magic was twisting through the air. They both looked over at me and smiled. I screamed for them, but it was too late. The last thing I saw was The Darkness breaking through their shield as I was hit with powerful magic. When I woke up in this magic-less land, I found the same diamond scar upon my skin that lies on yours."

She reached out to touch the place where his scar was and let her magic run through. Her eyes flashed while a non-existent wind rustled their hair. She dropped her hand and parted her lips. But before any sound could escape, a strange ringing started up.

CHAPTER SIX

"IT'S TIME!" Graham jumped up and ran over to the computer screens, fully replenished of life.

Eliana watched wide-eyed for a moment before quickly recovering and rushing to join his side. Everything seemed to stop as they intently watched. When nothing happened, Graham let the excitement pour out of his body.

"Come on! Let's get the box so we can bring it to the lab for the last tests!" he said with a slightly crazed look in his eyes.

He was bouncing almost imperceptibly while he waited for her to respond. It appeared he might explode if he didn't get moving soon.

"Actually..." Eliana started, taking a step back. "I'd like to stay here if you don't mind. I can see you on the camera and will come to help you if needed."

She did not know if the box would hold. And if she was honest with herself, she knew there was something Graham still wasn't telling her. He was undoubtedly a Fighter, though he had been oddly avoidant at expanding upon that subject. But her magic proved who he was every time they touched. And maybe this was all just a trap to get her rather than The Darkness.

She let her magic flow again to take on a new identity with a deep breath. Her soft, red locks suddenly receded and hugged her scalp with tight curls while taking on the color of the dark, stormy night. Her skin changed to ebony, and her eyes mimicked the tone of Graham's. Her muscles shifted beneath her flesh while other parts of her body filled out. As she finished shrinking down a few inches, her clothes changed from practical, earthy tones to colorful, feminine garb.

Graham stared at her with his mouth hanging open when she changed.

"Yes, you stay. That's probably for the best. If the Darkness sensed you and broke out... Well, let's not take that risk. I'll bring the box to the lab and then come back for you," Graham said with a detached look while he went towards the exit.

She frowned, "This isn't your lab? And won't The Darkness sense you?!" she finished with a shout.

"No, no, no. Observation room!" His fading words stated, ignoring the latter question.

Eliana frowned at his response but could only assume that the box was meant to somehow block magic, though it probably hadn't been thoroughly tested. Sighing, she suddenly realized how desolate the windowless room was without another heartbeat to fill the silence. It was just her, the gray walls, and the giant screen full of images. Before her encroaching thoughts could lead her mind astray, she walked over to the machine and hit a button to adjust the sound.

The speakers immediately groaned at the boom from the door slamming shut on the opposite end of the entrance, causing Eliana to wince and cover her ears. She removed one hand to adjust the volume when the sound cut out, hearing Graham whistling down the first corridor. The other hand fell away, and she laughed at the image dancing across the screen. Maybe he wasn't hiding anything important... Perhaps he really was just trying to help everyone selflessly.

"After all this time. ALL THIS TIME. We will see. Yes, we will see. My years of work," Graham stopped moving, and a solemn tone engulfed his words. "So, so many years."

He paused outside the room where the box sat, staring quietly at the doorway for a moment. An audible sigh filled the speakers as his lungs inflated and deflated. Leaning in to look closely at his muscles,

Eliana observed his tensed jaw and curled fingers rubbing what she assumed would be sweat on his palms.

"Well, here's where we find out if I just wasted twenty-five years of my life."

He stalked slowly like a cat while checking if the room held any threats. His back muscles were barely expanding from the shallow breaths he was taking. When his torso blocked the view of what his arms were doing, Eliana held her breath. After what felt like hours, he finally turned around, smiling and clutching the box to his heart. An awkward sound resembling a laugh escaped her relieved lips at the sight.

While being so close to The Darkness, Graham's unchanged form gave her hope that he had succeeded. When he returned through the maze of hallways, he turned in a different direction and disappeared from the screen. Frantically pressing buttons, the screen flashed in and out of communication with the cameras. As panic started setting in, there was a crackling followed by Graham speaking.

"Eliana, you still there? Press the left shift button so I can hear you when you talk."

She looked down at the keyboard and quickly found the button.

"Where did you go?"

"My lab. It's more equipped for handling this than the observation room. I built somewhat of a holding cell where I can monitor The Darkness while being close enough to react if need be. I need to run some tests from the lab, and then I will come back for you. Thirty minutes max. Maybe. Probably."

"Why can't I see you?"

"There's a camera recording outside the room, but I keep it on a secret channel, so if someone gets into the observation room, they won't see this room. I promise I'll be back as quickly as possible."

She frowned at the idea of sitting alone in the cold, desolate room without knowing what was going on. The trust he had gained was quickly faltering.

"Is there a secret camera inside of your lab that I can access so I'm not just sitting here twiddling my thumbs?" she asked with a thick coating of sarcasm.

"Oh. Hmm. I guess I should have thought of that before. There is, but you won't be able to access it without me." He started mumbling to himself, "... If I could just remotely...no, I disabled that one before. Shit. I wonder if I could — Nope. Blocked that, too," he laughed, then spoke more clearly. "It looks like I was overly secure. Honestly, I never expected to have anyone in the observation room while I was in the lab that might be trustworthy enough to see what I was doing in here. And if I needed to see in either room, well, I'm me, so that's obviously not an issue. But I guess if—"

"Okay! I get it!" she half shouted to get him to stop talking to himself in circles. "I'll just keep an eye on the other cameras while I wait. But could you at least leave your end of the communication on so I can hear what's happening?"

"Sure, sure, sure. Yeah. I can do that. Yes. An open line of communication. Yes. I'll open both sides, so you don't need to press the button, either."

She shook her head and reminded herself to unclench her jaw as she listened to his indecipherable murmurs.

"Keep it together, Eliana." She took a deep breath and focused on the odd sounds Graham was making.

Before long, his words melted away into humming. His deep voice soothed Eliana and helped her focus on the keyboard clacking. Then, closing her eyes, she willed her magic to be her sight. At first, her imagination fought to tell her what she was seeing, and then something shifted.

A glimpse of the house flashed through her mind. The rain was still beating down, but whatever provided her the sight was unaffected. She jolted herself away from her vision as she leaped up from her seat.

"A spider run by and startle you?" Graham laughed.

"Uhh. No. I mean, maybe. I dunno. It was nothing. I must have dozed off to your humming." Eliana smiled tensely towards where she thought the camera was.

She carefully sat down again and turned her focus to the screens, trying to hide her discomfort from the cameras with Graham watching. Then, closing her eyes, she attempted to call upon her magic again but was met only with darkness.

CHAPTER SEVEN

Graham watched Eliana, the undisguised Eliana, sitting silently in front of the screen with her eyes closed. She was the most curious Fighter he had ever met and seemed to carry abilities far beyond anyone he knew. A smile pulled at his lips as the glimmer of hope that he had been desperately grasping became more obtainable.

"Okey dokey. Just about ready to run tests. I'll let you know what happens." He watched her intently.

"Thanks." She offered a smile at the camera beside her.

Just as he had hoped, she let her guard down for a moment when she brought up a camera to the entire screen. Graham zoomed in on what Eliana was watching, just barely able to make out the shape of the house through the pouring rain. Filled with wonder, his eyes shifted back to her, and the world went silent. She was utterly captivating in every element of her being. She was stoic and compassionate with a fiery disposition that could easily command the attention of an entire room. He had almost forgotten how unpredictable people could be, and the curiosity of her behavior was the only thing that had been able to draw his attention away from the impending doom since he had started this fight.

A click from the box interrupted his thoughts, informing him it was safely locked in place and ready for tests.

"Here goes nothing," he whispered as his hand dropped.

Graham held his breath for a moment before turning his gaze back to Eliana. She was leaning into the speakers, and the tilt of her head told him she was no longer focusing on her screen. Her nose crinkled slightly as she leaned closer.

The soft whir of the machine increased gradually as it started working on opening the box. Graham had put several precautionary safety measures into the room in case something went wrong, but a sheen of sweat formed on his brow, revealing some of the anxiety he was trying to bury.

"I think it's working," he whispered excitedly, though he could hear the doubt in his own voice.

Years ago, when Graham had first started fighting The Darkness, he discovered they couldn't be defeated with conventional methods. There was a reason those gifted with magic were the ones who were fighting off this evil, so he tried to capture the essence of his magic for testing. It took many years, but eventually, he could get what he was sure he needed.

From what he knew, no one had ever actually defeated The Darkness. They had banished them for a while, but there was no proof of eradication of the form. The one thing he knew for sure was that The Darkness was made of magic, and his father had taught him that magic could be destroyed.

A hiss of air escaped as the box was relieved of its tight grip.

"Here we go," Graham said, barely loud enough for Eliana to hear.

The box's two halves had separated and smashed against opposite walls in a blink. Graham's eyes widened slightly when the dark blob formed into a human-like shape in front of him. The way The Darkness moved never ceased to amaze him. There were sounds of shoes making contact with the hard floor beneath it, but there was only smoke. The gigantic mass which made up the torso seemed to strain to hold one shape, flickering like a weak television signal while the spine twisted to impossible positions.

Graham desperately wished it were safe for him to get close enough and touch this life-sucking creature. But, as the curiosity took over the fear, he let his feet take charge. There was a chance that his equipment would not hold up, but the barring thoughts did not stop his movement. He made his way forward while The Darkness was angrily darting along the walls.

"Graham?" Eliana whispered to him. "What's going on?"

"I want a closer look," he replied, his voice almost detached from himself, wholly focused on The Darkness.

Squinting at the blur that filled the enclosed space, it suddenly stopped directly in front of him. He gasped and then held his breath while he looked at the details of the form. The face looked almost human, but the eyes were disturbed. Something about them chilled him to the bone, causing him to shiver. The expressions shifted into what he assumed was supposed to be a smile but with a hint of pain and sorrow. Suddenly, Graham was nauseated by the mere sight of this thing. It was either turn away or lose his dinner.

As soon as he turned, a horrible scream left The Darkness, and Graham was dropped to his knees. His entire body filled with pain while his hands covered his ears. Agony consumed him. He shouted, a failed attempt to shut out the shriek, the light around him fading as his lungs strained for air.

When his body finally forced him to breathe, he was unable to tell how long he had been shouting in anguish, but his throat was hoarse, and sweat dripped into his eyes, making them burn. As panic set in, his muscles tightened, and sound no longer left his lips. The pain took over and pulled him out from the world of the living.

Just when he was about to give up by uncovering his ears and letting his head explode, he heard a click, and the next phase of his experiment went into effect. The dark form was slammed against the wall and silenced, and air quickly filled his lungs once again as he was released from his agony.

Graham vibrated from the strain that had taken his body and mind captive. Feeling dizzy, he opened his eyes to a spinning room and tried to convince himself that everything was alright now. When he could finally release the tension in his jaw, Eliana's voice broke over the ringing that filled his ears.

"... GRAHAM! PLEASE ANSWER ME!"

Her words sounded garbled, but he could make out the fear that laced them, and it filled him with new determination. Shakily, he forced himself up enough to see her on the monitor. She was frantically mashing buttons. When he tried to form words with his mouth, nothing coherent joined the drool that left his lips when he spoke.

"Shit!" she yelled in response to his muddled noises.

Graham was falling away from consciousness again when he heard some rustling and a click coming from Eliana's microphone. Another wave of nausea hit him that forced him to close his eyes and focus on his breathing. A series of distinct beeps and clangs told him she was leaving the observation room, but that was impossible. He frowned and pulled himself back to the screen. This time he concentrated enough to search the observation room.

It was empty.

She shouldn't have been able to get out without him. His eyes had to be deceiving him.

A muffled groan from The Darkness temporarily tugged his attention from the screens. When he confirmed it was still held in place, he changed the view to all cameras and allowed his eyes to be drawn to the movement. He now saw Eliana's disguised form elegantly race down the corridors, successfully retracing the path he had taken to get to the lab. Her tight curls whipped rapidly as her magic flowed through her. When she was just beyond the doors, Graham hesitated a moment, then gave her access into the room before collapsing.

CHAPTER EIGHT

Eliana stared hard at the wall she had been led to through magic. She could feel Graham's presence so strongly, it was as if he were standing right next to her, but she could see no entrance. A moment later, the wall disappeared, revealing another passage. Ceasing her magic, Eliana's hair felt heavy against her scalp, and she confidently took a step to where the next opening was.

The wall behind her slammed shut, forcing the air to swirl around her for a minute before the door clicked. It creaked open as her fingers reached towards the handle, receding into the wall.

Eliana's eyes immediately fell upon Graham, who was breathing shallowly on the floor. Taking two leaping steps, she crouched down and thrust her magic through him. The Darkness thrashed wildly, pulling her attention for a moment. Her eyes widened, distracting the flow of her magic. As soon as she faltered, the strange gurgling sound stopped.

With a shudder, she turned her focus back to Graham. As she gently ran her fingers over his flesh, she sensed an alarming amount of exhaustion, though nothing was seriously damaged. When he moaned softly while smiling and shifted into her hands, she sighed with relief and cradled him in her arms. She placed her cheek against his forehead, feeling a warm tingling where their flesh met.

"I'm glad you're okay," she whispered to him, squeezing her eyes tightly to prevent the tears from spilling.

Graham shifted slightly, then traced his fingers softly down her arm until they closed around her hand. Squeezing back, she gently placed a kiss on his forehead.

"'M glad yer here. 'S warm," he said sleepily.

Eliana giggled, brushing his hair back and shooting another round of magic into him.

A deep growl immediately vibrated the glass next to them, and Graham tensed and then weakly attempted to move. Taking a deep breath, he seemed to have come to terms with his current situation.

"Can you help me up?" he asked apologetically.

"Oh. Yeah. Sorry," she replied awkwardly, suddenly feeling uncomfortable about their current position.

She quickly placed her free hand beneath his elbow. Even with most of his weight falling into her supportive grip, Graham swayed and struggled to stand. Eliana released his arm to roll the chair beneath him, and he plopped down and sunk limply into the leather, taking deliberate breaths. When his heart rate returned to a less strained rhythm, he gently moaned and started making small circles with his thumb upon her hand.

Eliana smiled and turned her attention to the struggling creature hugging the wall.

"When I was very young, my grandmother told me stories about The Darkness." She stared at the creature.

"What did she say?" he encouraged, setting his head on the desk.

She smiled, chewing her lip while letting the memories flood back.

"Grams would say that every dark form we fight was once one of us. They are born of magic and trained, but if we die at the hand of The Darkness, we get pulled to another dimension. The Darkness is a magical projection of our power — from our flesh. The reason that the movements are not always fluid is that The Darkness is growing tired. It is struggling to stay in this dimension. Moments are lost in another time or space to the void of nothingness where these things of evil belong."

"But if Fighters get pulled into this dimension to become an entity, where did she say the first one came from?" Graham prodded, lifting his head to look at her.

Eliana brought her focus back to him.

"She believed the origin came from a man who had become sick with the desire for power. I don't recall a name, but I know it was before we were labeled as Fighters. It was a time when those of us with magic would keep a balance in the world. Evil has always sought out the good — challenged it, tried to be an overcoming force. Luckily, the desire for people to survive and have a choice of what life they wanted to live always prevailed.

"But one Fighter let himself be consumed by what evil offered: power. The power to control others. The power to be invincible. To be strong. To consume all that is good...." Eliana let her words trail off and shivered.

"It was said that people saw flashes of what appeared to be a tattered black cloak around him," Graham continued for her, smiling wryly.

Eliana jerked her focus back to him.

"You know this tale, then?" she asked with a grin.

Graham laughed.

"You tend to pick up lots of stories when you spend your extended life hunting one thing, but it's nice to hear it from someone other than myself," he finished, putting his head back on the table with a gentle sigh.

She nodded with a vacant look but smiled before continuing.

"At first, everyone thought they were seeing things. Like when you think you saw something from the corner of your eye, but it's gone when you turn your head. As his magic grew stronger, his solid form faded into this malleable one. It was like he traded his soul to the devil. But—"

"But if The Darkness isn't here, how do we fight it?" Graham interrupted as he sat up, some life returning to his pallid flesh.

"Yes." She released his hand and moved to sit on the metallic desk in front of him.

"We bring the solid forms back to our dimension. If we can find a way to pull The Darkness back here, in their true form, eventually we'll find the origin, right? And if it's something we can fight that doesn't just go poof", he said, mimicking the sound with his hands, "then we know it's gone for good."

Eliana couldn't help but smile at the hint of hope she sensed in his eyes. Letting his words absorb into coherent thoughts, a frown quickly took over her face again.

"What exactly is it you built?" she asked with a feigned sweetness that oozed her annoyance.

Graham instinctively flinched away, shifting awkwardly, placing his hands on the armrests of the chair to sit up. As he plopped back into a straighter position, the chair rolled back slightly. He cleared his throat, using his heels to pull himself back to where Eliana sat waiting and trying to hide a smile.

"Well," he hesitated, scratching the side of his head while his mouth formed some vowels without making a sound. "I realized they aren't attracted to weakness, as I had originally assumed. They are attracted to power. So, this thing that I have made... well, it harnesses magic; amplifies it. I—"

"Whose magic? Where are you getting that magic from? If it's powerful enough to bring one life sucker here, then why not all of them? If they're so attracted to power, why did they go after my parents when they were at their weakest?"

Eliana quickly jumped from the table and huffed away from Graham. She was so used to not trusting anyone but herself since her parents' death. She reactively responded with anger, assuming he was hurting people to take their power and giving it to this thing he built. But when she turned back to look at him, the distrust left. A calm washed over her, and she yearned to give herself to him completely, again.

"Eliana..." Graham started.

"Stop."

Eliana sighed, shaking her body like a dog trying to remove excess water. A sudden laugh pulled her into focus. When she shot a glare at him, Graham immediately covered his mouth. His gaze remained on her while she took a deep breath to recenter. Shooting one last glance towards Graham before closing her eyes, she caught him as he lowered his hands, revealing a toothy grin.

She shook her head and settled into her mind. Shutting out her surroundings, she could hear no sound besides her breath to calm down. As peace came over her, she lifted her eyelids, and a soft aura encased her.

"Are you ready to hear what I have to say?" he asked her quietly.

She glanced back at The Darkness before nodding to Graham and taking a few steps back to the desk. As the dark shape watched her intently, she crossed her arms and remained safely separated from both of them.

"Let's start with your first question," he said before clearing his throat. "Right now, the magic is mostly my own. I may not be the most powerful person, but I know how to drain my magic into this," he said, pointing to a crystal that was hooked up. "It usually takes a few days or weeks to collect enough to attract The Darkness. When I first left, I had some of your parents' power stored up to go with mine, but I wasn't prepared for the strength of what I was up against. I guess I thought this would be easier than it turned out to be."

He snapped his mouth shut and cleared his throat, attempting to clasp his hands behind the chair. "Did you know that if magic is harnessed into a place like this, someone can use it as a weapon? Kind of dangerous if it falls into the wrong hands, but it saved me when I summoned over one entity. I would have never survived alone. You know, I was wondering if I would have to return home to rally up some people to use their magic. Things were starting to look pretty grim here, and I was not looking forward to that," he laughed awkwardly.

"Was?" she asked skeptically.

"Uhh. Well, yeah," Graham stated, rubbing the back of his neck. "After seeing what you're capable of, I am pretty sure I can just harness some of your power to defeat The Darkness once and for all," he finished with a grimace.

Holding her focus on him, she calmly digested what he was telling her. It was well thought out, and she understood now why he had left home. Had he stayed around to do these tests, she would have jumped up to help, but watching what one captured entity did to him made her glad that no one else was around.

A loud exhale from Graham forced Eliana back to the present situation. She spread her fingers in front of her diaphragm, turning them over to gaze into her palms. There were small sparks of magic dancing happily around. She nodded her head, dropped her arms, and closed the last of the gap between herself and Graham.

"What do you need me to do?" she asked, ready to take her place in the story.

He visibly relaxed but didn't immediately respond, so she took an extra moment to reconsider. But the more she thought about it, the clearer it became. This was the path she was meant to follow. Every loss, every pain, every struggle... It had led her to this moment. A confident calm replaced the anger that kept boiling up. She smiled gently at him and reached out to take his hand in hers.

"Well, I have to empty my magic into a crystal to make any of this work. The crystals absorb power when you touch them with intent. Then you use it as a wand — an obese wand," he chuckled. "Anyway, once I get enough of my magic into one, I hook it up to a satellite-type device I created. Then I can direct the signal out to the known areas The Darkness is drawn to and, hopefully, attract one to me. More than once, the satellite ran out of power before I lured The Darkness here. And even more times than that, I failed to capture them at all."

He paused to let it sink in.

"Does it hurt?" She asked.

"Which part?" Graham asked.

She stopped to analyze her question, contemplating passing it off as a concern about her safety. In reality, she wanted to know the adverse effect of these tests on him. She desired to ask him if The Darkness had ever harmed him. If draining his magic so wholly hurt. The more she imagined his pain, the harder it was to fight the urge to hold him in her arms.

"I... um," she hesitated, blushing slightly. "I guess I wanted to know if it's hurting you," she paused and shifted, "to do all of this testing.

Does The Darkness hurt you? Does it hurt when you're draining your magic?"

Her voice had gotten quieter. She rapidly asked him questions, embarrassed by hearing her worries out loud. Her fingers, unsure of what to do, twisted and wrapped around each other. In her mind, expressing emotions would make her seem weak. A Fighter could not afford to show any type of vulnerability. She sighed before dropping her hands and forcing her tear-laced eyes to meet his aureate gaze.

CHAPTER NINE

The way Eliana spoke caused Graham to falter. It wasn't so much that he thought of her as emotionless, but he never expected her to show this level of concern about him after everything.

"Eliana..." he started, unable to complete his thought as a tear trailed down her cheek.

When she opened her mouth to speak, nothing came out. Instead, she met him with a shrug and a sad smile before shutting her eyes again. With a squeezing pain inside of his chest, Graham felt all defensiveness fading away. While his body relaxed, he felt slightly exasperated, and a suppressed giggle burst from his lips. He quickly threw his hands over his mouth, trying to stop it, but she didn't even react to the sound.

His eyebrows knit together as he let his eyes navigate her body. He would have been able to quip back at her unrelenting passive-aggressive sarcastic remarks, but he was clearly unprepared for these raw emotions. The warmth he felt radiating from her words confused every element of his being, and her ever-changing moods kept him perpetually surprised.

Even as a child, Eliana had always been quiet and hard to read.

Their one-on-one interactions were minimal as she managed to shut down any conversation, and most of what he knew about her true personality came from talking to her parents or observing her from a distance. His mind raced for some memory of her that might help him now, but his time spent alone here had made his people skills a little rusty.

Eliana groaned softly, pulling Graham's attention to the forefront. His gaze followed her as the weight of her body fell into a wall. She was hugging her torso tightly with her eyes squeezed shut. A slight shudder traveled through her body. He lay a hand on her arm, using his limited energy to just provide whatever comfort he could.

He couldn't even imagine the insurmountable anguish she must have gone through growing up. Not just from losing hope when he left but also from the apparent loss of her parents. With a sigh, he turned his attention back to her face. Her glossy eyes pierced into him through the silence, and his chest ached from the tears he had been hiding.

Pressing his teeth together, he cataloged the fact that she was one of the most selfless people he had ever met, probably to a fault. Letting the pieces of her personality fall into place, he could only surmise that her fighting was not out of revenge or anger as she made it seem. Instead, it appeared her desire came from a strong need to take care of everyone that she thought incapable of doing so themselves. She was simply cleaning up what he left behind and blamed herself when she felt she had failed. He smiled sadly at her, wiping her cheek dry.

"Draining my power only hurts as much as fatigue would hurt anyone. I've learned to push my limits over the years, and I'm sure my magic has gotten stronger solely because I urged my body to heal quicker so that I could continue testing with less downtime. As for The Darkness? What you heard and saw tonight was extreme. I've never been affected by them this much. Usually, they decide that my weak magic is not worth their time, so they leave me alone. Of course, I'm also typically not trapping them and becoming a threat," he chuckled.

"Why is that funny?" Eliana asked with a frown.

"The Darkness has always seemed so unobtainable. I honestly thought I'd never succeed. However, since you arrived, not only has this whole thing seemed doable, but their reaction has also been displaying a type of weakness. Usually, they have the upper hand. When they drain their magic, they just disappear, but when most of our magic is depleted, we are left vulnerable. I've discovered that The Darkness needs to consume those who wield powerful magic to exist. I think that's why so often they fight us but take no lives. There aren't many worth their time. The part that has been worrying me recently is that no one has been taken from existence by The Darkness in the last handful of years. I think they are preparing for something big, and that scares me.

"I mean, what could make something so selfish and power-hungry that it doesn't even want to take the smallest piece of gold? It's almost like they have gotten so fat that they can't see the little guys anymore. Anything below their gut might as well not even be there."

He stopped and let his soft-focus melt away, watching the troubled creature in front of him. As it twitched and writhed, an idea came to his mind.

"Come," Graham extended his hands for Eliana. "I want to try something with your magic."

She carefully grasped him, providing support to his still weakened state. They trudged to the glass where The Darkness was still pinned to the metal wall. Graham guided her hand towards the window and put her palm flat against it. She glanced at him and frowned before deciding to place the other one next to it.

"I am going to ask you to try something," he started slowly, watching her body language, "but I will need to release the hold on The Darkness to do it. There is a slight chance that I won't be able to concentrate enough to restrain it again without your help. Do you think you can help me if it comes to that?"

She nodded, concentrating on the black form in the room for a moment.

"What do you need me to do?" she asked quietly, looking him in the eye with a fiery intensity.

"I need you to send your magic in there to hold The Darkness in place, just like I'm using my stored magic to do now."

He held his breath, waiting desperately for her to agree. He knew this was an opportunity that he would likely not get again.

CHAPTER TEN

Eliana hesitated. A quick frown danced across her brow. Graham's quiet stillness vibrated through the air. With a deep breath, Eliana looked beyond her hands to where The Darkness was. Using her magic, she could see Graham's magic from the crystal flowing around The Darkness, holding it captive against the wall. Her breath caught for a moment at the beauty of it. It was like a flock of small, golden birds darting in and out, creating a chain that locked The Darkness in place.

She released a small amount of her magic and watched it dance effortlessly with Graham's. When both streams pulsed with a brighter light, she smiled.

"Okay. Let's try this," she said gently.

Eliana watched Graham's unsure reflection in the window for a moment before turning to him.

"Go," she commanded.

With a terse nod, he walked back over to the computer. When she turned back to the glass, she could see him looking down at the keyboard, still hesitating. With a loud sigh, he closed his eyes and clenched his hand. Eliana felt her breath gripping tightly in her chest while she waited. It took him what felt like forever to raise his eyelids and place wiggling fingers over the keys. She braced herself, concentrating on The Darkness.

"I am ready."

Eliana's eyes sharpened, and everything came to a dramatic halt. She could hear the long clicks of the keyboard as time slowed the depression of each keystroke beneath Graham's fingers. The golden magic's hold faded as she increased her energy to keep The Darkness immobilized. Her teal magic weaved its way into Graham's, working to reinforce its grip on evil.

She felt a slight burn when The Darkness tried to break free. As more of her magic flowed, there were flashes of a face she didn't recognize coming from the dark form, and a voice called out through the static of the dimensions. Eliana forced a shield around herself to push back the prying evil threatening to consume her. However, the protection did not stop the fire in her body. While she continued to force her shield out enough to encase Graham, the fiery pain that pushed against her subsided.

Her magic cocooned Graham, keeping him safe. Eliana could feel every emotion he was feeling because of that. His heart was racing, and his breath was shallow, but the pain that existed when she first encompassed him had dwindled. His anxiety was the thing now taking hold of his physical actions. He was afraid but also excited and hopeful. She smiled when she felt the hope he carried.

Graham stood frozen, waiting. She saw the reflection of his widened eyes locked on her. She forced more magic into The Darkness before turning her head to speak to him.

"Graham, it's time," she said calmly.

Her magic always calmed her when she actively used it, and this amount of magic almost lulled her into a state of sleep. She felt the curls of her hair lift from the back of her neck and head as she urged more power to feed into the room. When Graham locked eyes with her, she nodded and let her gaze trace down the tensed muscles in his arms until it reached his hesitant fist over the keyboard.

"Do it," Eliana urged.

He audibly exhaled and unrolled his trembling fingers. Finally, he let his hand settle on what she assumed was the button to make everything set into motion. She spun her head back to look into the face of the evil trapped in front of her.

She unleashed another wave of magic, her feet no longer on the floor. She was now floating in the air. Her eyes flashed as she looked directly into the eyes of the dark figure. There were hints of the same face she had seen before. The pained human features seemed to be fighting to speak to her.

For a moment, she faltered and pulled back the intensity. At that moment, a horrifying scream filled the air. Eliana growled in response and pushed forward with new determination. She heard a click and saw Graham's magic pouring back into the crystal, leaving The Darkness for her alone to hold. Letting her eyes fall shut, Eliana felt her power perfectly blend to replace his. Relying solely on what she felt, she finally let go of herself into a trance.

CHAPTER ELEVEN

Graham watched with awe as Eliana rose a few inches above the floor. The air swirled around her, yet there was no breeze. He hesitated with his fingers resting on the button. For a moment, he saw her hair start to fall back against her skin but was jerked back to reality when The Darkness cried out. The pain from its scream forced his muscles to tense. He released all inhibitions and pressed the button, the click reverberating through his body.

Graham's fingers turned white from the force used to depress the button. He was unable to move while he waited for a change in the other room. The air kissed his wide eyes, forcing tears to form and blur his vision. When what looked like a face appeared, he blinked, shaking his head, and refocused his vision back to The Darkness. The glimpse of a human face had disappeared from the struggling black mass, and he wondered if he had imagined it.

Eliana grunted softly as her hair whipped around harder, and when his gaze snapped back to The Darkness, he realized he hadn't. A translucent face stretched and twisted through the dark form, passing between smirking and wincing. The powerful pull of Eliana called Graham's attention back to her, and he released his unnecessary hold on the button to stand next to her. She hummed. The electricity of her magic made the hair on his left arm stand.

The relaxed look that now painted her face was captivating. Graham slid his palm in front of hers, intercepting the direct path of magic through the special glass which separated the rooms. He willed limited magic through his fingers and watched as sparks flitted in the space he had left between their hands. He slowly wiggled his fingers. The electricity of the spell still dancing between their hands, trying to form a path.

When he went still, Eliana slid her fingers between his and squeezed. Jumping at the initial contact, he relaxed and followed her lead. Her eyes twitched behind her closed eyelids as she smiled softly.

"Let your magic intertwine with mine," she whispered.

He closed his eyes, shutting out every fear. When darkness should have taken over his vision, he was instead met with the beautiful dance of feathered lines of energy that flowed between them. The gold and teal paths circled each other like DNA before finally coming together to form a stronger connection.

Experiencing the flow of magic was almost too much for Graham to handle, but before the power overtook him, he felt Eliana guiding it away. With relief, he opened his eyes and saw that the dark figure in the room had become more human than expected. The face that was once twisted and unrecognizable represented someone grimacing in pain. His eyes widened, and surprise took over the fear when he saw him. He recognized this face.

"Francisco?" he murmured.

The form in front of him screamed out in agony, but this time mixed with the deafening cries, Graham heard his name from a masculine voice. It was faint at first, but the more Eliana's magic poured into the room, the clearer it was.

"Graham! Please! Please, help me! It hurts. I just want it to stop!"

Graham found it hard not to just stare at the face appearing in front of him. This was his friend. A human that The Darkness had encompassed many years ago. His friend's solid form was here — in this world. He wanted to release his grip from her hand and run to him, but Eliana squeezed tighter.

"No, Graham," she said calmly. "If you want to release evil's hold, then you must stay focused. Be present with me now. We can save him from this prison."

Graham knew she was right. He pushed more magic while gazing upon the flashing face of his friend. It was precisely as Graham had remembered it. Francisco remained unaged from the time he was consumed.

Francisco had always excelled at everything he did growing up. He had more often than not been the best at anything he tried. However, when he started his training as a Fighter, he wasn't top-ranked. It ate away at him more aggressively than anyone was prepared for. After that, there were rumors that he had begun practicing beyond the approved methods. Francisco drew power from places and objects that he shouldn't have.

In retrospect, it was all so obvious. Graham berated himself that he hadn't seen the change happen. He was sure he could have done something about it. He could have prevented the years of torture that his friend had suffered because of his insatiable need to be the best at everything. As guilt flowed through his veins, Graham's powers dwindled, and the face of his friend was consumed back into the dark form.

"Graham!" Eliana said sternly. "I need you to stay focused. You asked me to fight this, but I can't do it alone. I won't do it alone."

The softness at the trail of her statement untangled his thoughts. Eliana's eyes were filled with sadness and worry. His breath caught in his throat when a spark traveled through their connected hands. Her face relaxed into a smile before she leaned over to kiss his cheek.

As she pulled away, Graham reached across his face to touch the spot her lips brushed. The spark that had been traveling through his body from their hands seemed to settle where her lips caressed his skin. The tingle left behind made him believe that he should be able to physically experience something when his fingers ran over the 5 o'clock shadow that had failed to grow for years.

When he didn't feel anything on his cheek, he looked at his fingers, expecting to be able to see some sort of glow left behind, but there was nothing visible to his naked eye. Dropping his hand, he saw Eliana's hair whipping around more rapidly. When her extra surge of power reached their clasped hands, Graham tried to pull away from the discomfort it sent through him, but Eliana kept her grip tight. Taking a deep breath once more, he focused back on his old friend behind the glass.

"Francisco?" he gently prodded.

The twisted form in front of them screamed as it fought to split itself into separate entities. Graham pulled the last of his power and sent it down to the hand that was intertwined with Eliana's. The force of their full power combined sent them all flying back.

There was a deep growl and a whooshing sound amongst a black mist. A smaller blast reverberated through the room, knocking them to the floor. Then, like a vacuum, The Darkness dissipated while it screamed, revealing a frail body.

"Francisco!" Graham shouted.

Stumbling while pushing himself to stand, he rushed towards his friend and pressed his hands against the glass. The man didn't react to Graham's voice, but there was a slight rise and fall to his chest that allowed Graham to release his breath. Before he could make a move, Eliana had jumped up and smashed the button to open the door.

"Go."

"Thank you," Graham replied, running to the door.

He started the exit sequence of the current space, bouncing impatiently. Every step seemed impeccably long. With the last click, he squeezed through the door, not waiting for it to fully open as he rushed to the room and pulled the door open.

The atmosphere that invaded his nostrils practically singed the hairs working to protect his sinuses. He gagged as the thick, hot air entered his mouth, waving his arms around in front of himself, trying to move the stagnant air from his path. He blinked away the blur of tears. His eyes filled with the sting of something that smelled similar to manure, sulfur, and freshly chopped onions. Eventually, he stumbled his way to his friend and gently turned him onto his back.

Francisco's skin was pale, and he looked malnourished and exhausted. His cold flesh barely revealed the faint pulse. But there was still life in him, and that was all Graham could ask for at this moment.

"Eliana," Graham said calmly, looking through the glass where he had been only moments ago. “Can you come to sit with him while I grab some water and blankets?”

She nodded and strode towards the exit of the lab. A faint cough announced her distance.

“Sorry,” he mumbled. “Probably should have mentioned how horrible the after-smell of that whole experiment was.”

Eliana chuckled and shook her head, smiling as she let her disguise melt away. Graham’s breath caught when the face that was beginning to make a permanent home in his memories returned to reality. He watched her scrunch her nose at the smell before squatting down to touch Francisco and let her magic bring some of his life back.

CHAPTER TWELVE

Eliana could feel Francisco's power struggling to travel through his body. It was faint, but it was still there. He shifted with a groan, mumbling incoherently. She closed her eyes and resettled her magic, finding it difficult given the fact that she had just used the massive amount to separate this human from the dark. As her weakened magic poured into the body lying beneath her fingers, she felt a hand on her shoulder.

"Do you think it's a good idea to let down your disguise? What if The Darkness comes back?" Graham asked gently.

Eliana smiled but left her eyes closed for a few more seconds as she let a little more magic flow from her own body into the one that needed it more than her own. The man tensed beneath her touch as he quickly sucked air between his teeth. A frown formed across Eliana's brow. She removed her hands and opened her eyes, turning back to Graham. He was waiting patiently for her to explain, but the worry was still very prominent across his features.

"My ability to change my appearance at will consumes more magic than to let the magic change my form. If The Darkness appears, the magic that fills every Fighter will take over, and wait..." she paused for a moment. Her expression immediately changed with the realization. "How is it you have magic, but The Darkness hasn't affected you once when being this close?"

"I... uh... Let's talk about this after I get a few things for Francisco."

Eliana's frown deepened at the lack of an answer, but she nodded in agreement to wait. She absent-mindedly rubbed Francisco's cold skin, trying to stimulate more blood flow to his extremities while trying to find the answer in the past. She remembered what had happened to some other Fighters her age when they were around The Darkness.

As memories of all the Fighters back home flooded her mind, she searched for a single person besides herself who could control their appearance around The Darkness. Francisco groaned again, snapping her back to the present. She shifted her face into a gentle smile and spoke to him.

"Lie still. Graham went to go grab you a few things. I'm Li. Is anything causing you discomfort? Do you need me to do anything for you? Does anything hurt?"

Her words came out quickly, and when she was met with a vacant stare, she realized that he probably needed more time to let his mind process everything. Francisco looked up at her like she was the sun, and he was trying to blink her into focus while squinting. He opened his mouth to speak, but no sound left his lips. Clearing his throat, he attempted to find his voice again.

"Thank you," he replied in a raspy voice. "What happened?"

"The Darkness had consumed you, but Graham and I were able to separate you from it. Does anything hurt?" she repeated gently.

"No," he replied, slowly rocking his head sideways. "Feeling numb. Freezing."

"Well, I can take care of that!" Graham said as he entered the room with blankets, a pillow, water, and some snacks. A smile filled his face, and he quickly wrapped Francisco.

Eliana took the pillow and assisted Francisco in placing it beneath his head. She glanced over at Graham, wishing they were still alone so she could get an explanation, but his energy was wholly focused on Francisco now. She sighed quietly, using his distraction to go back through her memories. After flashing through several conversations with her parents, she finally landed on the one she was looking for.

I was sitting in the dining room staring into a handheld mirror as my features transformed. I laughed and wiggled my new nose. It was much too large for such a small face.

"Eliana!" my mother called.

"In here, Mom!" my tiny, eight-year-old voice replied.

"Oh, there you... ELIANA! Your face!" she said with surprise. Her eyes grew large enough to be a matching pair to my new nose.

"Isn't it neat, Mom? I showed my friends at school, and they said they can't do it. Why can't they do it?" I asked, pouting a little.

My mother smiled at me; all elements of surprise had washed from her face as quickly as they appeared. Her body relaxed, and she came over to run her fingers through my unbrushed hair.

"Oh, my little marshmallow. You're just special. We've always known that. You know how we've talked about how you might grow up like Mommy and Daddy to fight The Darkness? Well, only if you choose to do that you'll be extra special. I've known only one other person in my whoooooole life who was able to change the way they looked in danger. Or even at all. And he's pretty special, too. So, yes. You, my little love; you are special."

I giggled as she kissed my giant nose and ruffled my hair.

"Okay, Mom," I said, looking into the mirror again and changing my face back to my own.

I watched my mother's reflection walking away. She turned for one last glance before closing the door. She was smiling at me, but her eyes were filled with a sadness that I understood now.

"You can control your appearance, can't you?!" she shouted at Graham without thinking.

Both men looked at her with wide eyes, not even knowing that she had temporarily left them to search her memories for an answer. There were a lot of questions, and searching for memories that she might have was the quickest way to get the answer. Graham was holding the cup of water up to Francisco's lips and seemed like he had been the one who was talking before she so rudely yelled. Her face flushed as she realized she should have saved this conversation for later... whenever that might be.

"Would you excuse us for a moment, please, Francisco? We're just going to grab a few more things to make you more comfortable. Li?"

"Sure," she replied awkwardly, suddenly feeling extremely uncomfortable that they would be alone right then. "We'll be right back. I apologize if I frightened you — just rest. We'll be back in a flash," she finished with a genuine smile while swallowing her heart.

As soon as she stood, she felt Graham's hand on her back. He pushed her firmly, moving them both quickly out of the room. Eliana started sweating from embarrassment and guilt. Her stubborn impatience might have just caused a lot of issues for the future of fighting The Darkness. Graham kept his connection to her as he opened the door to the central part of the house with his free hand, an eye, and a phrase which she could not hear as she clenched her jaw in the discomfort of the whole situation. When the doors opened, he gave her one last forceful push into the hallway.

"What the *hell*, Eliana?!" he half-shouted at her once the door closed. "We don't even know if we can fully trust him yet. What made you think that would be a safe conversation to start when he was awake and coherent? I'm already uncomfortable enough with you showing him your true form."

Eliana blinked away the tears that threatened to coat her eyes. There wasn't an adequate answer for Graham. She knew she had made a poor decision. She wasn't used to being around people. Especially the ones where she couldn't just say what she wanted. Surviving this long had required finding the answers as quickly as possible, and anything less brought extreme irritability.

"I'm sorry," she said with sincerity, turning around to face him. "I don't know how I missed it. You claimed to be a Fighter, yet you weren't changing around The Darkness. The yelling was mostly anger at me for being too distracted to catch such a vital detail."

She paused for a moment, reaching for his hand, but when he pulled it away and clasped it behind himself, she sighed and rubbed the side of her arm before continuing.

"Anyway, while you were tending your friend, I searched my memories and came across one from when I was eight and realized I could change my appearance at will. When I asked my mother why none of my friends could do the same...., she told me I'm special, and... mentioned that there was only one other man she knew who could do the same thing. So, I guess I just assumed it was you." She searched his golden eyes for a hint. "Is it you?"

His face softened as she spoke but still looked stern. His eyes switched quickly between focusing on either of hers. Eventually, she saw his shoulders relax as he exhaled. Shaking his head, he released his hands from behind his back and took a step toward her.

"The short answer to this is, yes," he started, shoving a finger in her face. "But this conversation is far from over. You need to work on your patience if you want to beat The Darkness. I've been around longer than you, so I would appreciate it if you could at least try to trust that I know what I'm doing.

"We still don't even know if The Darkness can return to Francisco or if it's entirely gone. I don't trust Francisco fully yet, but I would like to get him comfortable. Corrupted or not, he needs to start healing in his human form. We may be able to remind him of the good he has, but we also need to be careful with what we talk about while he is in earshot.

"Which begs the point that I owe you an apology, as well," he continued, his voice much more subdued. "I shouldn't have questioned you removing your disguise in front of him. He could have just been listening to everything we said and feigning such frailty. So, I'm sorry, too. It's been a while since I've changed forms, so I guess I forgot how the magic feels when you change," he finished, running a hand over the back of his neck.

"It's fine," Eliana bit back more harshly than intended.

When Graham scowled at her, she calmed herself with a large exhale before continuing.

"Look, I'm not used to having to worry about the consequences of what I say. And, yes. It uses more magic to create a particular form than to allow the magic to assign me one. But I've felt your magic. I know it's there, so why aren't you changing every time you're close to danger? Did you figure out a way to control it without magic?"

After studying her sternly, he eventually conceded with a sigh."Let's walk and talk. I'd like to come back with a heated blanket, so it's not as obvious that we were hiding something."

Eliana followed closely but avoided touching him. When their magic had intertwined, there was a different vibe in-between that she didn't recognize. She didn't know what his magic was capable of, and her emotions were in turmoil right now. How could she not have immediately realized she was responding to the magic of a Fighter when he grabbed her arm? Groaning quietly to herself, she clenched her fists and grounded her teeth. When they got further down the hall, he started speaking again, pulling her from her self-directed rage.

"I discovered that by draining my magic to control The Darkness, I become ordinary, just like people without magic. The flow is so weak that when The Darkness arrives, they can't or won't sense that I have magic. Their draw to power leads to them basically being blind to me. Something in the ancient magic that helps us change feeds off the threat of danger, and because I can pass as a magic-less mortal, I'm invisible. It's a dangerous line I'm walking, though. My magic has gotten so used to being drained and working to replenish itself that if The Darkness caught me as my magic passed the threshold of grabbing their attention, I would probably be consumed. And before you ask, yes. I'm sure I could be a great Fighter with my magic, but my scientific brain is of more use to everyone at this point."

Eliana nodded silently, smiling at his accurate assumption that she would have asked that. Practicing her listening skills for once, she took everything in and sorted her thoughts while following Graham down a few corridors. Realizing how little she knew him, she didn't want to repeat anything stupid. He had given up his entire life to helping fight this thing, and she wanted to make sure she accounted for that now.

Getting lost in her own thoughts, Eliana crashed into Graham's muscular back, unaware that he had stopped moving. He chuckled softly, then opened the cabinet, grabbed a blanket, and maneuvered around Eliana without saying anything else. Her heart dropped at his apparent disappointment while he blatantly ignored her. At that moment, Eliana vowed to herself to do anything she could to make sure that she wouldn't elicit this response from him anytime soon after she fixed this.

"Graham, wait," she blurted, reaching out for his arm to stop him. "I know I keep making excuses for my frustrating responses to things, but this is just me trying to interpret the situation. And, I appreciate you being so honest. I will do my best from here on out to trust you and respect our conversations. I just... I don't want you to be upset with me all because I may be slightly out of practice in being able to work with someone. Instead of, you know... Just saving people or losing them. And then moving on."

She cut off her stubborn words when she heard him mumbling to himself. When he still didn't turn around to acknowledge her, she released Graham's arm and tried to double down with a new determination, focusing on bringing back the sincerity and confidence in her voice.

"Alright. No more excuses. Only improvement. I promise," she said. "Although, I am not confident I can keep this promise when we're in a quick decision-making situation. There's no stopping what I may do then. I will always do anything to protect as many people as I can. Even if that means hurting myself."

Eliana stopped talking again, cursing softly to herself for letting her words get away from her. Planting her feet and closing her eyes, she drew power from the trees outside to calm herself. While imagining the surrounding forest, she realized she was once again peering through eyes that were not her own. The muscles in her body tensed as she held her breath.

She was high in a tree, sheltered from the rain by the thick leaves above her. The creature she was sharing a space with darted its eyes quickly through the openings in the branches. When the line of sight passed over Graham's home, she gasped. Her tense muscles swayed with the vibrations of the earth, trying to keep her balance. The eyes continued to dart around, making it almost impossible to find her feet.

"The house," she whispered, desperately trying to gain some control.

No sooner had she spoken the words than her vision reached the back of the house. The stillness allowed her to find stability. Clarity returned to her mind, and she summoned the creature to come closer, calling it in her mind. There was a loud caw in response to her command.

Her breath caught again as she felt as if she was flying. Without thinking, she moved her head to look at her surroundings. The peace and freedom she felt cutting through the raindrops were unlike anything she could have imagined. As Eliana felt her human form less, she embraced the wings of the bird. As the last sensation of the earth was disappearing from beneath, she was suddenly slammed back into her human form.

Adjusting back into the weighted flesh, she realized she was no longer standing. Instead, a warm embrace engulfed her. Something familiar that she was unwilling to fight. As the last of the whooshing air left her hearing, she heard Graham calling out for her.

"Li! Eliana! What's going on? Are you alright?"

His voice strained and cut out. She tried to reply, but she wasn't fully back in her body. When her eyes, at last, found their home, she raised the skin which blinded her view of the world. Eliana focused on the face barely two inches from her own and smiled. The golden orbs peering down on her continued darting around her flesh, waiting for some sort of response. Eliana turned her head away from his chest and found the arm supporting her neck was gripping tightly to her shoulder while the other arm was trying to check for some typical vital signs.

Freeing her outside arm, she reached up to touch the hand on her shoulder. Graham jumped, flexing his muscles. She could feel his thigh and part of his shin beneath her upper back, supporting her to be somewhat upright. When she tried to shimmy herself upright, his body pressed into hers, pinning her in position.

"You're awake! Thank God. What happened?! Are you okay? Are you hurt?" he rambled while trying to brush her hair away from her face.

"Graham," Eliana interjected unsuccessfully.

She attempted to move her face away from his flailing fingers, but he continued his attack to shift her hair from blocking his view of her face.

"I thought you were behind me, but then you weren't there," he continued. "I didn't know—"

"GRAHAM!" she shouted to get the nervous babbling to stop.

She stared at him incredulously for a moment, waiting for him to pull himself together. Graham stretched his arm behind her neck to support her and wiggled his leg further up her back to gently place her head on his thigh. Eliana patiently waited for him to find an appropriate position and then continued speaking.

"Satisfied?" she said with more sarcasm than she had intended.

"Yes... Yes," he concluded. A hand reached back towards her face.

"I'm fine." She swatted it away from trying to check her eyes.

"Okay," Graham mumbled.

He let his hand fall to rest on her forearm, which was draped across her stomach. She wasn't able to separate herself from him physically, still shifting to test if he would let her up. She realized that whatever was in his pocket was piercing her side when she settled in. As soon as she grimaced, Graham quickly helped her get more comfortable while keeping her primarily horizontal.

With a sigh, Eliana finally looked up at the worry-ridden face, which was now at least half a foot away from her own. Her heart fluttered as she stared into his eyes, forcing a nervous laugh from her lips. His frown deepened into something almost resembling anger.

"I was outside," she blurted before he could think this was all just a ruse.

"You... what?" Graham replied with confusion, all other emotion leaving his face.

"Earlier...in the observation room... something happened," she hesitated. "I was trying to see if I could somehow use my magic to look at you while we were separated. And suddenly, I was looking at the world from eyes that were not my own. At the time, I told myself it was just some memory that I was recalling. But just now-," she shook her head in disbelief. "I think there is some part of my power that I didn't know I could access.

"I was trying to draw energy from the trees to calm myself and heal, and then, somehow, I saw through those same eyes again. So, instead of pulling out of it, I settled in. I let myself experience this unfamiliar sensation. I merged with the creature. At first, I was simply an observer. I saw what it saw, and nothing else, but then I saw this house. The darting eyes passed by it quickly, and I willed it to return."

Eliana paused, expecting some sort of reaction. When Graham remained unmoved, she took a deep breath and then continued.

"I was looking down at the house again. I had made the raven look where I wanted. Well, it sounded like a raven. I don't know for sure. Anyway, after that, I could control it. I was the raven. I was flying free, soaring through the space between each raindrop, so close to the house. And then... and then I felt you here. Somewhere, some part of me felt you calling to me, but I wanted so badly to stay with the bird. I was so free, Graham."

She sat up, digging her elbows into the flesh of his leg for support. Her eyes were threatening to overflow with moisture. The memory of the freedom crushed down on her heart. She had spent so much of her life taking care of everyone else that the feeling of being so free was affecting her more than she wanted to admit. He eased his arm up her back to help support her new position but otherwise remained silent.

Leaving Graham to his thoughts, she let herself merge with the bird again. Her body quickly lost awareness of her human form again, returning to freedom. The raven sat on the roof beneath the shelter cast by a large tree hanging over the house. Each time a drop of water forced its way through an opening, the raven ruffled its feathers. Eliana giggled as it snapped its beak at a gust of wind carrying the rain sideways. It cawed, and Graham shook her back to her body once again.

An annoyed sigh left her lips as she dropped back to her own flesh. All she wanted was to embrace the freedom the bird provided, but her reality just kept crashing back down.

Letting herself come fully back to awareness, she realized that Graham was now cradling her into his body. She turned her face, pressing her cheek into the warmth of his chest. His heart was racing, and his breath was quick and shallow. Eliana wanted to go back and stay there, but it wasn't possible while he was there. His immense worry for her was preventing any sort of attempt to run away.

Smiling gently at the peace she felt at being cared for, she placed her palms flat against his chest and used some magic to calm him, sharing some of that peace.

Graham's heart settled as her magic made its way through him. Eliana shut her eyes again, preparing to leave. But this time, as she faded away, she took him with her. His consciousness was fighting hard to stay focused on the house. Eliana could feel him fighting. She pulled him harder, but he suddenly removed her hands from his body, causing her focus to falter.

"Hey!" she shouted.

Graham's solemn expression halted her words.

"Eliana," he said as she sat up. "There's probably more about your parents that you should know. Specifically, your dad."

"What about my dad?" she interrupted, pushing herself away to face him with her legs crossed, allowing their knees to touch.

"Well, it's no surprise that you can link with an animal. Your father was actually quite good at that," he laughed, running his fingers through his hair.

"I don't understand. Why I don't know about all these special abilities Fighters have? You guys all made it seem like I was above and beyond and the only one who could save us. But, the more I learn about my surroundings, the less true that notion seems. Are you sure I'm special? It seems all that was just a lie to trick a fervent teenager," Eliana asked, her temper flaring again.

"Now, hold on," he said, taking her hand. "Just slow down a minute. You need to understand that each Fighter has some special ability that they rarely share... with anyone."

"But you knew!" she shouted, yanking her hands back.

"Yes, but it was necessary for my work. Long ago, Fighters figured out that The Darkness was drawn to more powerful beings, so the

Fighters hid their unique abilities. Over time, the reasoning was forgotten, but Fighters continued to uphold that mentality. Your family was no different.

"Your dad could project himself into animals. Your mom could heal wounds. I can control my appearance, as you now know. But you, you seem to have a collection of skills wrapped up into one nice little package," he completed with a wink.

She flushed slightly at the attention.

"Okay... But how do I know that you're not changing your appearance right now and lying about the curse?" she asked, doubting her immediate trust in him. "You knew it was me out there. How can I be sure that you didn't choose to look like a younger version of yourself to gain my trust?"

"You know the answer to that, Eliana. You felt my magic, but if you want me to prove it, use yours to feel mine as I change," he replied, offering a hand to her again.

"Fine," Eliana replied, taking his forearm and closing her eyes.

A tingle raced through her hand as the flesh beneath her palm shifted. When she opened her eyes, a small Chinese woman sat before her. Eliana let out a burst of laughter, then watched as Graham changed back into himself.

"Okay. I'll choose to trust you for now, but the part about me... You're saying that I am this prophesied whatever because I have over one special skill?" she asked, using her hands to emphasize her disdain for the categorization.

"Well, yes. The power you hold inside is more important than any special skills you display. Your parents allowed you to use your anger and loss to train and improve, but that also left you lacking in what you can still become. I've seen your natural ability, and not just today. You started showing signs of magic long before you should have been able to, but I never meant for you to fight this alone. I always intended to come back and help you defeat The Darkness once and for all."

"Oh," she mumbled, embarrassed that she let her ego believe this was all up to her.

"Eliana?" he asked gently.

"What?" she replied, rubbing her face and trying to find something other than Graham to look at.

"I don't think your parents died that night."

"What?! What do you mean? How can you say that?"

Eliana's legs unfolded, and she was instantly upon her knees. Making her way back to Graham in a blink, she sat back on her heels, staring at him.

"Well," he started gently. "You mentioned they passed away fifteen years ago, but your dad sent me a message through a raven some seven years ago saying that you were well on your way to finding me. And after fifteen years of training, you were more talented than anyone else he had come across."

"Seven?! Are you sure? Maybe your timeline is off," Eliana tried to convince him and herself. Something wasn't adding up.

"No. I'm sure. I still have the note that was attached to the raven. We had a code that we wrote in to keep information safe."

"Well, what else did it say? Where are they? Why haven't they tried to contact me?" she asked, coming closer.

"They can't contact you, at least not in traditional ways; it's honestly safer for everyone that they don't. And as for where they are... Well, that night when their magic sent you here, it also affected them."

"What do you mean?" she asked impatiently, not giving him a chance to explain.

"I mean, your parents weren't killed, but Tohe Darkness also didn't take them. They got trapped somewhere between these two worlds. Something happened that interrupted them from being able to carry all three of you across the different worlds. My guess is The Darkness had drained too much of their magic, and they weren't strong enough after everything. I don't really know. I can't pinpoint where they are, and they won't tell me. But I have every intention of getting them out, but I don't think that's possible until The Darkness is eliminated. There are a lot of unanswered questions, and I'm still working on mostly theories. Luckily, most of them have worked out... But for now, we need to get back to Francisco."

Eliana sat back, gazing into the distance. The guilt and embarrassment left as her thoughts switched to destroying The Darkness and finding her parents. Without a word, she stood up and started trudging down the hall back toward the lab. Graham shuffled behind her, gathering the items he had thrown aside to catch Eliana. He encouraged her slow walk by pushing the blanket gently into her back. The contact snapped her out of whatever trance she had put herself in, and her movements returned to normal.

CHAPTER THIRTEEN

The rest of the walk back to the lab was quiet. Graham found himself lost evaluating the capabilities of Eliana's boundless magic. No one person should have that many powers, but he supposed it made sense for someone who was supposed to bring back balance. Her skills had just opened a field of possibilities. If he could summon The Darkness by just harnessing his magic, what would happen with hers? And now that she was discovering more about her abilities, would she continue to find more, or to protect herself, bury the magic? Graham sighed as they walked up to the room where Francisco remained half-conscious on the floor. That conversation would have to wait until they could be alone again.

"Francisco," Graham said, passing Eliana to place the heated blanket on his friend. "How are you feeling? Are you still cold? Thirsty? Hungry?"

Francisco laughed weakly, which transformed into a coughing fit that had Graham immediately by his side, supporting him up slightly while offering him water.

"Thank you," Francisco managed to speak once the coughing subsided. "I'm okay. The cold is just straight through my bones."

Graham reached over to turn up the heat, and Eliana kneeled

beside them and adjusted some pillows for better support. Graham stared hard at her from across Francisco, trying to analyze her thoughts. She looked up quickly and gave him a half-smile, then gestured to focus on the victim. He nodded, then turned his attention down to his friend.

"Alright, Francisco. Do you think you're up for some questions, or do you need more rest?" Graham asked, eager to learn more.

"No, no. I'm alright, but could I get more water?" Francisco asked, holding his glass towards Eliana.

"Uhh, sure." She shrugged while looking at Graham.

"Follow the hall back to the first room, where I took you; there's a sink with filtered water across the room."

"Got it." She nodded once.

Graham caught Eliana's eyes when she stood. The worry and suspicion were evident on her face. He watched her walk away and then turned his attention back to Francisco, whose attention was still boring into Graham.

"Okay. She's gone, so?" Graham started, hoping his assumption was correct.

Francisco struggled to push himself to sit. When Graham realized, he assisted. Francisco held his hand in front of his face and wiggled his fingers. With a nod of approval, he finally spoke.

"It's been so long since I was in control of my magic. It's strange being able to feel it returning to my extremities," he coughed, then continued. "I don't know how long I've been trapped, but it felt a lot longer than how old you look..."

Graham laughed, "Let's not base this off on how I look. That's a story for another time. As for you, I thought you died thirty years ago... But if I'm right..." He paused to deliberate before proceeding further. "In my theories, they have killed no one. The Darkness simply takes over your body for use as a vessel of some sort. Right?"

Francisco's face scrunched.

"I remember getting cocky about my skills, and then some hooded figure kept running into me. There were too many coincidences. He must have been following me." He cleared his throat. "Anyway. I never saw his face, but he told me he could make me more powerful. He gave me a bit, but I needed more... I wanted more. After a couple of months, I was a stronger Fighter than I had ever been, but The Darkness seemed to be more and more attracted to me. In the end, they finally overtook me. I remember being pulled through icy blackness like I was being consumed by it. After that... I remember nothing," his voice dropped to just above a whisper. "It was like being stuck in a nightmare. The force tore me apart, separated me from my magic. It was excruciating. A kind of pain I have never felt before. I could see through my own eyes, but I couldn't control what I was doing. My body didn't feel like my own. Does that make sense?"

Graham heard a sharp breath behind him. Turning around, he saw Eliana standing in the doorway; her eyes focused on something in the distance. Recognizing the difference between this look and when she had transposed into the raven, he knew something Francisco had said sent her back into memory. Graham wondered how often this happened to her, then turned his attention back to his old friend, hoping to keep him talking.

"It makes more sense than you think," Graham replied, forcing a smile as he tried to distract Francisco from Eliana. "Can you tell if the connection is still there? Do you think we need to worry about The Darkness returning?"

Graham's questioning seemed to fall upon deaf ears as Francisco just continued to glower at Eliana, who remained in the doorway, completely disconnected from the surrounding reality.

"Is she okay?" he asked Graham.

"Huh?" Graham turned his attention back to Eliana, who was now swaying gently. "Oh, yeah. She's probably just reliving a memory for something."

"Reliving... a memory?" Francisco replied, his voice oozing with confusion. "Is that something that she frequently does?"

"I'm not sure," he replied, continuing to watch Eliana. "I don't recall that happening to her as a child. At least not in this frequency. But she'll be fine," Graham turned back and smiled at Francisco again.

"When she poured some of her magic to heal me, I could feel her power. If The Darkness ever got ahold of her... we would all be doomed. I'm not even sure she's aware of the magic hidden within her.

Most of us have a power that is buried so deep we never even realize it, but I learned how to sense it from The Darkness. I can't feel that part of my magic anymore. When you tore The Darkness away from me, it latched onto that. But I don't think The Darkness is coming back; I'm sure it can't. When I was taking on more power, it took months for The Darkness to get its full grasp into this dimension without me calling to it first. So, I guess, for now, you're going to have to trust that I won't try to call back on The—"

Francisco cut off when the glass Eliana was holding dropped to the floor. Graham quickly ran and did a baseball slide, barely catching her head before it hit the floor. Then, cradling her gently, he shifted to straighten out.

"Are you sure she's okay?" Francisco asked again.

Graham scoffed, trying not to sound worried but instead appearing slightly heartless. He cleared his throat and tried again.

"I'm sure she is. She's done this before," he replied.

Graham felt her pulse and wiped some sweat from her brow. Eliana groaned in response to his touch but slowly opened her eyes, sat up, and looked around. Her face flushed with embarrassment before jumping to her feet.

"Sorry. I'll get you more water." She rushed out the door.

"Eliana!" Graham shouted, trying to find his feet. "I'll be right back, Francisco," he said while running.

Francisco nodded and readjusted himself like he was sitting around a campfire, wrapping himself tightly in the blankets. Graham, approving of Francisco's newly situated position, raced out the door.

"Eliana!" he said, running up behind her.

She kept walking, so he reached out and grabbed her upper arm gently. Her eyes were wet with tears that threatened to spill out when she turned around.

"Eliana..." Graham repeated with concern, pulling her into a hug without thinking.

"I'm fine. I will be fine. It's okay. I just didn't — I wasn't expecting a memory to be triggered without me doing anything. Usually, I have to concentrate and use my magic. But this was different. It was like walking into a wall of the past," she replied, pressing herself against him.

"Has it ever happened to you before?" Graham asked, pulling away slightly and wiping a tear from her cheek.

"Maybe once or twice as a kid, but I've been pretty good at controlling when it happens. It was just a little unnerving. The worst part is that it wasn't even my memory.... It was Francisco's."

Graham immediately tensed.

"What? What do you mean it was Francisco's memory? How is that even possible?" he questioned, stepping away from her.

"I... I don't know. I heard you guys talking. He was explaining what it was like; how he felt with The Darkness, and I guess I just let myself get carried away into it all. The story and his feelings...," she paused and took a breath that shuddered in her throat. "That look in his eyes... he was there. Maybe it was my magic blending with his memories. I don't know." Her voice faded as her eyes remained unfocused on the present for a moment. Finally, she jerked her head up and looked at Graham. "You try it. Think intensely of a moment. Try to really go there. Let your magic take over a little. Imagine going to the place, really being there. Once you find that memory, it's just about focus. Let me try."

She started to fade away from the present again, so Graham took a breath and focused on a memory he would want her to see.

In the twilight hour, it was cold enough to send a shiver through me. The sun had left, and new colors were painting across the sky. Graham was talking to my parents. I went to step to get closer, but I had no legs. This form was just an entity existing unknowingly inside of memory, yet I felt the breeze that danced through the air. When I got within an inch of Graham, his skin raised with goosebumps, and he turned my way slightly before continuing to talk.

"Well," he smiled at my mother and then my father. "I guess this will be goodbye for a while. Are you sure you guys will be okay if I leave on such short notice?"

My mother and father both returned the smile. They stole a quick, loving glance at each other, then turned back to Graham. My mother reached out to squeeze Graham's arm before replying.

"Graham, you know we are perfectly capable of taking care of ourselves. Things have seemed difficult, but I have complete faith in your scientific ability," she paused a moment to brush a tear from Graham's cheek. "Whatever we come across from here on out, I have no doubt eventually, we will succeed in defeating all of it. And...." she hesitated a moment, frowning at the ground before looking back up into Graham's eyes, "as much as I hate to put this on her, I know Eliana will step into her role. The two of you will finally be able to end this."

My mother and father simultaneously reached out for one another's hand and linked their fingers. The love that so very obviously existed between them filled my heart with happiness. Seeing them alive and so unworried about putting on a fake smile for me was sort of calming in a way. Observing my parents believing so much in Graham and myself in this fight gave me a new sense of hope. And knowing that this entire plan was more thought out than I could have ever imagined lessened any anger I felt towards Graham and my parents.

"Thank you, both of you, for everything you have done and sacrificed. And everything you are about to sacrifice. I love you all more than I know how to express."

They hugged their goodbyes as my parents returned their love for Graham.

Graham snapped his eyes open when he heard Eliana sniffling. He hoped he hadn't caused her pain by showing her that memory. He had just wanted her to know that everything they were doing was more than just a whim of a plan. There was also a part of him that needed her to know that her parents didn't want this life for her, but they felt like there was no other choice.

"So, you saw the memory that I focused on, then?" Graham asked gently.

Eliana nodded and hugged him tightly, whispering a barely audible "thank you" in his ear. She quickly pulled away and wiped her tears from her cheeks.

"I'm sorry," she sniffed at him.

"For what?" he replied, brushing a tear from her cheek the same way Eliana's mother had done to him all those years ago.

"For judging and doubting you, I suppose. I've been letting anger drive me for so long. Perhaps, I didn't want to face my fears and pain. I have this compulsion to be strong and take care of everyone else around me, so most of the time, I forget about myself. When someone tries to change that hierarchy that I've created in my brain, I panic. Finding my worth in this is hard. In my mind, I'm doing this for everyone else, and that alone makes it all okay. Sometimes I need to feed on that anger so the fear and pain don't consume me. You know?" she asked him with a sad smile.

Graham nodded but said nothing as he processed her words. There was a lot more behind what she said, but he felt like he needed to just be in this moment for her right now.

"I think I understand what you mean. We've all struggled at one time or another, trying to find our self-worth. When you're left alone, it's harder to find that without practically killing yourself to get some sort of recognition that makes it all feel worth it."

"Yeah, something like that," Eliana replied, her body visibly holding tension.

"Look, I know you probably don't want to hear it, but your worth does not depend solely on what you are doing for everyone else. Just because it feels like there is so much riding on your shoulders doesn't mean that without your complete success, you can't be worthy of the existence you have in this universe. I mean, I know I've continually asked for you to help me since you arrived, but that doesn't mean that just being here with me as a person isn't one of the most pleasurable experiences I have had in a long time. Your wit and nuances that I'm learning to read have been more enjoyable than you realize. You're smart and talented, and I have always enjoyed spending time with you, even when you were a child. When this is all over, and we have finally defeated The Darkness, I cannot wait to get to know the person you are," he replied, placing her hair behind her ear.

Eliana smiled and let tears fall from her eyes again. She leaned in and gently kissed his cheek.

"I think if we can get Francisco to focus on a memory with The

Darkness, I will be able to gather more information on how to save everyone," she said, changing the subject abruptly as she pulled away.

"What?" Graham replied, trying to keep up with her alternative plan.

"I mean, we tested I can be a part of a memory that isn't my own. I exist in it as if I was reliving my own, but I can't touch anything or be seen. I only exist as an entity, an object of energy. I saw you react subconsciously to my presence in your memory, but you never actually saw me, right? If I can tap into his memory with The Darkness, maybe there's something more I can find."

"Okay..." Graham started tentatively. "But what if The Darkness can see you? They exist differently in time and space than we do. What if something happens, and you get lost with them?"

"I don't really have an answer for that, but what other choices do we have? We can't just keep draining your magic and hoping that The Darkness will show up here. That's going to take more time than I want to spend on this. It's been so many years and so many lost lives already... I just want it to end," she said.

"I wasn't planning on just sitting around and draining my magic forever either, you know. But I agree that the fewer people we drag into this, the better I'll feel. We can attempt this, but if you feel you're in danger at any point, I want you to separate yourself from the memory as quickly as you can, got it?"

Eliana scrunched her nose.

"I'll do what I can. If you think that it's getting out of hand, hopefully stopping Francisco's memory will release me as well, but I guess we'll find out."

Graham grunted disapproval and mumbled to himself about how he still didn't like this plan, but he knew they were running out of time.

CHAPTER FOURTEEN

Following closely behind Graham, Eliana's mind was racing through every probable scenario for what they were about to attempt. The worst case would be her getting overtaken by The Darkness. If they got ahold of her and her magic, she knew things would quickly turn against them. Graham would be left with the nearly impossible task of saving them, let alone everyone else.

When they reached the doorway where Francisco still sat bundled in his blankets, Graham continued forward while Eliana took a moment to stay just before the threshold of the room. She knew they were about to take a gamble that could end in utter devastation, but they didn't have a choice. Taking a deep breath, she accepted the knowing that this was the right choice for everyone. All she had to do now was be calm, attentive, and strong.

As the humming of the room got her attention again, Eliana tried to decipher the mumbles coming from the two men. Her eyes snapped to the movement when Francisco nodded blankly. He stared hard at something that she couldn't see.

"Do you think that's something you would be willing to do? I know I am asking a lot from you— especially in this weakened state, but you won't be alone. And since it's just a memory, you can easily snap out of it if you feel you're not safe."

"Yeah," Francisco replied slowly. "I think I'm more worried about letting The Darkness back into my thoughts and getting lost to that feeling of power again. Losing control... scares me the most. It's like I can feel them touching me, even in the memory."

Francisco shivered and looked up at Eliana. She stared back as his eyes studied her for a moment before smiling.

"I know this is going to be difficult for you, Francisco, and I want you to know that I'm going to do everything I can to protect you. Graham will be here to protect us, too. If something happens and we are both in danger, I will do whatever it takes to keep you from being harmed anymore. But I also need to do whatever I can to learn as much as possible."

Francisco and Graham both watched her quietly while she spoke. She could see that Graham wanted to stay steadfast, but fear subtly painted his features. Francisco just looked exhausted, but there was also a spark of hope that existed behind the dark circles which consumed his eyes. This dim light gave Eliana more optimism than anything else at that moment. The fact that Francisco could still believe in good made her feel that together, they could fight this.

"Okay," Francisco finally whispered. "If there's anyone I'm going to trust in this situation, it would be an old friend and the woman who helped rip me away from the grasp of The Darkness."

Graham straightened up, hope replacing the fear gradually.

With a gentle smile, Graham nodded and helped Eliana arrange the blankets for her to sit comfortably close to Francisco. Lowering herself to the floor, she crossed her legs and reached out to touch Francisco. A pulse of magic shot through her hand, and she watched his dark circles lighten ever so slightly.

"It will all be okay. We will protect you," Eliana said with a smile.

A frown replaced her expression as he winced slightly. She couldn't tell if she was hurting him or if he was just sensitive to her touch. Once she received two solemn nods in response, she retracted her hand and closed her eyes.

"Okay, Francisco. I need you to focus on a memory of The Darkness. Let yourself go there. It can be any memory at all, even from before they melded with you. Just focus on that moment, and try to remember every detail about being there," she guided.

It was a moonless night, blackness shrouding my surroundings. The cold forced my lungs to contract, but something felt off like last time. When I looked down to find my feet, once again, no form existed. I willed my mind to relax from the sensations it was being told that it was feeling and did my best to focus on my surroundings.

I searched around and saw two figures off in the distance. They were barely visible in the dark wooded area. As I shifted closer and realized that it was Francisco and The Darkness talking.

Francisco formed some sort of sphere of magic in his hand that flickered dimly. He reached out with his free hand and touched The Darkness, causing the ball to explode with power. I tried to shield where my eyes would be, temporarily blinded. As the light dimmed out again, I saw The Darkness reappear.

"You need to control the power I give you," The Darkness growled at Francisco as it came back into view.

"It just feels so good to access my hidden talent. I don't want to hold back," Francisco replied with widened eyes and a beaming smile.

I shifted closer, careful not to touch either of them. When I was within an arm's distance, everything went quiet. The air stilled, the bugs stopped mid-flight, and I quickly realized that time had frozen.

"Who are you?" the growling voice hissed into the air.

I froze and waited for the memory to continue, but it seemed no one existed at this moment except for me and The Darkness. The air grew denser. I looked closely at the form in front of me. The human that was buried inside was barely visible, but I could see him smile. I shuddered.

"I am a Fighter," I replied confidently.

"Well, obviously, girl. Who are you, and how did you get here? You're not of a form that exists in the present. Explain yourself," The Darkness continued with annoyance taking over.

"I came to find you," I said with a smile in my voice.

"You're testing my patience. How did you get here?" he repeated.

"Through a memory," I replied, regretting my honesty.

"THROUGH A MEMORY?! HOW IS THAT POSSIBLE WHEN YOU DON'T EVEN EXIST HERE IN THE FIRST PLACE?" the voice rumbled at me.

"I don't really think that's relevant," I replied, sending myself further away from where Francisco's frozen form remained.

The Darkness followed me for a moment, revealing the human whom it had consumed for just a flash. I tried to place the face, but I didn't recognize him. It appeared as though for The Darkness to control its entity in such a way, it would need its human attachment. Without the vessel, it would not be able to manipulate its surroundings. I tried to move further away again, but this time, it did not follow, flickering as it strained to exist in our world.

"Look, girl. I won't fall for any of your tricks. Who are you, and how do you exist in a place where you don't belong?!"

I laughed.

"What's wrong? Do you want to be the only one capable of existing somewhere in some time that you shouldn't? At least I don't have to suck the magic out of a living form to be here," I half-shouted.

The Darkness growled and shot forward at me again. This time, the human that it had consumed was revealed entirely. The fleshy hand reached out to grab The Darkness before it completely separated from his body. He glared where I existed and forced The Darkness back together with his solid form.

"Think you're pretty clever, don't you? I'll soon learn who you are. This form you have taken is simply made up of the pure magic which we all bury deep inside. It is a skill that I shall soon work on to make my own. I will search for every magical person that exists in this land. I will always remember your magical form. I will find you, and I won't stop until I do."

Eliana snapped back to reality with a sharp inhale, quickly reaching out and shaking Francisco.

"Francisco! Francisco!" she shouted.

He opened his eyes in confusion and grabbed onto her forearms.

"What happened? I was just barely in that memory...."

Graham glanced between them both, then looked down to check his watch.

"He's right, Eliana. Barely a minute passed."

She shook her head, closing her eyes tightly. After a moment to collect herself, her eyes snapped open. She rubbed her hands over her face as she stood.

"No. The Darkness froze the time within the memory... and apparently here, too. Everything is moving too quickly. I need a moment to think through this."

"Whoa, what do you mean, The Darkness froze time? How long were you in that memory?" Graham asked.

She paused a moment to take a deep breath.

"Graham, I think I know how we can stop all of them without having to defeat hundreds of entities."

"What? How can you have that much information? How long were you even there?" Graham asked, clearly puzzled.

"I don't know." She rested the back of her hands on her eyes in exhaustion, trying to slow down the thoughts. "At least five minutes."

"What?!" Graham exclaimed. He looked down at his watch again. "My watch says that you were only there for barely a minute. I don't understand."

Eliana sighed, pacing while her mind continued to race while the two men waited quietly.

"Look, I don't know how, but The Darkness could see me. In the other memories I have gone to, the people within them reacted as if they felt something, but there was never a full acknowledgment of my existence. The Darkness said that I existed in my pure magical form," she stopped walking and stood in front of the men. "I don't know if I froze time here as he froze it in the memory or if he did, but if he was able to freeze time through a memory...." Eliana faded off and put a hand to her forehead, her breath shallow.

"Then we're in more danger than we know," Graham finished for her.

There was a thick silence that grew more and more uncomfortable by the second. Just as the room felt like it would explode with the weight of the situation, Francisco spoke up quietly.

"But how does any of this help us stop them?"

"Because I know who it was," Eliana responded quietly. "I saw the human within The Darkness. He said he would spend as long as it takes to find me by my magic, so if we set me out as a trap or leave hints in memories we have with The Darkness, I think we can tell him where we will be at a specific time. Then he will come to find me, but we'll be ready for him."

"Are you insane? Do you want to be the prey? And, who is he? How do you know this is safe at all?" Graham asked in a protective tone.

"Sebastian."

"What?" Graham asked.

"I think Sebastian McMallum is the origin of The Darkness," Eliana replied.

Francisco froze, and Graham cursed under his breath.

"But how? How could a name we've all heard hide the fact that he is the creator of The Darkness?" Graham asked, slightly in awe.

"Well, I don't know if he created it. I think evil has and will always exist. It's whether we choose to acknowledge it that makes it so powerful. The stories always said that Sebastian spent his time calling upon darker powers to strengthen himself, and you mentioned that The Darkness followed those with the most talent and most profound insecurities. The Darkness knew he could manipulate those Fighters to crave the extra power. I've always assumed it was multiple entities coming after people, but I think it was always Sebastian, at least in the beginning. In Francisco's memory, Sebastian was controlling the dark form more than it was manipulating him. The Darkness tried to come after me, but he grabbed it and forced it to blend back with his flesh and bone.

"I think every entity that we see is just a piece of him. Clearly, we have been wrong about thinking that the entities projected here from another dimension while the human host stays behind. Whatever attaches The Darkness to their dimension needs the vessel to travel beyond. I don't know if defeating them is making Sebastian stronger or weaker or what happens to the humans when The Darkness is sent back, but I suppose I could look at memories over the years and compare his strength. Then that could take time that we don't have. If we focus on what we do know, we know he's controlling each of them through magic. But in that same thought, we don't even know if he gains power from the magic or the person. And then we have to wonder if he gives up a part of himself to have eyes everywhere and then only consumes magic in intervals when his minion entities return to him. Gah!"

Eliana paused, letting her frustrations settle as she spread her fingers across her temples and massaged gently, trying to slow her thoughts. The tension she felt in the air was palpable. She needed to calm her mind. She filled her lungs with air, then dropped her hands and looked up at them as she released them.

"Uhhh," Graham finally forced out. "I guess all versions kind of make sense. But are you really planning to capture Sebastian this way? Are you even really sure that he's the root of it all?"

"I don't know. I just have this feeling. Kill the supreme boss, and everyone else returns to normal."

Eliana laughed at herself and hoped that it could be like in the books she had read. If this solution didn't work, she would likely fall into complete hopelessness. When her laughter was met with only silence, she looked up to see Graham's wheels turning.

"What are you thinking?" she asked him.

"You know, you may be right. If Sebastian and his powers created this, then breaking his bond might be all it takes to destroy it. Do you think you have enough magic to drop into one of my memories with The Darkness?"

"Shouldn't we let her rest and build up her power?" Francisco cut in frantically.

"Graham's right, Francisco. I'm fine, and we need more evidence. If he can take me to a memory of an entity that isn't Sebastian, I might be able to taunt it enough to see where the power holds."

"Right!" Graham confirmed excitedly. "Now, all I have to do is find a useful memory with an encounter, and then you can head on in," he said before turning. "Francisco, I need you to monitor us. Help pull us out if anything seems off. Okay?"

"Alright... I will try," Francisco agreed hesitantly. The conversation happening around visibly confusing him.

"Great. That's all I can ask. Ready?" Graham asked, turning to Eliana.

She took a deep breath and nodded. Taking a quick inventory of her magic, she tried to access the hidden core. A wave radiated through her body, then stopped. She found it. The direct touch of the core warmed her body along with her surroundings, like a warm sunrise. As the power surged, her hair waved, and gravity started to surrender. She was no longer on the floor. With a satisfied smile, she released the flow of magic, settling back to the ground beneath.

Looking up at the two men, she couldn't help but laugh at their expressions. Graham was frowning, and Francisco was staring at her in awe. When she snorted, Graham frowned more, but Francisco tried to speak.

"What... how did you...how can you... um..." he sighed.

"What?" Eliana attempted to clarify.

"I can feel what you're doing. My body still aches for that magic that is buried so deep. I feel it every time you touch me, but I can't understand how you just tapped into it so easily on your own. It should be almost impossible. At least that's what The Darkness told me..." he trailed off at the end, his eyes glossing over.

He dropped his head into his hands and whimpered. Eliana went to console him.

"Look, we weren't taught as Fighters that we could access more powerful magic on our own. Maybe it was forgotten, or maybe it was purposely hidden to help keep us safe. Whatever the reason, it's something that I learned on my own and need to tap into now. I think Graham has unknowingly been doing it all along when he drained his magic to summon The Darkness. This is still all very new to me," she finished, placing a hand gently on his back and letting him feel some of that power.

The instant she released her core magic into Francisco, he went rigid and threw his head back, screaming in pain. Eliana immediately retracted her hand and stepped protectively in front of Graham. Francisco ceased his scream when her hand was removed, but his breath was labored.

"Francisco?" she prodded gently.

"Don't," he said between shallow breaths.

"Don't what?" she encouraged, taking another step towards Graham as they waited for a reply in the silence.

They both watched as Francisco calmed before speaking again.

"You can't do that. If you put that much power into me, they'll find me again. They are still connected to me. I could see them... waiting for me... Just waiting," he paused and shook his head frantically as a shiver visibly passed through his body.

"We're not going to let anything happen to you, but maybe we should be separated further while she goes into my memory," Graham said gently. "How about you go into my lab, and if The Darkness makes it through and we can't control it, lock us in? Can you do that?"

"I don't want to let either of you do this," Francisco finally said.

"I know, Francisco. Please understand that you're still a good person, even though you've been manipulated into doing horrible things. I trust you to take care of us the best you can. If you think we need to pull out of the memory, press this button to talk. If talking doesn't work, you might have to come in and shake me, but don't risk it if you think you won't have enough time to escape back to the safety of the lab. I will deal with touching Eliana. I don't want you to sacrifice any more of yourself."

Francisco's frown deepened, and his eyes filled with tears again. He pulled Graham into a hug and looked up at Eliana, and mouthed *I'm sorry*.

She nodded and smiled gently at him.

"Alright, Francisco. Let's go into the lab. I'll show you a few controls you might need. It's fairly simple to understand."

CHAPTER FIFTEEN

Eliana watched as the two men made their way into the other room. Her mind raced with every potential disaster that could occur during this. Still, there was a light fighting through the crushing weight of despair. *What if I fail, or worse, what if I win but lose him?* She looked at Graham as his arms animatedly explained something to Francisco, and there was an unfamiliar ache in her heart. As it bubbled up, she laughed and promised herself that she would do anything to protect Graham in whatever might happen.

For now, she would focus on what she knew. These entities were traveling across dimensions, so it only made sense that time travel was also possible. Now she just needed to figure out if memories were frozen moments in time for The Darkness as it was for mortals or if they could sense a change and refocus their existence to that precise time and place it in their timeline. If the memory could change, how would the actual moment be replaced in time?

"Eliana?" Graham's voice shook her out of her thoughts.

"Huh?" she said, glancing toward him.

"Okay. Just wanted to make sure the intercom was still working."

The muffled voices in the lab were barely a whisper from where she stood, yet The Darkness had been so clear to her in the other room.

With a quick scan, her eyes spotted the microphone in one corner of the room.

"Graham?" she attempted softly.

The murmur from the lab ceased immediately, and Graham stopped waving his arms about. He reached out to press the button so she could hear him once again.

"Is everything alright?" he asked with concern.

"Yes. Just making sure the microphone still worked," Eliana replied, pointing to the corner just behind her right shoulder with a smirk.

Graham nodded, smiling at her. The breath she was sucking in through her nose caught in her throat. The lump nearly choked her as she dreaded that this was the last time she would be able to see the smile that had been torn from her once before. The feelings she had once felt for him as a child had transformed and matured as she had, and now the weight of them threatened to crush her.

Eliana could remember only one other time she had allowed herself to open her heart enough for another that she felt this way. Wanting to recall this other person, she closed her eyes and imagined their smile. It didn't take long to recognize the similarities between her past lover's smile and the smile that Graham frequently wore. Though, beyond the mouth, their faces held no other likenesses. Where Graham was sharp and rugged, this other had soft, peach skin that stretched across defined cheekbones. The sharp, blue eyes that Eliana swore she could see through all the way to the soul. The long blond hair that cascaded over bared shoulders. The silk lips that were painted the color of a rose.

Eliana smiled at the memory, relaxing as the woman smiled back.

"I miss you, Fiona. I will always love you," Eliana whispered.

The image of the small woman in front of her replied I love you, too, but no sound left her lips. The tears that Eliana had tried to force back rolled down as Fiona faded away. The pain of her loss still felt fresh, and she vowed to never experience it again. Not this time... She was determined not to lose anyone else she cared for. The Darkness would soon meet its end.

"Eliana?" she heard Graham speak once again, this time more urgently. "Is everything alright?"

Wiping the tears from her cheeks, she replied with a nod and a soft smile. Both men were standing slightly more at attention, concern visible across their foreheads. The tension in their bodies pointed directly to the doors that would bring them back to her, and she briefly wondered how long Graham had been calling her name. With a deep breath, she shook her hands off to the sides of her body.

"Are you ready to do this?" she asked through the glass, ignoring their questioning gazes.

Graham relaxed slightly and turned to Francisco and shrugged, saying something she could almost make out. Her squinting eyes formed the words "ready," "this," and "okay if you're not." Francisco nodded his head in response to the statements. With a visible sigh, Graham turned his focus back to her.

"Okay. I'm coming back to you," Graham said over the intercom.

Eliana nodded, then watched Graham pull Francisco into another tight hug. When they separated, Graham left a hand on Francisco's shoulder and squeezed while giving a small nod. As Graham turned, both men took a deep breath in unison. Eliana let out a breathy laugh, and Francisco snapped his face to her. She could see his widened eyes filled with fear and tried to reassure him while Graham made his way back to her.

"Francisco, whatever happens in this memory, know that I will do everything in my power to protect everyone." She stepped towards the glass and placed a hand on it. "You won't be alone. Not even for a moment."

As she spoke the last of her words, she focused on her core magic and let it take over her. Just as her toes left the floor, Graham entered the room and walked over to her. Letting herself settle, she looked at Graham and watched him nod to Francisco with tears in his eyes.

"Okay," Graham whispered.

"Did you find the memory we'll need?" Eliana asked Graham softly when he took her hand as they walked back to the center of the room.

"I think so."

Eliana waited for more words to follow, but the silence that remained was never filled. Graham's jaw tensed, and his lips tried to form more words, but nothing came out. After a moment, he finally just shrugged and sat on the floor. She followed. Crossing her legs, she scooted slightly closer before reaching out to place her hand on him.

"Ready?" she asked one final time.

"As I'll ever be," he replied more nonchalantly than she expected.

The sky was dark. A gentle breeze moved a cluster of trees nearby. The clouds broke momentarily and let a splash of moonlight paint the path in front of me. As Graham looked frantically around, the light caught his eye, causing its golden hue to glow. His body became a silhouette against the soft light.

"I know you're here!" he shouted into the engulfing blackness.

I quickly scanned the area around me, sending out more magic to lure The Darkness out. Graham whipped around, looking directly where I was standing. His eyes looked through my entity, but he frowned as if his eyes were deceiving him. The Darkness charged out from the trees that were now behind him. I instantly willed my magic to freeze the moment, just as Sebastian had done before.

The Darkness shot from the body that it had taken up residence in, leaving the malnourished human behind. I didn't recognize them, but I did know the scream of The Darkness as it fought to stay in our world. The dark blob thrashed, making its way back to the host, writhing in pain.

Unlike Sebastian, the human form, whether blended with the entity or alone, was unable to move while time was frozen. The voice of The Darkness hissed through the mouth as if the lips were still able to move to form the words.

"What have you done? Who are you?"

I increased my power before speaking, watching The Darkness struggle to stay with the human it was linked to. It desperately wanted to reach me and my power but pulled itself to blend with the frozen flesh.

"Who I am is not important at this moment. What I need you to do is pass on a message to Sebastian. Let him feel what you feel. Tell him of my power."

I surged my magic once more, listening to The Darkness cry out as I forced it out of the solid body it controlled. The longer I let my magic leak through the air, the more I represented a human rather than a shape. I looked down at the fingers forming beneath me and was suddenly hit by a blow of power.

As I looked up, I was met with Sebastian's twisted face smiled through a shifting entity directly in front of me. I immediately released my hold on time, and Graham vanquished The Darkness that had charged him. As soon as Graham's threat was eliminated, my breath caught in my chest, and we ripped away from the memory. I looked up just in time to see Sebastian lunging forward at me.

As Eliana was smashed back into her present body, she choked on the breath that had been trapped during the memory. The hard, cold floor beneath her sent a shiver through her flesh, and finally, her vision adjusted back to the colorless room with Graham. She could feel some of her magic trickling out towards him as she regained control. He shivered in response as he was watching her inquisitively, following her lead as she stood.

"Did it work?" he finally asked.

"Mostly. The Darkness you fought isn't as powerful as Sebastian. He approached me wrapped in his Darkness where the other form couldn't even be separated from its frozen host without being in pain."

"What do you mean?" Graham asked.

"When I froze time in your memory, Sebastian appeared. He must have sensed my surge of magic — my core magic, or possibly it was the scream of The Darkness as it was ripped from the host you fought. I'm not sure. I unfroze time and let you end the fight before Sebastian could speak to me. He was lunging at me just as we faded away."

Eliana's voice grew quiet at the end, the fear of everything closing in. After a brief pause, she took a sharp inhale and continued with more hope.

"Anyway, what I mean to say is that I don't think the others can travel freely as Sebastian can. They can't control things the way he does. When I froze time, The Darkness was flung from the human host and struggled to get back before disappearing." She closed her eyes, trying to accurately recall every detail. "And I think when they scream, they are calling to Sebastian. There is a weakness that exists in their reliance on a Fighter's magic. I think Sebastian needs our magic, our bodies, to give entities that power, or maybe he is the power."

Eliana paused again, shaking her head as she squeezed it with her hands. There were multiple possibilities — too many unknowns. She still didn't know if The Darkness was of its own existence or just a part of Sebastian. Had his hate and desire for power materialized the entities? Or had he just learned to take control of the darkness that had existed since the beginning of time?

"Eliana?" Graham interrupted her thoughts.

She dropped her fisted hands from either side of her head and opened her eyes with a deep breath.

"There's too much I still don't know. If we fight Sebastian and win, are we certain that the rest of The Darkness will release their hold on their hosts? Or do we have to find the strength to do what we just did to Francisco hundreds of times? What if we can't beat Sebastian? What if—"

"Hold up!" Graham interjected, placing his hands on her shoulders. "You're spiraling. Let's focus on one thing at a time."

Eliana soaked in his touch and let it calm her, taking a few deep breaths. When she looked up into his eyes, he smiled gently and nodded before removing his hands and turning.

"Francisco, can you help clarify anything?"

"Maybe," he replied over the speakers. "I'm not sure I fully understand it all either, but I can confirm that things felt differently when Sebastian was guiding my magic. He must have given me part of his when he was showing me how to use mine. It always felt so much stronger with him, but when it was time to complete my training...." Francisco trailed off, his eyes filling with tears.

"The Darkness took over your body," Eliana finished for him, watching his reaction.

Graham spun around, frowning at Eliana. She stared back at him with emotionless eyes.

"Yeah," Francisco whispered in confirmation. "Sebastian made me believe I would find the power of my own. Subconsciously, I knew I was taking the side of The Darkness, but I guess it was a disillusion that I would be able to take control. If I had known that I was giving up all of myself to The Darkness, I never would have followed through. Although, now when I think about it, I am sure Sebastian probably would have killed me had I not completed the training."

"What?" Graham cut in.

"There's no way he'd trust someone to know his plans and walk around untouched. Besides, I think he needs our core magic so that he doesn't have to use his own to build an army, but I don't know what would happen if he's gone. The Darkness latches on to the people it takes over, but I think non-hosted ones are attached to Sebastian. And the ceremony to complete the training... Well, I only remember parts of it.

"The weather was gloomy like it always is there. The silence was bone-chilling. I wanted so badly to back out right before, but then he grabbed me. There was a pain that went deep into my core, similar to what I feel when Eliana touches me with her core magic, and then I passed out. I don't know how long I was out, but when I woke up, I was no longer in control of my body. I was being transported through time and dimensions far beyond what the imagination could comprehend," his eyes glossed over, and he paused for a moment.

Eliana opened her mouth to speak, but Francisco started up again, cutting her off.

"You know, Sebastian has been targeting more than just Placata Montis. I've seen more lands with magic than I can count, and most of them haven't survived. The hardest part for him is the amount of time he takes to convince someone to join him. It starts long before anyone even realizes it. He's the voice that whispers in the wind, telling you that you don't fit in, convincing you that you are better than everyone else, and they just don't understand you. He watches you for years and then feeds on your insecurities to pull out your power. If you don't concede, he attacks."

"That's horrible," Eliana and Graham said in unison.

"Sometimes, Sebastian would try to extract the magic from the non-compliant people, but no one ever survived, and he barely got any stronger from it. The amount of magic it took to drain their core was not worth the amount that he got out of it, but he can't always control his anger," Francisco stopped to laugh nervously.

Eliana looked over at Graham while he stared hard at his friend.

She made a mental note about Sebastian's inability to gracefully lose at anything, then turned her attention back to the conversation.

"Thank you, Francisco. Everything you're telling us is more helpful than you can imagine," Eliana said.

"Graham," Francisco continued as if she hadn't spoken, "if he knew you had found a crystal to store magic in and use later on, I think all would be lost. I hope they haven't been able to get a strong enough connection to me already to figure that part out. They might already be coming for you. He knows Eliana's magical form. He'll be able to track her down, eventually. I'd say sooner rather than later."

As Francisco finally went silent, Eliana and Graham looked at each other. There was tension humming through the surrounding air. Eliana knew they needed to hasten, but she didn't want to make any mistakes.

"Well, I guess we don't have a choice in this," Eliana spoke up. "If we wait, we lose any advantage we might have. If we jump in, we may not make the right choice. But either way, I think we all know that the only option is to move forward now to fight."

"What are you saying?" Graham inquired.

"I'm saying we'd better put together a plan. And a damn good one, at that. Francisco," Eliana said, changing her focus, "do you think you would be able to drain any of your magic into the crystal? I would really like to keep you out of this as much as possible."

"I—"

"Whoa," Graham jumped in, cutting off Francisco. "On what planet do we think it's a good idea to have more ammunition that Sebastian might get ahold of?"

"Look," Eliana replied calmly, "if we are going to have a chance at any of this, we're going to need to have the upper hand. Your magic is already weakened, but I can feel it building back up quickly. If you and Francisco drain your magic in a crystal, you can go mostly unnoticed and then help attack if I falter. If you have a crystal with not just your magic but whatever Francisco has to offer, you have that much more power."

"I'll do it," the voice said over the intercom. "I want to be able to help you in any way possible, but I know that the further away I am from this, the more chance you have of succeeding. If this plan allows me to do both, then I will give you everything I've got."

Eliana watched Graham nod with glazed eyes. He seemed far away in his thoughts, his breath ragged. She reached her hand towards his and let their fingers intertwine.

"Graham, this has all gone on for long enough. We can't keep searching for answers anymore," Eliana quietly encouraged, but her eyes were speaking a lot more than those words.

"I know," he replied, squeezing her hand. "I think I've known that for a few years now, but I kept waiting for something. You showing up on my doorstep is more than any sign I could have asked for. I'm just having a hard time processing that this is all finally about to happen," he finished with an awkward laugh.

The smile that remained on his face after he stopped laughing faded away, and his eyes clouded over. The realization of the situation came down like a heavyweight over the room again. Almost suffocating Eliana. Graham released his hold on her hand and absentmindedly rubbed his palms together. Staring off, he spoke again.

"One thing I cannot wrap my head around is how no one ever saw a hint of the human form these life suckers attach themselves to. You'd think with all the groups of Fighters throughout the years, someone would have seen something. In all of my research, I never discovered that the human host is actually here. I just assumed that we were defeating these entities. That it's just a cloud of evil latching on to the core magic that exists in each of us. Are they all just that well trained that they travel back to their dimension before they get weak enough to be separated?"

Eliana watched him go through his memories and hone on something, but she could tell his mind was racing despite his slow, methodical speech. His anxieties spiked her own thoughts, sending them on a rampage. Maybe there was something they were missing in this, or perhaps they were just wasting time. Before she could think too deeply into it, Francisco spoke up again.

"The Darkness is trained to leave before there is ever a chance to destroy their host. That scream you heard when you trapped us is a sort of the last line of defense. Usually, it kills the person who hears it.

Had it gone on for even a second longer, I'm not sure that Graham would have made it. Li, you saw the scream call Sebastian to it. I don't know how you blocked him from hearing the scream in that room, but somehow you did."

Eliana and Graham both nodded, taking in the additional information.

"Is there any way to stop the scream?" Eliana inquired.

Francisco hesitated a moment.

"If you have The Darkness trapped like you did mine, I think you can, but Sebastian is pretty quick to respond to a scream. I'm impressed with whatever you did to that room to stop him from coming, Graham. He refuses to lose the upper hand in any situation, so he has got to be pretty pissed that you two are figuring so much out. The other entities must have told him everything by now. I'm certain if he knew where I was, I wouldn't still be alive."

Eliana and Graham looked at each other apprehensively. They knew they had to act now, or they would have no chance of succeeding. Francisco's words came with more daunting truth. However, there was one last question that remained unanswered.

"Francisco, what part did my father play in your erm... uh... downfall?" Graham asked, struggling to find the right words.

The tension rolling from Francisco at that question could be felt all the way to where Eliana and Graham stood. His breath quickened, and a sheen of sweat glistened on his forehead. They watched as Francisco wiped his hands down his pants and darted his eyes around the room. Eliana flexed her muscles, preparing to defend them, then Francisco finally reached out to press the button to speak once again.

"Look, Graham. I don't want you to think that our friendship meant nothing to me, so please don't take it that way. Do you remember when I started coming over more, but then I would go run off to 'help' your dad?" there was a long pause. "He started showing me what The Darkness could do; how he controlled them. He told me I could learn to do the same. Sebastian had been following me for about a month before your dad reached out to me, and I just wanted so badly to be something more. I'm sorry. I was sort of hoping that you wouldn't ask," he finished with a grimace.

Graham and Francisco stared at each other. To an untrained eye, Graham appeared calm as he nodded, but Eliana had learned better. Even in their short time reunited, she could see the quick tension of his jaw. The flexed muscles in his back. The way his ear twitched slightly as he struggled to contain his neutral expression.

"Do I need to eliminate my father?" Graham finally asked in an icy tone.

Eliana couldn't stop the sound that escaped her lips when she heard the question. It was not something she had been expecting, and from the look on Francisco's face, he hadn't either.

"Well, um. I don't know that, uh, he would need to be eliminated, um, but I think he needs, uh, to be, errr, removed from a position of any sort of power," Francisco forced out.

Graham nodded, then turned to Eliana.

"I owe you a bigger apology than I thought. Not just you, but all of my people. Because that's what they should have been long ago. My people. Not my father's. I was foolish to think that he wasn't as big a threat as The Darkness. But he was among them. I expected everyone else to do a job that should have been my own. I was selfish in thinking all of this rode on my ability to make some stupid room to catch these things."

Graham spat the last word, then sighed and closed his eyes.

"Stop the pity party, Graham. What's done is done. You can now spend the rest of your days fixing this and making the world a slightly better place. The more time I spend with you, the more I realize how wrong I was to find fault in only you. I wanted someone to blame, but there have been centuries of choices that have led to this moment. Nothing falls on you alone."

Graham smirked at her, "You should listen to your own advice, sometimes, you know."

"Hush," she replied, unable to stop the smile that engulfed the word.

The silence echoed again. Eliana knew he was right. She hardly followed her advice yet expected everyone else to trust her word. And honestly, her guidance had seldom led anyone astray.

"So, what's the plan?" Francisco said, breaking the tension.

"I think," Graham started, looking to Eliana, "it's time for me to return home."

"What?!" Eliana replied louder than intended. "Why would you want to leave? You have built all this specifically to catch The Darkness and hold them here."

"Listen! If I go to my father, I can use whatever he has to call them there. He calls them there for a job. He doesn't bring them there to attack them, so they won't expect it. There must be something left in him that will want to do good. There's no denying that he's getting older. I've been checking in on him from time to time, and he's definitely slowing down.

"He should have already passed on the crown to me, but I'm not there, so he doesn't have anyone else. It's wearing on him, but I don't see him giving that power to anyone else, or he would have done so already. He will clutch on to his authority until death finally takes him, and then where does that leave everyone? No. I need to go back.

"*We* need to go back," Eliana interjected, emphasizing 'WE.' "I'm so tired of running. I thought I was chasing something, but I realize now that I've been running from my past. I didn't wish to face everything that I had left behind. I didn't want reminders that my parents were gone. I didn't want to feel like I had failed and just wanted to live in anger and focus on revenge... anything to mask the pain. Every dark entity that I took care of here, I counted as a win. I didn't need to know what was happening back home, no matter how much it haunted me every day."

Graham nodded at her and reached out to squeeze her hand.

"And I understand my magic now... All thanks to you," she chucked. "I was redirecting the wrong emotion to access my core. All I needed was trust, love, and hope to access my power, to access my core. The Darkness fed on his magic by using fear and hate, and I was using the same, where it should have been something Sebastian could never understand."

She understood now that the core of her magic lay within the core of her heart. The freedom she experienced as the raven, the trust Francisco had put in her, and the hope Graham had given to her lead to a gleaming light. The Darkness would never be as powerful as the light that has filled her now.

Graham smiled at her then turned.

"Francisco, I want you to stay here and let yourself recuperate. There's no more need for you to be involved if I can use my father. In a bit, I will show you how I have been checking in back home so that you can see certain things, but it won't last long, and you won't be able to see much. I need about an hour to put together everything required; then, I will come back to the lab. In the meantime, I'd like you to stay here. If there is any connection left to The Darkness, I don't want to take a chance for them to find you and pull information from you. This room will keep you safe," he smiled, then turned away. "Li, I need you to come with me to help prepare some stuff."

"Okay," Francisco and Eliana responded simultaneously.

CHAPTER SIXTEEN

Eliana smiled at Francisco as she followed Graham to the exit. She stepped through to the hallway and watched Graham engage each lock. Francisco wouldn't be able to leave, but nothing could get in, either. Graham pulled out his phone and unlocked it, changing the screen to the camera in the lab. Eliana saw Francisco spinning in the chair slowly, taking in the entire room as he went around. She suppressed a giggle as Graham grunted softly in approval and placed the phone back in his pocket.

The rest of the navigation through the hallways was quiet. Eliana was lost in her thoughts, and Graham didn't seem to be any different. The blurs of colors that they passed didn't register as anything more than the unfocused background in a picture. When they stopped, Eliana looked up for the first time since leaving the lab and let her eyes focus on the door in front of them.

It looked no different from the other doors down the hallway, but a strange beeping started when Graham put his hand on the doorknob.

"How many secret doorways do you have in this place?!" Eliana asked, laughing with surprise.

Graham simply turned slightly to look at her and shrugged with a half-smile. Once the door finished its beeping sequence, it slid open into the wall. Beyond the door lay yet another hallway, but this one did not attempt to look inconspicuous. The metal walls reflected distorted images of the two of them, and Eliana saw no evidence of another door. They walked a handful more steps; then, Graham put his arm out to stop her.

"Take a step back."

She moved back, watching as he squatted down. Eliana tilted her head slightly and changed her focus to the floor. When her eyes sharpened, she noticed a faint line running along the otherwise smooth surface. Graham's body turned at an angle to her as he scooted one foot back. He slid his finger along the line until it reached where the floor met the wall, then pushed a hidden button. The ground moved where his foot had been moments before.

"What... even is this place?" she asked incredulously.

Graham stood up, sucking his finger. His lips formed a smile around the limb, and she spotted a tiny pool of blood by his nail. Eliana whipped her head back to the supposed button and realized it had a blue glow to it.

"DNA reader," he shrugged.

He laughed at her open-mouthed stare as he turned away from her and descended the recently revealed staircase. Each stair activated before he stepped on it, bringing light to the otherwise darkness. Eliana followed behind and let the blue glow of each stair fill her eyes. She tried to catch a glimpse of where they were going, but the blue blinded her from seeing anything besides where to step next. When Graham reached the bottom, the floor above them closed, and the floor below them lit up and rippled on through the walls and ceiling until Eliana could see the space surrounding her.

The sight was breathtaking.

The walls around her cast off an inviting glow and revealed containers with labels. CR5C7. She frowned, trying to figure out what that could mean.

"What—" she began.

"Let me show you," Graham interjected.

He walked up next to her and slid the label aside. It promptly scanned his eye, and then he spoke another phrase.

"All that is soon will be. Take this power away from me."

Eliana scrunched her nose in confusion. She felt like she needed to be taking notes of the phrases he kept using to get in.

The container rotated in the wall to reveal an opening. When she peered inside, there was a large crystal. As Graham's hand went towards it, it pulsed, and the moment his hand wrapped around it, it hummed and came to life. He nonchalantly pulled it out and held it close to Eliana's face.

"This is one of the crystals I was telling you about, the ones that store magic. This one is categorized as a size 5 with a magic capacity of 7. That's what these letters and numbers mean," he went on, pointing to the label with his free hand. "Crystal: 5. Capacity: 7. It is the largest crystal that I have according to size, but the capacity isn't as great as it could be."

"I don't understand," Eliana began, gathering her thoughts.

"What part?" Graham patiently prodded.

Eliana laughed.

"Well, that's what I'm trying to figure out. I guess how you found them. What are they? How does no one else know that they exist?"

"Right. How about I just tell you the story of how I came across the crystals, and we'll move on from there?"

"I think that's an excellent choice...." Eliana replied slowly, never removing her eyes from the crystal.

"Indeed," Graham replied, laughing. "This all started about 24 years ago when I was first trying to learn more about The Darkness. One night, a fight had taken us, your parents and me, to the cliff over the river. You know the one that has a trail leading to your house?"

"I know the one," Eliana replied with a mischievous smile.

"Of course, you do," Graham laughed. "Well, after the fight was over, I stayed out there for some solace. The moon was full, and the way it was reflecting off the water was stunning. I watched some bats fly below me and then disappear into the stone. I don't know why I felt compelled to follow them, but I did. It wasn't far from where they had gone, and I could see several safe places to hang on to during the descent.

"When I reached the opening, there was a strange glow deep

within the cave. I called out before going any further than the entrance, but there was no reply. However, the light seemed to respond to my voice, and I felt a powerful pull to move toward it. My feet carried me further into the cave without me consciously willing them to do so.

"As I approached the light, I realized I was surrounded by crystals of all shapes and sizes. The source of light came from a single large crystal off to the right of the room. I reached out to touch an unlit one, not realizing that I had engaged my magic in defense. When my skin came into contact with the crystal, I felt my power released into it. I quickly pulled my hand away and noticed a faint glow coming from the once unlit rock. It throbbed with the pulse that ran through my veins. I had no idea what I had just done, so I turned and ran. I didn't know if my powers would return or if I would heal, or if I would be pulled back.

"Anyway, so, I bolted out of the cave, sending bats fleeing ahead of me. I scaled the wall and collapsed on the rocky ground above the cliff. I was dizzy and didn't have the strength to get up or call for help. I laid there for nearly an hour to regain my strength. However, when your body is that exhausted, it gives your mind more space to run rampant. So, I tried to process what had happened. There had to be a reason I was drawn to it, right? I was convinced of it."

Graham paused his story when Eliana reached out to place a finger on the crystal. He took a sharp breath and didn't release it. When she touched it and forced some magic into the crystal, it exploded with power.

They were hit with a blast of energy that threw them both backward. When Eliana pushed herself up and brushed her hair away from her face, she was speechless. The crystal remained precisely where Graham had been holding it moments before, suspended in the air with an aura that cast a new light around the room. It hummed and pulsed, and Eliana couldn't help but stand up to approach it. She now understood Graham's pull towards them.

"Eliana!" Graham shouted, jumping to his feet.

As her hand got closer, the crystal responded to her energy. She turned her palm to face the ceiling and placed it six inches below where it floated. The humming got louder, and the crystal gently fell into her hand. The moment it touched her skin, Eliana's hair shot out, and her feet left the ground. After a moment, the crystal cast no light. She had consumed all the power from it.

"Eliana?" Graham asked wearily. "Are you okay?"

She nodded at him, looking at his tense posture as he chanced another step closer to her.

"I'm fine. I guess I should have put less magic into the crystal," she laughed, trying to lighten the mood.

"I don't know that the amount of magic caused that reaction. That's not something I have ever seen, even when I have put an overload of magic into a crystal. I think it may have something to do with the way our magic blended," he said, gently stroking the now lifeless rock.

"What made you go back to the cave?" Eliana asked, ignoring his comment and how much she wanted to believe it was true.

He frowned for a moment but conceded when she merely stared at him with raised eyebrows.

"Well," he continued, taking the dull crystal from her, "when I woke up the following day, I could tell that my magic had been restored. I changed my appearance and turned it back. Nothing felt off, but I couldn't stop thinking about those crystals. So, I went back to the cave.

"My heart was racing as I climbed down and made my way through the lightless chamber. The crystals remained dark, aside from the two that hummed with light. The one I had touched still pulsed with my heart, but the one in the center remained still. Besides its pull on me to find it, it was not connected to me. I reached for the one with my magic, careful not to engage my defenses, and held it in my hand. This time, it drained nothing, and I was able to absorb it back... as you just did. It took me a while to figure out, though. Anyway, I left the original crystal that lit my way alone. I didn't trust the secrets it held, and I didn't want to lose the connection I had.

"After a few hours down there, I learned how to push the magic out of the crystal, making it more like a wand. I could shoot the captured magic rather than absorb it back into myself. I spent the next few weeks in the caves testing various ways of using the crystals. It was going well until one night, about a month later. After draining my magic into several of them and placing them back on the wall, I ran into some trouble.

"This time, when I reached the top of the cliff, The Darkness waited. Which makes sense now that I know my father had control over them. When I came up over the top, they didn't attack. They looked over at me for a moment, then turned their attention back to the other parts of the cliff. I didn't understand what was happening, but I knew I was too weak to fight them. My appearance didn't change when I was close to them, and I couldn't force the change. So, I quickly made my way past them, forcing myself not to run until I was out of their sight.

"The next afternoon, I found an alternative way down to the caves and tested a few more theories before confirming that draining my magic into the crystals allowed me to slip by undetected. When I got braver, I took the magic-infused crystal with me from the cave. Still, The Darkness did not detect me. After four months, the group of The Darkness dwindled to just one because of no threats during the time.

"It was my chance. I don't know what came over me. When I saw only one creature left to fight, I decided to practice pushing magic from the crystal. I needed to know what kind of weapon I had come across. If I could store my magic over time, could I use it later on for whatever I needed? Well, though it did work, I quickly learned how difficult expelled power was to aim. Luckily, I won my fight against the single one that night." He paused, staring at his hands like a samurai staring at his sword.

"I knew I had significantly limited my time on that cliff after that, so I immediately dropped back down to retrieve as many crystals as I could, including the one that first called to me. The rest of my testing had to continue elsewhere. I depleted that cave of two-thirds of its supply before I couldn't carry anymore."

He paused again to sigh, sadness taking over his features before he continued.

"I struggled immensely with the decision I made next, but I couldn't think of a better choice. So... I took some explosives that I had brought with me, and I set them off. I watched the dust from the rubble that had come crashing down deep within the walls. A few small rocks fell by the opening where I stood, but nothing more. The thing that would help save us was hopefully lost to anyone else that might stumble across the cave.

"When I made it back to somewhere safe, I fell to my knees and just cried. I had destroyed the cave with my own hands. But what else could I have done? How could I let them find what I had found? I hoped with every ounce of my body that they wouldn't dig past that rubble, and if they did, I prayed the crystals left behind were destroyed," he closed his eyes and took a few shaky breaths.

"Where did you take them?" Eliana gently asked when he took a moment to calm his emotions.

Through her now heightened magic, she could easily feel that he was reliving the moment more than he was letting on, so she didn't want to push too hard.

His water-laced eyes peered into her own and smiled minutely.

"Here."

"What? How?" Eliana asked sharply.

Graham laughed.

"I stumbled upon my ability to travel between worlds pretty early on. I thought I had imagined some places, but I would physically go there when I dreamed. I would excitedly tell my parents about my vivid dreams, but it was my mother who eventually caught on to what was happening and started sleeping with me. One night, I somehow took her with me as I traveled. She played along perfectly, convincing me we were in a dream together, and when we woke the next morning, she acted as if it was normal to dream the same thing as someone you loved that much. Anyway, shortly after that night, she gave me a necklace with some strange runes on it. She had told me it would protect me."

Graham paused and went to another container. He opened it and pulled out a smaller crystal that was scratched up and dull. As he brought it closer, Eliana realized it wasn't damaged. There were deliberate designs carved into all parts of it. He held it out to her, and she opened her hand to accept it. When the crystal contacted her flesh,

Eliana suddenly felt strange. Her equilibrium felt off, and her head felt like it wasn't attached to her body. When Graham pulled the crystal out of her hand, she sucked in a deep breath as though she had been underwater for some time.

"What the crap was that?!" she hollered.

He chuckled.

"That, my dear, was the crystal that saved my life for many years. My mother made it to dampen my magic. It kept me from traveling to another world and getting lost there, and it kept The Darkness from discovering that I had powerful magic before I could learn to control it. Remember when I told you I was unsuccessful in the training of being a Fighter?"

"Yeah," she answered, recalling their conversation from just a few hours ago.

"Well, I had been wearing the necklace my mother left for me. I refused to ever take it off. I didn't know that it was made from magic, so even when I hated magic and my mother, I continued to wear it. Something about it comforted me and probably protected me from The Darkness that my father had summoned, preventing them from sensing my magic."

"But how did you figure out that the necklace was stopping you from using your magic?" Eliana asked.

"I didn't. It was your grandmother. We started training, and the first few weeks were rough. Like, I couldn't even make a spark on the wick of a candle. I was frustrated, and I wanted to give up, but some part of me wouldn't allow that. I knew I was born to protect others, but I also felt this hole where a stronger sense of self should be. One day I was taking a break, holding the stone beneath my shirt and whispering my annoyance, and your grandmother saw me. She asked me to show her what I'm always grasping so tightly when I'm feeling out of control. So, I showed her, and I clearly remember the concerned look on her face. 'Take that off and let me hold it. I want to see it closer,' she had said. I hesitated only briefly before I handed it to her, and she shivered slightly the moment it touched her flesh. Then she smiled at me and told me to keep trying while she went to grab a magnifying glass to inspect it.

"I thought she was absolutely crazy having me try again, but I trusted her like a mother. So, I closed my eyes, took a deep breath, and forced my magic out." He paused a moment, his face red with embarrassment. "Then I didn't just light the candle; I blew it up... and set the drapes on fire."

Eliana let out a hearty laugh. "What did Grams do?!"

"What do you think? She put out the fire! As soon as we got it out, she explained to me what the crystal was. While I was busy almost burning the house down, she had gone to grab an old book. Together we found a page with the carvings that my necklace had. The runes pair with a vessel to drain the magic from a person, and then it would slowly release it out over time. All I had to do was have it close to me, and it would do its job.

"Your grandmother did not know where it came from, but the runes told her the story of what it did. When I stumbled upon the full-sized ones a decade later, it took me longer than I'd care to admit to put two and two together. But without the runes, I had no idea how it was working or if it was even the same crystal. The one I wore around my neck never glowed like this. It never showed any signs that it was holding my magic," Graham paused and stared at Eliana, studying her face.

"Okay..." she started slowly. "Are you planning to use it again? Can you teach me how to travel between worlds? Are you going to add magic to the crystals? How many are already filled? Wouldn't your ability to change and your ability to travel suggest that your magic might be just as powerful as mine? Who's to say that you're not the one to defeat The Darkness?"

Eliana's words sped up as her brain started racing, trying to formulate a plan with all the information she was given.

"Hold on! There are still a few more things that you should know."

"Fine..." Eliana said hesitantly.

"When you asked what I did with all the crystals, and I said I brought them here, it was because this was one of the most frequent places I dreamt of going. After I released my magic, I took your parents here many times, and I even brought you."

Graham paused for a moment and stared at Eliana. She didn't say a word, but she was sure her expression spoke loudly enough.

"When I first got these crystals, I didn't run back into town. I didn't trust that I wouldn't be followed, and I didn't want to put anyone in harm if I didn't need to. So, I went down by the river to what I thought was an abandoned house and went inside. I only had a moment to catch my breath before someone came down the hall with the light. A little old man, who looked utterly harmless, slowly came towards me, asking what my business was. I quickly explained that I just needed a place to make sure that The Darkness hadn't followed me, and I meant him no harm. So, he dropped the weak and helpless act, stood up straight, and removed a jacket that he had stuffed in his shirt to make his back look hunched over.

"We ended up talking for hours, and I learned that he had once been a Fighter. He went down to that house to escape the clutches of Sebastian, whom he just referred to as the most powerful of The Darkness. In his younger years, this man has been hunted by The Darkness and almost succumbed to the desire for more power, but then he stumbled upon the crystals and released his magic into one, saving himself from their grasp."

"The one that glowed in the cave," Eliana extrapolated.

"Precisely. That one crystal saved his life that day. He left it, hoping it would do the same for another. Then he took a few others with him and wandered along the shoreline until he found this house. The outside had remained unloved so people wouldn't assume anyone was there, but on the inside, it was cozy. He had been there for almost forty years at the time and had avoided any human contact. When I asked why he didn't warn everyone about what The Darkness was doing, he explained he had tried a few times unsuccessfully. Things weren't as bad back then, and he hoped that hiding, it would help to keep it that way.

"When I explained how things were and how you were our greatest hope for defeating this, he passed on the knowledge he had gained over years of being alone. I told him of my plan to take the crystals to the land of my dreams and study them there.

"And he explained he could place a curse on me that would stop my aging while I was away from this world. If I could stay in my prime, I could come back here and be strong enough to help you defeat The Darkness. Everything seemed to be happening the way it needed to."

Graham paused to put the crystal in its place and silently watched its flickering light before continuing.

"I came to this world, purchased this land, and started building. I traded the gold coins I had for their currency and had more than enough to hire hundreds of different people so that no one man saw the full plan. The entire project took just under two years to finish. They actually put the last piece into place about eleven days before your birthday." He paused, but his eyes continued the story of helplessness.

"I went down to the old man on the day I was to leave, but I wasn't careful. After he placed the curse on me, The Darkness showed up. I cried out as I watched the man be consumed by The Darkness while I faded away to this land. I had enough time to stash my stuff and get the resources I needed before one of The Darkness found me. So, I continued running and fighting for the next few years. So much lost time and life because of my carelessness."

He sighed and shook his head.

"Graham," Eliana said, reaching out to him, "you can't blame yourself for the way things happened. Yes, things might have gone along smoother if we all didn't hide things from each other, but how could we know who was actually on our side? We all saw the truth the way we wanted and felt that it was solely on our shoulders to end this war. Now it's pretty damn clear we were never meant to fight this alone. What's done is done, and we are stronger now than we ever were before. So, let's get this plan together and get back to save our people."

"You're right," Graham nodded, straightening up. "This is the fight we were meant to win together, so let's win it," he paused and slumped down again. "However, there are a few things I need from you."

"Of course. Anything," Eliana replied.

"Sebastian knows your magic. He's going to be looking for you the second we leave the safety of this house. So, I need you to wear this when we're out of the protection of my home," he said, holding out the crystal rune necklace to emphasize his words.

"Fine, but how will we get back to our world if I can't use my magic? Aren't you too weak?" she asked as she watched him place it into his bag after she agreed.

"I shouldn't be, but I have a few spare crystals that I can replenish my magic from if I need to. Though I used quite a few on that last test to break Francisco free. I also left some aside in the chance that I ever succeeded and needed some extra assistance."

Eliana watched him walk to the other side of the room and open six more containers. Gently taking out the glowing crystals one by one, he placed them in a satchel. The last case had a crystal so large that he had to use both hands to lift it out.

"This is the one that called to me in that cave. It has multiple people's magic in it, and I have yet to see it overload like what you did with that one," he said, nodding towards the drained crystal.

"Can I...?" she started.

"Please, do," he said, tipping the crystal towards her.

Eliana stepped over and placed her hand on it. Closing her eyes, she focused a small stream of magic into the crystal. This time she paid attention to the hum that it let off, trying to gauge when it would overload. As the vibrations sped up, she was sure it was going to levitate. She removed her hands and opened her eyes to a glow that was now almost blinding. Graham gasped at it, tapping it lightly a few times before grabbing it and moving it to his bag with the others.

"I will use the smaller crystals to reabsorb my magic so that I can get us safely back home."

"Wait, if it's not the right amount of magic, will we end up wherever my parents are? Didn't they get trapped somewhere by not having enough magic to travel here? Couldn't we—"

"Slow down, Eliana! I promise we will find them after this is done. Yes, there is a chance we could end up where they are, but I taught your parents everything I know about traveling across the worlds. So, even if their magic ran out, they probably aren't somewhere I hadn't taken them before. They refused to tell me their exact location until we had completed our task, so there's not much to do except utilize my already limited resources to find them."

"Alright..." Eliana accepted, "but promise me that no matter what happens, you will find them. If I don't make it through this..."

"Don't say that. We will find them. Together."

Eliana stared at him as she absorbed his words and bit her tongue. She had to get information from her parents and wondered if she could use the raven somehow. They needed to know that someone would be coming to save them. Whether it was her or Graham, someone would get them.

"Okay," she said tersely.

"Okay... So," he hesitated again. "If you see me pull out this large crystal at any point in time, promise me you won't try to intervene with whatever I do."

"What? What do you plan to do with it?!" she half yelled at him.

"Eliana, this crystal contains a collection of magic that may not be easily controlled. Not only did you fill it, but four more people have drained their magic into it before you."

"Four?!" she asked.

"Me, the little old man, and your parents," he replied.

Her mouth twitched as she stared at the floor. Her eyes filled with tears at the thought of being so close to something alive that belonged to her parents. It took everything to stop her from pulling their magic from it and absorbing it into her own body. She longed to feel them there, but she knew they gave some of their magic for a more significant cause. There was a barely noticeable nod of her head as she brushed away a tear.

"Thank you. If I'm bringing it out, there is a good chance that it's because I am starting to fatigue. So, if you see me struggling to use it, trust that I'll get a hold of it. We may not need it, but I need to make sure we have backup plans."

"Alright, I understand. Can you tell me where we're going? Or what the plan is to get the upper hand? How do you know it will be safe?"

Graham laughed at her. He went around the space, locking everything up, then motioned her to follow as he went towards a hallway.

"Remember when I said I had been checking in? Well, I talked to a few trusted people. Everyone at your house is still trustworthy. I was impressed that no one had been taken to the dark side of this, but I guess when my father learned how to transform himself into other people, he did not need to recruit anyone else. Yours and your parents' bedrooms should have remained locked aside from when they were being cleaned, so I think we will be safe going to either of those. As for having the upper hand... There is a tunnel from your house that—"

"Goes to the castle. I know," Eliana interrupted.

"Of course, you do," Graham smiled, "but did you know that your parents and I were the ones who created it? It wasn't always there because it wasn't necessary to have, but I don't think my father knows it's there. We never told another person about it, except for you, apparently."

"No one told me. I was following a firefly one night, and it led me there. It lit my way through the entire tunnel. When I reached the end, I heard you talking to someone. I was too scared to get close enough to see anything, but you were saying something about moving on. It all makes more sense now...."

"I can't even feign surprise at this point," Graham chuckled. "Well, I guess that makes me feel better. Did you tell anyone about it?"

"No. Who would I have told? I never hung out with anyone at my house."

"Mm," Graham nodded. "I suppose that's great for us. Anyway, the plan is to go to your parents' house, take the tunnel, find my father, and use him to summon Sebastian. We must make sure you have the necklace my mother gave me on at all times. If you remove it too early, Sebastian will no doubt find us, and we will lose the element of surprise."

"And if your father refuses to help? Or sabotages us to help Sebastian?" Eliana inquired.

"Hmm."

Graham paused a moment to open a door hidden within the smooth metal walls that had surrounded them for the last hour. As Eliana's mind continued to race, she was hit with a wave of exhaustion. She wasn't surprised, as she hadn't slept in almost 33 hours. While Graham continued down the next hallway, Eliana took a moment to lean against a wall and rest.

"I'm hoping at 79, there won't be much that he'll be able to do. The last time I checked, his health was already degrading. And as soon as we get what we need to summon Sebastian, I'm using a crystal to send my father back here," Graham said, turning to look at her. "Eliana! Are you alright?" he asked, rushing back.

"Yeah," she said with an airy tone. "I just needed a moment to rest. Exhaustion hit me like a ton of bricks."

She yawned, and Graham placed a hand on her solar plexus. He pushed a tiny bit of his magic into her body, passing on the rejuvenating aspects that sleeping would have provided her at that moment.

"I could have done that myself, you know," Eliana said, blushing at his touch. The feeling of his magic traveling through her made every ounce of her body tingle. She shook the goosebumps off her arms and wiped her sweaty palms on her pants.

"I know," he whispered, brushing the hair from her cheek, "but I wanted to help. Especially after asking so much from you tonight. When was the last time you slept?" he inquired.

"It's been about a day and a half at this point. Even then, the sleep I had before wasn't great. I've been on the go so much the last week, so I just sneak in naps when I can."

"I'm sorry. I should have paid more attention. I don't think I've slept at all in about thirteen years. The curse literally froze my body in time."

"WHAT?! How is that even possible?!"

Graham shrugged.

Eliana shook her head, chuckling. "I guess I didn't know as much about the capabilities of magic as I thought. Since arriving at your door, I have been humbled by what it can truly do. So, I guess it's a good thing your body wasn't trapped in a state of exhaustion, eh?"

"Well, yeah. I knew that was part of it, so after I spoke to your parents about leaving, I went and took a nap, ate some food, then headed down to the old man."

"Wait... when was the last time you ate?" Eliana asked, trying to process everything.

"It's not that my body doesn't function," Graham said as he walked again. "It's just that I don't feel hungry or tired because technically, I'm not. I can sleep if I want to. And eat, which I actually do... a lot. Have you ever thought about how much food you would eat if your body were unaffected by it? I never did until I realized I had formed a habit of bored-eating. And if I came back, and the curse was lifted, but I was still eating as I had been? Well... I'm not as young as I once was, even in this body. I'm still the 38-year-old that I was then."

"Well, I think you look amazing no matter what age you are now," Eliana mumbled somewhat quietly, blushing behind her hair.

"What's that?" he asked, turning around to look at her.

"You never answered my question," she deflected loudly.

"What? Oh! Right. I believe I ate dinner just before you started causing a ruckus outside! I think the better question here is, when was the last time you ate?" he inquired, raising an eyebrow and placing his hands on his hips.

As if answering for her, Eliana's stomach growled. They both laughed, and she tilted her head slightly, raising her eyebrows and pulling her lips into a pout with a smile tugging at the edge of her mouth.

"That answers that. Let's stop by the kitchen to grab you some food before we head back to Francisco!" Graham exclaimed before turning around to open another door.

CHAPTER SEVENTEEN

Eliana followed, watching the shiny metal walls transition into wooden paneling. After some time, she found it strange that there had been no security measures besides the touchpad on the first door out of the room with the crystals. Lost in her thoughts, she walked directly into Graham, not realizing he had stopped.

"Oof! Sorry," she said, looking at the surrounding space.

Her jaw dropped as she stepped into what she realized was the kitchen. The greenish-blue granite countertops lined three out of the four walls. The stainless-steel fridge was three times the size of a normal one, and the sheen of its dark metal mimicked the walls of the previous room. At the end of the wide refrigerator, there was a door leading to a walk-in freezer. On the wall next to the fridge, there were two massive ovens at torso height. The center of the space contained an island with a gas range stove built-in. A mechanical belt stored pots and pans slightly above, weaving around the hood.

Eliana stepped further into space and saw a glass door on the floor that led down to what she assumed would be a wine cellar. As she stood next to the island, she could see that the stone sink was deep enough to hold a toddler. The current lighting made it seem like the entire room was filled with twinkling stars, complete with a light that hung over the stove, mirroring a full moon on a clear night.

"Eliana?" Graham called out from the front of the open refrigerator.

"What?" she asked, mouth still slightly agape from taking in her surroundings.

"I asked if you would like a sandwich," he repeated, smiling at her.

She swooned momentarily, sighing as she gazed upon his silhouette.

"Yes, please. Turkey, if you've got it. If you just show me where everything is, I can make it," she replied, heading over to him.

"Condiments are here," he said, pointing to the door. "Any other fixings are in the drawer above the drawer that says *Meat*. I will grab a knife and cutting board for any veggies you might want on it. There's also some fruit here that you are welcome to have. Cheese is with the meat. There's a spice rack on the counter over there. Drinks. I have juice, wine, soda, tea or—"

"Water is great," she cut him off.

He nodded and went off to collect things. Eliana opened drawers and started pulling out ingredients. After a decent fridge raid, she had gathered a sourdough roll, turkey, chipotle mayonnaise, mustard, sliced banana peppers, olives, tomatoes, lettuce, some pepper and Italian seasoning, a side of blueberries and chips, and her glass of water. Graham sat with her at a table that folded out from the wall, placing his cheek on his fist as he watched her inhale her entire meal within three minutes.

"Impressive," he said as she popped the last blueberry into her mouth. "A little hungrier than you let on?"

"It's been a while since I wasn't eating off the land," she replied, blushing.

Graham smiled at her, reaching up to gently brush away some breadcrumbs that remained in the corner of her mouth. Eliana blushed again, feeling more alert with some nutrients in her body. As her eyes studied his lips, she suddenly felt nervous. The false moonlight of the kitchen made him look radiant, and for a moment, she forgot about the fight and let herself crave for more of him.

Eliana was worried that there wouldn't be another moment like this and tried to weigh her options. She was convinced that one of them wouldn't make it out of this battle alive and was already regretting the time they wouldn't have in the future. As her eyes continued to trace his face, frowning at the thoughts racing through her mind, he quickly cupped the back of her head and pulled her into a kiss.

Without hesitation, she pulled his body close to hers, causing them both to stand. Her hands traced up the muscles of his back and rested on his scapula. Forcing his lips to separate, she traced his teeth quickly with her tongue before it met his. His hands slid down her body, cupping her ass and pressing her against him. When he hardened against her, she released him abruptly, stepping away. As she breathed heavily, he looked at her guiltily.

"I'm sorry. That was inappropriate."

He cleared his throat and tried to subtly adjust the bulge in his pants. Eliana watched him for a moment, chuckling at his sudden discomfort.

"Um...," he started, rubbing the back of his neck as a blush painted his cheeks.

"I'm sorry. I'm not laughing at you. Well, I guess I kind of am but not in a bad way."

"Alright..." he started slowly, frowning deeply at her. "So, what are you laughing at?"

"You," she started, pausing to take another deep breath, "apologizing for something that we both very clearly wanted. There are just so many lives at stake, and I started to think about all the consequences of letting that go any further would have. But don't get me wrong!" she quickly added. "You are very adept at making it difficult to have those thoughts, and to be fair, you interrupted me arguing with myself about how much I wanted to initiate that kiss. I mean, what if we don't get another chance?" she finished quietly.

He stepped towards her, taking her hand in his own.

"I understand. Mostly. I don't understand why it was so funny, but I get your reasoning for pulling away," Graham gently replied.

"Because you were thinking the same thing. Apologizing for it not being appropriate... I don't know. I guess it's been a while since I could be honest with someone I was attracted to. I'm so used to burying part of myself to be happy."

Graham nodded and squeezed her hand, changing the grip so that he could interlace his fingers into hers.

"I get that completely. I haven't even thought about another person in that way since I left. I've been so caught up in making sure that we can beat this that it wasn't really on my mind. But you... You have brought out so many parts of me I had forgotten were once there. I was worried about how long it's been that I completely misread your cues, so I'm glad that I wasn't just some perverted, horny, depraved man."

Eliana laughed again, but this time it was a befitting amount.

"You know, you still might be," she quipped with a wink. "In all seriousness, though, you've always held a special place in my heart. And how often does your childhood crush stay that exact age that you fell in love with them at?" she laughed.

"Fell in love?" Graham asked her with raised eyebrows.

"Oh... Uh... Well," she stuttered and blushed furiously and pulled her hand from his to wipe the nervous sweat from her palm.

"Eliana... Li. Your feelings are entirely valid. We can't always control who we fall in love with, and sometimes we don't even realize that it's happening. So, I promise you, there's no need to feel embarrassed," he chuckled lightly, taking her hand back into his own and taking a deep breath. "With that in mind, don't get discouraged that my feelings may not yet be as strong as yours in that sense. Remember that the last time I saw you, you were just a child. I never thought of you that way. You were just my best friend's amazing kid, and while I always hoped that you would be able to find the perfect partner, I never thought that I would be in that timeline with you. Though I can say with some confidence that you have grown into an amazing woman, and the physical attraction is most definitely there. I just want to make sure that there is more than that. I'm no spring chicken."

Eliana nodded, not trusting her voice. His words hurt her ego a bit. She wanted to hear that he was already madly in love with her, but she knew that was poppycock. He was mature and honest and everything that someone would want in a partner. He was forcing her to take a moment and re-evaluate whether she was thinking with her brain or her genitals.

"You're not helping my desire for you by being so logical, but I get it. You've been around longer than me, and it's hard to convince myself that you have a good twenty-five years' experience on me when you look like this. I also seemed to have opened some flood gates by letting myself open up to the world for a moment, and I saw how sexy you are... I mean.... damn," she finished with a flirtatious whistle and a wink.

Graham laughed heartily.

"Thank you?" he responded before laughing again.

She interrupted his laugh with a quick kiss, then shifted her focus back to the mission.

"Let's put some snacks in your bag. I think I will probably be famished when this is over. Do we need to bring anything for Francisco?"

Graham shook his head, "There's a mini fridge in the lab that should have plenty to hold him over until we can come back. Also, if you don't mind, I have an insulated backpack I'd prefer to put food in. The less blocking the crystals, the safer we are, and the longer we can keep perishables cool, the better. Who knows how long this will take?"

Eliana nodded, following him to where the backpack was and taking it from him. She stared at him for a long moment before sighing and moving on to her task. The dread was starting to take over her again, and she did her best to shake it off. While she loaded up the backpack with whatever food sounded good, Graham pulled out his phone and called into the lab. She listened to the one-sided conversation between Graham and Francisco and grabbed a handful of fruit snacks to throw in as he said goodbye.

"Ready?" he asked.

"Yup," she replied, zipping up the pack and swinging it over one shoulder, then maneuvering her arm through the other hole.

The bag felt surprisingly light, considering how much she had shoved into it. Graham clipped two buckles from the backpack around her chest and waist, taking a moment to brush a hair from her face, letting his thumb trail down her cheek and along her jawline to her chin. Eliana's breath caught, expecting another kiss, but then he dropped his hand.

Eliana sighed and tucked her thumbs into the straps around her shoulders, and let her elbows hang heavy as she followed behind. After a few hallways, she forgot she was wearing a backpack. Its weight was so evenly distributed that it felt like her own. Eventually, she let her arms swing free as she fell into a trance, listening to Graham's humming.

CHAPTER EIGHTEEN

When they reached the lab, Francisco was pressing different buttons on the computer. Eliana watched as he frowned at each depression of a key.

"We're back! Having fun?" Graham asked, chuckling.

"Whoa!" Francisco shouted, jumping out of his seat. "I didn't even hear you guys come in."

They laughed, Francisco awkwardly joining in. Graham turned, his hand brushing Eliana's, causing her heart to skip a beat. The distraction that Graham had become made even the most benign task difficult. So, Eliana stepped away from him to lower the chances of him making contact with her again.

"Sorry to frighten you. I thought you'd heard the doors," Graham started. "Anyway, a few things before we part ways. I don't know how much wandering you're going to want to do, but there is a door in the back corner," he said, pointing behind where Francisco sat. "Inside, you will find a small bedroom with clothes, a bed, a full bathroom, a TV hooked up to your basic cable package, and a drawer full of snacks in the dresser next to the bed. Out here, there is a mini fridge built into the desk and a toaster oven that you can use to cook pretty much anything."

"I don't have much appetite yet, but the bed sounds nice," Francisco replied.

"Great. I just have one more favor to ask of you," Graham said, making a slight face when he paused.

"I will help however I can," Francisco replied without hesitation.

"Alright, I have some crystals in here that I was hoping you could try to drain your magic into. It might slow your healing down, but it will definitely be the most helpful to us along the way. It will also help keep you safe longer, although nothing should be able to sense you from this room. Anyway, let me just go grab the crystals real quick, and let's see what you have to offer!" Graham finished as he shuffled to a corner that opened into a room.

Francisco turned and smiled awkwardly at Eliana as they waited for Graham to return.

"So...," he started, "you and Graham, then?"

Eliana choked, spitting a little as she attempted not to laugh. Her face turned deep red as she tried to find her words.

"Uh. Sorry. I didn't mean to assume. I just— It seemed like you two had something going on...," he trailed off, looking to the room where Graham had disappeared.

Eliana gathered herself and replied.

"No, you're fine. The quick answer is, maybe. I mean, technically, he's about a quarter-century older than I am, and it's weird to think about. I don't even know what happens when we go back home. Is he going to gain all of those years back? Will he just be stuck in this age forever? It's a lot to process, but I know he held a very special place in my heart growing up. Reflecting on the years since he left, I realize I was trying to find someone just like him to fill the void.

"I just never expected that he would someday be an actual possibility. Part of me wants not even to question any of it and just let it happen. Especially after I spent too much time hating him and blaming him unnecessarily. Then there's also this logical part of me that thinks about how this man was my mother's best friend growing up and how he should have never even been a tangible possibility. Though, I guess people fall in love every day at all ages. I don't know.

It's just all very confusing!" she finished, blushing furiously that she had said so much.

"Uhhh, yeah," Francisco started.

"Got 'em!" Graham exclaimed as he reappeared from the wall, breaking the awkward tension that had built.

Eliana flushed again at the sight of Graham but almost felt better having talked through her worries. The only remaining hesitation was what her parents might think. She hoped they would understand that this was her desire and wouldn't think that Graham had been thinking of her in any sort of romantic way as a child. She groaned a little at her unique talent of overthinking everything and losing touch with the present. However, she kept wandering down its path of worry and anxiety.

She continued to watch Graham and Francisco work at draining magic into the empty crystals. She tried to imagine what her mother might feel if she came back to her best friend and daughter being something more than just friends. The world around her became nothing but a murmur of sound and a blur of scenery. Rejection of this relationship appeared in the distant future. The cold floor beneath made her feel numb, and she melted into her false reality. As she let go of her hold on her magic, she felt herself being pulled into what felt like a memory but was a moment that had never happened in the past. Just like that, she was gone.

There was no distinct color, and the surrounding space was barren and lifeless. I could feel no air kissing my skin as I walked around, yet the dust twisted through as if it was caught in a gust of wind. There was a sandy path that led between two mounds of dirt in front of me, so I followed it towards an unknown place. As I passed to the other side of the piles, the dust settled, and I could see remains. It looked like remnants of a town that once existed.

I approached the rubble and was hit with an actual gust of air. As I blinked away the dust from my eyes, I saw vibrant colors. The building that seconds ago was in shambles was now full of life; the cracking ground was now covered with lush greenery. The air was fresh. Did I make this? Whose memory was this? A group of voices coming from a large house at the end of the path interrupted the chain of thoughts. I cautiously listened and moved towards the sounds.

"Hello?" I called out, making sure I had somewhere between the buildings to take cover if they were dangerous.

I paused for a moment to listen, tensing my muscles as I waited. There was a silence followed by some soft murmuring and then a reply.

"Who's there? How did you get in here?" a woman replied.

"My name is Eliana, and I don't even know where I am. If you'd be willing to chat with me. I think you might have something important that I need to know..."

"Eliana?" the voice repeated back with some skepticism.

I sucked in a sharp breath and stood up straight. The way the woman said my name sounded just like... but, no. It couldn't be.

"Mom?" I asked, my feet taking me closer.

I saw the curtains move at a far window and jumped when the door slammed open. I froze in place as two figures inside crossed into the light. As I blinked away the sun, I saw the faces that I knew better than my own, but they had aged since the last time I saw them. My parents came running towards me, not even hesitating. As their bodies slammed into mine, the shock of seeing them vanished, and I collapsed into them, crying.

"How are you here?!" my father asked.

"I don't know!" I exclaimed.

"Wait!" my mother shouted, separating us.

I desperately tried to keep clinging on to them, but I was fading away. I saw the worry on my parents' faces, but their words were jumbled with a third voice. I could hear Graham vaguely blending with them, and I felt the touch of someone shaking my physical form.

"I'll come back to you! I promise!" I shouted just before I jerked back into my form.

"Goddamnit!" Eliana shouted in Graham's face.

He froze but left his hands on her arms.

"Li?" he gently prodded.

"I had them! They were right there!" she continued to shout.

"What? Had who? What are you talking about? Where did you go?"

Eliana threw Graham's hands from her body and quickly came to be standing. When she paced and growled in frustration, Graham stood and took a moment to talk to Francisco.

"What were you talking about before I came back out here?" he asked, pulling Eliana's attention slightly.

"Well..." Francisco started, catching Eliana's stare and shifting uncomfortably. "You."

After a long silence, Graham spoke again.

"Aaaaaaaaand?"

Eliana caught Francisco's eye again while she continued to talk to herself and flail her arms about as she paced.

"And.... her parents," Francisco finally said.

"Ah. Ok. Um," Graham replied. "Eliana?"

"I TOUCHED THEM! I FELT THEIR BODIES AGAINST MINE!" she yelled louder than before.

"Who? Your parents?" he calmly asked.

"Yes, my parents! WHO ELSE?" she spat back with sarcasm.

"In a memory?" he continued patiently.

Eliana rocked her head. "No, no, no, no. I saw them where they are. Alive. Now."

With that, she came to a sudden stop. Her breathing was shallow, and her eyes were crazed. She stared off into space, thinking about the words she had just said.

"Alive," she repeated in a whisper.

And then she broke down. As she collapsed forward, Graham caught her. He sat with her and held her close as she sobbed into his chest. Rocking her gently, he rubbed her head and crooned until she quietly dozed off.

CHAPTER NINETEEN

"How?" Francisco asked.

Graham simply shrugged and shook his head. "I honestly don't know. When I travel places, my full form goes there. I don't leave any part of my physical being behind. If she could go there, then she existed in two places at once. I wonder how much of her existed there. If she died there, would she have died here too? In the memories, she never existed as more than energy. But touching them? Feeling their touch?"

Graham stopped and shook his head. He squeezed Eliana in tightly, his heart aching for how much unnecessary pain she had suffered during her life. He kissed the top of her head and sighed.

"I'm so sorry, Eliana."

The three remained in silence aside from the occasional sniffle or hitched breath that came from Eliana. There didn't seem to be any words that could be said to make something that seemed so impossible any better. Until Eliana gave them more information, there was nothing more that could be said. While he trusted his friend, this man had been manipulated once before. And if he did leave the protection of the lab, there was no saying how quickly Sebastian might find him and get what he wants.

When Eliana finally relaxed, Graham turned to Francisco.

"I think I should get more details about what happened somewhere that you can't hear. If she confirms some piece of vital information that may cause Sebastian to have the upper hand, I don't want the chance of giving away all that. Right now, all you've heard is my speculation. That can easily be brushed off, but if she confirms anything...."

Graham trailed off, shrugging slightly as he looked back down at Eliana.

"Okay," Francisco said softly, standing and making his way to the other room.

Graham watched as Francisco shut the door behind himself and glanced back to Eliana. The lab was protected from all sounds unless Graham pressed a button to speak, and the space kept Francisco protected from being detected by Sebastian. It was a smart move, and Graham was pleased that Francisco stayed somewhere safe, but he still went to double-check that his microphone wasn't locked on. He reached up to press the button on the keyboard to talk.

"Thanks, Francisco. I'll try to be quick. I think we can probably still get a little more of your magic into these crystals after this. I'd like to have it spread across them all if possible."

"Sounds good!" Francisco replied, getting comfortable on the floor.

Graham released the button and watched for the microphone symbol to display that it was no longer active. When it did, he turned to Eliana and pulled a tissue from his pocket.

"Eliana?" he asked quietly.

She moaned a little but didn't respond.

"Li," he repeated a little more loudly. He wished they had a moment for her to sleep, but they just didn't right now.

This time when she groaned, she lifted her head to look at him. He smiled down at her and used the tissue that was still in his hand to wipe the tears and mucus from her face. She squinted and blinked her slightly puffy eyes. Graham removed the arm that was still wrapped around her, and she sat up, rubbing her face.

"Sorry," she started, yawning, "I guess that took the last of whatever energy I had left."

"No need to apologize, Eliana, but I would like to talk more about what happened. You said you felt them where you were, but I could still see you here. Was it a memory?"

"I don't think so. Not unless Francisco had been in that exact place before, and I just didn't see them, Graham. It didn't even feel like a memory; it was too real for that. I was no longer just a ball of energy floating around. I was the full-bodied me that is able to walk with their own feet and use their voice. And my parents... They were able to see me and respond to me and *touch* me. What happened to my form here?" she asked.

"It was like a robot version of you waiting for some sort of instructions to move. I just don't understand how if you sent a projection of yourself somewhere that you could feel and touch someone. It's like you traveled to a different place without taking this physical form. I wonder if the magic we used to change forms allows creating a second physical form wherever you send your consciousness. This could be a beneficial move against Sebastian. But we need to make sure your original form remains safe."

"I guess all makes sense," Eliana slowly replied, squinting her eyes. "I just don't understand how I had so much more ability buried within me I never accessed until now."

Graham laughed.

"You know, as much as the anger helped to train you physically, I think it prevented you from accessing the power that you hold deep in your core."

Eliana yawned and nodded. Graham watched as she closed her eyes and activated her magic throughout her body again. When her eyes opened, the dark circles had almost disappeared, and she seemed more alert.

"My parents," she mumbled as her hair settled back down onto her neck.

"Yes, Eliana. You found them?" he prodded.

She nodded.

"They're safe. They have some sort of protection spell around where they are living, but why haven't they left? Why haven't they come to find me? Why are they just sitting around in some other dimension hiding behind a wall of magic?"

Eliana's nostrils flared as she huffed, quickly standing and pacing around. Graham saw Francisco watching Eliana with concern as he stood. When their eyes met, Graham nodded to let him know it was okay.

"Eliana...." Graham started. "Your parents didn't just settle down and forget about you. That place that you found... it took them years to find. If you hadn't been distracted by your parents, I'm sure there would have been others you could see. Your parents have a natural way of leading people without becoming a ruler. Others want to follow their lead. That spell protecting them is a combination of the magic of many people there, but not all of them have magic. Your parents have been working on a way to get everyone out of there but keeping up that mirage drains them. Besides, if they left to come to find you, they might never get back there, and you know damn well your parents will always do what they can to protect as many people as possible."

"I don't understand. How can you know so much? I thought you hadn't heard from them in years," she replied, nearly yelling.

Graham cleared his throat, shifting awkwardly.

"Uh, yeah. Well. Do you know how I said I heard from your dad seven years ago? Um, your mother contacted me much more recently."

Quickly turning and reaching toward the desk, he unlocked a drawer, pulled out a letter, and handed it to Eliana. Graham silently watched her read her mother's words.

And finally, Graham. I need you to do us a favor. I trust you will know when the time is right to share this information. Tell Eliana that we love and miss her more than anything. We wish we could have been a part of her growth to become the best Fighter that she can be, but it's just not feasible right now. We watch her often and are so proud of the woman she's become. We want nothing more than to be with her now, and I know soon we will be able to... I can feel something big coming. There is a shift that you may sense, but here, we live it. We've collectively had to use practically all our magic to keep an inhabitable place. It's draining, but I know that someone will come for us when the time comes. Much love to you, Graham.

I look forward to hearing from you.

Love, Delilah

Graham watched as Eliana stared at the letter long after her eyes finished reading it. He wanted to give her more answers, but he also didn't want to push her beyond what she was willing to hear. Half expecting anger again, he was surprised when she looked up at him with only curiosity. The peace that painted across her face caused him to tilt his head in wonder at what she had taken from that letter.

"Why did you keep this from me? What makes you think this is suddenly the right time and not before when you were letting me think they've been dead? Or when you told me you had been in contact with my father? I don't understand. If you've all been watching me, why couldn't someone tell me? Have you been to see them? Do you know where they are?" she asked, urgency in her voice.

"I know. I should have. And I'm sorry. This is all a bit delicate, and I'm doing the best I can. I'm sorry I didn't tell you that they're still alive. I was trying to let you live your life until everything was ready, and I suppose I could have gone about all of this in a better manner. But no. I haven't seen them since the day I left. I only have descriptions and could guess where they actually are. They won't tell me, and I've failed at any attempt of tracking them."

He held up a finger to pause the conversation and went over to press the microphone button.

"Francisco?" he beckoned.

"Yeah?" the voice responded.

"Have you been to the in-between? Were you thinking about it when Li, uh, zoned out?"

He slowly nodded.

"I knew Eliana's parents were there somewhere. I didn't know exactly where they were, but I was trying to remember some clue about where I had seen them a few years before they disappeared. The Darkness frequently roams that land. It was always an easy target for anyone that got trapped there, but then they became harder to come by."

"Thank you, Francisco. We're almost done," he replied through the microphone.

"So, my desire to talk to my parents and his desire to remember where he had seen them allowed me to create some sort of portal?"

"It would seem so," Graham interjected, "but that doesn't explain how you were able to materialize a duplicate physical form. I wish we had more time to learn about it, but since we don't, please be careful if you use it against Sebastian."

"I will try," Eliana replied.

"Good. There is one more thing."

"Sure," she replied with little emotion.

"What were you and Francisco talking about?" he asked.

Eliana blushed furiously and laughed before turning away to cough.

"Let's just get this going, so we can defeat Sebastian, and I can have a conversation with my parents without being pulled away. Yeah?"

"Alright...." Graham agreed hesitantly. "Come back so we can finish up," he said as he pressed the button.

"Wait, Graham. How did Francisco know they are my parents?"

Graham quickly pressed the button again.

"One more thing, Francisco. How did you know who Li's parents are?"

Francisco turned bright red.

"Oh, well. I just kind of put two and two together. She's a perfect blend of Scott and Delilah, and when you kept calling 'Li', it only made sense that it was short for Eliana."

Eliana sighed but accepted the explanation. Anyone who actually knew her parents would immediately recognize the similarities in their appearance. She nodded to Graham, giving him the go ahead to let Francisco out.

"Ah, got it. Still wise, I see. Glad The Darkness couldn't take that from you," Graham chuckled.

"Yeah. I guess not."

Graham reached to unlock the door and turned back to Eliana. When Francisco passed out of sight behind a wall, she placed a gentle kiss on Graham's cheek. As she went to step away, he caught her wrist and pulled her back. With his other hand, he cupped her neck and kissed her back. He felt her melting into him, then pulled back when Francisco cleared his throat.

"Sorry," she mumbled, scurrying away as Graham laughed.

"I'm not," he said loud enough only for Francisco to hear.

Francisco smiled at Graham as he passed the last two crystals for him to move his magic. Graham glanced over at Eliana and watched her rearrange the backpack at least four times. She shot a glare at him when he chuckled softly, then she went back to her bag. With a longing sigh, he turned his attention back to his friend.

"Alright, Francisco," he said, placing the last crystal in his bag. "Last thing before we head out. I'd like you to know how to check in on things."

"Are you sure it's wise to give me a link where Sebastian might learn what you're up to?" Francisco asked.

Graham took his friend's arms in his hands and looked him directly in his eyes.

"Even if I don't fully trust you yet, I don't think you're evil or intentionally wanting to harm us. I'm aware you've had some urges to do things that give you more power, but since I have yet to see you follow through with any of it, I'm willing to give you a chance to help. Besides, once we leave this house, we are putting ourselves in more danger than you could possibly manage."

Francisco looked down and shuffled his feet like a scolded child that had been caught doing something they shouldn't have. Graham released his arms and went to sit down at the computer, accepting the response as an answer for Francisco to do his best not to screw them over.

"Thanks for your kindness after everything I've done," Francisco finally said.

Graham simply nodded. He had seen when Francisco attempted to keep a crystal for himself, only to return it shortly after. He had seen Francisco attempt to leave the microphone on before going into the observation room. He saw the way Francisco glanced at Eliana when he thought no one was looking, and Graham saw the camera footage of Francisco being alone in the lab. There was nothing that Francisco had let stick, so showing Francisco that he still had good in him was more important to Graham than reprimanding him further.

"Before I made my journey here, I left behind several crystals in different parts of town. I have used all but one to check in. That one resides within my father's home. Be forewarned that the effects of the crystal will be short-lived, and you won't be able to interact with anyone while you are there. Once you trigger it, you will have precisely 364 seconds to observe an area. The—"

"How do you communicate with people if this doesn't allow you to interact with anyone? And why such a random amount of time?" Eliana interrupted.

"The same way your parents communicate with me," he replied shortly before continuing. "The time is just what it is. I have no control over that. Anyway, I have set the computer up with a shortcut that will take you through a program to trigger the crystal. All you will have to do is double click this icon here and then type take me to the crystal in the box. Press the enter button, and voila! The work will be done for you."

"How can you possibly use a machine to trigger magic in a completely different land?" Francisco asked, clearly dumbfounded.

Graham laughed.

"Well, there are certain channels set up, but mostly it's just using the power of the internet, which has been amplified by a few other things I built, which then project my voice to the crystal via a device that I left near it. The phrase that it speaks activates the crystal!"

Graham cleared his throat, realizing he was letting his excitement get out of control. While his love for learning encompassed science, history, engineering, and anything else around, he figured it might not be the same for everyone. He glanced over at Eliana, who was smiling brightly at him, and hoped that she genuinely appreciated it.

"Okay. So, I click the icon that looks like a star and type the phrase and hit the button that says enter, and just look at the screen? Are there ways to change the angle? Or does it only show me that one spot?" Francisco asked.

"If anything is happening nearby, the crystal will guide you. There is literally nothing else you'll need to do," Graham beamed.

"Well. How will I know when to use it?" Francisco inquired.

"You won't," Graham said. "This is not quite an exact art. If you set it off at a time when nothing is happening, then that's that. The crystals don't refill their magic on their own, but it gives you eyes into the castle, long enough to possibly hear or see anything helpful during those approximate six active minutes."

"But how would I warn you of anything that I may find if this is my only connection?"

"A-ha! For this, I present you with a satellite phone which has been-—"

"Modified to communicate across the different lands?" Eliana finished with a smirk.

"Yes. Precisely that," Graham agreed.

He was impressed that she was catching up so quickly. Her intellect cast her in a new light. Never in a thousand years could he have asked to have found a more perfect woman. Her abilities continued to surprise him yet kept him wanting more, and he couldn't wait to pick apart her mind for years to come if she'd have him.

"Sooooo," Francisco started, interrupting the long silence as Graham and Eliana stared at each other. "I use this phone and send you a warning of anything if I find it. How do I reach you?"

"Well," Graham stated, turning his attention to Francisco, "I will set up a shortcut to a message between these two phones. It is encrypted, and you won't be able to see a number... Or do much on the phone in general. Anyway. Safety precautions. Send a message. Don't call. Calling.... does strange things still," Graham vaguely finished while putting information into the phone.

"Thanks," Francisco replied, taking the device.

"You're welcome! These are the lock screen options. I set you up on your profile. You can set your lock password to whatever you want. You will use it to unlock the phone and contact us. Make sense?"

"Yeah. I know how a phone works. I wasn't completely cut off from the world; I just didn't have much chance to use these things."

"Right. Sorry," Graham replied, grimacing at his over-explaining.

Francisco took a moment to create a password on the phone. After a few moments, the charcoal pocket of Graham's slacks buzzed. He pulled out his phone, looking at the new message.

Got it

Graham laughed. "Great. I guess all that leaves is goodbye, then."

Francisco smiled at Eliana and Graham with tear-laced eyes.

"Thank you for everything. Truly. I never imagined that I would live my own life again. Even if it's just for one night."

Francisco pulled Graham into a hug as a tear rolled down.

"It won't be one night, my friend. Eliana and I will make sure of that. Just promise me you will do everything you can to keep yourself safe," he paused and took a deep breath. "And if I don't return, take care of the house. You should have enough resources to last you quite some time."

"Graham..." Eliana started.

"No, no. I just mean I will probably need to stay and lead the people of Placata Montis. So, if I don't make it back for a while," he pulled away from Francisco, "I want to make sure everything is taken care of!" he said, trying to cover the cynical words.

Francisco wiped his eyes, and Graham shot Eliana a look that told her not to argue what he'd said. She nodded and went over to hug Francisco goodbye.

"Thank you for all that you've done to help us. I know it will help us win this war," Eliana smiled at him as she pulled away.

"Good luck. I wish you both the best."

Graham gave Francisco's arm one last squeeze.

"Thank you."

CHAPTER TWENTY

Graham picked up his olive-colored bag and silently headed toward the door across the lab, passing through the hallway. Eliana quietly followed until he took out a key and unlocked the door manually, which brought on a fit of laughter.

"What?" Graham asked with a half-smile.

"I guess I've just gotten used to all of your extravagant methods of entering rooms that having a door with a key to unlock it seemed too rudimentary."

"Oh. Ha. I just never got around to changing this to anything more," Graham replied lightheartedly.

"Mm."

He chuckled and opened the door, reaching in to quickly turn on the ceiling light.

Eliana took in the surroundings, trying not to comment on the extravagance of it all once she realized it was his bedroom. The massive four-post bed had burgundy cloth draped down to just above where his head would reach. The vaulted ceilings barely provided enough space for its height. There were intricate carvings of what appeared to be Norse mythology on each mahogany post and the headboard. The comforter was a sage green with a silvery sheen of swirls embedded throughout and the five pillows that adorned it.

Aside from the grandiose bed, which sat upon a shaggy Venetian red area rug, the room appeared ordinary at first glance. Two of the walls were built-in bookshelves that went from floor to ceiling, complete with a rolling ladder. An empty desk that matched the carvings on the bed captured reflections of the light on its sheen top. A matching nightstand stood at each side of the bed, holding matching lights. The shades covering each of the ornate lamps had black trees painted on the ivory material that surrounded each bulb. Brazilian walnut floors blended beautifully with the different shades of wood that tied the room together.

As her eyes scanned along the wall, Eliana saw the doorway leading to an en suite. The darkness on the opposite side of the room didn't allow her to see much, but she could assume that an equally elegant bathroom was probably beyond the dimly lit door. The simple, gothic chandelier that hung down in the center of the room was just bright enough for her to see some sort of marble or granite vanity and the sheen of what looked like a tile floor. As Eliana let her eyes scan back into the room, she watched Graham close a drawer and zip up his bag.

"Well, I think that's everything now. Are you ready? Is there anything else you need to do before we go?" he asked.

"What did you put in there?" she said, nodding accusingly towards his bag.

"A few items that I never leave without. A necklace that my mother always wore with a picture of her and me inside, a dagger that your mother gave me to always protect myself even if there was no magic, and a letter from my father that reminds me that there must be some good in him."

"Oh," Eliana replied gently.

She hadn't expected it to be mementos.

A silence hung in the air as Eliana tried to understand her immediate defensiveness against what he had put in the bag. She had no reason to think that he would be trying to hurt or deceive her in any way. Still, her instincts rarely led her astray, so she cleared her throat and walked over to him.

"Do you mind if I see the dagger from my mother? It would be nice to hold something that she thought would be special for you."

"Sure," Graham said, smiling.

He removed the bag from his shoulders, and Eliana peaked in as he opened it up. There was nothing out of place, but something still felt off, and she couldn't figure out what. As he pulled out the dagger, Eliana held out her hand to accept it. The moment it touched her flesh, the aura of the dagger pulled her somewhere else. She was no longer in the present with Graham.

I found myself standing in the woods, but my body was present, unlike the memories I had been cast into before. Unsure of when or where I was, I crouched down and slowly made my way forward with the dagger still clutched in my hand. The wind blew gently above me, carrying muffled voices with it.

Using the surrounding trees, I changed my vantage point to be above what might be a dangerous situation while gripping the dagger, afraid of what might happen if I let it go. I softly leaped from tree to tree, allowing the voices to guide me. As the familiarity of the forest started sinking in, the hours I had spent in these trees rushed back. Images clouded my mind while I continued concealing myself, shifting slightly around the tree to get a better look at the owners of the voices.

"You know, you really shouldn't keep tossing that around. You're going to cut off your damn finger!" I heard a female say in a playful "mom" tone.

"Oh, come on, Delilah. You know I'm more careful than that."

I froze at the mention of the name, leaning in to hear some familiarity in the voice.

"Don't you 'Oh, come on' me! How many times have you accidentally hurt yourself, hm?"

The man sighed dramatically.

"Fine. Take your dagger back then. You're taking away all the fun anyhow."

"Graham, sometimes you are more dramatic than everyone I know combined."

"Holy shit," I whispered to myself, losing my grip on the branch.

As I shifted, the wood creaked beneath my weight. I failed to grab a new branch as my support gave way, dumping me on the forest floor. The pair instantly went into a defensive stance— the woman pointing the dagger in my direction. I pushed myself to my knees, brushing off some leaves, and then raised both hands in the air, refusing to release my grip on my own dagger.

"Who are you?!" the woman shouted.

"I'm, uhhh," I started, wondering if I would change my future if she knew who I was or if this was just another memory of some kind.

"Well?" the younger version of Graham asked with annoyance.

I flushed, finding myself affected by his presence.

"I'm not sure how much to tell you. I don't know where or when I am, and I don't know how you perceive me."

"What?" Graham and Delilah asked in unison.

"What color is my hair?" I asked.

"Red. Are you feeling alright? Why were you up there? Were you spying on us? Did you hit your head as you fell?" Delilah inquired, concern peeking through her stoic stance.

I laughed at the similarities my mother, and I had.

"No. I'm fine. I'm just..." I paused, collecting my thoughts. "There's a lot I've been learning about my powers that I wasn't aware I was capable of. I know this may sound strange, but you know me. Eventually. In your future. I, uhh. I can show you the dagger I'm holding. It's the same one that you have."

"Ok, so you're a Fighter. Is there something else that you can tell us that might give us more proof?" Delilah asked.

"Yeah, sure. How old are you right now?" I asked.

"I'm 24," she replied with a frown.

"Ok. Based on the weather, you recently married Scott. You may or may not have discovered that you're pregnant. Your mother's name is Francine, but she goes by Franny. Graham, you only just discovered the strength of your powers as a necklace from your mother had prevented you from properly accessing it for years. My G— Franny was the one that finally figured it out."

"You're pregnant?!" Graham immediately turned to ask Delilah.

I spit out a laugh that he so quickly believed what I told him.

"I've only just found out yesterday, myself," she blushed. "I brought you out here to tell you..." she smiled at him before turning back to me. "Alright, you know things that most people wouldn't know, so why are you here?"

"I'm not sure. Graham's future self handed me this dagger, and the next thing I knew, I was standing in the middle of the forest."

"Can I see it?" Delilah asked.

"I'm afraid if I let go, I will disappear back to my own time, but if you trust me to hold it, you are welcome to observe it."

Graham and Delilah shot each other a look, but ultimately, they both made their way toward me. I stayed on the ground, not daring to get up. When they got close enough, Delilah came over to the dagger in my hand and looked it over. She traced her fingers and shrugged in surprise.

"This is my dagger, but it seems to be a few decades older than mine," she announced. "You said Graham gave this to you?"

I simply nodded. Seeing my mother so young and knowing that I was growing inside of her was a little unnerving. I couldn't understand why the dagger took me to this moment in time, but I was sure there had to be something behind it. As the silence continued to grow, Graham stepped between us to help me up.

"Well, I suppose if I gave it to you, then you must be special. Though, how did I end up with it?"

"My m— Delilah gave it to you. To keep you safe."

"Safe from what?" they both asked.

"Probably best to not say any more on the subject," I replied, laughing nervously at their repeated unison.

"Yeah, you're probably right," Graham agreed.

I smiled at this younger version of Graham. He indeed was a beautiful human through and through. When I opened my mouth to speak again, my entire body was thrown from where I stood. The wind was knocked out of me as I was slammed against a tree. The ringing in my ears made the muffled shouts indecipherable. As I used my magic to heal, I heard Sebastian speaking to me.

"Not wise returning to such a prominent moment in your life. I could so easily end this for you by killing your mother."

I turned my head to see my mother and Graham, both frozen in time. My mother's magical form shifted, clinging tightly to the dagger, and I could see the hair on her arms standing with the promise of a fight. Graham was in a position to protect her but also appeared to be activating his magic. I growled at Sebastian's dark form, calling upon all the magic I could. His human body stepped away from the dark shape and started walking toward me.

I had a choice to make, attack the dark entity, or attack him. As he stalked towards me, calling upon his magic, I threw everything I had at the dark form he left by my mother and Graham. His face was painted with fear as he watched my magic soar past him. I used the distraction to lunge forward and shove the dagger deep into his side, causing him to howl in pain as both forms were hit simultaneously.

Quickly recovering from the flesh wound, he swung his arm and struck me across the face hard, knocking me backward. As I landed on the ground for the third time, my mother and Graham unfroze and shifted back to themselves. Both of them turned to me as I touched my bruised cheek and watched the slick blood dripping from the dagger.

"Are you ok?!" my mother asked.

"I'm fine," I said, brushing myself off again as I stood.

"Are you sure? Your head is bleeding," Graham pointed out.

"It's nothing I can't take care of," I replied tersely.

"But—" Graham started.

"I think I did what I was meant to do here. Delilah, take this dagger. I believe you need to keep both for me to leave."

She hesitated a moment before reaching toward me.

"Thank you... for whatever you've just done."

I shut my eyes as she grabbed the dagger, holding my breath.

"ELIANA?!" Graham shouted.

Eliana slowly cracked one eye open, not sure where she was going to find herself. She let out a sigh of relief when she found herself back in Graham's bedroom. Looking down at her hand, the dagger was there. She was sure that her mother had taken it from her but guessed it was good that history didn't seem to have changed by her going to that moment. It must have been a time she was meant to return to.

"What the hell?" Graham asked.

"Uhhh," she started. "I don't know... What did you see?"

"You turned into robot Eliana again. I tried to let you just go along with it a little longer this time, but then blood started dripping down the back of your neck, and you got a bruise on your cheek."

"Aw, shit," Eliana said, touching the wet spot on the back of her head.

She closed her eyes and let her magic flow through her body to heal more than she initially realized was injured during that short time there. When she finished, she opened her eyes and looked at Graham. The worry still laced across his face. He reached out and gently ran his thumb across her cheek where the bruise had been. When he sighed and placed his forehead against hers, cupping the side of her face in one hand, Eliana could feel his fear traveling into her body and forced some magic out to calm him.

Once he relaxed a bit, he dragged his nose up her forehead and kissed just below her hairline. He took the dagger from her and placed it back in the bag.

"So, can you tell me what happened this time?" he inquired solemnly.

"Well, as soon as I touched the dagger, I was pulled into the past. I think it was always supposed to happen, but it's tough to tell. Anyway, I heard some voices, so I followed them. It was you and my mother in a forest. You were playing with the dagger and—"

"The day I found out she was pregnant with you," he said, his eyes glossing over. "That was you that day?! I—"

"Yeah. Anyway, so, Sebastian showed up," she cut him off.

"He WHAT?!" Graham shouted.

Eliana flinched away slightly.

"That's who I stopped. The Darkness that showed up was him. He froze time and threatened to kill my mother and the fetus me."

"How did you stop him?" Graham interjected.

"He separated from the entity and came toward me. While he was in a weaker state, I sent my magic at The Darkness he left behind and shoved the dagger into his side."

Graham stared at her incredulously.

"You stabbed him?" he finally said.

"Yeah. He disappeared after that, and I gave the dagger back to my mother. When I opened my eyes, I was back here."

"This is all a lot to process, but I guess it's good that we're able to learn so much before we go to fight him. One thing that we learned from this is that you will get hurt in both forms, so we need to make sure you don't get killed in either place if you end up traveling this way. Do you feel you have enough control to use it against Sebastian safely?" Graham asked.

"I mean, as far as I can tell, I will be able to control everything. It all feels different from before. It's like I was trying to do magic with my eyes closed, but now I can see everything. I don't have to think about steps. It's like the magic knows what I need to happen before I do."

Graham nodded. He put down the bag and went over to her, taking her hands in his own.

"Can you promise me you will do everything you can to stay safe during this? Please?"

Eliana furrowed her eyebrows together, fighting back the tears as she saw the pain take over his features.

"I will do whatever is necessary to save us all from Sebastian, but I promise you I will do my best to stay alive."

Graham frowned at her, clearly not pleased by her avoided promise.

"Eliana, this fight was never about you giving up your life to save everyone. I won't have you sacrificing yourself just because you think that's the only way to win."

Eliana dropped his hands, becoming annoyed with him.

"Look, Graham. It's my choice how I will win this fight. I've promised to do my best to stay alive, and that's what I can give to you. I won't try to sugarcoat any of it. There's no point in lying about my intentions when there's a chance neither of us surviving this. I appreciate your concern. I do, but don't insult my intelligence by assuming that I am just going to go out there and give up my own life. I've already given up so much just to get to this moment. I won't give up anymore."

Eliana was almost yelling by the end of her speech. Graham had dropped his eyes and was looking at his toes as they shifted on the floor. His discomfort was growing more apparent by the second. His following words came out strained, though he tried to hide it with a joke.

"You know, one would think that you were the one who had spent the last two decades learning everything about anything that mattered, and, yet, here we are." He paused and took her hands in his once more. "You are wise beyond your years, and you are completely correct in everything you've said. It was wrong of me to try to tell you what choices to make. I guess I've really just been bossing you around all night, huh?" he laughed. "I appreciate your willingness to trust the plans that I keep throwing together. I truly do just want what's best for the masses in these choices I'm making. When the time comes, and you choose to ignore everything and trust your instinct, then I will do whatever I can to assist you. You've already proven multiple times that you are far stronger than me."

Eliana laughed and shook her head.

"You are all over the place right now. Stop thinking about such extremes. I know you're probably afraid, but I'm sure my feelings aren't much different from yours. I'm trying hard right now to stay calm and focused, but I don't think I can do it for both of us."

Graham sighed, pulling Eliana into a tight hug.

"You're right. I'm projecting my worries into everything that's going on. But really," Graham paused to pull away and look at Eliana, "you're making this all extremely difficult with all your curveballs. There is so much information that I never in a million years thought that I would have before going into this fight. I mean, could you have imagined any of the things you've done in the last twenty-four hours alone?"

Eliana laughed, "No. I guess not."

She took a moment to study his face before laying her head against his chest and letting his heartbeat take over her senses.

"Give me that back!" I laughed, chasing Graham to retrieve the sandwich that he had taken from me.

"If you want it that badly, then you're going to have to catch me!" he playfully shouted back.

"Is that a challenge?" I asked.

"Could be," he replied with a smirk.

Eliana jerked her eyes open, trying to understand what she was seeing. This clearly wasn't something that had happened, yet here she was experiencing it. It felt different from a memory, somehow lighter, more refreshing. Before something could change, she rested further into Graham, hoping to go back to that place.

"Oh, you're on."

I watched Graham's body tense to his left ever so slightly and threw myself to where I hoped he would be going. I crashed into him, sending both of us to the soft grass that had been beneath our feet not a moment ago. I was able to retrieve my sandwich during the fall before landing on my side. I immediately rolled myself to sit on top of him and show him the sandwich triumphantly.

As I was pulling in the sandwich to take a bite, he grabbed my wrist. Before I could protest his denying me of eating my lunch, his lips found mine. I resisted slightly at first, really wanting to take that bite of my food, but instead melted into his touch. I released the sandwich and ran my hands along his chest. A groan escaped his throat as I slid my hands up the insides of his thighs. He quickly reached for the button of my pants, releasing its hold.

Eliana pulled away from Graham, gasping for air.

"Are you alright?" he asked.

"Yeah, but apparently not my sandwich," she said sarcastically.

Graham blushed furiously, rubbing the back of his neck.

"I... uhh. Heh. You really should ask before invading someone's mind, you know. You might end up seeing something you don't want to."

"I think the only thing I didn't want to see from that scenario was my sandwich going to waste!" Eliana joked.

"Oh, right. Yeah. I guess, I uh. *ahem* I will make sure to imagine the sandwich landing on something to keep it sanitary next time," he finished with a wink.

"Much appreciated. Now, if you'll excuse me for a moment, I'm just going to use the bathroom before we head out."

"Oh! Yes, of course. Right over there," he said, pointing.

"Thanks," Eliana laughed.

When she closed the door, she let out an audible exhale. She was having a hard enough time controlling her lust, let alone feeling Graham's. As she relieved herself, she wondered if she could blame some of it on the impending doom that was quickly closing in on them. Accepting the idea, she went over to the sink and splashed her face with cold water before washing her hands. She dried her face and hands, took one last breath, then went back out to join Graham.

"Feeling better?" he asked with a breathtaking smile.

"Sonofabitch," Eliana mumbled to herself, finding it harder to control her body's response's to him. "One hundred percent!" she continued loud enough for him to hear.

"Great! Are you ready, then?" he asked.

"It's now or never," she shot back, mimicking a superhero taking off in flight.

Graham laughed, but it quickly faded away as the worry replaced his momentary relaxation. Eliana's body tensed in response. She desperately hoped their plan would succeed.

"Alright. Well, I guess it's time. So, put this on, and try not to access your core magic," he said, holding out the necklace to her. "I have a feeling that it won't be completely effective against you, and I don't want the chance of getting intercepted while we're traveling back home."

Eliana nodded, holding it in her hand for a moment. As her head passed through the chain, a wave shivered through her body. It felt like part of her existence was lost. Her core begged her to fight against this alien feeling the crystal gave, but she effortlessly controlled the urge with some focus.

"Ok," she eventually said. "I think it's doing what it should. Ready?" she asked, reaching out her hand to Graham's.

"Not really, but I'm glad that I get to do it with you," he responded, taking her hand and smiling.

CHAPTER TWENTY-ONE

As Graham took a breath, Eliana could feel the tingle of his magic traveling through her palm up to her elbow. The necklace lit up as she unconsciously responded with her magic, so she quickly repressed it again. When he didn't react to the potential danger that had just occurred, Eliana let her body relax and absorb his magic. It perfectly blended with hers, like it was filling the empty spaces left from the pain and struggles of her life. An intense wind encased her body, and the whooshing sound permeated her ears. She sucked in a sharp breath at the profound stillness that followed.

"Okay, we're here," Graham whispered.

Eliana swiftly opened her eyes, desperately needing to take in her surroundings of home. Her chest tightened. Everything precisely as she had left it that night her parents sent her to the other land was a little eerie. She stole a glance to make sure Graham hadn't aged twenty years, then continued exploring her room when she confirmed he hadn't.

Crossing the room, Eliana went over to the window, noting that aside from some plants and trees being more substantial, there weren't many changes. She never expected that she would be able to return to a home that was still so loved and cared for. The emotions threatening to consume her were brushed aside when Graham spoke again.

"It doesn't sound like anyone is out there, but I want to make sure," he continued in a hushed voice.

Eliana turned from the window and watched silently as he unlocked and carefully opened the door. His hair rustled slightly as the air from the hallway forced its way into the room. Fighting the urge to assist him with magic, Eliana carefully made her way to where he was. When she arrived at the door, they heard someone coming down the long hall. Graham closed the door as quickly as he could without making a sound, and the two took a step back. As the footsteps came closer, both of them held their breath. The humming passed through the cracks in the door and then faded away. Graham turned to Eliana and smiled brightly.

"Who was it?" she whispered.

"Louisa!" he replied a little louder.

Eliana smiled at the mention of the name, feeling slightly embarrassed that she hadn't known who it was.

"Oh, of course, it was," she flushed.

Louisa was the only person she had ever known to rise with the sun and be cheerful enough to cast a warmth more considerable than it. Wherever she went, joy seemed to follow. The world would definitely be a slightly darker place when she left it, but Eliana was ecstatic to know that she hadn't.

"Come on," Graham said with his head poked out the door and his arm motioning her over. "Let's get to the tunnel!"

Eliana nodded and followed, impressed at how well he knew the house that had been in her family for generations. Before her parents, her Granny Franny and the grandfather that Eliana had never known lived there; and before them, five generations of her bloodline stayed in this house. The massive home had always felt so cozy, with her parents and grandmother to fill every corner with love, but in this twilight hour, the shadows seemed to taunt her. The only time she felt a cold emptiness in her home was in the months following the passing of her grandmother when she was almost twenty. She often wondered after she thought her parents had passed if they would all still be alive and together had her granny not passed on.

Despite the actual emptiness of the house, Eliana felt some warmth and life filling the spaces as she passed through with Graham. While knowing that she could soon share these walls with her parents lit up her eyes with the hope she had not known still existed within her, there was something about seeing a man whom she was falling in love with all over again walking through with such comfort and grace. Even though she knew his obligations would probably force him to live in the castle, the tunnel that connected their homes made it just a quick eight-minute walk to be together in either house.

As Graham opened the door that would lead them down to the basement, Eliana was hit with how real all of this had become. Everything that she had spent the majority of her life fighting for was about to resolve. Eliana stopped a moment and forced the breath that had caught in her lungs to be expelled from her body. Clearing her mind, she took the first step leading into the basement, knowing that there was no turning back now.

CHAPTER TWENTY-TWO

Graham's racing mind could barely keep up with the adrenaline pulsing through his body as he finished his descent into the basement. Everything he gave up, everything he learned; it was all about to come together, whether for good or bad. When he reached the cold cement floor at the bottom of the stairs, Graham closed his eyes and took a deep breath, trying to slow his body's natural reaction to the imminent danger.

The warmth of Eliana consumed his left arm, and he smiled and reached out to where he hoped her hand would be, successfully grasping it. Her presence calmed his mind, if only for a moment. When his palm tingled with her magic, he quickly released their hands, opening his eyes.

"Sorry...." she breathed.

"It's alright. We're both still learning how powerful you are. It is amazing how easily you can push past that necklace. I wonder how many times you've tapped into your core magic without knowing." Graham brushed the hair from her face.

"Now that I know what it feels like, I know I've done it a few times before, but I was never in control of it like I am now. I think acting out of anger so often prevented me from fully letting go and trusting in my abilities, but I guess it's never too late to redefine who you are." She laughed.

Graham nodded at her.

"The choice still belongs to you, you know. There's no promise of what will happen during this fight. Is this really what you want?" he asked gently.

"I think it's beyond me having a choice. Not because it was made for me, but who else is going to make this happen? And in all honesty, I would never be able to forgive myself if I stepped down and we lost or more people died. That sort of guilt is just not something I would ever be able to let go of. Besides, even if we do fail, I think that you will at least get some closure with your father."

"That would be nice, but I think I've accepted and moved on from everything he's done. I just hope the damage to our home has not been so great that we can't bounce back." Graham sighed.

"Shit. I guess everyone lost all the powerful voices of reason around the same time." Eliana laughed awkwardly.

Graham watched her brow furrow deeper and deeper in the silence and assumed from her slumping shoulders that she was placing that burden of guilt upon herself. He couldn't blame her, though. His guilt started to weigh him down further. His mind began to wonder if he could have done something differently. He shook off the thoughts and tried to focus on what he could do in the now.

"I suppose they did," he replied softly after the long silence. "But I do not doubt that everyone leaving at once allowed Placata Montis to come together stronger than ever before, even if just in secrecy. From the talks that I've had with people, there were some improvements simply because there was no need to use magic actively. The attacks were happening next to never, and without my father seeing anyone left behind as a genuine threat, some lightheartedness came over the land."

"Oh," Eliana replied tersely.

"Not to say that they are better off without us!" Graham quickly clarified. "It's just that the focus of my father to destroy magic resides dominantly with your family. Your lineage has always produced a powerful voice. When my grandparents led the kingdom, your great-grandparents worked with the people hands-on to keep things safe. And your ancestors did the same.

"And when my father stepped up to be the king, the relationship with your grandparents became cold. The friendship that used to exist between our families was thrown aside because my father didn't have magic. Everyone else before him could use it; that's why I think he tried to prove his strength in terrible, hurtful ways.

"I wasn't just brought up to hate magic in general. When I started talking to your mother, my father was beyond pissed because your family was the essence of what it meant to have magic. He probably felt inferior to your mother. So, I hid our friendship for a long time, though I'm sure he knew more than I thought. Anyway, his desire to be the best at everything made him a poor father and a lousy leader. Without you and your family there to make him feel insignificant, I think it suppressed some of the pressure he put on himself."

"I suppose that all makes sense," Eliana replied slowly. "I never realized how much our families were linked over the years. I mean, this tunnel alone should have tipped off some of that!"

Eliana laughed, and Graham joined in.

"I didn't know the complexity of our families until I started researching everything that I could about The Darkness and the history of our land. Knowing now that Sebastian is the root of all of this makes so much sense. I can't understand how he managed to hide his identity, but I would assume he used magic somehow.

"Sebastian originated from Placata Montis, so, of course, he would be keen to return here and help my father. Besides, The Darkness traveled around to try to get people to revive the core magic that they crave, but most places would turn out to be a complete waste of time. Those were the places that were destroyed. So, having someone to call him to powerful magic, Sebastian must have been giddy."

"Do the people where you hid have magic?"

"The land runs rich with powerful energy, but everyone is too distracted by everything else to notice. Though, sometimes, they accidentally tap into it. I didn't just choose that place on a whim to do my work," Graham stated.

"Why didn't I notice it, then?" Eliana asked.

"You probably did at a subconscious level. When you started tapping into your core magic, you were allowing yourself to be pulled by the surrounding energy. If we had been somewhere that the magic was completely dead, I'm not so sure you would have been as successful."

Eliana closed her eyes and placed a hand on either side of her head. Graham regretted telling her about it when they were trying to go into what he hoped would be the ultimate battle, but he waited patiently for her to absorb the information. She was breathing evenly, and there weren't any signs of significant stress visible like before, so Graham allowed his guard to drop.

"Was my magic calling to The Darkness? Were they in danger because of me?" she finally asked with her eyes still closed.

"No. If anything, I'm the one who put them in danger. Though I did my best not to."

Eliana opened her eyes and dropped her hands back to her side. Graham watched her silently as she nodded slowly. Her head suddenly stopped in a tilt, and her eyes squinted.

"When you picked that land, did you know there was a certain level of protection?"

"I did. Had you escaped to a place where magic was completely dead, you would have been a light calling to The Darkness."

Graham smiled softly as Eliana visibly relaxed. He wished he had time to show her all the planning that he and her parents had done. So many precautions were taken, and although there had been some pieces left to chance, Graham made sure that there was a failsafe to protect as many people as he could.

He knew that he wasn't leaving Placata Montis weaponless. Eliana and her parents were more powerful than any combination of Graystin's before them. Delilah and Scott had passed on all of their traits and then some to Eliana. Of course, during the time of planning, Graham and her parents had no idea how powerful Eliana would become, but there had been so many moments leading up that gave them hope.

"You know, when you thought The Darkness took your parents, I checked in back home as often as I could." Graham clarified while walking ahead. "I passed on a message to trusted informants to limit their magic use and see if the frequency at which The Darkness came around dropped. It did. In fact, most of the people left behind thought that things were finally over. Even my father didn't know the threat of magic remained, so he stopped creating attacks against people," Graham added when Eliana stayed silent.

With the knowledge he had now, he assumed Sebastian got bored with the apparent lack of powerful magic left. Though, with the number of entities that had kept chasing Eliana and himself, he guessed the scent on their trail was more critical than anyone left behind.

"Well, I'm glad that you were still working behind the scenes to try to take care of everyone," she finally said. "I wish that I hadn't been left in the dark for so much of it, but I can understand the need for me to activate my hidden talent. The desire to take care of everything you left behind pushed me to train pretty hard in the beginning, but I would have to say that thinking my parents had died pushed me more than anything else I had known before..." she trailed off.

"Yeah. I'm sorry you had to endure that heartbreak, but I'm glad it helped to prepare you for this moment."

"Ha!" she gave a short laugh. "Thanks, I guess."

Graham smiled at her and shrugged, shooting her a quick wink. He watched the subtle pink paint across her cheeks before she spun away to clear her throat. The sudden change in the mood as her body slightly tensed caused him to follow her stare down the long tunnel and shiver at the unknown journey ahead.

"Graham?" she inquired.

"Yeah?" he asked, taking a step to be directly beside her.

"If something happens to one of us," she replied, turning her head to look him in the eye, "I want you to know that this time with you has been one of the happiest moments of my life. And I hope that we can continue whatever this is, but just in case... I needed you to know."

"Eliana, I—" Graham began.

"No," she quickly interrupted. "There's nothing to argue. I don't want to pretend that this isn't dangerous. We both know it is. If I don't make it, please let my parents know I love them. If you want me to pass anything on to anyone, tell me now, and hopefully, that's something I can do if need be."

Graham gently grabbed her, pressing his lips to hers. He felt her weight increase as she relaxed into him, slowly wrapping her arms around his body. She followed his lead, and he let his hands slide down her arms until they wrapped around her waist, closing the space that had been between their bodies. She moaned softly as his hand traced gently up and down her spine, eventually stopping to grab her backside roughly. Separating for a moment to gasp for air, Eliana threw her head back and groaned. Graham kissed down her neck, tracing his tongue along her pronounced collarbone. He watched her goosebumps and smiled. Trailing his lips up her shoulder and neck, she shivered and then sighed, setting her head against his chest.

"I'll be sure to pass that on..." she said in an airy voice.

Graham laughed heartily and slid his hands back to her waist, pulling Eliana flush to him and placing his cheek on the top of her head. He was falling hard and fast for her and wasn't sure how to feel about it. Part of him wanted to resist everything, knowing it would be a distraction in a fight, but the other part of him wished to just pause all the heroics and spend time with her. Being alone for so many years had taken more of a toll on him than he had cared to admit. The warmth of her body alone against his own calmed him, but he wanted to be sure he wasn't falling for her just because of loneliness.

Turning to kiss the top of her head, he pulled her away and looked into her eyes. The fierce drive that had always been there seemed to be amplified. Her eyes flashed with an intensity that perfectly blended with a calm aura. She was powerful, confident, and strong. There was nothing about her that wouldn't have drawn him in had he not known her before this lifetime. It was all strange to him. He had been there for her birth. He had watched her grow up for almost thirteen years, and now, twenty-two years later, a remarkable woman stood in his arms.

Graham separated the two lifetimes in his mind. The Eliana that he knew before was no longer the timeline that he existed in. Everyone he knew and grew up with would be twenty or so years his elder. The detachment that he had had from the current state of things would separate them even more. He would have memories of his childhood, but the life he was entering back into would be drastically different. The effects of it being a curse cast upon him were starting to sink in fully. The worry of what life would be when he returned never really forced its way so actively into his life, and now that it was here, he felt like a newborn horse trying to find its legs.

"What's wrong?" Eliana asked, dropping her arms and interrupting his thoughts.

"I was just thinking how different the world I'm returning to would be. I've been frozen in one moment in time. Everyone has lived a life without me here. I just feel like I won't connect with the things I knew anymore. There are twenty-two years of life and experiences that everyone has had, and all I've gained is more knowledge. There aren't any moments I can say I've lived since I left. I just stayed in my timeless bubble and focused on one thing. It's kind of strange to think about."

Eliana nodded at him.

"A part of me understands what you mean. Being in that other land felt like I was mostly just fighting to get back to a place and moment when I knew who I was and what I was meant to do. While I stayed behind in Placata Montis after you left, I don't think I will fully connect with anyone I hung out with before either. I didn't live there as many years as you did before you left anyway. But, of course, at least everyone I knew would all still be my same age, eh?" she finished, elbowing him playfully in the side.

Graham laughed.

"Yes. You have that going for you. Too bad there's not much else," he quipped back, making a fake face of offense at Eliana.

"Hey!" she said, nuzzling and pushing him.

He laughed and pulled her into a hug once more. He was stalling and didn't want this moment to end. The truth of what was at the end of the tunnel was frightening and unknown. There were so many possibilities, and he didn't know if he would be around to see the success. He desperately hoped that everything he had done to prepare for this moment would be enough.

"Alright," he said, pulling away one last time. "Are you ready to do this?"

Eliana nodded and reached out to take his hand. They simultaneously turned towards the tunnel and took a deep breath before starting their descent.

CHAPTER TWENTY-THREE

When they reached the end of the tunnel, Graham released Eliana's hand and motioned for her to stay behind him, hugging the wall. She followed his direction with minimal eye-rolling, causing him to stifle a laugh before turning around to continue walking. Quieting his breath, he listened for any other signs of life in the space before them. There were some muffled voices in the distance, too far to cause him any worry.

Graham carefully proceeded, deliberate with each step. Glancing behind, he saw Eliana intensely watching his feet, and he smiled. Taking a breath, he hesitated briefly as he tried to remember where to step, not to cause the boards to creak, before he continued ambling up the stairs. Eliana stayed slightly behind, carefully replacing his invisible footprints. At the top of the stairs, the grandiose area flooded his senses. He rarely took time to appreciate the beauty of the lesser-traveled halls. Eliana stepped beside him, running her fingers over the cold Quartz, tracing intricate designs that swirled behind the smooth finish.

Graham watched her for a moment and smiled.

"I'm guessing you've never been to this part of the castle?" he asked.

Eliana shook her head.

"I never really had a reason to go beyond the main living space, and I was too afraid to come up the stairs from the tunnel. Your father wasn't the most welcoming, especially after you took off."

Graham grimaced when he caught on to the bite in her words. Despite their undeniable chemistry, there would be some feelings that would need to be dealt with when this was done. Any resentment that Eliana might have been harboring for twenty-two years would probably need a little more than a physical desire to erase.

"Yes. I know," he said solemnly after a pregnant pause, "But to my knowledge, there was no other way. I regret that you weren't informed more. Had I known how much I meant to you, I probably would have told you more before I left. Although, even when you were a child, I think you may have understood love better than I. There was a time when I first met your mother that I thought I was in love with her, but when I saw her with your father, I knew that while I loved her, I didn't want her companionship beyond friendship. There was something between them that I knew wasn't there for her or for me."

Eliana's face stayed surprisingly neutral as he spoke, but the necklace dimly lit up as he finished speaking. Graham held his breath when he realized what he had just revealed to her and took a step back to give her space, and tried to relax. His attempt for a deep breath was interrupted when she burst out in laughter.

"What?" Graham choked out.

"That magic wasn't for me. It was for you. Your high level of stress and guilt makes it really hard for me to suppress my magic," she laughed again. "I don't care that you thought you loved my mother romantically. I realize that thirteen-year-olds rarely know what love is like, but I think the connection goes down to the core of our magic. If you had ended up with a child, they might have been the one I'd desire, but I'm not going to question the path the universe has sent us down. Even if these are our only moments to be together, I know it's meant to be this way. Our magic compliments each other too well for it not to have been a track we were meant to follow."

Graham resisted the urge to grab her and kiss her again. Instead, he closed his eyes and absorbed her words. Their partnership was greater than sexual tension. He felt his hair ruffle with magic. He jerked open his eyes and realized that he had also started to levitate.

"Eliana, that's not safe," he lectured as he came back to the earth.

"Uh. None of that was me," she laughed.

"Pardon?" he asked with exasperation.

Eliana shrugged.

"All you, my friend. Guess someone else found a part of their core magic that they didn't know existed. Welcome," she finished by bowing mockingly and holding out a hand to guide him to her side of the room.

"But—" Graham started.

His words were cut short by someone coming around the corner. They froze. They had foolishly let themselves get distracted, and there wasn't time to dive out of sight.

"Graham? Is that you?" the woman asked.

"Hey, Felicity," Graham replied in his practiced calm voice, his body still tense.

As she continued walking towards them, Graham motioned to Eliana behind his back. He didn't know what might happen to him upon his return home, and he didn't want to drag her into it. Graham heard Eliana sigh quietly as she moved behind him. His tense body relaxed as soon as Felicity pulled him into a tight hug. As he returned the hug to the older woman, he felt her tears soaking his shirt.

"Felicity?" he asked, pulling away.

"We never thought that we'd see you again. We thought we'd have to appoint a new person to be in charge," she replied with a sniffle.

"What? What do you mean?" Graham asked, trying not to assume the worst.

"Isn't that why you're here?" Felicity asked, taking a step back and wiping her tears.

"Well, it is part of my hope that I can stay here and take my rightful place, yes. But why are you so upset? What happened?"

Felicity looked at him incredulously.

"Your father, Graham. He passed away last night," she hitched. "I was by his side. Someone was supposed to contact you. I just figured.... I'm sorry," she said, covering her mouth as she started to cry again.

"Oh," was all Graham could manage as he handed Felicity a handkerchief. He'd taken too long. He knew his father hadn't been well for some time but never thought he wouldn't make it back in time to mend things.

"He wanted me to pass on that he was so sorry for everything that he'd done. He said he left something where you and your mother would play before she got sick," she added after wiping more of her tears away.

"Thank you. Did he say anything else?"

"Yes," Felicity started with a frown. "He said, 'Ah. They're together. I can hear their screams.'"

"Who?" Eliana poked her head around to ask.

"Oh! Eliana! Hello!" Felicity shouted excitedly, some sadness leaving her face as she pulled her into a quick hug. "That's exactly what I asked him!" she continued as she pulled away.

"And?" Eliana encouraged.

"Well, he said your names, Graham and Eliana. And then he smiled and closed his eyes."

Graham shot Eliana a swift look, trying to read something in her body. He assumed by her lack of reaction to Felicity knowing who she was that he shouldn't worry, but he still did. Eliana had rarely come to the castle when he had been there, and he doubted that she would have at all after he left. Though, Felicity had a gift for remembering and knowing everyone in Placata Montis, so he brushed off any worry and focused on the conversation again.

"What time did he pass?" Graham asked.

"I'd say it was around 11:30 pm. Why?"

"Can you excuse us, Felicity?" Graham smiled.

"Sure." She frowned.

Graham grabbed Eliana's arm and took her back down the stairs before pulling out his phone. Eliana quietly watched him access files of camera footage from the last day. He chose the one which contained the footage from the lab and set a timeframe of 11:15 pm-11:59 pm. As they watched in fast forward, he paused when he and Eliana blended their magic and expelled The Darkness from Francisco. The timestamp read 11:34 pm.

"Holy shit," they said in unison.

CHAPTER TWENTY-FOUR

"Graham, how could your dad know what was happening?" Eliana finally asked after a long silence.

"I don't know. It doesn't make any sense. Let me text Francisco that we're safely here, and then I think we need to go talk to Felicity more about it..." he replied, turning to head back up the stairs, his phone being held limply in his hand.

"Wait!" Eliana said, grabbing his arm. "Are you ok?"

Graham paused for a moment before turning around to respond.

"I don't know. There is a lot to work through, but I will probably know more when I go look for what my father left behind."

Eliana simply nodded and squeezed his arm. He gave her a sad smile, kissing her gently on the cheek.

"Thank you. Let's go back up," he said, taking a quick pause to send Francisco a message.

She sighed quietly, slowly following behind him.

"Graham!" Felicity called when they reappeared upstairs. "Is everything alright?"

"I'm not sure. Where is my father now?" he asked.

Felicity looked a little uncomfortable at the question.

"He's still in his bed. We didn't want to move him in case you could get here quickly."

Graham smiled and gave her a quick hug.

"You did just fine. I appreciate everything you've been doing since I left. Was there anyone else in the room with you when he passed?"

"No..." Felicity replied slowly. "But he seemed to keep talking to someone that I couldn't see. Can I ask why he thought you two were screaming? I mean, he was correct about you two finding each other. If you don't mind me asking, that is..."

Eliana blushed furiously at the underlying assumption, and Graham laughed before quickly replying.

"He wasn't referring to us screaming, but can you do me a favor and not tell anybody that we're here? I'm not sure if I trust what's happening just yet, and I'd like to see what my father left before I get bombarded. I also need a moment to say goodbye so that you guys can properly handle his body."

"Yes, Sir. Of course. Also, not to be too much of a nag, but the sooner you can let the people know there is, in fact, a king, I think the better off things might be. There's been some tension throughout the land since you left. No one has truly been at ease since you disappeared. We all had to constantly tread lightly, and no one with magic felt like they could truly be themselves."

Eliana felt Graham tense at the comment, but he kept his smile gentle.

"Yes. I deeply apologize for that. We will move as quickly as we can. Before you go, can you put a few important numbers into my phone so I can contact you?"

Felicity nodded, taking the device from him and quickly typing some information.

"I've added myself, Billy, and Felipe for now. If you need anyone else, you can just ask me."

"Thank you."

"You're welcome. Now, go. Stop with the lollygagging."

Felicity smiled and turned down the hall while Graham and Eliana went in the opposite direction to where his father was. The silence was heavy, and she wanted to take his hand but decided against it. When they got to his father's room, Graham closed his eyes outside the door, taking a deep breath. She could see the pain painting across his features and gently squeezed his arm.

"I'm right here," she whispered.

He opened his tear-stained eyes and gave her a nod with a tight smile, then reached for the handle. As the door opened, they saw The Darkness standing over Graham's father's body. Eliana went to tear the necklace off to fight, but Graham quickly reached out to stop her.

"Don't," he whispered.

They both watched as the entity circled the body, completely unaware that there were now others in the room. It seemed to be looking for something and was getting frustrated when it couldn't find it. When its back was to them, Graham took a slow step forward, and the floorboard creaked beneath his foot. The entity whipped around and screamed just before it disappeared.

"Shit!" Graham shouted.

He spun around and took off down the hallway. Eliana immediately followed, keeping in stride and quietly running beside him, falling behind slightly when he took two quick lefts. She caught up just as he was pushing open the doors, which led to a garden. The full moon lit up space and revealed a giant tree, taking over the entire view as they exited the building. Eliana wordlessly joined Graham, staring up at the massive branches.

"My mother used to take me to this tree," Graham said, panting. "She would say that it was born of magic and would guide me to the truth. Funny how, at the end of it all, she's probably more correct than anyone ever thought."

"Women usually are," Eliana joked.

A small smile pulled at Graham's lips, but his eyes remained locked on the tree.

"What do you think your father left here?" Eliana asked.

"I'm not sure," Graham started. "Can you keep an eye out? I don't need The Darkness sneaking up on me while I'm looking."

Eliana nodded. She took a moment to absorb her surroundings as

Graham stepped closer to the mass in front of them. The stone walls that surrounded the garden were entirely concealed by vines with vibrant purple flowers sprouting from them. To her left was a large fountain filled with lily pads and a statue of a falcon.

Letting her gaze fall back to Graham, she observed him run his fingers over the bark, opening a knot and pulling out an oddly shaped crystal. The moment his hand cleared the space, a squirrel ran out of the now exposed hole, and he smiled at the distraught animal before replacing the cover on its home.

"What is it?" Eliana asked, her eyes darting around the garden again.

"It's another crystal," he replied, frowning. "It's different from the ones I have, and it's been carved into the shape of a bird."

"What kind of bird?" she asked, taking a step towards him.

"A falcon, I think?" he responded, unsure.

"Like that?" she asked, pointing to the statue.

"Oh. Yes, actually," Graham laughed lightly.

"Graham... How long has that statue been there?" she asked slowly.

"A few hundred years, I guess. Why?"

"Is Sebastian related to your family? How much do you know about your mother's birth parents?"

Graham stopped and stared at the statue.

"I don't know," he finally said.

"I read once that the falcon is used to teach one to guide souls back to the land of the afterlife. They also help to—"

"Invoke magic..." Graham finished for her.

"Right. Do you think Sebastian helped your dad invoke magic through that crystal? And if that belonged to him... Then this is probably his statue."

"I honestly don't know," he replied, still eying the crystal. "In all of my years of research, I never thought of looking into my mother's true family lineage. It never made sense to. This has always been about you and your family."

Eliana leaned over the crystal and looked at it more closely. It glowed faintly and revealed intricacies she couldn't quite understand.

She went over to the statue in the fountain and looked for similarities. When she reached out to trace the words which appeared to resemble Latin, they dimly glowed in unison with the necklace around her neck and the crystal that Graham held. She jerked her hand back and held her breath, hoping that she hadn't activated something.

"Eliana? What did you do?" Graham half-shouted.

"I'm not sure that was me...," she replied slowly.

She remained tense with her hand clutched tightly around her necklace, stepping away from the statue. The glow that had been there moments before showed no sign of returning. Graham rushed to her side, causing her hair to flutter in his wind, and then he stepped away. He stretched his arm, holding the crystal towards the words on the statue, but nothing happened when the two touched.

"Hmm," he said.

Turning to Eliana, he brought his crystal closer to her, and it pulsed in time with the statue and her necklace.

"What the hell!?" she shouted, jumping back.

"Eliana?" Graham asked tentatively.

"Yeah?" she asked with a wavering voice.

"How much do you know about *your* family lineage? Did your father's parents die when he was young? I'm honestly a little embarrassed to say that I never met his family, and your mother always told me about her strong bloodline. I never thought your father might be the connecting factor in this."

Eliana shook her head, trying to remember a specific moment from her childhood to help answer him. Her breath became short as she focused hard on trying to find something, anything. Juggling through memories like searching for a needle in the haystack, but she could vaguely remember something...

"There was a book," she started with a whisper in between hitched breaths. "He was fostered," she said, answering Graham's question. "From what they used to tell me, he stayed with foster care until he was about twelve. He had been friends with my mom for a few years at that point, so my grandparents offered to take him into their home. At first, he said no, and then he slowly stayed longer each time he was invited over. Eventually, he never left. He and my mother had become inseparable and started dating when they were fifteen. He took mom's last name when they got married because he wanted an identity that he knew and not something that was assigned to him."

"Oh... Well, I don't know why I never asked that before. I guess I just assumed when they told me his parents died at a young age that he always just lived with your family. I never really thought he was on his own before that." He cleared his throat. "Do you know anything else?" he prodded, clearly uncomfortable.

"It wasn't something that he talked about. I only knew because I used to ask my grams about his parents' whereabouts. She would tell me all about how my parents met in school, and she knew immediately that they were meant for each other. Every time my mother invited him over, Grams would ask him to stay. He was so quiet — so shy. When he met my mom, he hid behind her outgoingness, but eventually, she helped him find the person he was. There is another moment... I'm struggling to recall it."

Graham set the falcon crystal down and walked over to her. Eliana frowned at him, not catching on to what he wanted to do. When he reached for the crystal around her neck, she smacked his hand away.

"What are you doing?!" she shouted at him.

"You need to access a memory using your core magic, so I'm going to remove the necklace. If you keep trying to remember like you have been and the necklace is blocking you, it's going to be more dangerous for both of us. Please, just try to be careful. I don't know how well I can protect you. Especially when danger is already lurking."

"Graham—" she started.

"We have to. It's responding to you for a reason. If it were my family, I would have caused a reaction the moment I touched it, but I didn't. You did. The only other person I ever brought back here was your mother, and I never saw anything like this happen. So, I can only assume that it's something you inherited from your father."

"Okay," Eliana nodded.

Graham reached towards her again and closed his hand around the necklace. He took a deep breath, and Eliana saw the reflection of her uncertainty in his eyes just before he lifted it. The moment it passed over her head, the falcon crystal and statue both lit up, throwing her backward.

I was back at my house, running through the long hallways, but everything looked massive. My little legs were carrying me as quickly as they could before I slowed to turn into the library. I giggling as I waddled over to a dark corner with a locked armoire. My toddler body reached up and used magic to release the lock and open the drawer.

I recalled that this was the third time I had attempted to retrieve the item that was hidden away. The first two unsuccessful attempts had been in previous months and resulted in my mother locking it in this drawer. Something about the forbidden book had drawn me to it at a very young age, and despite her multiple attempts to get me to leave it alone, I never could.

I raised up to my toes and clasped my hands around the leather binding, letting out a small breath of air as it hit me with some force. I giggled again while I plopped to the ground, crossed my legs, placed the book on the shelf I had created, and carefully flipped through.

The first few pages were filled with pictures of cut-out faces from my mother and father's immediate families. As I flipped further through, the photos turned into paintings, and the faces became harder to see, having faded over time. The images of my mother's family ended shortly after they started, while my father's family continued.

Eventually, I reached the family tree that went back almost three hundred years. The child version of me was looking through the book giggled at the faces, but my current body screamed as I saw a name and face that I recognized. I froze the memory and stared at the page that was about to turn.

Taking control of the memory, I reversed it and followed the names, trying to understand where the change happened. One page back, it was apparent where the change was made. The illegitimate daughter of Sebastian claimed her mother's name, and the remaining members changed the entire family name. His parents. His siblings. None of them wanted to share his name. An entire family knew what Sebastian had become and hid it from the world, including my parents.

Frustrated now, I followed the lineage all the way back to my father and let the memory go forward again.

The pages slowly turned, the sound of my giggles getting distorted by the decelerated time. When I made it back to the page with Sebastian, I froze on it once more. I stared at the cold eyes that pierced through the page, studying his face for similarities to myself or my father. My anger built, so I released the memory and returned to the present.

CHAPTER TWENTY-FIVE

Eliana jolted back, gasping for breath, pulling the necklace from Graham and placing it around her head again. She instantly relaxed as she felt her magic cut off from her awareness. The beads of sweat that had formed on her forehead during the memory stopped growing. She wiped them with the back of her hand and dried them on her pants. Graham watched her with fascination, waiting for her to say something. Finally, she looked into his eyes with concern.

"He's my family," she whispered.

"From your father?" he asked gently.

"Yeah. My father... How could they hide that from me? From everyone. Did they know who he was? What he had done? Why wouldn't they tell you? Wouldn't that have helped?!" Eliana said, yelling and causing the necklace to glow.

"What did you see?" he asked, taking her hand in his and brushing the hair away from her eye as he placed his palm against her cheek.

She sighed, letting his touch distract her from anger.

"I remembered a time when I was a child. There was a book they always tried to keep locked away. It was filled with my family trees, mostly from my father's side. As it went further back, I saw him," she hesitated. "Sebastian. His entire family changed their names after he took on The Darkness. He had a daughter, and that is the bloodline that my family came from. So, I guess it makes sense that I would have some same powers as him. Do you think what I have is strong enough to defeat him?"

Graham nodded without emotion as she spoke, dropping his hand from her cheek. His eyes were unfocused, but his frown gave away that he was deep in thought. There was a heavy silence between them that remained unbroken by anything around them. It was as if the entire garden was holding its breath.

"Let's get back to my father's room before we do anything," Graham finally started. "I don't want to rush into using this information. I still don't know how my father knew we would be together, but the fact that this crystal responds so strongly to you tells me that my father must have known a lot more than he ever let on."

"Do you think my parents knew that it was Sebastian that created The Darkness?"

He shrugged.

"I want to hope that isn't something they'd keep from me knowingly, but maybe they had a good reason for it."

"Is there anything else in the hole?" Eliana asked, not wanting to think about her parents having more secrets.

"I'm not sure." He released her hand and walked back towards the tree.

Eliana scrutinized him, making sure she kept her distance from the crystal and statue as they headed back towards the tree. She watched his hand disappear into the hole, followed by his forearm. He frowned for a moment, then made a sound and yanked out a piece of paper. Running over to him as he unfolded it, Eliana's mind started racing with the possibilities of what it could be.

"What is it?" she asked.

"Let's get back to my father," he said while he folded the paper up and went over to grab the falcon crystal.

"Okay?" replied questioningly.

Suddenly feeling panicked, Eliana turned and headed back inside, not waiting for Graham to say anything more. She hadn't gotten close enough to see the paper, but if he had seen something to make him react this way, she would not question it. With a quickened walk, Eliana made her way to the king's room. Something in the way he spoke told her she needed to just go, and by the time she got to the last corner, she was running. When the door was in sight, she removed the necklace and tossed it aside.

She let her magic pour into the room before she saw anything, and it collided directly with The Darkness, forcing the entity out from the human for a moment. It wasn't Sebastian, but with the scream that it released when she hit it, he was sure to show up soon. The dark cloud snapped back into its human host and mobilized towards her, growling. Anger was still boiling inside of her, so she collected it all, then called her core magic, let out a scream, and shot The Darkness back out with a wall of magic. The entity was separated again, this time with a greater distance between the forms. Eliana took two long strides to stand over the body that now lay on the ground, blocking the pathway back. The Darkness screamed again as it was pulled back into its own world, struggling to reach out to the woman lying on the floor.

Eliana dropped to her knees, shivering, trying to catch her breath.

"Li...," Graham started, unable to leave his position at the door. "What was that? Did you just expel The Darkness on your own?"

She nodded, her body still shaking with adrenaline. There was a groan next to her, so she turned her attention to the woman.

"Whoa, whoa," she said, making sure to not access any more of her core magic as she helped the woman get more comfortable. "Just lie still. You'll be all right."

Graham ran to the closet to grab some thick blankets and tossed them over the woman.

"My name is Graham," he said gently. "Just try to relax. You're going to be fine. What's your name?"

The woman curled herself into a ball and started crying, unable to respond. Eliana placed a hand on her to release some elemental magic to calm her as she started convulsing.

"Go to your father," Eliana whispered.

He nodded and walked away while Eliana continued a consistent stream of magic into the woman beneath her hands. The shaking stopped, and her breathing evened out.

"Jamie," the woman finally said weakly.

"Jamie. Nice to meet you. My name is Li. Can I get you anything?"

"Where am I?" she asked, wiping the tears from her face.

"You're in the castle of Placata Montis."

Jamie looked around, "Oh," was all she said.

"I'm going to grab someone to take you somewhere more comfortable. I'll be right back, ok?" Eliana said with a friendly smile.

Jamie nodded, and Eliana quickly made her way over to Graham. When she got close to him, the crystal in his hand lit up the room.

"Shit." He quickly tossed it further away from her.

She grimaced as it landed next to the king's head.

"Sorry... Do you think you can call Felicity and have her come get Jamie?"

Graham pulled out his phone and sent a quick message.

"Hopefully, she's not far. I would like to go over this letter a little more closely," he said.

His phone beeped, and he read the reply, then went over to Jamie with Eliana again.

"One of our helpers is coming to take you to a room to get you more comfortable," he let her know.

"He knows you," she whispered.

"What?" Eliana and Graham said in unison.

"Sebastian," she replied weakly. "He knows who you are, Eliana. He knows your magic."

Graham and Eliana looked at each other uncomfortably.

"Oh," Eliana replied, grabbing the necklace to put back on.

Jamie started laughing, causing Eliana to take a step away from her.

"He can't feel you when you wear that, you know. Don't you want him to find you?" Jamie asked, pushing herself up to sit with a crazed look in her eye.

"Eventually, yes. I suppose that is exactly what I want. How long ago did you let him consume you?" Eliana asked.

"I knew your great-great-grandfather," she said with a wheeze. "Sebastian wanted him, but he was weak. It was too bad. He would have been great for us."

Eliana and Graham watched the woman and saw the evil that still poured through her.

"I don't want Felicity taking this woman anywhere alone," Eliana whispered to Graham.

"I already contacted someone else to help. He'll be here shortly."

Eliana's nod was barely noticeable in response to him.

"So, he killed people who refused to join him?" she asked Jamie, trying to get as much information as she could while they waited.

"Only the ones who had powerful core magic and refused to give it to him. I think that's pretty logical if you ask me," she smirked at them, her voice becoming more stable.

Jamie was fully sitting now, the blankets falling from one shoulder. Dark circles consumed her eyes, and she looked less human by the second.

As Eliana opened her mouth to speak again, Felicity and a man came through the door. Without a word, the man went over and helped Jamie to stand. Felicity stayed by the door, watching for anyone else coming down the hall.

"Where do you want her, Sir?" the man asked.

"Take her downstairs, Billy," Graham said. "And make sure that she gets plenty of food and water. I don't know how permanent this behavior is."

Billy frowned as the woman laughed but bowed to Graham and helped her out the door.

"It's good to see you again, Sir," he breathed as he passed by Graham.

"You, too, Billy," Graham said, smiling sincerely.

Felicity let them pass before coming in to grab the blankets that had been left behind.

"Wait!" Graham stopped her. "Please make sure that no one else knows we're here still. I told Billy, but I don't know what Jamie is going to say to people."

She nodded.

"Of course. I will stay with them both downstairs."

"Thank you, Felicity. You have been extremely helpful."

She smiled at him, closing the door as she left.

Alone again, Eliana and Graham stepped back to the bed. She kept her distance from the falcon, though she would have less effect on it now as she was wearing her necklace again.

"What does the letter say?" she asked, never taking her eyes off the king.

"I don't know."

"What?" she said, looking at him with exasperation.

"I can't read it. It's in an unfamiliar language."

"Well, why did you make us rush back here then?!" she half-shouted.

"I don't know," he said. "Something just felt off, and I didn't trust being out in the garden."

She nodded.

"I felt it, too."

Graham smiled at her, reaching out to squeeze her hand.

"Can I see the letter?" she asked.

Reaching into his pocket, Graham pulled out the letter, hesitating a moment before passing it over to her.

"If by some chance you can read this, I need you to hold off on doing it out loud. Okay?"

"I think that's fair," she replied.

Graham went to grab the falcon crystal again and placed it in his pocket as Eliana opened the letter. The words looked like the same language that was on the falcon statue and crystal. She let her focus grow soft, and the gem she wore around her neck lit up. Graham reached over and shook her shoulder.

"Hey! You're accessing your core magic."

"Sorry," she said, flushing.

"It's fine, but we need to be careful. Did you see anything?"

She nodded.

"When I access my core, I'm able to understand what the words mean. I think if I take off the necklace, I can go through it quickly and translate what it's saying."

Graham thought for a moment. He looked over at his dad and then back at his phone.

"Okay, but let me message Francisco. I want to have him trigger the last camera while you do this. It should give us a warning if someone or something comes. It's off this hall."

Eliana watched him as he typed on his phone again. When he finished the message and looked back up at her, she took a breath and removed the necklace. Quickly bringing the paper up, she focused and let the words speak to her. After a couple of minutes, Eliana pulled the chain back over her head and stood by Graham.

"This is the incantation for the falcon to call upon The Darkness. Whoever speaks the words, magic or not, can summon them here. That falcon crystal paired with the statue creates some sort of satellite that can project the words. The person who says the words has control over any of the minions, but if Sebastian is called, he can't be forced to do your bidding."

"Is that all the crystal can do?" he asked.

"No. This looks like it was specifically written by Sebastian for someone. I'm guessing that whoever erected that statue in the garden probably made use of this quite frequently, but the crystal and statue themselves simply contain stored magic to help power the incantation."

"Why does it respond so strongly to you?" he asked.

"From what I can tell, it's because it was made from my bloodline. I don't know for sure, though. This doesn't tell me everything. I'm kind of just going on feeling at this point."

"We should have asked Jamie what she was looking for..." He cursed quietly to himself.

"I have no doubt that they are looking for the crystal and this letter. I don't think he can bring himself somewhere with it, but I assume he probably has someone that will read it for him," Eliana squinted her eyes in deep thought.

"Do you think he meant for Jamie to read it?" Graham asked.

"No," Eliana shook her head. "I don't think The Darkness can read it. I think it has to be someone fully made of flesh and blood."

"Mmm," Graham replied, his eyes unfocused.

Eliana shifted uncomfortably in the silence. It felt like they were missing something. As she let her eyes carefully trace over the room, she noticed something that seemed purposely out of place. Without saying a word, she walked over to the nightstand.

Glancing at the matching one on the opposite side of the bed, she realized there was a slight difference between the two. Letting her fingers trace along with the carvings on the side, she felt a nearly imperceptible indentation. Tilting her head down to analyze the area more closely, she recognized a circle around the design and pressed it in. With a click, the side opened up, revealing a box.

CHAPTER TWENTY-SIX

"Graham?" she breathed, pulling him from his thoughts.

"What?" he quickly replied, his eyes focusing on the present again.

"I found something."

Eliana carefully pulled out the box, holding her breath as she waited for something to happen. Then checked thoroughly in case there is a hidden compartment. When she found nothing else, she turned to Graham. The blood had drained from his face, leaving another pale, rigid form with her.

"Graham?" she prodded.

While she waited for him to respond, his phone dinged and buzzed multiple times. Tilting her head to read the screen of the phone, Eliana read the messages coming from Francisco.

Someone's coming. I can't tell who it is.

Graham?

Scratch that. Two people. Seem to be in a hurry.

They're being chased.

Two people being chased by a woman.

"Graham. I think Jamie is no longer being detained..."

Within seconds, Felicity and Billy went running by. Graham dropped the box on the bed, snapping out of his daze, while Eliana removed her necklace. When they bolted towards the door, Jamie ran directly into them and stumbled back into the hallway from the force. Eliana used her magic to bind the woman, freezing her in place.

Graham sighed.

"Well, a lot of good that did. I guess we can ask her who read this now, though," he finished with a tight smile.

Eliana frowned at him. Without a word, she put her hand on his chest and pushed him back into the room, using her magic to shut the door behind them before throwing the necklace back over her head again.

"Open the box," she demanded.

"I can't," he said sheepishly.

"Why not?!" she half-shouted.

"It was my mother's. I watched my father burn it when she died. He threw it directly into the fire. I watched it burn..." he faded off.

"Okay, well, either he didn't burn it, or this is a different box. Either way, we don't have much time. I'm sorry to seem insensitive, but if there's something important in there, we need to know. Whatever feeling led me back here to stop Jamie also led me to that box, and something else is coming quickly."

"Okay," he said, smiling and gently taking her arm. "Thank you for keeping me focused. I was trying to repress my emotions until after we defeated Sebastian, but this box..." he trailed off, dropping his hand.

Eliana linked her fingers through his.

"We'll open it together. You don't have to do any of this alone. Okay?"

He nodded, giving her a melancholic smile. His phone buzzed once more, and this time he looked down at it. Releasing Eliana's hand, he replied to Francisco.

Yes, sorry. We're ok. Everyone is ok. You were extremely helpful!

Placing his phone in his pocket, he stepped over to the bed and picked up the box. Eliana reached up and squeezed his shoulder to let him know she was there for him. His knuckles turned white as his grip tightened on the box. Taking a deep breath, his finger slid along the lip of the box for a moment before pressing a concealed button similar to the nightstand. The lid popped up, and Eliana watched while Graham's hand shakily took hold of the top and lifted it.

Glancing inside, Eliana saw a collection of unique items. Another locket that she recognized from a picture of the queen. A ring that the king had always worn. Some children's toys that she could only assume belonged to Graham. A pair of jade and ruby earrings. A woman's wedding ring. Pictures of his parents' wedding, Graham's birth, and the three of them laughing by the tree in the garden. Behind the photographs lay a letter that looked much newer than the other items. Graham frowned and picked it up, setting the box back down on the bed.

Graham,

If you are reading this letter, then I most likely passed on. I wish I was able to tell you everything in person, but I know I did a lot of terrible things that might make you never want to speak to me again. I hope that someday you can forgive me for everything. I am sorry I didn't ever apologize to you in person, even if you didn't want to hear it.

I hope you found this box when you need it the most. If time is limited, maybe skip to the end. With that out of the way, I was never the one hurting your mother. After she had you and her magic was revealed, I went into a jealous rage. There was yet another person in my life with magic while I was nothing special. My bitterness made me horrible and angry, and I can only hope my last years have made up for some ways I treated everyone.

The night I found out your mother had magic, I came to the garden. I started throwing rocks, and one revealed the hole in the tree, then I found the crystal and the spell. When I took them, sat by the fountain, and did my best to read it, I summoned Sebastian. But I lost who I was that night. Before then, I simply resented those with magic and vowed to keep myself separate from them when possible. I had no control over when The Darkness came. I spent my life trying to prove that I could be more influential without magic, but having access to his magic changed things.

Despite my rage, I still loved your mother and found it hard to stay away. I would think that maybe magic wasn't so evil when I looked at her, but then Sebastian began poisoning her, driving her mad. He wanted me to believe that magic was worse than I already felt. He would plan things to happen so he could prove that point and eventually caused me to fear my wife. He used my terror to convince me he needed me to bring him the most powerful Fighters so that he could dispose of them properly. It wasn't until the Graystins were gone that I realized the mistakes I had made and what Sebastian had done.

He had poisoned me, too. Not in the same way he did to your mother, but the effect was the same. He used his words to change my views on things. He tricked me into giving him people with powerful magic. He gave me the power I so desperately craved, but he took away everything that I loved. I can never apologize enough for it all. I am so sorry, Son. I did so many terrible things that I regret now. The potions that Sebastian taught me to make to hurt people... I hope there is forgiveness wherever I end up.

I'm sure by now that you have found the crystal and the spell. If not, they're in the tree in the garden. Use them. They call Sebastian without The Darkness being attached to him. There is something about the way he controls them that prevents him from being able to travel across the dimensions without them unless called. So, take control. Plan your attack as best you can. The more of an upper hand you and Eliana get, the better chance you have to win this all. I know with her, you will be strong enough to defeat him.

I love you, and I am genuinely sorry that I let things happen this way. Everyone deserved a better life and a better leader. Please send my apologies to everyone, especially the Graystins.

Much Love,

Your Father, Claude

Eliana stood behind Graham, reading the letter and trying to process all the words. The more she learned about Sebastian as a person, the more confident she became that she would defeat him. His drive for power would be his demise.

"Well..." Graham started, pulling her from her planning. "I guess he knew about the plans to have you defeat The Darkness. And assuming the rest is true, it's nice to know."

"You don't think it is?" Eliana asked.

"I don't know. It's going to take some time to process and compare memories to what he's telling me. Though, it makes sense for the stories my mother used to tell me about when they first met. She always begged me to see the good in him. Of course, at the time, I didn't think it was him poisoning her. That came later. I wonder if she knew who it was...."

Eliana stood there, not knowing what to say. Graham had gone through a lot, and she was probably the only one who could relate to him right now. Seeing him in pain, she bent down and hugged him tightly to her.

"Thank you," he whispered, slipping his arms around her.

"You're welcome," she said, smiling to herself.

He separated slightly to pull her into a kiss. As she let herself sink into him yet again, he stood and pulled her body against his. Breaking the kiss much sooner than Eliana would have liked, he squeezed her tightly in one last hug.

"Let's take care of Jamie, so we can get to Sebastian," he said.

"Okay." Eliana smiled, still feeling frustrated.

As she went to walk to the door, Graham stepped over to the bed once more. He placed the letter back inside the box, closed the lid, and stared at it for a moment before taking it back to the nightstand and hiding it away once again. Before heading back to the door, he knelt down and gently pressed his lips to his father's forehead.

"I forgive you," he whispered.

Eliana quietly watched with her hand on the doorknob, smiling sadly at him. When Graham's attention turned back to her, she could see the tears lacing his eyes, but he seemed determined and focused.

"Let's do this," he said.

Eliana simply nodded and opened the door. As soon as they stepped into the hallway, Jamie made muffled noises that had inflections that Eliana was sure would have been a chain of curses had she been able to speak.

"How long will it hold?" Graham asked.

"Until I let her go," Eliana said with a smirk.

Jamie's eyes grew large, and the muffled sounds became more urgent.

"You think Felicity and Billy are willing to give it another shot? Taking her downstairs, I mean?" Eliana asked Graham.

"Might as well ask," Graham replied, pulling out his phone. "I suppose if they don't want to, we can run her down."

As soon as Graham finished his messages, they heard a ping from around the corner. Felicity immediately poked her head around. She smiled; phone in one hand and Billy's elbow in the other.

"Oh, good! I'm sorry we let her get the slip-on between us. I'm not sure what happened. She's just a terrific actress," Felicity frowned. "We won't let her get the upper hand this time!"

Graham laughed.

"There is no need to apologize. None of us could have known what she would do, but Eliana cast a spell on her that should prevent her from causing either of you any problems. She'll be stuck like this until we return, so you two shouldn't need to do much. Though, we were thinking about asking her who the traitor is here."

"I don't think we will get any useful information from her based on those sounds. Billy, Felicity, if you could just be very careful and don't trust anything that anyone else says unless you hear it directly from us-—"

"I'M SO SORRY!" Billy blurted, interrupting Eliana.

Eliana and Graham laughed heartily together.

"It's not your fault, Billy. You'll be good now. Go ahead and take her downstairs. She's of no use to us anymore."

"Yes, Sir," Billy replied, bowing to Graham.

Graham and Eliana watched them walking away with the frozen Jamie, and the tension in the air grew. There were no more distractions at this point: just them and the short walk back to the garden. The two let their hands find each other, their fingers intertwining.

"You ready?" Graham tried again.

"As I'll ever be."

CHAPTER TWENTY-SEVEN

Adrenaline was rushing through Eliana's body, causing her heart to race. The moisture between their clasped hands had become unbearable by the time they reached the door to the garden, forcing Eliana to release the grip and wipe her hand down her pants. Even with the separation, the tension coming from Graham had the hairs on her arm standing on end.

They each took a breath and stepped across the threshold in a single unison step. Their arms, now touching, allowed Eliana to take a moment to match her breathing to his. It was calming and helped her feel more connected to him without magic.

They continued to walk silently to the statue, their hands brushing every few steps. Eliana's eyes traced the garden, analyzing the best place for them to summon Sebastian. Graham followed her as she walked around the backside of the statue, quietly finding the best vantage point for them. When Eliana opened her mouth to speak, she was cut off by another.

"I'll take that crystal if you don't mind," the deep, sinister voice said.

Eliana and Graham both froze. Eliana turned towards the sound, discovering that the words came from a man standing along the stone wall. She poked Graham. When he looked back at her, she lifted her eyebrows in question. Graham moved around and looked over to the man, squinting.

He appeared to be slightly older than the age Graham would be had he not been frozen in time for over twenty years. Eliana failed to recognize him, but Graham made a sound that forced her to look his way.

"Elijah....," Graham said through clenched teeth.

"Ah, Prince Graham. So kind of you to remember me," he replied, the words pouring off his tongue like venom.

When he stepped out of his shadowed corner, Eliana swore his eyes flashed. They were a neon green that contrasted completely against his slicked, chin-length, black hair. Streaks of gray shimmered as he passed through beams of the sun. The menacing smile that stretched across his face as he sauntered closer revealed an under-bite that forced his pointed chin to show more prominently. In his hand was a jagged dagger that he pointed towards them but held low by his thigh.

"Now," he started again once he was close enough for them to make out the details of the scars across his face, "I said, I'll take that crystal."

Eliana shivered.

"So you're the one they think is going to call upon Sebastian, then?" Graham replied, ignoring his demands.

"Look, boy. I don't have time for your games," he spat, creeping closer to them. "Give me that crystal!" he shouted, emphasizing his point by thrusting the dagger towards them.

Graham moved his arm in front of Eliana protectively, forcing her back.

"From what I recall, Elijah, you never gained your powers to become a Fighter, right? So, all I can see as a threat from you right now is a dagger and a practiced tone. You realize all it would take is a flick of my hand," Graham said, waving his hand and stepping towards the man, "to disarm you."

Elijah's eyes grew slightly as the dagger was flung out of reach. He quickly recovered and pulled a gun from his belt, firing it without skipping a beat.

"NO!" Eliana shouted, reacting without thinking.

Her core magic immediately engaged, causing the crystal she wore around her neck to explode. Pieces flew in all directions, an exceptionally bulky shard lodging itself in Elijah's cheek. When the bullet reached Graham's forehead, it ricocheted off with *tink* and was sent flying in a different direction. During the split moment of chaos, Eliana stepped to Elijah and did a roundhouse kick to the hand that held the gun, then landed a punch directly where the crystal had embedded itself into his face. Her hair whipped rapidly in response to her surge of magic, seemingly casting off sparks of electricity.

Elijah continued to scream in pain as he writhed on the ground, which covered the sound of Graham's warnings. Eliana, not wanting to attract any more attention to them, used her magic to silence him. The second his screams ceased, she heard Graham.

"LI! The crystal!"

Turning around, fully expecting to apologize for destroying his mother's crystal, her words left her as she saw the falcon he held lit up in unison with the statue.

"Shit," she said.

"Awww, and here I thought you'd be excited to meet your family," a sickly sweet voice said from nearby.

"Sebastian," Eliana growled, her eyes frantically searching for him.

Graham ran by Eliana, collecting the gun and dagger that Elijah held moments ago. He stepped next to Eliana and held both options out to her. Taking the blade, she moved around the statue and spotted Sebastian leaning against the tree with his arms crossed. Eliana tossed a hand behind her, freezing Elijah as she had done with Jamie. The blood that had formed on her knuckle after punching the crystal dripped off the tip of her finger as her arm swung forward.

Graham stayed behind, opening the backpack to retrieve the stash of crystals that he had. Eliana stopped on the other side of the statue, her magic lifting her from the ground as her anger took over. Sebastian smiled at her, pushing off the tree with his back to stand up tall. He held out his hands to the side.

"Well? Here I am. You called, I answered."

"I didn't call you," Eliana spat.

"Didn't you, though?" he replied, lowering his arms and taking a slow step forward.

"I never read your little spell," she answered with annoyance.

"Oh, but you didn't have to, my dear child. Your magic was enough. Each time you activated the statue, I heard you. Sure, you stopped it in time to prevent my arrival the first time, but that last surge of power... Oh, if only I could have a little taste..." he said, his eyes crazed with hunger.

"I don't think so," she growled.

Even though she had spent years using her anger to guide her magic, she couldn't allow it to cloud her judgment now.

So, she took a deep breath to let her power settle and regain control. As her hair fell and her feet touched the ground, Sebastian faltered in his confidence. Irritation now took over his features, and his nostrils flared with rage.

"Now, you listen to me," he hissed. "I gave you that power. It came from ME! Don't you get it? My blood runs through your veins. Everything you have, everything you can DO, that is all thanks to me!"

She laughed.

"I am nothing like you." Eliana stalked confidently toward him.

He flinched almost imperceptibly. His unkempt, dirty blond hair rustled in a slight breeze, and he snarled at her. She noticed the wound on his body from her mother's dagger hadn't healed yet, and this time she thrust Elijah's dagger forward, aiming closer to his heart. Sebastian took advantage of the moment of distraction and sent magic to Graham's back.

"NOOOO!" Eliana shouted for a second time.

Without the crystal diluting her magic, a surge of power shot through the area. Graham was thrown backward, slamming into a wall. His head immediately bled as he lay motionless on the ground. Eliana focused on the sound of his shallow breath as she let her magic carry her to where Sebastian stood. Directing her magic at him this time, he was able to block her attack with a shield of his powers, but he missed seeing the kick that was aimed directly at his head.

The contact of her shin crashing against his prominent nose caused her to wince slightly, but the depression from the force made her smile. The momentum spun her in a quick circle, and she twisted around in a blink to see Sebastian stumbling backward. Throwing a binding spell on him while the blow incapacitated him, Eliana ran over to Graham and placed her hands on his face. Not wanting to waste too much magic healing him if he didn't need it, she stopped as soon as he groaned and shifted.

"Graham. Graham! Are you alright?" she whispered urgently.

"Absorb this," he replied, slamming the largest crystal into her chest.

"But—" she started.

"No. Please trust me. I have smaller ones to help you, but you need this."

Eliana nodded as she took it from Graham. He immediately reached into the bag that still looped around his arm and pulled out a smaller crystal, pointing it over Eliana's head. Sebastian made a little OOF but quickly recovered, laughing at the attempt.

"You think that has any sort of effect on me when her magic can barely hold me?!" he laughed again, his hazel eyes appearing almost yellow.

"Absorb it, Eliana!" Graham shouted, tossing one crystal aside and grabbing two more.

"Okay," she said, turning around to face Sebastian as the magical bind broke away from him.

"Shit," she mumbled.

Time seemed to slow as the intensity behind her focus begged to tap into her core magic, but she resisted releasing it yet. Two streams of magic on either side of her came from the two crystals that Graham had pulled out, and a slow growl grew into a yell as she forced the magic out of her own crystal. Eliana continued sprinting towards where Sebastian now stood, racing to keep up with the streams that went by her. Sebastian dodged the power from one of Graham's crystals but not the other. When he was struck, Eliana was only a few feet away from him. Sebastian flinched when she screamed louder, absorbing the power of the crystal in his moment of weakness, expecting to end it all right there.

CHAPTER TWENTY-EIGHT

There was a flash of light and a loud whooshing sound followed by blackness and a suffocating aura. Eliana's buzzing head caused disorienting vertigo. A moment later, her feet found the ground, and the world started to reveal itself around her again. As the shapes of the land came into focus, she recognized where she was, but before she could complete another thought, a wall of magic tossed her backward into a hill.

Sand flew around her, creating a barrier that allowed her to take in the surroundings. A glance to the right revealed precisely what she was hoping for: her parents' hideout. The momentary excitement was quelled when she turned back to Sebastian and saw him flanked by three dark forms.

"Thank you, Eliana. I could not have asked for a better location for you to lose this fight," he laughed, baring his pointed teeth. "Not only did you separate yourself from help, but now you have taken us somewhere that I have some!"

Eliana unclipped the buckles of her backpack, dropping it to the ground as she stood. She rotated slightly to place her parents' current hideout behind her and took a confident step forward to flatter ground. Sebastian nodded his head at where she stood, and an entity came towards her, screaming. Unphased, Eliana tapped into the shared power that she had absorbed and directed a part of it at the entity and the other to send a stealthy message to her parents. Once the message was sent, she redirected everything to the entity that was now struggling to reach her.

With her focus entirely on The Darkness, she saw the human form separating. She walked towards the two shapes, and as soon as her magic separated the human, she grabbed him, placing herself between him and The Darkness. Sebastian's mouth was agape, and Eliana smirked and froze the freed human before he could run. The Darkness screamed vigorously as it failed to return to its host. She covered her ears, watching Sebastian intently. Her smile grew as he screamed in agony, both of them dropping to their knees in pain. The Darkness disappeared from the drab desert landscape, and Eliana watched the two remaining entities flinch while Sebastian continued to thrash in pain.

She smiled smugly at them, standing to run during the distraction, and dove across the protective magic of her parents' new home. On the other side, she completed her roll and quickly stood up, nearly knocking down her mother.

"Eliana!" her mother shouted, pulling her into a tight hug.

"Mom! Dad!" she responded, hugging them both.

"We assume the message was from you?" her mother started, brushing Eliana's hair from her face.

"Yes. Sebastian and a couple of The Darkness entities are beyond your protection spell. The longer I hide here, the more danger I am putting everyone in, but I need your help. Graham was left behind when I used the crystal, and it brought us here. I can't fight Sebastian alone. Will you be able to help?"

Her parents looked at each other, smiling and linking their fingers.

"We would love nothing more than to help you, honey. With the danger gone, these people will be able to return to a safe place," her mother explained.

"Good. Then let's—," Eliana started.

"Hold on!" her father interrupted. "How do you plan to exit without making it look like there is a protective spell here? I don't want to risk anyone's life behind the barrier, no matter what happens to us."

"You're right. Is there an exit that exists on the sides?" Eliana asked.

Her parents nodded in unison.

"Quickly. This way," her father said, leading the two women.

The three ran along the edge, Eliana watching as Sebastian blew up dunes looking for her. He and his minions were getting unnervingly close to the wall. A moment later, she saw Sebastian tilt his head, reaching out his hand to touch where the wall was.

"Shit!" she shouted, throwing herself sideways through what should have been an unbreakable wall.

"Eliana!" her mother shouted.

Turning back to where she had just come from and seeing only desolate land, she sighed and ran faster, making sure to reappear from behind a dune. She took the wide arc to get around the small hill, finding solid ground and gave an extra push to get closer to Sebastian.

"Hey!" she yelled, shooting a burst of magic at his hand just before it crossed the wall.

Sebastian growled and sent both entities at her. Eliana dove behind the mountain of sand, desperately hoping that her parents would be close. Without the additional magic, she wasn't sure she would be able to take on those two at once. As the two dark figures came to her side of the dune, her parents came running towards her. Coming to a stop, she slid down to a crouch and spun around to face The Darkness.

Focusing part of her core magic on each entity, she closed her eyes and concentrated entirely on the task. Trusting that her parents would have her back, it wasn't hard for her to let go of everything. Her magic was pulling the Fighter that was trapped within The Darkness, but she searched deeper for anything else that she might not have accessed yet.

As she tried to dive further into her core, it felt like an invisible wall was blocking her. Sweat formed along her brow as she grunted, driving her will to get beyond the barrier. Taking in a large breath and trying once more, the resistance let up, and she exhaled with a wind of relief. The magic that danced wildly beyond the blockade responded with ease. Opening her eyes just as her parents joined her, Eliana smiled and took their hands.

"Follow my lead," Eliana told them confidently.

The three of them took a deep inhale in unison before forcing a blast of magic forward. Much quicker than before, The Darkness was expelled from each person and screamed. The Graystins released their hands, dropping to the knees to cover their ears. When the screech of The Darkness faded, they heard the pained calls of Sebastian not much further away.

Eliana pushed herself up from the sand, sending a quick burst of magic to freeze the two released humans before brushing her hands on her pants. She turned around to quickly help her parents up as their older bodies struggled to move as swiftly as she did. Suddenly, Eliana paused, frowning at her parents.

"What is it, honey?" her father asked.

"Why did none of us change when The Darkness was so close?" she asked in a weary tone.

"Magic here works differently," her mother replied, smiling gently. "Didn't Graham tell you?"

Eliana closed her eyes, trying to breathe away from her annoyance. How could he possibly have thought that it was a good idea to hide any information from her at this point?

"No. All he told me was to absorb the magic in the large crystal, so I did. Did he know it would send me here to you?" she asked, annoyance exuding from her every atom.

Her parents glanced at each other.

"Well, yes. That was part of this whole thing. When it was over, if anything happened to him, the large crystal brought you to us. I'm surprised he let you bring the fight here." Delilah frowned.

With that, everything clicked. Graham hadn't wanted her to be so close to Sebastian when she used the crystal. He had expected her to use it right after he passed it off to her. He knew that if she used it when she was still by him, he could travel back and finish the fight alone.

"I'm gonna kill him!" Eliana shouted, both of her parents looking at her with surprise.

"I'm sorry?" Scott asked.

"He didn't think I was going to be able to do it. He didn't think it would work. He was trying to — GRRRRR," Eliana cut herself off, growling in frustration.

She focused some of her anger on Sebastian and shot a blast of magic while he still struggled to find his footing in the sand.

"What?" her parents asked in unison.

Eliana turned and looked at them with passion-filled eyes. Her parents responded with fear and confusion. She thought back to how her magic had intertwined with Graham's earlier and knew there was no other choice. The last thing Eliana saw before closing her eyes was her mother reaching out as her physical form disappeared.

CHAPTER TWENTY-NINE

Graham sat in the garden with the still frozen Elijah, dozing in and out of consciousness. The wound on his head bleeding profusely. His thick hair could not contain the pooling of blood for long, and he soon found himself covered. With a groan, he tried to heal without using the last three crystals. He desperately wanted to make it to Eliana to help, but he was unable to focus long enough with his injured head.

As he dragged himself away from the wall towards the fountain, he attempted to keep track of how much time was passing. However, he kept on losing consciousness every few minutes, eventually failing to remember exactly when he was in each moment. When he got to the fountain, he reached out to scoop the icy water and poured it over his wound, screaming out in pain as it flowed over the deep gash.

"What the hell, Graham?!" Eliana shouted at him.

Graham froze. It couldn't be. How had she gotten back to him so quickly? Was it quickly? Why was she alone? Had she ever even actually left?

"Eliana?" he asked, trying to rotate weakly to see her.

Before he could focus on her face, everything went black again. This time when he woke up, he felt the warmth of someone's touch, and the pain in his skull mainly had subsided. He groaned and reached up to grab the hand that was on his forehead.

"It doesn't hurt anymore," he said, awkwardly smiling.

"Good, because when this is done, I'm going to kill you myself," she said with a flash in her eye and tension in her jaw. "But right now, I need you to help me. Can you stand?" she finished in a much gentler tone.

Graham grimaced a bit, not looking forward to her barrage of questions that were sure to follow this complete debacle. He nodded to her and stood with a soft groan, looking deep into her eyes. He assumed that she had put all the pieces together and figured out that he had expected to finish the fight against Sebastian alone. Of course, in total Eliana fashion, she instead had tried to use her absorption of the crystal to force Sebastian back and sent both of them to what Graham hoped would be a safe place for her. He sighed at himself for not explaining precisely what the crystal would do when she took on all of its power.

"Your magic feels strong enough to travel back to my parents. Can you help me get you there?" she asked, interrupting the long silence.

"I'm sorry, Eliana. I didn't expect you to take him with you."

"Now's not the time, Graham. My parents could be in danger. Either answer my question or shut up and hold on," she bit back.

"Yes, I can help," he responded timidly.

"Great. Grab the crystals," Eliana said shortly.

Graham reached down to put the remaining crystals in his pocket, then closed his eyes and took in a deep breath before being pulled to the other dimension.

CHAPTER THIRTY

Eliana and Graham landed gracefully between Sebastian and her parents. Sebastian was still dragging himself slowly around the dune, almost recovered enough to be fully standing. So, Eliana quickly shot another small blast of magic, forcing him to face plant directly into the ground.

"Graham!" Delilah shouted, running and throwing her arms around him in a tight hug.

"There's time for that later," Eliana interjected before her father could also jump in for a hug. "Graham, give them a crystal."

Graham flushed slightly, handing Delilah and Scott each a crystal. Eliana watched as he smiled at them and mouthed, *I'm sorry* before returning to her side. He leaned over and kissed her cheek, causing Eliana to immediately turn red, spinning around to avoid her parents' reactions.

The instant she dropped her defenses, Sebastian took advantage and hit Eliana with his magic, though it was only enough to cause a sting to her skin. She growled and took a step forward to confront him, but Graham slipped his hand in hers, snapping her from her blind rage. She relaxed, turning to stare into Graham's eyes for a moment. With a deep breath, she calmed down, then reached out to her mother's arm, careful not to take any power from the crystal that she had been holding.

"Take each other's hands," Eliana said while peeping at her parents.

When they happily obliged, the group started walking towards Sebastian just as he was pushing himself fully upright. He glanced up at the group coming toward him and started laughing again.

"I see you finally figured out that you can't defeat me alone, Eliana," he coughed as he brushed the last of the sand from his body, then cracked his neck.

"That's the point, Sebastian. I don't have to. This has nothing to do with me being powerful enough to defeat you alone. Besides, I am not alone, and I never was. So, yes. I would rather have people who choose to fight with me because they love me rather than followers who are only there because they fear me. What kind of life is that? What has all of this power gotten you? Years of loneliness? Did you learn anything about yourself?" Eliana replied.

She felt Graham squeeze her hand and looked over to see him beaming at her. She couldn't help but swoon a little at the moment, but instead of getting completely lost in his eyes, she stored away the feelings and used them to fuel her confidence in everything she had just said to Sebastian.

"You and your father, Scott, are just diluted versions of me," Sebastian spat back, hissing her father's name and aiming some magic at him.

Scott doubled over in pain as he was struck in the side. Sebastian's laugh filled the air, increasing in volume when Delilah broke their formation to help Scott recover more quickly. The group paused for a moment while Eliana kept a glare on their enemy.

"Even combined, there's no way you can be anywhere near as powerful as I am. I've had years of practice— years of training. I have felt what power can be at its strongest, and I'm sure if you lend me your power, I could show you what it truly means to be my descendent," he finished with venom-laced words.

"You're wrong," Graham interjected before Eliana could respond. "I know the history of what you've done. Even if I didn't exactly know it was you until yesterday, I know your story. I know the paths you've taken. You use hate, manipulation, and fear for tearing down the strongest of people. Eliana is right; you've forgotten that love will eventually always overcome fear and hate. When people come together in love, they are there as a choice. They aren't there because they feel that they have to be. Do you think they worship you? No! They are there out of helplessness and loneliness, just like you. A miserable, weak loner. You may have strength, but you are alone. We are strong AND together. Not because of the power we hold inside, but because of the love and support we have in our lives. That love will always be stronger than your hate."

"You shut up!" Sebastian shouted, sending a stream of magic directly towards Graham.

Eliana screamed, releasing her magic to block the incoming attack. Having her loved ones with her fueled the wall of protection enough that it sent Sebastian's magic back at him. He dove to the ground, successfully dodging the deflection.

"Whoa," Scott said.

Eliana blushed slightly at his response.

"I'm sure you could do the same thing if you tapped into your core magic, too," she whispered to him.

"Nope. Definitely not," he replied. "I learned to use my core magic years ago. I'm nowhere near as powerful as you."

"You realize I can still hear you, right?" Sebastian said, pulling himself from the sand once again.

"And just what do you plan to do about it?" Delilah asked.

Sebastian rested on his knees. He was obviously tired and injured, but his maniacal laugh was still frightening. Eliana frowned but made sure not to let her guard down. There was no way he would be this weakened so early on. She sent some of her magic through each hand, silently begging Graham and her mother not to let their guard down either as she passed along a message.

On my cue, release everything you've got against Sebastian.

Barely a blink later, Sebastian stood up, yelling and sending all his magic directly at Eliana.

She took in a sharp breath, holding it captive as she used her magic to slow everything around her. Narrowing her focus, she watched the pulsing black stream coming towards her much more aggressively than anything else she had experienced. She placed a shield around herself before shouting to the group.

"NOW!"

As soon as the words left her lips, the three crystals were raised and pointed at Sebastian. His eyes widened, and Eliana screamed as she fought to keep her shield up. Within seconds, Sebastian's magic had once again bounced off her protection and directed itself back to him, striking him at the exact moment as the magic from the crystals hit him. The cry that left his lips when it all hit him was inhuman, but it didn't cause any of them to keel over in pain. Eliana watched in awe as the surrounding earth seemed to vibrate, mimicking the pulse of his scream.

The group continued to walk towards Sebastian at a slower pace, the tensions high amongst them. As they got closer, Eliana could see Sebastian's exposed flesh start to shift and bubble while gurgled noises escaped his throat. His young skin quickly lost fluids and elasticity as he rapidly aged, and even still, he was laughing. Even on the verge of death, he wanted to be in control. He winced in pain between his bursts of laughter, but he seemed to be enjoying his death. A sinister smile stretched across his lips.

"You continue to claim to be so virtuous, Eliana, but I know the truth. That part of you died along with Fiona," Sebastian attempted a laugh, coughing up blood and baring his reddened teeth. "You were never going to give me a chance to redeem myself. Not after what Bradly did to the love of your life."

"Shut up!" Eliana shouted, letting him get the better of her emotions.

"See? She won't even let me speak my final piece! You're weak. You're nothing. You couldn't save the one person who mattered the most to you... All because you chose to trust someone you barely even knew! Yet Fiona knew, didn't she? She knew something was off, but you were so sure that you were right. Just like always. Just like now. You never stopped to question it. You just came to kill me, not even taking a pause to imagine another possibility. May you forever now live with the guilt of your choices, the guilt of never knowing what I could have given you with my power. You might have even been able to save her," Sebastian choked, gasping for air as a final sinister laugh left his weakened body.

Eliana shivered at the words that he left her with as she watched him writhe. His muscles dissipated, causing his skin to cling to the bone while his eyeballs rolled back and sunk into his skull as his flesh melted away. The exposed bones continued laughing until they, too, turned into nothing but dust. A sense of relief passed over her as she watched the last of him blend with the sand that danced through the air.

"Don't listen to anything he said, Eliana. You know he was just trying to get into your head. That's Sebastian taking advantage of the vulnerability. That was what he did. There was nothing you could have done differently in this," Graham whispered.

Eliana nodded, not trusting herself to speak. A part of her knew he was right, but there was also something in Sebastian's words that stung deep. Trying to distract her mind, Eliana crouched, staring at the settled sand. She took a handful and watched it effortlessly fall through her fingers. It was done. They won. After these years, the fight against The Darkness was over. It felt so surreal; she was sure it had to be a dream. Never would she have imagined that she'd be standing with the man whom she was sure she would continue to love for the rest of her life and the parents that not 24 hours ago she thought were lost to her forever. Finally, happiness overtook her, and tears fell from her eyes.

"Eliana?" Graham interrupted her quiet thoughts.

When she looked at him, her heart was overfilled with joy. Closing her eyes, she took a deep breath, allowing herself to realize fully what all of this meant. A tremendous weight lifted off her. She had survived to a moment where she could begin life, hopefully with the person she'd always dreamed of. She sighed again, opening her eyes.

When Eliana saw Graham's face, his golden eyes were pouring love into her. She forgot her parents were still there and pulled him in from the back of his neck, roughly pressing her lips to his own. Her tongue forced his lips apart, and she groaned lightly as she let it explore his mouth. While Graham gave in initially, he became rigid as soon as she moaned louder. When her mother cleared her throat behind them, Eliana quickly pulled away, wiping her mouth before turning around.

"Uhhh," Eliana said, her face burning red.

Eliana's mother stood with her arms crossed and eyebrows raised, shooting the pure definition of a 'mom look' at them. When Eliana quickly glanced at her father, he was pretending to see something extraordinarily fascinating off in the distance. She couldn't hold back a laugh at his response, throwing a hand over her mouth to try to muffle the sound. Delilah immediately turned to look at Scott, smacking his shoulder and gesturing back to Eliana and Graham.

"Ow! What?" Scott said to her, rubbing his arm. "They're both adults. I mean, I would appreciate it if you two would keep the kissing a little more PG in front of us, but I get it. They have fought well and probably needed a touch of reality. I mean, none of us thought we would make it through this."

He winked at Eliana.

Delilah huffed slightly but pursed her lips and didn't address it further. Instead, she stood quietly for a moment; then, a smile spread across her face. Turning to Scott once again, she grabbed the collar of his shirt and pulled him in for a kiss.

"Oh, Mom! Come on! I didn't mean anything by it!" Eliana turned away from her parents.

Graham laughed at her, brushing a chunk of hair from her face. She gazed into his eyes and sighed once more. He was making it challenging for her to control her primal urges again, but she would do her best for her parents' sake. Instead, she raised up on her toes and kissed the tip of his nose. When she turned back to her parents for their response, they were groping each other.

"I get it! Geez," Eliana crossed her arms and pouted.

Delilah finally responded by laughing and pulling away. Scott now pouted slightly when she separated from him, clasping his hands in front of himself awkwardly. He turned around, finding something else that was extremely interesting again.

"Well! Would you look at that sky," Scott said.

Delilah quietly laughed, then pulled Eliana into a tight hug.

"I'm so proud of you, and I truly hope you don't let Sebastian's words get to you. There was no saving that man from evil, and we never wanted you to feel like this was the only option in life you had. We wanted you to find happiness and love, and it almost appears maybe things were meant to happen this way," she asserted, pulling away to glance between Eliana and Graham with her eyebrows raised. "I wish that we had been able to tell you sooner than we were okay but know that we were always keeping an eye on you. Your father and I were so thrilled when you finally made your way to Graham yesterday."

Eliana couldn't hold back the tears. Pulling her mother back into a tight hug, she started shaking as she fought to keep her tears silent.

"Shhh," she said, petting Eliana's hair. "There's no need to hold it back anymore, darling. You don't always need to be strong for everyone. You were never meant to fight this on your own, and you aren't expected to be strong every time for everyone, okay? Let it out."

Eliana nodded, burying her face into her mother. Breathing in her scent helped her to calm down slightly. There were too many times that she had held back, especially when she was younger, and now her inner child felt safe. It wanted to let go of every weight Eliana had been carrying for far too long. And when she finally was able to release her burden, the tears couldn't have been contained even if she tried.

Her mother remained quiet, allowing Eliana to absorb all that had transpired until she found a point of calm. When she finally lifted her head, she blinked away the tears and wiped her face on the sleeve of her shirt. She saw her father and Graham talking a few feet away and smiled at the privacy that they had given to her at this moment.

"Are you going to come home with us?" Eliana asked with a sniffle, sounding more like a child than she intended.

"Of course we are! Between our house and the castle, we have space for everyone here to live comfortably until we can build homes for them if they choose to stay. When we're not expending all our power to keep this shield up, the ones of us that have magic are more than enough to get the whole group back to Placata Montis. I will just need to talk to everyone and give them time to collect what they need to move. Some of us have been here a long while, so it will not be easy to leave it behind," she finished gently, placing her hand on Eliana's cheek.

"Yes, of course," Eliana replied, placing her hand on her mother's. "Take the time you need. I know where you are now. I can come back anytime I want, so it's not that hard to leave you. And I'm sure if we worked together, we could probably figure out how to transfer entire homes to some of the open spaces back home," Eliana suggested.

"Oh! You're right! That could be a possibility! Especially if we fill up some of these crystals and use the magic to help!"

Eliana laughed. She'd forgotten how excited her mother got when coming up with new ideas that could help others. Her selflessness was something that Eliana always hoped that she had inherited. Though spending so much time alone made it hard to gauge.

"Exactly," she continued to laugh before something her mother had said clicked. "Wait, what did you mean you were thrilled when I found Graham yesterday?" she asked, frowning as her thoughts caught up to real-time.

"Did you ever notice that a few ravens frequently followed you?" her mother asked.

"Oh..... OHH..." Eliana shouted with a realization.

Delilah laughed.

"Yes. Your father and I have kept a close eye on you for a long time. Though you did kick him out of the raven when you started taking over," she finished with raised eyebrows.

"Ha, oh..." Eliana managed. "Well, um, I'm sorry?"

"Don't be. It was only confusing for a moment, then your father realized what happened and was so excited for you!" her mother replied, beaming.

"Well, that's good, I suppose," Eliana replied, shifting in the discomfort at the positive feedback. "Anyway, we should let the boys know it's safe to come back," Eliana said, changing the subject as she started to walk toward them.

"Hold on!" her mother said, grabbing her arm. "Is this something real?" she asked, nodding towards Graham.

Eliana felt her face get hot before she glanced over at Graham and sighed.

"I've been questioning that, too, and as much as I want to say yes, it's honestly hard to tell. It's been less than a day since we were reunited. We have discussed it a few quick times, but I don't know. I want it to be something, but I don't want to create some fairy tale relationship in my mind of what I want it to be and not what it is..." she faded off.

"Well, you were always very attached to him when you were younger. It will take me a moment to get used to the idea that now it could be something. But, I promise, I will do my best not to let my judgments get in the way," her mother said, putting a dampened chunk of hair behind Eliana's ear.

Eliana blushed again and looked away.

"That was different, Mom. I was just a kid, and you let me hate him for so many years."

"Yes, I did. There are some decisions that I regret making, but us not telling you why he had left to help seemed to fuel you more than anything... So, I convinced your father not to tell you," she sighed and glanced over to Scott. "Although he pushed us to tell you so many times," she finished solemnly.

"I think it was meant to happen this way. This is the path that our lives are on now, and I want to focus on the future, not the past. And I know Graham is your best friend, and that might make things kind of awkward for you, but you're also right. I think our timelines aligned, and he feels the same way. If things were different and The Darkness hadn't been the driving force of our lives, I'd probably be with his child instead of him," Eliana finished with a shrug.

Delilah laughed.

"The infatuation that you had with Graham as a kid definitely would have been redirected to his son or daughter," she winked, laughing again.

Eliana shrugged, joining in.

"Maybe. Or maybe he would have made hideous children," Eliana added, laughing harder.

"Alright, kid. Let's get the boys," Delilah finally said, putting her arm around Eliana's shoulders.

As they walked up to them, it sounded like Scott was giving Graham the "if you're dating my daughter" talk. The look on Graham's face as he turned around confirmed Eliana's fears. She groaned.

"Daaaaad. Come on! We're both adults!"

"I can still take you, Graham." Scott poked a finger into Graham's chest. "Behave yourself."

Graham nodded furiously before stepping by Eliana and placing his arm around her waist.

"I so do wholly promise never to hurt your daughter. And if I do, all three of you have permission to kick my ass!" Graham said quickly with one hand raised.

"Oh lord," Eliana muttered. "All of you stop. We've got business to take care of. Mom, Dad, get back to your little town and talk to the people. If we don't hear from you in a couple of hours, we're coming back. Got it?"

"Alright, Miss Bossy Pants. You're not the queen just yet," her mother joked.

"Yeah, yeah," Eliana started to joke back. "Wait! No. I can't be a queen!" she shouted with fear.

"Whoa!" Graham said, throwing both hands up. "Let's take this one step at a time. I haven't even agreed to be the king yet! If I decide to agree to that, then we will discuss if you're the queen material," he finished with a wink directed towards Eliana.

Eliana quickly turned away from her parents to punch his arm gently. He smirked at her, and she swooned, her eyes flashing with passion.

"Anyway," Scott started, clearing his throat loudly. "We'd better get back to everyone and let them know the plan," he paused, then turned to his wife. "What's the plan?"

Delilah laughed.

"I'll explain along the way. Come on, darling," she said, linking her hand through his arm.

Eliana smiled so big that her cheeks were starting to hurt as she watched her parents walk away. The moment they disappeared behind the shield again, Graham pulled her around into a kiss. Letting herself be engulfed at the moment, Eliana shifted to straddle one of his legs. As his hands traced down her body, she ground against his thigh, turning her hips slightly to rub against him simultaneously. Graham grunted and pulled away just enough to talk breathlessly at her.

"Eliana, we can't do this right now."

"Whyyyy?" she half whined at him, forcing his lips entirely against hers again.

"Your parents and—" he started.

"They're not paying attention to us," she said, kissing around his face. "So, why can't we just take a quick moment behind a dune?" she asked as she smashed her lips into his.

"Because," he said, separating again, "I really hate sand."

With that, Eliana burst out in a fit of laughter and stepped away from him.

"Fine, but I'm coming for you later," she said with fire in her eyes, reaching around to squeeze his ass.

Graham made a sound that was somewhere between a squeak and a moan. Then shook a leg to the side and shifted between his feet, trying to adjust some discomfort in the tightening crotch in his pants. Eliana laughed at him again, running her fingers through his hair to calm it down from all the excitement.

"And don't think for one second you're getting out of explaining to me what in the hell you were thinking trying to send me off so you could fight Sebastian alone," she said more loudly than intended, shoving a strong finger into Graham's sternum.

"I know," he sighed, taking her hand to his lips to place a kiss on it. "I am sorry about that. Kind of dick move, eh?"

"Yes, actually. It was. Didn't you trust I could do it? You could have died, Graham," Eliana asked solemnly, fighting back the tears as she shrugged.

"Of course, I did," he said, wrapping her in his arms. "But when I saw you with Sebastian, I got caught up thinking about the life I had taken from you. All that time you lost being a child. All the time you lost with your parents, it was all because of me and my father. So, I was selfishly trying to redeem myself without thinking about the repercussions beyond that. I want to reiterate that if it weren't for you, a lot more people would have gotten hurt," he pulled away to look at her. "Can you forgive me for my moment of weakness?"

Eliana saw the pain in his eyes. She slid an arm out from his hold, smiling softly as she placed a hand on his cheek.

"I think we'll just blame this moment of complete idiocy on the fact that you had a concussion and were bleeding profusely from your head, yeah?"

Graham laughed heartily, a tear rolling down his cheek. He tilted his head further into her palm as he placed his hand over hers.

"Alright. I can live with that, but one quick question; what are we going to do with these three?" he asked, pointing to the humans that were still frozen.

She looked around to where he pointed.

"Oh. Right. Forgot about them," her blush returned when she realized they had a perfect view of her and Graham. "Well, can we bring them back with Elijah and Jamie? I think it might be easier to deal with them in one place."

"Mm, yes. I'll do that. Be right back," Graham said.

Eliana stepped away to her backpack right as he disappeared with the first frozen body. In a blink, he was back and grabbing the other two. In a flash, he was back by her side.

"Is everyone safely back home?" she asked, throwing on her backpack before reaching out to him.

"Appears to be so," he replied, taking her hand. "I brought them to the garden with Elijah. I didn't want to take the time to get them with Jamie just yet."

"Well, I figured that. You ready?" Eliana asked, smiling at him.

"Let's do this," he smiled back, squeezing her hand.

CHAPTER THIRTY-ONE

Eliana's chest tightened as she whooshed through the darkness once again. When her feet hit the solid ground, she expelled a loud breath, still gripping Graham's hand tightly. The buzzing passed through her senses, causing her to shiver. Graham chuckled, pulling her attention. He was smiling at her with widened eyes, excitement painted across his face.

"What?" Eliana asked, confused by his slightly crazed look at her.

"It's done. It's done. And I have to PEE! The curse! My body! I can feel it all working again! WAHOOOOOO!" Graham danced around with a huge smile.

Eliana burst out laughing, choking for air as she keeled over. She waved him away from her when she felt his hand on her back, unable to stop. Through her tear-filled eyes, she watched him run to the bathroom, cutting his happy dance short.

Wiping the water from her eyes, she calmed her fit of laughter and removed her backpack, setting it on the ground and sitting on the bed. Taking in the room, she suddenly realized that they weren't back in Placata Montis. The bathroom door opened, and she snapped her head up to find Graham.

"Why are we back here?" Eliana asked, yawning.

Graham walked over to her, gently brushing the hair from her eyes before sitting beside her on the bed.

"I wanted to talk to you with no one else around. The castle has too many people stirring. There are a lot of decisions that need to be made, and for years, I thought I would make them alone. But honestly, I'm having a hard time imagining going through any of it alone now."

"Okay?" Eliana asked, leaning back on her hands.

Graham clasped his fingers in front of him, rubbing his thumbs over each other as he sat quietly for a moment. Eliana felt her face flush when she realized what he was saying. Her relaxed posture tensed as she sat up and rubbed the back of her neck.

"I don't want to ask anything else from you, Eliana. You have so much time to make up for with your parents and the life you lost to all of this. We've only been reunited for a day, and it just feels wrong to ask you to choose to spend the rest of your life with me. I just—" he cut himself off and shrugged, smiling softly at her.

Eliana's infamous frown took over her face again. Her mother had already gotten her wheels turning, and they never stopped.

"When I was growing up, I spent my time watching you. I listened to my parents talk about you. My grandma always said she wished she'd had another child so that you might have found love, too. I created an image of you based on all the positive things I heard and saw. You were the perfect prince charming. And now, I'm not sure what's real and what is my painted fantasy of you." Eliana sighed, skeptical. "I can't say that we'll be good together, but I know that I would like to try. There's no law saying that you can't be the king without a queen by your side, right?"

"No, I guess not," Graham replied, sounding disappointed.

"Okay. Well, then I can keep my role of leading the people as a Graystin, and maybe we just slow this down a bit. Are you ok with that?" she asked hesitantly, trying to hide the embarrassment she felt from trying to rush it all before.

Graham took her hands in his own.

"I need you to understand that I fully believe in whatever this might be between us, but I also respect whatever you wish to do. I know you felt it when our magic combined. It was like you filled all the parts of me that have been missing. The pain, loneliness, weakness, flaws. Everything. The only problem is that I really can't tell if it's because I want it to be true or because it actually is."

"Yeah," Eliana replied softly. "I felt the connection, too, but I wish my mother hadn't said anything to me. I feel like I'm overthinking it all now," she laughed awkwardly, her heart aching as she thought of him not wanting her.

Going into this fight, Eliana hadn't expected to survive. She was vulnerable and open and let him experience parts of her through the magic that no one else before him could, and now she was trying her best not to let her words hurt him. Logic said that he was wise and considerate, and if she was honest to herself, it only made her fall harder for him. The willingness to pause and make sure that this was something that would work for both of them gave her a sense of permanence that she craved for. But at the same time, she wanted him to fight for her. She desired for him just to tell her she needed to be with him.

"What is it you wish to do now?" he asked, pulling her from her spiraling thoughts.

"What?" she asked, tripped by his question.

"Well, there seem to be a few options. I'm sure you'll want to spend time with your parents and help all the people currently trapped. If you wish to assist me, a queen would have duties I would, of course, make sure won't limit you to the castle. There's also this land which could probably use some help to find the magic that has been lost throughout the years."

"Oh," Eliana replied, blinking. "I didn't even think about the people here. With The Darkness and Sebastian gone, they could reawaken their magic safely, right?"

Graham nodded.

"According to my research, yes. But I also need to talk to Francisco about his stay. I think it would be better for him to have something to make him feel like he's redeeming himself without having to explain anything to anyone back home. Besides, I have tools that pick up the smallest signs of magic anywhere in this world."

"You what?" Eliana interrupted. "Does that mean you always knew I was here?"

"Well," he flushed, "I didn't know for sure that it was you. The Darkness puts off a pretty powerful signal, and when you were not being threatened, your magic became dampened like the others here. OH! I bet if we looked back at the records of you tapping into your core magic, the results would be off the charts!" he finished with an almost crazed look in his eyes.

Eliana laughed. How could this man be tied down to being a king? There was so much more he could offer everyone. His love for knowledge and innovation had made him invaluable, especially in places with magic.

"Graham..." Eliana started with hesitation. "Do you *want* to be the king?"

Graham laughed.

"I mean, I don't have much of a choice."

"Says who?!" she replied more loudly than intended.

"Eliana," he started after a stifled laugh, "do you know the role of your great-grandparents to the king and queen?"

"They were like advisers. The ones who did the most of the work with the people of Placata Montis while your grandparents made the rules and final decisions," Eliana replied with some disdain.

Graham chuckled.

"Kind of. But, before my father, our families were equals. The family which held the title of king and queen would manage funds, put together events, solidify laws, listen to the people, and do what they could to maintain peace. Your family would work with them by being more hands-on with the people. They would get out and defend, enforce, and explore, but they always had as much power as my family. There was never meant to be only one ruler. It was intended to be a single voice with the consensus of many.

"If we end up blending our lives, I want it to be in a way that works for us and everyone in Placata Montis. It's not fair for anyone to have things continue in a way that isn't conducive to everyone moving forward... Even if that means I'm only an interim king," he finished quietly.

"It's true that we need someone as caring and level-headed as you in charge. There has been so much lost already, and I'm sure once things settle down, we can come back here frequently. But tell me honestly. Is it truly something you want? Do you really want to be the king? You never actually answered my question," she tried again.

Graham chuckled.

"You're right. I didn't. The simple answer is yes. I feel drawn to my obligation, but with everything that I've experienced in life, I also feel drawn to finding solutions to fix things. My time spent in this home," he said, motioning to the space around them, "has taught me so much. I just worry now that being the king will limit my ability to play and build!"

"I'm just going to take this opportunity to point out how much time your father had to become obsessed with destroying magic," Eliana said with some sass.

"Haha. Okay... You may have a point with that one, but remember that required your parents and me to step in a little more to help fill that void."

"Great! So how do we get ahold of your dad's brother and sister to see which of them might be willing to help? I'm sure they have children and grandchildren that might want to come back here. Right?" Eliana inquired, trying to stay hopeful about their future.

"Hmm, I suppose so. There are going to be a lot of long explanations, but I guess they'll want to know that my father has passed, anyway. And maybe some of them will want to come for his service, even though he was the one that cut ties."

"Perfect! So, let's go talk to Francisco and then keep moving these plans forward from there. We are not short on options," she finished, yawning again despite her current adrenaline rush.

She paused for a moment, realizing that almost five hours had passed since they left this house initially.

"We will talk to Francisco soon. But first, are you hungry?" he asked, reaching for her backpack.

The sound of two empty stomachs growling filled the room, answering Graham's question.

"Well, alright. Let's have some food you packed," he said as Eliana giggled.

The two quickly devoured a meal with a brief conversation. As soon as they finished, Eliana brushed some crumbs she had left on the bed and struggled to fight the exhaustion that was taking over her body. She attempted to shake away her heavy eyelids that were trying to force their way closed. After another enormous yawn, she went to use her magic to re-energize, but Graham stopped her.

"No," he replied firmly. "I need to talk to Francisco alone, anyway. Just lay down for a bit. I promise I will come back for you, alright?" he finished more gently.

Eliana sighed but couldn't fight the exhaustion taking over her body. A quick nap would get her through quite a few hours.

"Whatever. You'd better come back to me," she replied, turning to fluff a pillow.

"I will!" Graham half-shouted with a toothy grin.

Eliana glared at him for a moment, taking in his dashing smile. There was no way she had the energy to argue it, so she sighed and took off her shoes.

"Fine," she fully resolved.

Graham beamed, folding down the blankets on the opposite side that she sat before scooping her in his arms and placing her under the covers. Eliana took in his scent before he separated from her and tucked her in. She hoped that whatever was existing between them now would continue because she was pretty quickly getting used to his presence. Her heart warmed when Graham kissed the top of her head, and a calm wave washed over her.

"Sleep well, Eliana," he breathed.

Eliana moaned in response but could not form any words before fading off.

CHAPTER THIRTY-TWO

Graham smiled at the woman sleeping in his bed, sighing softly before he switched off the light and gently closed the door. The restlessness raging through his body caused him to shiver. His muscles were still stiff, and his head still throbbed slightly. He sighed again heavily before stepping away from the door, pulling together his emotions, then painted a smile before crossing the hallway to join Francisco.

Silently entering the lab, Graham found Francisco anxiously switching between checking his phone and trying to navigate through the cameras on the screen. Chuckling, Graham opened his mouth to speak right as the view changed to show both men, and Francisco shouted, tossing the phone from his hand.

"GRAHAM!" he yelled, running over to hug him.

"Hey, Francisco," Graham replied, returning the hug.

"You didn't reply to me!" Francisco thundered after they separated.

Graham pulled his phone from his pocket and saw the notification for sixteen unread messages. He assumed all were from Francisco.

"Oh, wow. Sorry! I probably didn't have service. And I was also unconscious for a brief amount of time," Graham recalled nonchalantly.

"Uhhhh. Unconscious? Where is Eliana?" Francisco inquired.

"Heh," Graham replied awkwardly. "Eliana is fine. She's sleeping across the hall. As for the rest, I'm sure you want to know, Sebastian is gone, and I was unconscious after I hit my head when I was thrown to a wall."

Francisco stared at him incredulously for a moment. He blinked rapidly and shook his head multiple times before finally responding.

"How?" he managed.

"Which part?" Graham asked for clarification.

"Sebastian!" Francisco shouted.

Graham shrugged slightly.

"Eliana has his bloodline, and somehow she ended up with powers comparable to his own. We, me and her parents, assisted her in the last fight, but it was his own magic that destroyed him. Eliana deflected it back at him as we assisted with the crystals and our magic."

"I felt him die, you know," Francisco whispered.

"In what way? Did it hurt you?" Graham asked gently.

Francisco nodded, his eyes glazing over.

"It was like when The Darkness was separated from me. It burned and felt like a part of me was being torn away, but I had no idea what was causing it. Although, unlike the emptiness that The Darkness left, this left an emptiness of who I had become after meeting Sebastian. But I think some of my core magic is returning now. I'm interested in seeing if Eliana's magic would still cause me pain..." he trailed off.

"Do you want me to try?" Graham asked.

"What? You can access your core magic, too?!" Francisco asked with surprise.

Graham blushed lightly.

"Well, yeah," he said.

"But... Huh... No. I guess that would make sense. Most Fighters can't control their appearance because they can't access their core magic, but you've been doing that for years, right? So... when you were draining your magic into the crystals?" Francisco paused.

"I was putting my core magic into them. That's why The Darkness never noticed me. It wasn't just that my magic was weak; it was that the magic they wanted was well hidden," Graham finished.

"Yeah, okay, that would make sense. I don't know why I didn't catch on to that earlier…."

"Things were moving quickly. It's still complicated," Graham explained. "So, shall I give it a try?"

Francisco nodded, pulling in a sharp breath. Graham placed his hand on his friend, hoping he wouldn't hurt him. Francisco flinched, and Graham took a moment to study Francisco's face as it pulled tightly together. He was trying to explore the aftereffects of Sebastian's death in his body, but he couldn't find anything on the surface. When Francisco relaxed beneath his touch, Graham closed his eyes and took a breath to force out some of his core magic into him. Graham's body stayed tensed as he waited for Francisco to react in pain, but there were no screams, only calm. Graham removed his hands and opened his eyes.

"How do you feel?" he asked Francisco.

Francisco was relaxed, but a tear ran down his cheek.

"I can feel my magic again. All of it. Nothing you did caused pain. I belong fully to myself again," he paused to sniffle and wipe some of his tears. "I never thought that was something I would get back, even after you pulled me out."

Graham comforted his friend for a moment before turning his attention back to the task at hand.

"Francisco," he started, "Can we discuss a few things?"

"Sure. What's on your mind?" Francisco asked, sniffling and smiling.

"Well, I guess my first question would be if you want to stay here or return home now that everything is over."

Francisco's eyes darted around as he thought through his reply.

"I never thought that home would be an option for me again. Being a part of The Darkness didn't allow any hope of a normal life again, and when you released me, I honestly thought that my body would give out in a few days. But now that Sebastian is gone, the heaviness isn't crushing me anymore. However, even with life returning to my body... There's so much more out there in the vast expanse of space. Our world, our home, it's just a speck. I have been thinking about it for a while. This world feels like it has so much more to offer me, you know?" Francisco concluded.

"I think so?" Graham tried to make sense of what Francisco was telling him. "If I understand you correctly, you want to stay here to find a new purpose in your life and be able to explore. Am I correct in that assumption?" Graham asked.

Francisco laughed.

"You are more right than you know. Going back home feels like I would walk back into my weakness. Here," he said, stretching his right hand to emphasize his point, "the magic is weak. I can feel it, but it doesn't provide enough to tempt me to go overboard. I think I can have a much more fulfilling life here."

"I was hoping you'd say that," Graham responded, smiling at his friend. "I actually came in here to ask you if you'd be willing to continue living here. This place has so much potential, and I'd hate to see it all go to waste. The people here are trying so hard to find the magic in their world without even realizing the potential. They can sense that it's there, but it's so hard for them to find it amongst the fear and hate that surrounds them. They don't understand what they feel when they tap into the magic."

Graham took a minute to reevaluate his thoughts before addressing Francisco again.

"Would you be willing to stay here and possibly help people to find the good in the power that they feel? With Sebastian gone and some of the ugliness that existed here without him meddling... I'm just worried that the same evil that consumed him will start up here, and I'd rather have smaller battles instead of centuries of fighting something that was damn near impossible to defeat."

Graham felt some of the tension leave his body as the words left his mouth, realizing that the fear of evil in this land weighed more heavily on him than he had cared to admit. He sat quietly and watched as Francisco slowly nodded, taking in the words that Graham had spewed at him.

"Being consumed by The Darkness back at home preserved me in a young state. Now with The Darkness gone, all this knowledge and wisdom paired with a strong, youthful body feels like a blessing."

"I know exactly what you mean," Graham interjected, laughing.

"Right," Francisco started again. "So, I want to do some good. I want to balance out the terrible things that I was forced to do... And, of course, the ones I did on my own. But I am not sure if I am qualified to guide people into using their magic for good...." he faded off.

Graham nodded.

"How much do you know about Jamie?"

"Jamie?" Francisco repeated.

"Yeah, we separated her from the entity like we did to you."

"Oh!" Francisco replied. "She was around quite a while before me, so I don't know really anything about her life from before. The human parts of us are buried deep within The Darkness. You would rarely see the glimpse of what the human was like within them unless it was during a fight, and then it would mostly just be screaming."

"Well, that makes sense," Graham said, still trying to formulate a complete plan with the information he had.

"Why do you ask?" Francisco finally said.

"Well, I didn't know if she was redeemable like you. She seemed like she was full of her own darkness that might cause some negative situations. I was trying to figure out if she was worth trying to reform or if it was better just to keep her locked up. We have three more that Eliana separated, and who knows how many more that were off doing tasks," Graham explained.

"Oh. I think there were only fifteen or so of us left... Some humans had completely given up, and if they felt the pain of being torn away from The Darkness and Sebastian at the same time, I don't think they would have fought back or survived," he finished with some sadness.

"Shit..." was all Graham could manage to say.

"Yeah... I hope that you can help more of us. I was lucky to have a face that I knew fighting for me. No one else would have had that luxury," Francisco stated.

"I wish I would have known more about how to help sooner. Maybe we could have saved more people..." Graham said with frustration.

"No, I don't think so. Being separated from my entity without my core magic probably would have killed me in a few days. So, while you may have been able to provide some of us with a better quality of life for a few days if Sebastian was still alive, I don't think the survival rate would have been high."

"Oh," Graham said, some of the weight lifting from him with that information. "Why were there so few of you? Were the numbers always so low?" Graham inquired.

"Creating the army consumed Sebastian's core energy. If the human he was draining magic from wasn't strong enough, he would have to supply some of his power. That's why he stopped going after Placata Montis after some time. The ones with the power that would feed him had all left. Eliana's parents were trapped somewhere else. You were here constantly draining your core magic, and Eliana was unconsciously suppressing hers," Francisco replied.

"Oh! That reminds me! I wanted to look at Eliana's core magic readings," Graham interjected.

"There's a tool for that?!" Francisco asked incredulously.

Graham laughed heartily.

"Well, there wasn't until I made one. At least, not that I am aware of. Do you mind?" he asked, gesturing towards the computer.

"No! Please! I would love to see this!" Francisco said, shooting up from his chair.

Graham sat down, rolling his head around and shaking his shoulders slightly before placing his fingers on the keyboard and typing several commands to get to the camera footage. As he scrolled through, he wrote down the times when Eliana was tapping into her core magic that he knew about. He tracked when she helped release Francisco, when she went to see her parents, and when she overfilled the crystal.

Next, he opened the program that tracked the readings of high magical usage and compared the data to the times he had marked down. His heart was fluttering with the excitement of it all.

"Hmmm."

"Did you find what you were hoping to?" Francisco asked.

"Mostly," Graham replied. "Overall, the results were as extraordinary as I assumed they would be, except for this one piece that goes beyond the others. I just want to double-check what might have caused it."

Francisco nodded quietly, watching the footage with him inside The Darkness intently. Graham turned back around to focus on the screen, split the data and the video on the screen so he could watch both for the answers he was looking for.

"It's so amazing...," Francisco said quietly.

"Yeah," Graham agreed. "I just wish I had this tool with me when Sebastian was using his magic against us. It would have been so great to see how her magic compared."

Francisco laughed.

"I don't know how you're going to survive being trapped in a stuffy castle when you become king, Graham," he said.

Graham scrunched his face.

"Now you sound like Eliana. I don't plan to stop this life of science and engineering. It will just have to come second to serving people," he replied.

"Yeah, you always did help everyone else first, even if they didn't realize you were putting them first. You know, when you ran, your father told Sebastian that he had succeeded in getting rid of you as a threat to their plans, but Sebastian didn't believe him and kept following you."

"That was Sebastian's idea?!" Graham shouted.

"Well, yeah. Your father was busy trying to get the Graystins out of his way."

"Huh," Graham said. "I always thought my father sent The Darkness after me...."

Since the time Graham found his father's letter, things were revealed that showed his father indeed did have good in him. But the more Graham learned about his father, the harder his death hit. He thought back to the letter he had found and yearned to let his father know he forgave him. He hadn't even had enough time with his dead body to mourn. Things were always focused on one task, and while Graham had always put others first, this time, he regretted not putting his own pain from his strained relationship with his father first. If only he had arrived there a day earlier... A tear fell on the keyboard.

"Graham?" Francisco asked, gently placing a hand on his back.

"My father passed away," he forced out between breaths.

"I'm so sorry. When?" Francisco inquired.

"Around the same time that you were released from The Darkness," he said, turning around to look directly at his friend. "I think he felt Sebastian's pain."

Francisco nodded.

"Yeah, he probably would have. Sebastian poured more magic into him to set everything up to defeat you and Eliana," he stated.

"Of course!" Graham shouted. "That makes so much sense how he would know that I was successful. Though I'm still not sure how he knew I was with Eliana..." he faded off.

"Lucky guess, maybe?" Francisco suggested.

"Yeah, maybe...." he said, getting lost in his thoughts for a moment. "How long have I been here?"

"Uh, about 35 minutes; why?" Francisco responded.

"I wanted to let Eliana sleep enough, but I promised I wouldn't leave her behind, and the next steps require me to return home."

"What do you need to do? Maybe I can help?" Francisco offered.

"Well, I need to make arrangements for my father and contact his family. I also need to figure out what to do with all the frozen humans we left behind. I don't think I can free them without Eliana...." he trailed off for a moment. "I should also text Felicity to check in on things. She could probably help me make better decisions on where to start."

"All right..." Francisco replied.

"In short, I'm not sure what you can do. Most of what needs to be done is back home."

Graham gave a slight shrug, then pulled out his phone. The sixteen messages had grown to twenty-two. Felicity had messaged Graham to update him about everything there.

"Shit. Hang on."

Thank you so much, Felicity. I'm sorry for my lack of reply. Things have been a little crazy. I promise we will be back shortly. There is much to discuss and plan.

"Anyway. I don't think there's anything else you can help with right now, though I will probably try to find some people to come back here and join you so that you're not alone. Eliana's parents plan to bring back the group of people they were hiding with, and I have a feeling some of them will want to actively participate in the fight against evil. I mean, if that's something that you want," Graham quickly added.

"Thank you. I would love some company around here. The silence is harder than I anticipated," Francisco finished quietly as he paced around.

"Alright. That is all beneficial information. I will try my best to not leave you alone for very long," Graham said, walking over to join his friend. "And thank you again. Really. You have been extremely helpful in all of this. I will try to let you know the plan when I know, though it might be a few days. I've got a lot to catch up on."

"I get it. You've already done far beyond what I could have ever expected from anyone. Thank you, Graham."

The two men hugged for a long moment before Graham pulled away and patted Francisco's back.

"Right, then. I guess I'll be in touch," Graham said.

Francisco nodded, then watched as he exited the room. Outside the lab, Graham felt much more relaxed. When he crossed the hall, the smile that painted his face was natural instead of forced. Not only because he was heading back to Eliana but also because things seemed to be carefully falling into place.

Taking a quick moment to enjoy the feeling of relief, Graham quietly opened the door and found Eliana still softly breathing under the covers. He carefully closed the door, trying not to make any extra noise. Stepping to the desk, he bent down, unlaced his shoes, and slid them off. As he made his way to the opposite side of the bed where Eliana was, she moaned quietly. He paused where he stood, waiting to see if she was stirring awake or merely adjusting. When no more sound or movement came, he continued his journey to the bed.

Gently climbing on, he slid over the top of the covers to lay close to her. As soon as his body was within an inch of her, she rolled towards him and slid an arm over his chest. He grinned and turned to face her, wrapping her up in his hold. The slow rhythm of her breath and the peaceful look on her face lulled him quickly to sleep.

CHAPTER THIRTY-THREE

The repeated vibration of Graham's phone startled him awake. Throwing his hand into his pocket, he blinked rapidly to focus as he pulled the device closer to see who was calling. *Felicity*. He sighed and ran a hand over his face before sitting up to glance over at Eliana. She shifted slightly but did not seem to be disturbed by the call.

"Shit," Graham whispered while his vision tried to adjust to the brightness of his screen.

Felicity had sent three messages asking for an estimate of what time he would be coming back and if he wanted dinner. When he hadn't responded for over an hour, she tried calling. Graham shook the sleep from his eyes, then replied.

Yes, sorry. Dinner would be great. Fell asleep after I messaged you, but we should be headed back in the next half hour or so.

Sighing, he dropped the phone next to him on the bed and turned to Eliana, who was now staring up at him and smiling.

"Sorry..." he said in almost a whisper as he slid her hair behind her ear. "I didn't mean to wake you."

"Nothing to apologize for. I haven't woken up next to someone so beautiful in a long time," she said with a flash in her eyes.

Scooting towards him, she placed her head on his chest, causing him to roll to his back. He wrapped her tightly in his arms and placed a kiss on the top of her head.

"Did you sleep alright?" he asked, suppressing a moan when she traced a finger along his torso.

"Mm, yes. Thank you. This bed is like a cloud. Do we have to go soon?" Eliana asked, smiling innocently up at him.

"Yeah, we probably should," he replied, his heartbeat increasing.

"Okay. Did you get what you needed from Francisco?" she inquired, letting her fingers travel down his thigh.

"I think so," he replied breathlessly. "There are a few things that I can't predict before going home, but I think he will be fine here with some help. We've just gotta see who wants to do that."

"Yeah," Eliana said as she pushed the covers from on top of her.

Once her leg was free, she slid herself on top of Graham. His body pulsed with her heartbeat.

"So..." she started, slowly undoing the buttons on his shirt.

"Yeah?" he asked, sliding his hands over her curves.

"How much time do we have before we have to be back?" she asked in a sultry tone.

He groaned and tensed slightly as she slid a hand down his inner thigh. Grabbing her face, he pulled her down to him for a kiss before answering.

"Thirty minutes," he said in an airy voice.

"That'll work," she replied, quickly removing her shirt.

Graham fought off the thoughts that told him he had other responsibilities to take care of, unable to avoid the dreamy gaze of the woman sitting over him. Her red curls falling over the sides of her face caused a shadow that made her green eyes smolder. Her pale skin glowed with a pink hue as the blood coursed through her body, radiating heat into his own. When she bent down to kiss his collarbone while unbuttoning his shirt, he lost all control.

"Fuck," he whispered into her hair.

Suddenly, things weren't moving fast enough for him. His lips were craving for hers, but his eyes were still thirsty for her body. He paused and gazed at the dim silhouette of the woman above him, shuddering as she reached down towards his chest. He swiftly helped

Eliana unbutton his shirt, then moved to help with her pants. As she was finishing kicking them off her feet, he shifted to be on top of her and removed his pants and undershirt. When the initial urgency passed with the removal of his last article of clothing, he allowed himself to let his eyes study the flesh of the woman that now lay beneath him.

"Graham..." she started, destroying his resolve.

He dove down towards her, feeling his mouth pressing against hers, sucking her lip between his teeth. As his hands started to explore her skin more, she moaned loudly, a feral growl traveling through her body before she threw herself at him, taking control once again. This time, he let her. Releasing all inhibitions over to her, he let himself just enjoy everything. Her touch. Her breath. Her crying out.

They both plunged into a rhythm as their bodies intertwined. His hands traced her body as her kisses traced his. The feeling of their flesh touching sent him off into ecstasy more than once.

After what felt like forever, yet also not long enough, they collapsed beside each other on the bed. Both breathless and sweaty, they turned their heads and smiled. Their hands linked, then Graham reached over to remove a hair from Eliana's forehead. When he went to lean in to kiss her again, his phone vibrated.

He sighed and pecked her cheek before reaching over to answer it. After a few moments of blindly searching, he released Eliana's hand and peaked over the side of the bed, spotting it on the floor. He yelped when she grabbed his ass as he leaned over to retrieve it. She giggled, then played innocent as he rolled back onto the bed to look at her. He rewarded her with a crooked smile and a long kiss.

Another missed call from Felicity. He looked at the time since his last missed call from her and choked on a laugh that tried to escape. It had been almost ninety minutes.

"What?" Eliana asked, propping herself up onto one elbow.

Graham internally groaned as his eyes traced along her naked body, desperately wishing they could just stay here together.

"We're late," he said with a quick smile. "We should also probably shower," he added as he went in to sniff her and plugged his nose with a smile.

"Hey! You're no rose either!" she playfully shouted as she flicked his side.

"Ow!" he shouted back, pulling her hips towards him and giving her ass a quick swat.

The look that flashed across her face with the contact was not quite the one he expected. The hunger that now filled her face told him he would be in trouble if they didn't get out of bed immediately. When she started to crawl over him, he quickly rolled from the bed to standing.

"I'll start the shower!" he said, trying to hide his hardening member.

He needed no more excuses not to tackle her again, and he was sure she would comment if he gave her a chance. Turning on the water, he immediately jumped in, closing his eyes and letting the cold water soothe the heat pouring from his body. As the water started to warm, he opened his eyes to watch as Eliana glided through the doorway. Holding his breath for a moment as she got in, he instantly regretted suggesting that they shower together.

Not only was the bright light revealing every part of her that he had failed to miss before, but every chance she got, Eliana ran her hands across his body. Eventually, he just let her wash him and enjoyed the touch of another human, shivering when he found release yet again. Once she was done, Graham returned the favor and helped clean her up, taking in her form and laughing that just a day ago, he was wondering if her hands were as soft as suede. They were. She pouted when he laughed.

"Your hands are soft," was all he said to her.

"Thank you?"

As the last of the soap was rinsed from their bodies, Graham retrieved some towels. He wrapped her up tightly, kissing her before he pulled away. Quickly drying himself, he wrapped the towel around his waist and went to grab a clean outfit from the bedroom. Once they were both dressed again, Graham turned to Eliana.

"I should probably call Felicity..." he grimaced.

Graham grabbed his phone and selected the most recent missed call from her to call back. It had been two minutes ago. He held his breath as the call connected, flinching slightly when the first ring was abruptly cut off.

"*Graham Joshua Norbury*!" the voice from the other end shouted. "*Where are you?!*"

"Sorry, Felicity. We're on our way."

"*When now? In a few days?*" she retorted.

"Haha, no. No. We'll be there in thirty seconds. I promise."

"*You had better, young man.*"

"Bye," he said with another grimace.

"Whoa," Eliana said when he hung up.

"Oh," he turned around to look at her in the doorway. "You heard that?"

"I think Francisco probably heard that," she laughed.

He groaned a little before he reached out for her hand.

"Can we go, then?" he asked.

"Sure," she said, taking his hand.

CHAPTER THIRTY-FOUR

Still on a blissful high, Eliana was not prepared to leave, but she was glad to be with Graham wherever he went. In a blink, she left the cozy room and found herself looking at the king lying peacefully on the bed. Before she even had a moment to process being in a new place, Graham pulled out his phone and frantically typed a message. Eliana could only assume it was to Felicity and suppressed a laugh. Turning back to the king, she reached out to touch his arm. Not sure what she was trying to find, she closed her eyes and focused.

After a few moments, she sighed and opened her eyes. She looked up and saw Graham watching her intently.

"Anything?" he asked.

Eliana simply shook her head.

"I figured not, but thanks for trying," he breathed.

"I'm not even sure what I expected to happen, but it seemed like something called for it," she replied, walking over to take his hand.

"WELL, IT'S ABOUT TIME!" a voice boomed into the room.

They both flinched. The gentle older woman she had met earlier was frightening now. When Graham tensed completely, she had to turn away to disguise her laugh as a cough.

"Felicity," Graham started.

"No more excuses! Do you have any idea what's been going through my mind?! I went to look for you here, and you were gone. Then I went to look for you in the garden, and I found a trail of blood, and Elijah is frozen, but no sign of you! Then you don't reply to me for hours! How was I supposed to know you were alive, and it wasn't someone else pretending to be you, hm?!" she said in the best mom voice Eliana had ever heard.

As Felicity finished talking, she took a few determined steps towards where they stood. Her voice is still booming in their brain, disturbing the waves. With a lightning-fast motion, Felicity reached out and slapped Graham across the face, then broke down in tears and hugged him tightly.

"Don't you ever scare me like that again! Do you hear me?!" Felicity garbled into his shirt.

Eliana stared with her mouth open at the two. She couldn't believe this woman had just walked up and slapped the king across the face. Repressing a laugh, Eliana observed Graham. His lack of response to the slap almost stunned her more than the action itself.

"I'm sorry, Felicity. I didn't have time to think about what my disappearance might look like, and I honestly hadn't planned on taking so long to get back here. I didn't expect you to go to the garden," he said as he continued to hold her tight.

"Well, what was so important that you couldn't find a moment to reply to me, hm?" she asked, pulling away.

Graham's glance over to Eliana, paired with Eliana's intense blushing, was all Felicity needed to put two and two together. Eliana turned and stumbled into a table, desperate to be further from the eye of the storm.

"I see. Well, next time, I expect some knowledge of your well-being before you have a moment for yourself. If you don't mind," she finished, adjusting her clothing and clearing her throat.

"I will do my best to remember that," he said with a half-smile.

"And I'm sorry for slapping you. That was uncalled for. Slightly," she stubbornly said.

Graham and Eliana both laughed at that.

"No need to apologize. You're right. I should have let you know I was alright as soon as we defeated The Darkness. Can you forgive me?" Graham asked with his best puppy dog eyes.

"Defeated the— I oughta slap you again!" she joked. "But, yes. Of course, I can forgive you," the woman who at one time was only a handful of years Graham's elder replied. "And if you try and pull something like that again, I'm comin' for ya!" she finished, poking a finger at him.

Graham threw both his hands up in defense.

"Hey, I meant nothing by it this time, but I will make sure you are the first person I call if anything goes wrong." He smirked.

"Hey!" Eliana cut in.

Her quick reaction caused a roar of laughter to break out. Eliana was glad the tension was broken and was pleasantly surprised when Felicity pulled her in for a hug. For a moment, things felt like they could be normal, whatever *normal* meant. As Felicity released Eliana, she grabbed her arms and looked her in the eyes.

"You two take care of each other, alright? There's too much ugly in this world for something this beautiful not to thrive."

Eliana blushed again but nodded profusely.

"Alright, with that out of the way, I've got some questions you still need to answer, Graham," Felicity started in again.

"Yes, I'm sure you do. I have lots of answers and plenty of other things that I need to share with you so we can prepare the castle. Why don't you start first?"

"Thank you. My first question to you is, do you need time to mourn your father before stepping into a role as the king?" she asked gently.

The question was not what Eliana had expected, and from the quick rise of his eyebrows, she wasn't sure that Graham had been expecting it either.

"Oh, well. No, I don't think so. I would like to address the people. There is no reason to continue hiding anything. We all know that I am going to be the king, at least for the time being. I honestly think staying busy is going to be the best thing for me right now. Too much has happened. It's going to take longer to sit down and process it all," Graham said.

"Alright. That's entirely acceptable. When would you like to address the people and do the memorial for your father? And what in the heck do you expect me to do with all of these frozen people down in the dungeons?" she shot off.

Eliana snorted as she tried to stifle a laugh, earning a wink from Graham before he answered.

"I would like to address the people tomorrow morning. Hopefully, this will give us time to take care of some other matters. The memorial will need a few days, at least. I am hoping to get my father's sister and brother here, along with their families, and that might require a bit more time. And Eliana and I will get to the frozen people in a moment. Do they all seem to be alive?" Graham asked hesitantly.

Eliana shot him a glance but didn't say anything.

"As far as we could tell, yes. There appeared to be gentle breathing coming from each of them, though Elijah seems in pretty awful shape," she finished.

"Oh, yeah. I did some damage to him," Eliana quietly remembered.

"Don't worry, dear. I did my best to clean his wounds, and I was able to stop the bleeding with a few quick stitches."

Eliana grimaced.

"Thanks. It was self-defense," she defended.

"I'm not here to place blame. I'm just here to help," Felicity responded with a kind smile. "Now, what is it I can do for you right now, Graham?" she continued.

"If you could find the contact information for my aunt and uncle and maybe a few of my cousins, that would be extremely helpful. I also need as many rooms prepared as possible. There is a group of people coming, and I'm not sure how many there are," he paused and frowned for a moment.

"That shouldn't take long. Do you want to move your father down to be prepped for his burial?" Felicity asked.

"Oh, yes. If you could send someone to take care of that in half an hour." Graham replied, staring at his father, "I think that will be enough time for my goodbyes." He whispered.

"Of course. I will get started on all of that now," Felicity said, exiting with a curtsey.

The room fell silent. Eliana was unsure of what he needed, so she sat beside him and held his hand. They sat in silence for a few minutes before Graham took his father's hand.

"I wish I had known things sooner." He finally spoke. "I wish you would have sent me that letter while you were still alive. But you were probably right in thinking that I wouldn't have been ready to hear your truth. I suppose it's too late to let you know I forgive you. I hope you and mom are reunited somewhere. I hope you get to live the lives that you were never allowed in this body."

The room fell silent again after echoing trembling words hushed.

"Graham," Eliana started gently, but he simply shook his head.

"I forgive you," he finally spoke again. "And I love you, D... dad."

Then he finally let everything go. His emotions poured from his eyes, and his body shook. Eliana squeezed his hands, comforting him with her magic.

"I love you," he mumbled. "I will do everything that I can to help restore this land. The people will learn about your mistakes and how you couldn't mend some, and someday, they, too, will be able to forgive you. Goodbye, Dad," Graham finished, a tear running from his chin onto his father's temple.

Leaning down, he pressed his lips to his father's cheek, just below where the tear had fallen. Wiping his face with the back of his hand, Graham opened the side of the nightstand to retrieve the box they had left. He clutched it close to his body, then stood, staring blankly at Eliana as she stood by his side.

"Let's put this box in my room. It'll be safer there," he said after a moment.

"Alright. Lead the way," Eliana said, trying to hide the worry from her voice.

Graham nodded and passed her to exit the room. He continued to stare off into space as silent tears slid down his cheeks, not acknowledging the few people they passed. Eliana nodded solemnly at them, hoping they would understand his lack of response. After the long mosey down the unknown halls, they finally entered a new room. It looked much the same as the room they had just left, with a door that seemed to lead directly outside to a space just beyond the garden.

Graham walked over to his dresser, opened a drawer, lifted a false bottom, retrieved a key, unlocked a larger drawer, and placed the box he had been holding inside, leaving his hand to linger on it for a moment. Eliana stepped and embraced him from the side. Graham turned and threw his arms around her. She held him tight as he cried, hoping to heal him a bit. She had felt the pain of losing a parent, but no one had been there to console her. She wasn't sure she even ever dealt with it.

Squeezing him tighter, she shut her eyes and sent more of her magic to console him. His breathing stabilized gradually, and he pulled away, wiping his face before smiling down at her and pecking her on the lips.

"Thank you," he said just as his phone buzzed.

It seems your uncle passed on a few years ago, but his wife would love to talk to you. Your aunt, her husband, and their children have all been missing for some years now. I am trying to track down more information on that, but it may not be possible. Dinner will be ready in twenty minutes if you're hungry. Let me know if you need anything else.

Graham responded with his thanks and let her know they would do their best to be at dinner on time.

"What's the plan for us next?" Eliana asked, relieved she could finally have an answer.

"Let's go check on Billy. I'm not sure I trust that the people you froze are all as fine as Felicity says," he replied, taking a deep breath.

"What makes you think they're not?" Eliana asked.

"Francisco mentioned that the pain that he felt both when being separated from The Darkness and Sebastian might have been too much for some people to survive. He also mentioned that there should be about ten others that were still consumed by The Darkness."

"Oh," was all she could say.

"Come on. I'll explain the rest on the way," he said, taking her hand. The tension in his body started leaving when they touched.

As they made their way to the deeper parts of the castle, Graham explained everything that Francisco had told him. Eliana felt better knowing that things had happened in one of the best ways that they could have. She fully believed that Francisco's speculation that he would not have survived long after being separated from The Darkness was correct. She had felt the pain from the emptiness inside of him when his core magic was still being held captive by Sebastian.

"I'm glad you were never able to successfully separate anyone before last night," she said when Graham finished.

"Me, too," he said with a small smile, his eyes still puffy and red.

Shortly after, they reached another door. Standing silently in front of it, Eliana hoped that they could save the five frozen humans, but deep down, she knew that wouldn't be true for all of them. As she resolved that trying to save at least one of them was better than none, Graham reached out and opened the door. The pair stepped in and found Billy watching the bodies closely.

"Sir! What are you doing down here?" Billy asked, startled by their presence.

"We came to try to talk to them," Graham replied.

"Oh. Does that mean you'll want to put them in individual cells?" Billy asked.

"Please. And you shouldn't have to be down here much longer. I'll have someone relieve you soon," Graham said.

"You don't need to do that, Sir. I'm fine."

"Don't be ridiculous. It's not your job to guard the holding cells. We can rotate shifts," Graham replied.

"Alright, thank you, Sir," Billy said, bowing. "Do you need help moving 'em?" he asked.

"If you could, that would be wonderful. Then I want you to go grab something to eat. I'll ask Felicity to find someone else to replace you."

"Thank you," Billy said, blushing lightly.

The three of them quickly moved the bodies to a bed in separate cells, making sure they were locked as they exited. When they were done, Graham thanked Billy again, forcing him out, and then secured the door behind him. Eliana smiled as Graham shook his head, chuckling for a moment.

"Let's start with Jamie," he said after a brief pause.

She nodded and walked over to the cell where the woman lay stiffly on the bed. With a small blast of magic, Jamie was released from her frozen state . She angrily stalked over to the cell door where Eliana stood and shouted a string of curse words.

"I don't think that's going to help you," Eliana replied calmly.

"Yeah? What the fuck do you know about helping me, hm? Do you realize the things that I have done? I murdered my family! I probably murdered one of your friends along the way, too!"

The incoherent cursing continued as Jamie paced the cell. Eliana sighed, rolling her eyes before glancing back at Graham, who was watching the other woman with a look of disgust. As he absentmindedly reached up to scratch his stomach, Eliana remembered something that Graham had told her about during his visit with Francisco.

Stepping closer to Jamie's cell, Eliana reached in to grab one of the flailing arms and released her core magic before Jamie even had time to react. The cursing immediately stopped, and Jamie took a breath like a weight had been lifted off of her chest. She paused, looking around with confusion.

"What did you do?" she asked in a much more civil tone.

"I helped you heal. With Sebastian gone, your core magic should start returning. I speculated our friend could probably feel his return more quickly than you because he was consumed by The Darkness for a lesser time than you," Eliana stated.

A tear rolled down Jamie's face, and she went back to her bed to sit. Eliana unlocked the door, holding out a hand to pause Graham before he could stop her. Leaving the door opened behind her, she went to where the woman sat and held out her hand. Jamie looked up at her for a moment, then placed one of her hands into Eliana's.

This time, both women closed their eyes, and Eliana released enough magic to heal Jamie and explore the darkness that lived inside of her. She felt how much this woman had been through and desperately hoped that the years of manipulation could be reversed. But, for now, it seemed that Jamie could be saved, and that alone was enough to lift Eliana's spirits.

"How do you feel now?" Eliana asked gently.

"Human," Jamie said. "It's like a part of me that was missing has been returned. The part that cares about other people."

"Good. I hope that feeling stays, but for now, please forgive us for leaving you in the cell until we can know for sure," Eliana said.

"Of course. I understand," Jamie said. "I feel like I need to sleep for a while anyway," she added with empty eyes and a sad smile.

Eliana nodded, squeezing the woman's shoulder before exiting and locking the cell. As she went back to Graham, he smiled hopefully at her.

"If you unfreeze two, I should be able to help with one. I was able to help Francisco," he offered.

Eliana frowned, then reached out to touch him. As she let her magic flow through him, she felt his core magic radiating. Pleased with the amount of power that had been restored, she removed her hand.

"Okay," she agreed.

Moving on to the following cells, they found two of the bodies of the entities Eliana had fought in the other dimension. Unfreezing them, they both let out a scream before finding silence and taking in their surroundings. Eliana and Graham squeezed each other's hands before stepping into their separate cells. Quickly passing some core magic, the demeanor of the men instantly changed from intense to more relaxed.

"Where am I? Who are you?" the man asked Eliana.

"You're safe now. You are free from The Darkness forever. What's your name?" she gently asked.

"Cole," he said, still darting his eyes around the space.

"Nice to meet you, Cole. My name is Li. Do you know how long you've been a part of The Darkness?" she asked gently.

"Not long. I was one of the last. Where's my brother? Is he here?" he asked as tears started to form.

"I'm not sure. What's his name?" she asked, unsuccessfully attempting to reach out and push more magic into him.

"Davey. His name is Davey," he said.

"Graham?" Eliana shouted.

"Yeah?" she heard him reply.

"Who are you with?" she asked.

She heard some mumbles, then saw Graham accompanied by a young man at the door of the cell she was in.

"Davey," he said. "He tells me that you might be with his brother Cole?"

Immediately the two men ran to each other. They squeezed each other into a tight hug, both sobbing. As they stood there, Eliana looked over to Graham and gave him a shrug, trying to see if he agreed that they could finish the job of healing the two young men while they were distracted by each other. He nodded slightly, and they stepped towards the men.

As soon as Graham and Eliana released their magic into the boys, they calmed down. The intense crying became silent tears as the death gripped hugs became a gentler embrace. The shifty eyes and mistrust relaxed. After a few moments, the men separated, and Eliana explained what had happened and why they would need to stay locked up for just a little while. The two nodded, accepting their temporary fate calmly.

"Can we stay together?" Cole asked in a shaky voice.

"Sure. There's a cell with a bunk bed just over here," Graham replied, shooting Eliana a look.

The two young men made their way to the cell with no resistance, and just like Jamie, Cole, and Davey both quickly fell asleep after they were locked back inside. Eliana and Graham then stepped over to the last two cells, staring inside. Graham stood outside of Elijah's cell while Eliana found herself in front of a much older man than the previous two.

"Graham?" Eliana asked.

"I don't think we should release him yet," he said, watching Elijah in his room.

"Alright. You can help me with this one, then," Eliana said gently.

Expecting the scream of pain this time, Eliana stayed further back to use her magic to unfreeze the man. When the shouts left his lips, she opened the door and quickly went to him. Placing a hand on his arm, she released her magic, but the man blasted her to the wall.

"Shoulda let me die!" the man shouted at her.

"Eliana!" Graham said as he ran to her. "Are you alright?!"

"I'm fine," she replied, letting him help her up as she rubbed her head.

"Shoulda let me die!" the man repeated as he sat on the floor crying and rocking.

"Why?" Eliana asked.

"'Cuz all I do is hurt people," he responded.

"What's your name?" she asked, stepping closer to him.

"Jeb," he replied, hugging his knees more tightly.

"How did you force me back?" she asked, squatting down next to him.

"Core magic. Thas mah trick. Sebastian didn't want it for 'imself. Said he would keep me to protect 'im," he said in rhythm with his rocking.

"So, he never took over your core magic?" Graham asked.

The man shook his head.

"Always lived in me, but never mine to control," he said.

"What do you mean?" Graham asked.

"He left it in me, but he was controllin' The Darkness, and The Darkness was controllin' mah body. When I wouldn' use mah magic the way he wanted, he had The Darkness hurt me. Always hurtin' me."

"Can we try to help?" Eliana asked.

"Ya can't help me! Shoulda let me die!" he repeated.

Eliana looked over at Graham with concern. She stood and walked over to talk to him quietly.

"Do you think you can help me try to heal his mind?"

"I think so," Graham said.

"Alright, good."

"Jeb," Graham started. "Do you think we could try something?"

"Ain't gon' do no good. No good!" he said.

Eliana grasped Graham's hand and took a deep breath before they each placed a hand on Jeb's head. Closing their eyes, the magic started to flow. Eliana smiled as her magic intertwined with Graham's, and she experienced what he had described to her earlier about it filling the holes she had inside. Latching on to that feeling of peace and wholeness, she forced more magic into the man on the ground. Half expecting to be thrown back again, Eliana prepared her body. But as an extensive amount of magic was released into him, the man fell silent.

Opening her eyes, Eliana removed her hand and looked down. She was suddenly worried that she had taken away this man's life by trying to give him too much of her own. Jeb stared off into the space in front of him, his eyes flashing with magic. A smile slowly spread across his face, and he started to laugh. Eliana and Graham simultaneously stepped away.

"The pain. You removed it," he said.

"Jeb?" Eliana asked.

"Thank you," he whispered, dropping his head into his hands and crying.

Eliana looked over to Graham, glaring. He responded with a shrug and went over to the man.

"Can I help you onto the bed?" Graham asked gently.

"Yes, thank you. That would be wonderful," Jeb said with a sinister smile.

"Get some rest. We'll be back to check on you later," Graham said, tucking the man in.

Jeb nodded and let his eyes fall closed. As Graham turned towards Eliana, he shrugged again, catching her arm as he passed to push her out in front of him. When they reached the hallway, Graham quickly turned and locked the door, then pushed Eliana further away from the room.

"Something's not right. Can you freeze him again?" Graham asked.

"What? Why?" she asked, freezing the man before getting a reply.

"I don't know, but the fact that Sebastian let him keep his core magic... I need to talk to Francisco before we let Jeb go anywhere."

"Okay. Did you ask Felicity to send someone down?" she asked.

Graham shook his head.

"I don't want anyone down here. They can stay on the other side of the door. I'll grab Felipe. He's strong and smart and won't ask too many questions. Billy is smart, but he lacks confidence. I'm worried that will put him in danger."

"Alrighty... I'll just wait here while you grab him," Eliana said, still unsure of what she was missing.

"No. Wait on the other side of the door. I don't want you in here alone," Graham said.

Eliana rolled her eyes.

"Fine."

They exited the hallway together, and Graham turned to lock the door, taking the key with him. Eliana held back a laugh at seeing him use a regular lock for this situation. Then she froze. When he turned around and looked at her once more, there was something in his eyes that made her stop and think about what he was doing.

They both knew a key was pointless against magic, and the people in the other room wouldn't need a key either when their powers returned. Staring at the door that separated the previous Darkness army, she quickly cast a spell that any of them would have a hard time breaking through.

Listening carefully to the three that remained unfrozen, she heard steady breathing that told her they were still asleep. She released her breath and tried to relax. Suddenly feeling vulnerable, she looked around the space. Before she had a chance to scan the entire area, Graham returned.

"Eliana! This is Felipe," Graham said, pulling her attention.

"Ma'am." He nodded.

"Nice to meet you. Please, call me Li," she smiled, offering her hand.

"Likewise. Please just call me Felipe," he said in a surprisingly deep voice.

She chuckled.

"Everything ok down here?" Graham asked.

"Yup. I sealed the door up nice and tight. Felipe shouldn't have any issues." She winked at Graham.

Graham beamed at her.

"Perfect! We should get to dinner, then. I don't want Felicity to think we're avoiding her," Graham said with an awkward smile.

Eliana laughed.

"Definitely not. Thank you again, Felipe."

"Not a problem, Ma'am. Enjoy your dinner," he replied with a friendly smile.

Eliana returned the smile and nodded, turning back to take Graham's extended hand.

"I knew you'd figure out to protect the door with magic," he whispered to her as they left the cold cells behind.

She couldn't help but giggle as his nose brushed her ear.

"It probably took longer than it should have, but I got there eventually," she said back quietly.

He simply smiled and squeezed her hand before turning his focus back toward their next destination.

CHAPTER THIRTY-FIVE

Eliana and Graham entered the massive dining hall just as the last part of the meal was being set out. Felicity saw them and smiled brightly.

"Ah! Thank you for your punctuality!" she said to them.

"Well, I said that I would be where I promised to when I promised," Graham said with a smirk.

"Don't push your luck, kid," Felicity said under her breath.

He frowned, and Eliana laughed.

A handful of people in the room stopped and bowed at Graham, welcoming him back. Eliana watched as he greeted each unknown face by name, hugging a few when they paused to say something. Most of them nodded towards her with a "Miss Graystin," but a few shook her hand with excitement. She wasn't sure what they had all been told or how they knew her name, but she couldn't find a moment to ask if it was Graham's doing.

"Come on," he said, taking her hand and guiding her to the seats that had been set out for them.

"This looks and smells delicious. Is it just us eating?" Eliana asked no one in particular.

"I asked everyone to give you privacy for at least this one meal. I'm not sure that you'll continue to have that type of luxury for a long while after tomorrow," Felicity answered with a wink.

"Oh. Thank you," Eliana said as she let the words sink in.

"Alright!" Felicity boomed. "Everyone out. Let them eat in peace. You'll all have plenty of time to catch up later. Shoo!"

Eliana laughed at the appreciation she had for this woman, which somehow increased immeasurably each time they had an encounter. She couldn't even imagine the seemingly timid woman she had met initially anymore. Graham's trust in Felicity to take care of everything was completely understandable. As the last of the people left the room and shut the door, Eliana released a breath she hadn't realized she was holding.

"Are you alright?" Graham asked gently.

"I think so?" she replied. "I'm still a little unnerved by everything that happened in the cells, but I can't tell if that's from you or something I felt," she frowned.

"I appreciate you going with me on that. There was just something about Jeb... I feel like we should have paid more attention as to whether he was actually frozen or not. He seems to be pretty powerful," Graham finished.

"Yeah. Hopefully, Francisco can help. It all happened so fast, but his magic definitely radiated in a way I've never felt before," she said.

"Agreed, but for now, I say we eat. We will not get far on an empty stomach!" Graham exclaimed.

Eliana laughed, then took in the spread of food that surrounded her. It was, indeed, a feast. There was prime rib, mashed potatoes, gravy, green beans, salad, eggplant, steamed carrots, fresh rolls, a Dutch apple pie, and four different wines. Overwhelmed by the amount of food, she grabbed a roll and took a bite out of it, not bothering to cut it open and put butter on it.

"Mmmm! This is amazing!" she said, inhaling the scent of the warm bread as she chewed.

Graham laughed and filled his plate with a mountain of food.

"I have no doubt. The castle always had the best chefs. I'm honestly glad to hear that hasn't changed. I love food!"

"Better be careful. You're going to have to put in some work to maintain this now," Eliana laughed, patting his belly.

"Yeah, yeah. I'm sure we'll get plenty of exercises," Graham shot back with a wink.

"Well then, you'd better eat up!"

The rest of the meal comprised playful banter, laughs, and a few moments of drawn-out silence. Eliana struggled between enjoying the moments and worrying about everything else going on. From time to time, she would glance over and catch Graham frowning slightly and could only assume that he felt the same.

"What do you want to do now?" she asked to break one of the long silences.

"We should probably go check in with your parents. It's been a little longer than the few hours you said you were giving them to prepare things. I'd also like to let them know we arranged space for multiple people, but I don't even know how many people are there!"

"Oh, right. A lot has changed since we left... And I'm sure I could get some rooms ready at my house, too, if we need them," Eliana added.

"I know Louisa has kept things in tip-top shape," Graham agreed, wiping the corners of his mouth with his napkin. "Ready to head out?"

"Shouldn't you let Felicity know you're leaving?" Eliana asked with a smirk.

"Oh, yeah," he said, quickly pulling out his phone with a light blush painting his cheeks.

Eliana laughed, shaking her head as she pushed herself to stand.

"Done!" he announced.

"Great," she said, reaching out her hand to him.

The moment her skin touched his, she was standing on the sand. Her overstuffed stomach not appreciating the form of travel, she suddenly became nauseated. Placing her hands on her knees until her stomach settled, she groaned quietly and then came back to standing.

"You, okay?" Graham asked with a furrowed brow.

"Definitely," she smiled. "I've just gotta remember that traveling on that full of a stomach is not the best idea."

Graham laughed.

"Yeah, you did eat quite a bit...."

"Oh, shut up," she said, smacking his chest lightly. "Let's go."

As she passed through the invisible doorway, she was greeted by around fifty people. All were roaming around hurriedly. They were working together seamlessly, like a colony of ants. Eliana was in awe at the difference in liveliness from the first two times she had entered. Letting her eyes scan for a familiar face, she quickly found her mother in the sea of people.

"Mom!" she shouted over the bustle.

"Eliana!" she shouted back, waving her over.

Eliana stole a look back to make sure that Graham was still with her, then took his hand and made her way to her mother.

"So, I assume everyone is willing to make the journey to Placata Montis, then?" Eliana asked excitedly.

"At least for a little while. There may be one or two that aren't fully committed to leaving, though. But without our magic protecting this area, they might have a change of heart," Delilah replied. "What brings you back so soon?"

"Well, a few things. First, Eliana told you we'd be back for you. Second, I was hoping that we could talk somewhere with fewer ears," Graham cut in.

"Sure! Follow me," Delilah said, heading towards their house.

Eliana and Graham kept their fingers linked as they followed her mother on the short walk to where she resided. Once inside, she called for her Scott.

"What's up?" her father asked, wiping his hands with a towel.

"Hey, Scott," Graham said with a smile. "I was hoping I could talk to you two for a moment before we start moving people there. First, do you have a list of everyone here? I'd like to try and keep families together as much as possible. Beyond that, an estimate of how many people want to keep these homes and bring them to Placata Montis. And also.... If you think anyone with magic is willing to live with Francisco and help. He's going to be staying at the house I built and mentor people there to start tapping into their magic again."

"Wow, Graham. That's really great," Delilah said, squeezing his arm. "I know some who would be willing to start a new life helping

Francisco mentor. Only about half of us have magic, but maybe only thirty-five percent of that half know how to tap into their core magic. As for a list, I just finished making one up not too long ago! I can make a copy of it. I will need to double-check about houses, though. I think most people wanted to make sure they like Placata Montis before fully committing to moving their house, but I would say there would probably be about twenty-three houses that might need to be moved. Let me go grab that list for you. I'll be right back," she said in one breath and sprinted away as soon as she finished.

"Sure. Thank you," Graham said to her leaving shadow.

"You two staying out of trouble?" Scott asked as soon as Delilah left.

Eliana choked, but Graham remained calm.

"Of course! Lots of work to get done!" he smiled coolly.

"Mmhm," Scott said, looking to his daughter, then back to Graham.

"Daaaaad," Eliana said through gritted teeth.

"What?!" he asked, feigning innocence.

"Stop it, Scott. You leave them be," Delilah said, handing a paper to Graham.

He looked it over, suppressing a laugh as Delilah gently smacked Scott.

"What?" Scott repeated.

"You know what. They're adults. If they want to get into trouble, that's on them," Delilah said with her hands on her hips.

Scott sighed, looking down. When he looked back up, he had tears in his eyes.

"I just feel like we missed a lot of significant years. We never even got to meet Fiona," he said sadly.

"DAD!" Eliana shouted. "Were you spying on me?!"

"Not spying!" he quickly corrected. "We just wanted to keep an eye on you and make sure things were okay."

Eliana shot a glance over to Graham and watched his eyes shoot up from the paper while his head stayed down. He looked between Scott and Delilah but did everything possible to avoid looking at Eliana.

"Scott! Would you relax?! None of us are going anywhere. We're all healthy and have many years ahead of us to spend together," Delilah said, squeezing his arms in assurance.

"You're right," he said, wiping the tears that fell. "I'm sorry, Eliana."

"It's fine, Dad," she said as she walked over and hugged her parents. "I'm sorry you guys didn't get to meet her either. You would have loved her."

Graham made a weird noise, and Eliana suddenly felt extremely uncomfortable talking about someone else she had been in love with. When she released her parents and turned to apologize, the look on his face stopped the words from coming out.

"Graham?" she said, touching his arm.

"Delilah," he said, ignoring Eliana, "these names here... are they correct?" he asked, pointing.

"Of course, they are. I made this list myself!" Delilah said smugly.

Graham whipped back around to Eliana with excitement painting his face.

"Eliana!" he shouted in her face.

"What?!" she shouted back, laughing awkwardly.

"My aunt and her entire family; they're here!" he replied excitedly.

"They what now?" she asked, checking that she heard him correctly.

"Delilah, how long has the Sulina family been here?" he asked.

"I'd say just around twenty years or so. Sebastian had been trying to coerce other members of her family to join him, and when they tried to run, we brought them here. Then shortly after, two of the younger men in the family got taken over by The Darkness. The rest of them were able to fight and hide until Scott and I arrived," she said.

"What are the names of the men? Do you know?" Graham asked quickly.

"Mmmm. I believe it was something like Clay and David," she said.

"No, no," Scott corrected. "Cole."

Eliana and Graham looked at each other, their mouths both slightly agape.

"Cole and Davey?" Eliana clarified.

"Yes! Wait, how do you know that?" her mother asked.

"They were two of the people trapped in the entities we fought with Sebastian. They're back at the castle," Eliana explained.

"My family," Graham whispered.

Eliana smiled at him, squeezing his arm.

"I tell you what, my dear," Delilah said to Graham. "How about I take you to your aunt while I get more solid numbers on who is ready to go tonight?"

"That sounds great. Thank you," he said, hugging her. "Eliana? Would you like to join me?" he asked, taking her hand as he stepped away from Delilah.

"I would love to," she said.

As they followed her mother back outside, Eliana's heart started to race. The thought of meeting Graham's family seemed like a big step, but she tried to convince herself it wasn't. Graham squeezed her sweating hand and smiled at her when she looked up at him. The group continued to walk in silence for several minutes until they reached a decently sized home with a large plot of land behind it.

"Rose!" Delilah called out to an elderly woman in the field.

"Delilah!" she turned around, smiling. "What can I do for you?" she asked happily, leaving a streak of dirt as she tried to wipe the sweat from her forehead.

"I have someone that I think you'll want to talk to," Delilah said, grabbing Graham's arm and pulling him around in front of her.

"Oh?" she said, wiping some dirt from her hands and coming closer to the three.

"Rose, this is your nephew, Graham. Your brother's son."

"My wha —?" she paused, her eyes scrutinizing him. "You sure have aged well, young man, haven't you?"

"Yes, Ma'am. With the help of a bit of magic, I could freeze my aging for about twenty years," he informed her.

"Interesting," Rose said, staring at him. "You have your father's eyes."

Eliana covered up her laugh with a cough, and all three people frowned at her. She put a hand up and shook her head, making noises instead of saying actual words. An explanation about those golden eyes was not something she felt like sharing at that particular moment.

"Well, I need to go off and collect some information from everyone. I'll be back to check on you guys in a bit!" Delilah said, hugging Rose.

"Thanks, Delilah! See you soon. Would you two join me inside?" Rose asked the pair.

"We would love to!" Graham replied.

The simple home was inviting from the moment they stepped through the doorway. Rose shuffled around the room as they sat on the cozy couch. She also offered them various drinks and snacks, eventually settling in next to them.

"What's your name, dear?" Rose asked.

"Eliana. I'm the daughter of Delilah and Scott. It's nice to meet you," she said, shaking the woman's hand.

"Ah, yes. I see their features on your face! How did you meet my nephew?" Rose asked with a coy smile.

"Well, actually, he's my mom's best friend," Eliana said, blushing.

"Okay. So, what brings you two to my doorstep?" Rose asked with little emotion.

"Well, I was trying to get a hold of you earlier today. My father... Ummm. Your b... brother passed away late last night. I know your relationship wasn't always great, but I thought we could try to mend things. It would be great to have more family back home, and honestly, I wouldn't mind the extra help. I'm not sure I'm cut out to rule a kingdom alone. I know that's a lot to ask, especially when you guys don't even know me, and my father treated you so poorly, but if you would at least attend his memorial. It would really mean a lot to me," Graham replied in a respectful tone.

"Your father did a lot to this family," she replied icily. "He caused us a lot of pain. Mother and Father were heartbroken when he took over as king and kicked us all out. We did our best to keep up with everything happening back home, but eventually, it became too difficult. The Darkness started coming after us. They brought us here, and we did everything we could to ward them off. We didn't know that Sebastian had already manipulated two of my grandsons—"

"Cole and Davey," Graham interrupted.

"You know them?" she asked, her anger faltering.

"Yeah. Eliana actually saved them earlier. They're back at the castle," he said.

Rose paused to analyze Eliana a bit. "Well, it sounds like we'll need a few rooms in the castle then," Rose replied brightly after a few seconds. "I'm not sure what the rest of the family will say, but I would like to help you, and possibly your friend, as much as I can."

"Thank you. This means to me more than anything. I sincerely hope we can mend this family," he shifted and hugged his aunt.

"Of course, my dear child," she said, gently returning the hug. "I suppose it would be wrong of any of us to hold your father's transgressions against you without at least giving you a chance. Besides, if you were best friends with Delilah growing up, I doubt you could be that terrible."

They all laughed, and Eliana felt like she could loosen up a bit. As much as she wanted to trust this woman, she was worried about the bite of some of her words. She had no idea what the extent of the damage the late king caused, and there were too many unspoken words in the silences that kept her on edge.

"Where's the rest of the family?" Graham asked as he settled by Eliana again.

"Well, your uncle Jackson, the stubborn old man, went off to help some of the older families pack up. Our two daughters, Mae and Lina, are with their families. Mae and Jude had one daughter, Molly. She married Samson, and they had twins, Eli and Jess. Lina and her husband, Mark, have had some struggles since their boys were taken by The Darkness. They tend to keep secluded from the rest of us, but I'm sure hearing that Cole and Davey are alive will help soothe their pain," Rose explained.

"Wait, you're all here?!" Graham exclaimed.

"We are. We all lived together. My brother, God rest his soul, and his wife moved further away. I almost wish we would have followed," she replied, her eyes glazing over.

"Um, Aunt Rose?" Graham started.

"Yes, dear?"

"There's probably something else you should be aware of before we head back," Graham paused.

"Well, on with it, child!" Rose demanded.

Eliana sharply glanced at the woman, feeling protective of Graham as Rose spoke to him.

"Cole and Davey...," he started, stumbling over his words for a moment. "The way The Darkness exists worked differently than here or back home. Time moves differently. Neither of them has aged since they were taken."

"I see," Rose said.

"Anyway," Graham said as he shifted awkwardly after a pregnant pause, "I think it's safe to assume that you should let the rest of the family know the news on your own. We can meet up in the morning for breakfast before I address the people. I'm not entirely sure if Cole and Davey are going to be okay, so they're in a cell back home. But we can let them stay with their parents tonight as long as you're okay with Eliana adding some protection to the door."

"Yes. I think it's best I talk to everyone alone, especially Lina. I'd love to say there aren't any hard feelings in any of this, but there are. When we found out that you ran and deserted your people—"

"You lost all hope and became blinded by anger?" Eliana interrupted, hoping that this would explain the reason Rose was harsh towards Graham.

Rose looked at Eliana with a subtle offense for a moment, then her face relaxed, and she spoke again.

"Yes, actually," she answered before turning back to Graham. "I knew your mother. We used to be close growing up. I'm sorry you didn't have more time with her; she was a kind soul. What she saw in my brother was lost to the rest of us. We were all hoping that you would be the one to set things right, but when we heard you took off... Everything just seemed lost."

"I'm sorry he was so unkind to you all. I didn't have the best relationship with him, either," Graham practically whispered.

"You know, Claude, your father, wasn't necessarily cruel growing up, but his words were. The way he would talk to people having magic," she shook her head. "It was almost scary, yet sometimes I would catch the pain in his eyes when he thought no one was looking. Our parents were often too busy to see how he truly was towards those with magic.

My dad was convinced that he was just practicing taking on the role of a king at a young age by not even showing leniency to his own family." Eliana could see anger replacing the pain in her eyes. "Your father was given full control as a king far too early. Then he banished us. He said that we were only sticking around to rub it in that we had magic, and he didn't."

"I... am sorry. It must be horrible being deserted by the person you cared for so much," Eliana said when Rose paused for a moment to wipe a tear.

"It was. We never meant to hurt him, but he did on purpose. I just hope that you weren't treated as poorly, Graham," she said, reaching out to place her hand on his.

"He didn't know that I had magic for a long time. My mother protected me with a necklace that dampened it. I also tried to be secretive when I started training with Delilah."

"I remember that necklace," Rose chimed in. "Your mother was wearing it when she was found after her parents were taken by The Darkness. I think it was the last thing her parents did to protect her. She only ever removed it to shower."

Graham sat back against the couch, an unfocused look in his eyes. Eliana shifted her body so that she could reach out to comfort him. She let him process the information he was learning about everything and turned to talk to Rose while clinging to Graham's hand tightly.

"Did your family know what the statue in the garden was capable of?" Eliana asked.

Rose frowned.

"Capable of?"

"Your brother found a crystal with a note in the tree. It instructed how to summon The Darkness. The crystal provided whoever read the words with magic to cast the spell, even if they didn't have magic," Eliana explained.

"But how do you know all of this?" Rose asked.

"He left me a letter," Graham spoke, leaning forward to join the conversation again.

"Oh?" Rose encouraged him when he stopped talking again.

"He was angry when he discovered my mother had magic, even

though her magic saved us both. She had removed the necklace when she gave birth to me, unknowingly allowing her magic to flow," he whispered. "My father was livid when he watched it happen. He stormed out to the garden and started throwing rocks, which knocked out the knot in the tree and discovered the crystal with the spell inside and used them. When Sebastian came to him in his vulnerable state, any hope that might have existed of him not being completely against magic ended."

"How can you know that's the truth?" Rose asked.

"What reason would he have to lie to me when he knew he was dying?" Graham replied with a shrug.

"Graham," Eliana quickly said before anyone else could talk, "do you think that Sebastian was poisoning your father the way he poisoned your mother?"

"What would make you think that?" he asked.

"Well, your father knew he was dying, but he wasn't that old. So, what made him so sick? I mean, it kind of makes sense that Sebastian would be mad at him for stopping his attacks... Right?" she finished hesitantly.

"I don't know. That's a lot of speculation, but I guess it's possible. I don't even know for sure what was wrong with him. While I kept an eye on things, I was only able to receive bits of information. When I caught him on the cameras, he never really showed any signs of frailty, so I just kind of assumed that he was making it seem worse so that he could stay out of the eye of the public more," he replied with a sigh.

Eliana wrapped her arms tightly around Graham for a moment, then pulled away to kiss him on the cheek. He turned to smile at her for a moment, then turned back to Rose.

"I think maybe it's time for us to head back and get everything ready for those arriving tonight. I hope that we can all get to know each other more. Please make sure that Lina and Mark understand that Cole and Davey are being held in a cell for their safety. If you want to reach me at any time, here's my number," he said as he pulled out a card with his information on it and handed it to her.

"Thank you, dear. I'm sure they'll come to understand. The most important thing will be for them to see their children again. Even if the rest of us don't make it back tonight, I think they will probably go eventually. I can't guarantee that they will want to stay, but I know that if someone had found my children, I would go to them immediately."

"Of course," Graham said, standing to hug his aunt. "I really appreciate your kindness and willingness in this. Thank you."

"I've seen enough ugliness to last me several lifetimes," she replied, placing a hand on his cheek as they separated. "Don't let your father's mistakes drive you. Let your real self lead the way."

"Thank you," he replied.

Eliana saw a tear escape the corner of his eye before he quickly turned to wipe it away. She smiled and took his free hand, squeezing it gently. Rose led them back to the door and saw them out, giving them each one last hug before they left. When they had walked a reasonable distance away from the house, Graham spoke again.

"Let's find your mother, then head back home."

"Alright," Eliana replied, fighting the urge to ask him more questions.

The two silently made their way through the town, and after a few turns and weaves, they ran into Delilah again.

"Perfect!" Delilah shouted. "I was just heading back to you two. Here's the list of names. I made notes of who is ready to head back tonight and who would rather come in the daylight so they can see what it is they're getting into. It's going to be about half, so Scott and I will probably stay until the rest are ready to head there tomorrow."

"Thank you, Delilah. This is extremely helpful. Do you think you'll need help getting them home?" Graham asked.

"Yes, I think we will need help with both groups," she replied.

"Alright. How long do you think before the group is ready tonight?" he asked.

"I'd say we probably need an hour or two. I'll stop by with Scott to get you before we bring everyone. I need to make sure we're not too rusty traveling between lands before we try to take a group back with us," she replied.

"Sure, sure. We can do that," Graham smiled.

"We'll see you soon, Mom," Eliana spoke up as she stepped over to hug her mother.

"Yes," she said, smiling as they pulled away. "You two be safe and try to get some rest."

"We will," Eliana replied, stepping away from the scuttles of humans.

"Shall we?" Graham asked Eliana when they reached a quiet area.

"I suppose we should," she said, patting her less full stomach.

Graham laughed and took her hand.

CHAPTER THIRTY-SIX

Graham and Eliana arrived back in the dining hall. All the food and plates had been cleared, and there was an eerie quiet. Graham quickly pulled out his phone, jumping when a hand squeezed his shoulder from the opposite side of Eliana.

"Oh!" Felicity laughed gently as she jumped, too.

"Felicity!" he replied with a laugh. "I was just about to call you. I have a list of the people that are planning to come here tonight. If we don't have enough space, Delilah and Scott said we could use their home."

"Let me see," Felicity said, holding out her hand.

"Oh! And I found my aunt. She was hiding with Delilah and Scott, but she and the rest of her family should be coming a bit later," Graham recalled.

"Perfect! Have you called your uncle's wife?" Felicity asked.

"Not yet," Graham replied. "I suppose I could do that before we take care of a few other things. Has there been any trouble downstairs?" he asked.

"Not that I'm aware of," Felicity replied. "Go take care of what you need. I can get spaces started up. I'll send Louisa a message to make sure there are some rooms ready over there, as well."

"Perfect. Thank you. Please excuse me while I make a quick call," Graham said, heading off into one of the side rooms.

He spent longer than he cared to admit simply staring at his phone, working himself up to make the call. When no one answered, he wasn't sure if he felt relieved or upset. After leaving a lengthy voicemail followed up by an even more verbose text, he sighed and made his way back.

When he re-entered the dining space, he found Eliana alone, staring up at the massive chandelier that hung at the center of the table. Taking in her sense of awe, he tiptoed back to her. A warmth took over him as he observed her revel in the pure beauty of light. When he got close to her, she glanced sideways at him for a moment before she smiled back at the fixture.

"What?" she asked, keeping her face up.

"Just admiring. Felicity head off to prep the rooms?" he asked.

"She did. The silence was nice," she said before turning to Graham with a frown. "What if this all blows up in our faces? What if none of these people are actually good? I want so badly to believe it's over, but I just don't know if I can trust any of this yet," she finished with a sigh, staring at the void.

"Honestly, I'm struggling a bit with it all, too, even with my Aunt Rose. I was worried about some of what she was saying, and I saw you scrutinizing her," he laughed gently.

"Oh... I thought I was subtle," she grimaced.

"You were, but the electricity you were putting off tickled the side of my body."

She shrugged.

"Old habits die hard," she said nonchalantly.

Graham gave a hearty laugh.

"What!? I can't believe you haven't fully let go of your old ways! It's almost been half a day now!" he half-shouted sarcastically.

Eliana pouted at him, crossing her arms. He laughed at her, pulling her into a tight hug and kissing her.

"I'm glad I have you to help me get through this," he whispered.

"You are pretty lucky, eh?" she joked, returning the hug.

Graham smiled but didn't release his hold on her. He appreciated her ability to joke, but he also wanted to have this moment just to treasure her. Taking in a deeper breath, he absorbed her scent. With one last squeeze, he finally released her.

"Very lucky," he said in a deadly serious tone.

She blushed and looked away, causing him to laugh yet again.

"Oh," she replied, scratching her head and looking anywhere but at Graham. "I feel the same way."

"As you should!" he said, trying to break the tension.

She smirked at him, rolling her eyes dramatically.

"Come. Let's go see if Cole and Davey are willing to talk to us," he said, taking her hand.

The silent walk seemed to move too quickly as Graham observed Eliana admiring the space more while they walked through. Her fascination forced him to notice the beauty that was around him in a way that he had forgotten. When they reached the door, Felipe was reading a book, unaware of the constant blast of magic that was happening on the other side of the wall. Eliana squeezed Graham's hand, and he quickly nodded to her.

"Hey, Felipe," Graham said with a smile. "How's everything going?"

"Hello, Sir! It's all been fine. They're a quiet bunch. Almost feels like I don't need to be here at all," he said with a laugh.

Graham laughed with him.

"Eliana and I are going to head in there for a bit. Could you do me a favor and make sure Felicity doesn't need extra help? I will send you a message when we're done," Graham said calmly while his palm started to sweat into Eliana's.

"Not a problem. Anything you need. I'll be back as quick as I can when you need me," Felipe said with a slight bow.

Graham nodded his head and clenched his jaw as he smiled, watching the man walk away intently.

"Elia—"

"I'm on it," she interrupted.

In a blink, they were both on the other side of the door in front of Jeb's cell. Graham heard the man grunting, followed by an almost imperceptible bang on the door. It was as if he had attached a silencer to his magic to dampen the sound of his attempt to escape.

"Help me freeze him," Eliana quickly whispered.

Their magic traveled through the air, swirling through the bars before slamming into Jeb's body. The man growled but seemed unable to move. Graham's instincts had been correct that Jeb wasn't really frozen before. With a huff, Eliana swung the door open, and the pair walked through.

"Grab him," Graham said.

In a blink, they were back in the lab. Graham tossed Jeb further into the room and sealed the door behind them. Eliana stayed by his side as they went to the other side of the glass room, where they saved Francisco.

"What's he doing here?!" Francisco shouted.

"Okay, well, that answers my first question. Will this room hold him if it can hold The Darkness?" Graham asked quickly.

"Well, yeah, but weren't you using stored magic to hold The Darkness in there?"

"I suppose. If he breaks out of that, he shouldn't be able to escape. Probably," Graham replied.

"Will I be safe in here?" Francisco asked.

"I'll tell you in a moment," Graham said truthfully. "Tell me about him."

"He was Sebastian's first follower. He took on The Darkness with his power. Like Sebastian, he could control the entity more than it controlled him. I'm honestly surprised he let you capture him," Francisco said, never taking his eyes off the frozen man.

"Yeah, I think Jeb thought it would help him somehow."

"Graham, should we let him live? I mean, we didn't give Sebastian a second thought, and Jeb seems like he's basically the same," Eliana chimed in.

"I don't know. Francisco, do you know how often he was involved with hurting people?"

Francisco shook his head.

"I think he was more involved with the manipulation rather than the killing, but I honestly can't be sure," he replied.

Graham and Eliana sighed in unison.

"Alright. Well, I can't justify destroying Jeb without knowing the extent of damage that he's caused. Being powerful doesn't necessarily mean that he's evil." Graham moved away. His muscles tightened. "Francisco, do you feel comfortable staying in here still, or do you want me to set up another space for you?" Graham asked.

"No. I want to stay here, but I need you to seal the exits," Francisco requested.

"What? No. That could be your death!" Graham shouted.

"It could be," Francisco said solemnly. "But it could also be my chance to start redeeming myself. If I can talk to Jeb and learn more about all of this, maybe I can extract the good from it all."

Graham sighed in frustration. He didn't want to leave his friend alone with someone who seemed dangerous, but at the same time, he didn't even know if Francisco was still dangerous.

"Would it do any good to try and fight you on this?" Graham asked.

"Not one bit," Francisco replied.

Graham sighed loudly.

"Fine, but Eliana and I are going to fortify all of the doors. Okay?"

"Sure. I can agree with that. And Graham?" Francisco started.

"Yeah?" Graham replied.

"Thank you for everything you've done for me. I hope to see you again soon."

"You will!" Graham said. "I might have found you a few people to guide magic here! So, don't you go getting yourself killed, alright?" he said louder than intended.

"I'll do my best," Francisco replied, chuckling.

"Thanks, old friend," Graham said, hugging him tightly. "Alright, Eliana. Let's seal off these doors and get back."

Eliana nodded but said nothing. The two quickly went through the room, intertwining their magic to fortify the surrounding space. When they reached the main door, Graham looked at Francisco once more and nodded. Francisco smiled at them as the door closed down. With one last blast of magic, space was fully sealed off. Graham closed his eyes for a moment, trying not to let his thoughts go to the worst-case scenario, then turned to Eliana.

"Let's get back to the others," smiling tersely.

"Alright," she said, taking his hand.

Another blink, and they were back home looking at the cells they had left not long before. Without a word, they both went to Cole and Davey. Graham opened the door, knocking on it as they entered to announce their presence. Cole whipped his head up to look at them.

"Why are you back?" he asked wearily.

"I just wanted to make sure you're comfortable," he paused for a moment. "And to let you know your parents should be coming tonight or tomorrow. We still don't know the full effects of The Darkness on you, but I think you should be safe to stay with them with some supervision when they get here."

"Our parents?! Cole shouted, waking his brother.

"Your mother is my cousin. Your grandmother is my aunt. This land, this castle, is your home should you want to stay," Graham explained to the young men.

"Oooooooh. You're *that* Graham," Davey said with a smirk.

"Yes, I suppose I am," he replied with a frown as the young men cackled. "Anyway, I just wanted to let you know, but I will be keeping you down here until they arrive. I don't have time to monitor you right now. Sorry."

"Eh, no big deal," Cole replied with a shrug. "I ain't got nothin' better to do but sleep anyhow."

Graham laughed gently. He was glad that they were in better spirits now. Like Francisco, the longer they were separated from their entity, the less evil took over their personality.

"I'll have to take your word for it. I look forward to getting to know you both soon. Rest well," Graham responded with a genuine smile.

"Sure thing, boss," Davey said, flopping back down. "Catch ya later."

Graham looked over when Eliana laughed and shrugged. He smiled with a quick wink as they made their way out of the cell, locking the door behind them. Pulling out his phone, Graham messaged Felipe, asking him to return.

"Felipe is on his way. Let's get out of here," he said to Eliana.

"Can do."

In a blink, they were back on the other side of the wall, only having to wait a few minutes before Felipe came back.

"Sorry! I'm here!" Felipe said, out of breath.

"Did you run all the way?" Eliana asked with a laugh.

"Kind of, Ma'am," he said with a half-smile.

"Well, that wasn't necessary, but I'm glad you're back. Thank you again. Please let me know if you need someone to replace you," Graham said.

"I will, Sir," he replied with a subtle nod.

CHAPTER THIRTY-SEVEN

When Eliana and Graham arrived in the primary space, Eliana's parents were waiting for them.

"Oh," Eliana started. "Has it already been that long?" she asked.

Her mother laughed.

"We're early. The group tonight didn't want to wait much later. Do you have any rooms ready?" she asked.

"I've got about six rooms ready here, and Louisa has four," Felicity answered as she came down the hall.

"Oh! Hello," Delilah smiled. "Thank you! I'm—"

"Delilah, yes. I'm Felicity, and you're Scott," she responded with a smirk.

"Sorry," Delilah blushed. "I didn't think you'd recognize me."

"Of course I do!" Felicity replied, going in for a hug.

Eliana laughed at the older woman who had yet to falter when she saw a face.

"Well, it's good to see you again. Thank you for getting rooms ready," Delilah said with a smile as they separated from the hug.

"It's the least I can do! I had some extra snacks prepared in the kitchen, as well. Did you and Scott want to grab a quick bite before you get everyone?" Felicity asked.

"Oh, no. I think we'll wait to eat with everyone else," Delilah replied.

"Alright. You just have Graham let me know if you need anything else," she smiled.

"We will," Delilah smiled back.

"When did you want to head back?" Eliana inquired.

"Now, if you're ready," her mother replied.

"Sure. We can do that," Graham chimed in. "Felicity, would you mind hanging out in this general area to assist when we return?"

"Not a problem, Sir," she beamed back, gazing at him.

"What?" Graham asked her.

Eliana quietly laughed at the frown that had taken over his face.

"It's so nice to see you in charge," she replied proudly.

Graham blushed.

"Come on. Let's not leave those people to wait any longer," Eliana interjected, taking her mother and Graham's hands.

Graham stiffened slightly, puffing up his chest as Delilah reached for Scott's hand.

"Yes. Let us take leave!" Graham shouted playfully, recovering quickly.

Eliana chuckled, shaking her head, then the next moment, they were back where her parents had spent far too long.

"Who —?" Eliana started, interrupted by her father's excitement.

"Whew!" her father exclaimed. "I was worried I wouldn't still be able to do that!"

"I knew you'd be able to, honey," Delilah said with a smile, placing a gentle kiss on his cheek.

"So, all four of us can take people then?" Eliana confirmed.

"Seems like it!" her mother replied.

"Great! Who all is going back with us?" Graham asked.

"Us," said a voice from behind them.

"Ah! So, I see!" Graham animatedly replied as he turned around to see a group of about thirty people. "Well, alright, then. I'm Graham, and this is Eliana. If you guys could split off into groups, we'll bring you to our home. Eliana and I can do larger groups. I think Scott and Delilah will probably want to keep it limited to a few people. Am I correct?" he said, directing his question to his friends.

"Yes. I would say we could probably do four or five each. I don't want to risk more than that," Delilah replied.

"Alright. For those of you who have never traveled this way, the best thing you can do is try to relax as much as possible. You'll probably feel a little dizzy and possibly nauseated when we arrive, but that's perfectly normal. It will pass. Is everyone ready?" Graham asked.

The surrounding crowd murmured, but it sounded to Eliana that there was a consensus of an agreement to being ready. When a decent-sized group formed around her, she looked them each in the eyes and smiled.

"Hello. My name is Eliana. I'm the daughter of Delilah and Scott, and I promise to take care of each of you. Hold each other; make some sort of contact. I will send my magic through the chain of connections to guide us all back to Placata Montis. You all good?" she asked.

Most of the group seemed uncertain still. Their eyes darted quietly to the other people in the group. One young girl finally spoke up for the group.

"Oh my gosh, yes. Yes, is what they mean."

Eliana laughed at the girl's dramatic eye roll, whom she guessed was probably about fourteen or fifteen.

"Thank you...." Eliana paused, waiting for a name.

"Shoshana," the girl replied, releasing her grip with one hand to shake Eliana's.

"Shoshana. Excellent. Thank you," Eliana replied, taking the hand closest to her own. "Everyone, take a deep breath with me," she said as she loudly inhaled. "And let it slowly out," she said, moving to the middle of the group during the exhale.

"Whoaaaaaaa," a small boy exclaimed a moment later. "A CASTLE!" he shouted shortly after.

Eliana laughed.

"Yup. We are here... In the castle," she acknowledged.

There were some mumbles and looking around, but no one seemed to have suffered from the quick trip. As the group was greeted by Felicity, Graham and Delilah's groups arrived almost simultaneously.

Graham looked happy seeing everyone safe and sound. But a quiet voice somewhere in the crowd grabbed his attention.

"Graham?"

"Yes?" he replied.

Eliana watched as a middle-aged woman came through the crowd. Her chestnut hair had streaks of grey blended in. A man with salted black hair followed closely behind her. As the pair got closer, Eliana saw the dark circles that encased their reddened eyes.

"You have our boys?" she asked in a shaky voice.

"Lina and Mark, I presume? Yes, we have Cole and Davey. They're safe and back to normal as far as we know," he replied gently.

Lina burst into tears, throwing herself into the comfort of her husband's arms. Eliana felt her eyes tear up as she watched life return to their faces. A moment later, Lina turned to throw herself into Eliana's arms and then Graham's.

"Thank you both. For everything you've done. My mother and Delilah told me what you've sacrificed over the years. I'm so grateful for you," she finished with a sob as she turned back to her husband.

Graham gave a nod to Mark and then cleared his throat.

"Of course. It's the least I could do for family."

Eliana smiled, stepping away to give them a few moments while she made her rounds to check on everyone else.

"Where's Dad?" she asked her mother quietly.

"He had someone who wasn't sure they wanted to come tonight. He was telling them they didn't have to come now, but the rest of their family was. He said just to go on ahead. I wouldn't worry for a few more minutes," she said, squeezing Eliana's shoulder.

"Alright...." a worried approval came out.

Eliana watched as Felicity and a few other workers came to help guide the group to the kitchen. At the mention of snacks, not one person said no to the offer. Delilah joined them, leaving Graham and Eliana behind to wait for Scott.

"Do you think he's ok?" she asked Graham.

"I know he is," Graham said, brushing her hair back.

She nodded at the ground, frowning.

"Yeah, I'm sure you're right."

Graham laughed and pulled her into a hug. The comfort of his warmth removed all negative thoughts from her mind. She sighed and relaxed into him. This was something she could get used to. As she squeezed him tighter, she felt a breeze behind her.

"Dad!" she said as she turned around.

"Am I late enough to be fashionable still?" he laughed.

"Hmmm. I guess I'll allow it. Is everything good? Everyone alright?" she asked.

"We're fine," a young man that looked to be in his late teens replied curtly.

"Daaaaaaaad. I'm hungry!" a small boy said, pulling on another man's arm.

"Well, we have just the thing to fix that! There are snacks in the kitchen!" Eliana replied.

"I know where it is," Scott said. "I'll take them."

Eliana nodded to him and let her eyes fall on Lina and Mark. They were still standing quietly at the edge of the room.

"I assume you want to just see your boys?" Graham asked.

"Yes, please," Lina sniffled.

"Follow us," Graham answered, taking Eliana's hand.

"Is the rest of your family coming tomorrow?" Eliana asked to fill the awkward silence.

She received a stiff nod in return but no other words. The tension during the rest of the quiet trek made it hard for Eliana to not just run down to the cell where the two boys were. Luckily, the walk was short.

"Oh, hello, Sir," Felipe said, quickly coming to standing when the group came close.

"These are the parents of two people we've got in here. We're just going to bring them through the door to see them," Graham said.

Eliana, catching his oddly worded response, removed the magic barrier from the door. She had felt no magic since they had gotten close to the cells, so she figured the danger of being attacked was low. When Felipe stepped aside, Graham opened the door and led the group in. Moving to the cell with Cole and Davey, Graham knocked, then opened the door.

Lina and Mark didn't even wait to see if these were their boys; they simply ran in, shouting excitedly through their tears.

"Let's just give them a moment," Graham said quietly while leaving them behind.

Eliana nodded, watching the smile that pulled at Graham's lips.

"I hope this all works out," she mumbled.

"Me too. I've got a good feeling about it, so I'm going to trust it," Graham smiled.

"Can we bring them up to our room?" Lina asked, clinging to her sons as they headed to the entrance.

"Yes, but we're going to put up a barrier to just make sure that everyone is safe," Graham replied.

"Yes, yes. That's fine," Lina replied between the kisses she was attacking her sons with.

"Mooooooooooom," the boys shouted in unison.

Graham laughed heartily, his eyes twinkling with joy.

"Great. Li, will you grab them some snacks while I take them to their room? Have Felicity bring you to the twin connecting room. She'll know what that means."

"If you say so," Eliana replied with uncertainty.

Graham laughed again.

"Felipe can take you to the kitchen. Felicity should still be there."

"Alright. I'll let Felicity know about the rooms. See you guys soon," she said, leaning in to kiss Graham on the cheek.

Before she could pull away, he pulled her in for a tight hug, returning a kiss on the top of her head.

"Be safe," he whispered into her ear.

She squeezed him, then whispered back.

"You, too."

With one more frown, Eliana looked at Graham's cousins. Then she stepped outside the door to where Felipe sat.

"Can you show me to the kitchen, please? Graham said he'd hang out down here to watch things while you run me over there," she said, doing her best to not come across as demanding.

"I sure can, Ma'am!" he said with a smile.

"Great. Thank you. And please, call me Li," she smiled back.

"That'll take some work, Ma'am. My father trained me to always address a lady of the castle with complete respect, but if that's what you prefer, I can put in the work," Felipe replied, unbothered by her request.

"It would be most appreciated, Sir," she quipped back with a wink.

He chuckled, his eyes sparkling brightly with joy.

During the rest of the short walk up the stairs and down a hallway, Felipe never stopped talking. He told stories about how his father had worked in the castle before he passed when Felipe was just thirteen, and he remembered Graham always making him feel welcome. His face was wildly animated when he spoke about what an influential leader Graham was before he left and what a fantastic leader he would make now.

"Anyway," he said, finally taking a breath, "this is the kitchen. I hope you find everything you need, Li," he finished with a subtle bow.

"Thank you, Felipe. I can tell we're going to be great friends."

He blushed, bowing again, then quickly making his way back to Graham.

She watched for him for a moment with a broad smile as he walked back down the hallway, wondering what he had been told her title was. Or if he had even been told anything at all. Either way, if she chose this life, that sort of acknowledgment would have to be something that she got used to. Sighing quietly, she turned her attention back to the door to the kitchen.

Letting her hand rest on the intricately designed doorknob, she placed a smile on her face, turned the handle, and pushed it open. The room was filled with people, but none of them paid much attention to her. Laughter and joyful conversations were taking over every corner of the space. Taking a moment to let her senses adjust, she eventually found the face of someone she loved.

"Mom!" she shouted over the waves of noise that vibrated her ears.

When her mother didn't respond, she stepped closer and tried again.

"MOM!" she shouted with all her strength.

Still, her mother did not respond to her.

"DELILAH!" she tried one last time from just a few feet away.

"Eliana!" her mother finally responded, turning to hug her.

"Do you know where Felicity is?" Eliana asked.

"I do! Please excuse me," she added, touching the arm of the woman she had been standing with.

"Oh, sorry," Eliana said to the woman. "I didn't realize you two were talking."

"Not a problem, Ma'am. You two go take care of what you need," the woman smiled.

"Thank you," Eliana replied sincerely.

"This way," her mother said, wrapping her palm around Eliana's elbow.

As they walked through the kitchen, Eliana compared it to the one back at Graham's other home. Though the one in the castle was more substantial, it wasn't nearly as elegant as what had been built for the home that he had designed for his tastes. She smiled to herself as she analyzed the other house through her memories, realizing now how much of its quirkiness was just a representation of who he was.

Eliana was torn from her thoughts when her ears suddenly stopped vibrating from the noise. She observed that they had turned down a corridor that was off the central part of the kitchen.

"She's just through here," her mother informed, seeming relieved to be able to not shout.

"Great," Eliana replied, still trapped in thoughts of Graham.

Her mother opened a massive wooden door that led to the exact place where Eliana and Graham had eaten earlier. Eliana chucked.

"What?" her mother asked.

"I don't know why Graham didn't just tell me that the kitchen was off the room that we ate earlier," she said.

"Well, he probably didn't know that Felicity would be back here. It is much quicker to go from the hallway you entered if someone is in the kitchen, and there are quite a few doors off the corridor to choose from," Delilah stated.

"Eliana! Delilah! What can I do for you two?" Felicity walked over to the doorway where they still stood.

"Hey, Felicity," Eliana replied. "I'm supposed to see if we can get some snacks and bring them to the 'twin... connecting room,'" she said with air quotes.

Felicity laughed at the explanation.

"We can do that. Let's grab a few things, and I will take you there."

"Did you want to join us, Mom?" Eliana asked.

"I'd better stay with the group. We should probably start bringing them to their rooms soon, anyway. Once we get everyone settled, your father and I will head back to sleep and see if anyone else is ready to come in the morning," Her mother said while turning back.

Eliana nodded.

"Okay. Are you going to be back in time for Graham's speech?" she asked.

"His speech?" her mother asked.

"He's going to talk to the people and announce that he will step into his role as the king. It would be nice if the rest of his family could be there to see that," she replied quietly.

"We will be here. What time?" her mother asked.

"Late morning," Eliana clarified.

"Alright. I'll talk to them tonight and make sure we get here in time," Delilah smiled.

"Thanks, Mom."

With one more quick hug, Delilah made her way back down the corridor, leaving Eliana alone with Felicity.

"Come on, dear. Let's make our way to the room you need."

"Do you need any help?" Eliana asked as she noticed an enormous basket in Felicity's hands.

"I've got it. I'm stronger than this old skin claims," Felicity smirked.

Eliana laughed as she followed, expecting to go back through the kitchen, but instead was led down a different corridor than the dining room. After a dozen or so steps, Felicity stopped in front of a door and pulled out a key.

"Don't want anyone wandering into an occupied room accidentally from the kitchen," Felicity said without turning around.

Eliana laughed lightly, unsure of what to say in response. Once they had both entered the room, Felicity locked the door again behind her.

"Best not make that a door anyone will use again," she said with a knowing nod at Eliana.

Eliana frowned at her but quietly used her magic to seal the door. The room had two gigantic beds, three dressers, a couch, two sitting chairs, and four other entries. She could see that one led to a bathroom, but the other three were closed. She followed Felicity further into the room, watching as she set the food down on the table. Before she could ask anything, a knock came from one of the three unknown doors.

"Come on in," Felicity called out.

The door opened, followed a moment later by Graham's smiling, floating head.

"Everything ready in here?" he asked.

"Almost," Eliana replied, sealing the remaining two doors.

She nodded, and he responded with a wink before opening the door all the way.

"Felicity, these are my cousins Lina and Mark and their children, Cole and Davey. They'll be staying in here all night. Eliana and I will grab them for breakfast in the morning," Graham said carefully.

"Sounds good. I'll leave you the keys for when the rest of your family comes," she replied, giving him the ring of keys, including the one she used to unlock the back door. "Food is on the table. Towels are in the washroom. There are some different sizes of clean clothes in the dressers. If you need water, there are cups next to the sink. If there isn't anything else, I'll be on my way," she added.

"Thank you," multiple voices replied.

She gave a satisfied nod, then headed towards the door that the group had come through.

"Alright, if you think there is anything else you might need outside of this room, let me know now. Otherwise, we're going to seal the doors," Graham said as soon as she closed the door.

"I think we'll be good. I don't see us needing anything else for the night. I think we'll probably just want to catch up and rest," Lina replied, squeezing Cole and Davey's hands.

She got some nods of agreement but no verbal response aside from that.

"Don't hesitate to give me a call if you need anything before morning," Graham said.

"Thank you," Mark replied as he reached out to shake Graham's hand.

"Goodnight," Eliana chimed in.

"Goodnight, Queeny," Davey said with a smirk.

Eliana blushed and rushed out the door, catching the smile pulling at Graham's lips. As he locked it with the key, she used her magic to seal the last of the exits. The two stood silently in front of the door for a moment, their hands interlocking. Behind them, the sound of people coming down the hallways filled the air, but no one came by where they stood.

"Hmm," Eliana said quietly.

"It's just noise traveling," Graham laughed. "Would you like to see your room now?" Graham said with a smirk.

"My room?" Eliana asked with a frown as she turned to face him.

Graham laughed, placing a gentle kiss on her lips.

"OUR room," he corrected, rolling his eyes.

CHAPTER THIRTY-EIGHT

Eliana woke the following day to the warmth of the sun kissing her face. With a satisfying stretch, she rolled over to find the space next to her cold and empty. She sat with a start, suddenly wondering if she had simply dreamt the entire night. Her eyes scanned the room, taking note of the story told by the trail of clothing that led to the bed. Flashes of their bodies colliding passed through her mind, and the urgency of her body craving for him started bubbling up again.

She shivered in pleasure and lay back down, giving in to the bed as it begged her to stay with its engulfing warmth. Letting its cloud-like quality support her entire body again, she yawned happily as the silken sheets caressed her naked skin. Her eyes fell closed while her flesh danced along the bed, stimulating her senses and forcing a moan from her lips.

"Shall I give you a moment?" Graham's teasing voice suddenly said.

"OH!" Eliana exclaimed, reactively pulling the sheets to her chin as she sat up.

As she processed that it was just Graham, she relaxed, letting the sheet fall. Before she could make an attempt at seducing him back to bed, her stomach growled loudly at the food he was holding.

"Mmmm," she said, closing her eyes and enjoying the scent. "Felicity made me breakfast in bed?" she asked.

Graham scoffed.

"No, I did!"

Eliana laughed heartily, enjoying the boyish pout that had taken over his face.

"Well, pardon me. I guess I just assumed that a *king* wouldn't be allowed to make food for a strange woman he brought home," she winked.

Graham laughed, shaking his head while he walked over to place the tray on the bed. Eliana scooted back towards the padded headrest, tucking the sheets beneath her arms and flattening out the comforter on her lap. He leaned in and kissed her on the cheek while setting the tray over her, then stood tall again, smiling down at her.

"Will there be anything else you might be needing, m'lady?" he said with a dramatic bow.

Eliana responded with a pout.

"You're not going to stay?"

Graham reached up and traced his thumb along her lips, resting the palm of his hand on her cheek with a gentle sigh.

"I wish I could, but I'm still working on the speech I'll be giving soon. All the information we learned about my father and The Darkness kind of changed my plan to just go out there and talk. I just want to make sure I'm not speaking any of it from a place of resentment, especially since there really hasn't been much time to process any of it."

"I wish you could stay longer, too, but I won't be the one to hold you back from your duties," she replied sincerely.

She settled her hand over his, turning to kiss his palm then placing her face back into his flesh for a moment. With a sigh, she let her arm drop and tilted her head away from his touch. Graham reacted immediately by pulling her face to his for a kiss that ended as quickly as it started. Eliana was surprisingly okay with it. There was no sense of anxiety that it would be the last. Instead, it merely filled her heart with happiness.

"Thank you for breakfast," she whispered. "I'll try to get ready quickly in case you need any help."

"I appreciate that, but there's no need to rush. It's still fairly early."

"Is it?" she asked.

Graham laughed.

"Indeed. It's only 8:43 am."

"Oh," she said with a frown. "What time exactly are you supposed to give your speech?"

"I called to have everyone come by 11. Hopefully, the messages are being received well…." Graham faded off.

"I'm sure they are. Go on and finish up. I'll eat and get cleaned up and dressed, then come find you." Eliana replied gently.

He nodded, seemingly lost in thought.

"Thank you. I'm not sure what I've done to deserve you, but I refuse to question it."

He placed one last kiss atop her head, then made his way back out. As he left the room, Eliana finally looked down at her food. It smelled divine. He had made her some kind of quiche and paired it with a bowl of fruit and tea. The professional presentation was brilliant, making it hard for her to want to eat it. As soon as she placed the first fluffy bite in her mouth, she melted. The smoothness aroused her to finish eating it all in one go. It was the best-tasting breakfast she had eaten in years, if not her entire existence.

Too quickly, Eliana found herself at the end of her meal. She glanced at the last drop of the tea with disappointment, then laid back down to let everything settle for a moment. Turning her head towards the giant window, she watched the birds and squirrels darting around the lush greenery. The beauty of the garden seemed too good to be real.

"Was it always so breathtaking?" she asked a small rabbit that glanced her way.

With a wiggle of its nose, it tilted its head at her before hopping away. A smile pulled at her lips before she accepted the fact that she should get up. With a resigned sigh, she tossed off the covers, her naked flesh responding with a few goosebumps. Shivering, she sprinted her way to the bathroom, grabbing a robe and taking care of all morning essentials.

Once her hair was tidied up a bit, she made her way back into the bedroom. The worn outfit she had felt inadequate for the occasion. Even though she didn't have a title, she couldn't wear something like that as Graham announced that he would take on his role as their king. As she was looking around for something that might be more acceptable, a knock on the door surprised her.

"Come in!" Eliana responded a little more loudly than intended.

"Hello, dear," Felicity said. "Graham mentioned that you might need some fresh clothes to wear, so I asked Louisa to bring some options over. I hope you don't mind."

"It's like you could read my mind! I was just wondering if there was something a little more appropriate for me to wear. Thank you so much!" Eliana replied happily, taking the basket of clothes from her.

"It's nothing, dear. Did you want me to take your old clothes and give them some love?" Felicity asked.

"Could you? That would be great," Eliana smiled.

"Of course. It would be my pleasure. Is there anything else you'll be needing?" she asked.

"I don't think so. Thank you again," Eliana replied.

"Not even a bother. Just give me a holler if you need anything else," Felicity said as she took the old clothes.

"I will."

When Felicity closed the door, Eliana immediately started digging through the clothes that had been chosen for her to pick from. There were some dresses, everyday clothes, a few classy shirts, and a dressier pair of pants. She went to a mirror and held up a few options, eventually going with one of the blouses and the more fashionable pants. Glancing over at the clock, she saw it was now half-past ten.

"Shit," she mumbled, getting dressed as quickly as possible.

With one last glance at herself in the mirror, she nodded and made her way to exit the room. Practically throwing the door open, she nearly walked directly into her parents.

"Whoa! Hi!" she shouted.

Her parents laughed in unison.

"Felicity said we might find you here. We just wanted to let you know we brought the rest of Graham's family. They wanted to come to watch his speech, and we happened to run into him first. So, Graham brought them to Lina, Mark, and the boys," her mother replied.

"Oh. Are you staying?" Eliana asked, trying to hide the concern in her voice.

"Yes. We're going to stay and support him while he gives his speech and then head back to get the last handful of people to where they want to go. They don't all seem like they want to come back here..." Delilah trailed off.

"Oh. Okay. Well, I'm glad his family and you guys are here to support him. He seems pretty nervous about it all. I just hope everyone takes the news well," Eliana responded.

"I'm sure they will. We just wanted to make sure we caught you before you guys went out. Go be with him. He's in the dining room. We'll be cheering you both from the crowd." Her mother brought her in for a hug.

"What she said," her dad chimed in, wrapping his arms around them.

They all laughed, and Eliana was overcome with overwhelming happiness.

"I'm so glad I have you back," she whispered, tears lacing her eyes.

"Oh, honey. We are, too. More than you could know. Now go on," Eliana's mother encouraged, wiping an escaped tear.

With a sniffle and a quick nod, Eliana made her way down the hall, tracing the steps she had taken before to get back to the massive dining hall. When she finally got there, she found Graham talking to himself and pacing. His back was to her, so he didn't notice when she came in and sat down to observe him. After watching him argue with himself about three different sections of his speech, she eventually interjected with some advice.

"You know, I think it was better the way you had it the first time," she said coolly.

"Eliana! How long have you been there?" he asked, startled.

She chuckled.

"Long enough to know that you're going to be great," she replied, standing and walking over to him. "There is no better man to lead these people. You have proven that time and again. You are about to prove that once more when you'll speak your words of truth to them."

Graham took her hands in his own and smiled.

"Thank you. I sure hope you're right."

"Of course I am! Why wouldn't I be?" she quipped back with a wink.

Graham laughed heartily, visibly relaxing. He checked his watch, pulling out a handkerchief to wipe the sweat lining his brow.

"It's almost time," he started, taking a moment to breathe. "We should head outside... Unless you'd rather be with your parents as part of the crowd?" he asked, uncertainty lacing his voice.

"No. I don't want to be anywhere besides right next to you." Eliana squeezed his hands reassuringly.

Graham nodded, taking a deep breath before switching his grip to interlace his fingers with one of her hands. Eliana sent magic to him to ease some of his anxiety as they silently walked to the main entrance of the castle. Graham's muscles tensed as he paused before the door.

"You've got this. I won't leave your side even for a moment." She looked up at him, beaming with pride.

"Thank you," he softly smiled back. "I can only hope that everyone else is as quick to forgive me as you have been."

"Even if they don't at first, I'm sure they will come to understand. I will make sure of it," Eliana assured.

Graham leaned down to kiss her, cupping her neck with his free hand. Their lips separated not long after, and he rested his forehead against hers. She felt his thumb gently caressing her cheek while his breathing fell into rhythm with her own.

"I could have never imagined going through this moment with anyone, but now that you're here with me, I couldn't ever have it any other way. Thank you," he finally said in a gentle voice.

"You're welcome," Eliana choked out, swallowing the tears that fought to come out yet again.

With that, he separated from her, taking one final breath and nodding at the door. Eliana released their hands to smooth out his vest and fix his hair, then smiled brightly at him as she opened the doors.

For a moment, the initial shock of the entire town waiting outside made her freeze, but Graham stood slightly taller as he grabbed her hand and walked out onto the oversized landing.

The crowd almost instantly went quiet as Graham made his way to the edge. Eliana broke their connection and stepped aside, turning to acknowledge him with pride. With a quick smile at her, he took a breath and then beamed proudly at the town. A wave of cheers came from them, and Eliana couldn't help but smile with pure joy. She looked down at the sea of faces cheering at the man they hoped would be their new king. As her focus made its way back to Graham, she saw his eyes tear up slightly as a grin took over his face.

"Thank you! All of you! I can't even begin to describe my relief at your reaction to seeing me again." He finally spoke. "I know I abandoned this town, and I can never apologize enough for that. I can only hope that you now understand that I had to do it to protect you all. Not only were the tests I was completing potentially dangerous to those with magic, but my presence here played a part in the aggressive behavior that The Darkness exhibited. I hope someday you all will come to forgive me, but for now, I will simply do my best to lead you all as your King. That being said, I have some news to tell you all..."

Eliana watched as the crowd responded to Graham's news about accepting his role as King, his father, The Darkness, and Sebastian. Graham told them about the land he had gone to and the work he hoped to help Francisco completely. He acknowledged Eliana, her parents, Felicity, Billy, Felipe, Louisa, and his family and gave a general thanks to a few other names that she didn't catch through the cheers.

"I also ask you to accept our new friends. Show them the same warmth and kindness that you have shown me. Show each other how easy it can be to work together to build the future we all want. I will do my best to find you work that suits your lifestyle and help all of us thrive together. I hope that you will choose to make Placata Montis your home and that it can truly feel like home."

Eliana searched for her parents, knowing they would be near the people they had brought back. The look of hope amongst them filled Eliana with pride. There were still hints of uncertainty from a few of them, but the fact that Graham had captured the hearts of so many so quickly sent her soaring.

"With all that out of the way, I would like to make it clear that anyone and everyone is welcome here. I will do my best not to judge anyone by their differences, and I hope you will do the same. The people that Eliana and I saved from The Darkness may not be capable of pure kindness yet. I don't know if it will last forever, but I want to remind them how magic can be used for good. I want to teach those of you who have the gift of magic how to access your core magic properly. We thought we were protecting ourselves by burying it so deep, but in the end, that core magic saved us all. I know it will be scary, but I promise you it will only provide you more protection should anything ever try to come at us again." Graham paused, giving everyone a moment to digest. Eliana could sense his anxiety before he continued and reached out to him with her magic.

"My one last request for you is to find forgiveness for my father. I am very aware of the terrible things that he did to each of you. I was not immune to his poor behavior, but I do firmly believe that a good man was buried in there. He never faced his demons of feeling inadequate. He was riddled with the fear of not being able to protect his family because he had no magic. He dealt with it poorly, yes, but I don't want to continue with trends of fear and hate. Our differences do not make us lesser or greater than our fellow man; they merely make us who we are. Whether that be different from the group, or the same, I guarantee that there is someone out there who feels the same way you do.

"The things that make you who you are when you feel weak are the same things that will teach you to be strong. My father's battle was with his fears of being alone without magic. That fear consumed him in the same ways that someone who has fought in wars and watched people die would be consumed. Our bodies don't recognize the difference. Your traumas are just as valid as someone else's, and if we can learn to support each other and work through them, we can start to fight the darkness before it becomes its force of evil."

Eliana listened to his words, taken aback by how he had used his father's struggle to bring everyone together positively. His words took her back to her struggles of depression and anger. She had never really acknowledged her emotions since everyone else had it worse than her, or at least she believed that to be the truth. She understood how hard it must be for him to publicly acknowledge all of this; she didn't know if she could have been able to. But he did it, somehow. And it was so eloquent. Listening to him talk about it... was giving her strength more than her core magic to see the validity in her path.

"In two days, there will be a celebration of life for my father." Graham continued. "I want this farewell ceremony to bring us together to recognize all the good in our lives. I want you to use it to be grateful for what your struggles have taught you. Appreciate the differences that made you special. I want you to smile, cry... To live, not just exist. Be your true selves and be okay with that, even if it means going off into a room alone to sit quietly. And until then, if you need to talk to me, I will do my best to be available, but for now, I hope we can all actively practice choosing love over hate. Thank you."

As he finished, Eliana wiped the tears from her eyes, then clapped and cheered as loudly as she could, her shouts quickly swallowed up by the boom of everyone observing Graham's speech. After a quick nod to acknowledge their acceptance, he turned and smiled brightly as he came over to engulf Eliana in a hug and wiped her fresh tears. The comfort of his arms around her brought a hope that she had not realized was possible. This man who had struggled and sacrificed more than anyone here still found the capacity to give such beauty and peace to everyone. In that, Eliana realized Graham was indeed the King.

ABOUT THE AUTHOR

While DLM Johnson is new to the world of publishing her written work, she is not new to the world of writing, or even sharing her art. She holds two bachelor's degrees, one in Computer Engineering and one in Dance. Just like her degrees might allude to, DLM never wants to be boxed in by one label. What better way to break down walls and apply a plethora of skills than writing?

When DLM is not filling her free time with creativity in its written form, she spends her days working as a Software Engineer for an augmented reality company, and her nights she splits between teaching dance and **GYROKINESIS®,** attending rehearsals for both aerial and modern dance works, playing RPG, and catching up on TV. When she finds a moment to spare, she also enjoys taking motorcycle rides with her husband, being out in nature, and going on hikes.

If you want to keep up with more of the happenings inside of her mind, subscribe to her blog https://tinyurl.com/dlmjohnson, follow her on Twitter @dlmj18, and follow her explorations on HitRecord https://hitrecord.org/users/damnielle01/records.

www.ingramcontent.com/pod-product-compliance
Lightning Source LLC
LaVergne TN
LVHW091113080826
845145LV00008B/1891
* 9 7 8 1 7 3 2 9 6 6 2 6 0 *